A LIGHT IN THE DARK

Miranda Sapphire

About

Beast has been lost in the dark for two hundred years...

Claire is desperate to prove she belongs in the light...

But the shadow of ancient crimes might just swallow them both.

Beast has been locked away in his manor for two centuries to pay for the crimes of his past. Haunted by his failures, he is cursed by the fae mage he wronged to spend all of his days lonely and unloved. When a beautiful quester named Claire arrives at the manor, insisting she's there to help him, he's confused—he's not supposed to be helped, after all. But like a moth to a flame he can't stay away, even if he knows he'll only wind up hurting her.

Claire is the youngest daughter, the unwanted child. Determined to live her own life, she defies her father's expectations and takes up a life of adventure with the illustrious Questing Guild of Cillure. Right away, she's drawn to a strange quest that has been long-neglected, determined to help in any way she can...assuming she can even figure out what on earth is going on. As she gets closer to the manor's somber inhabitant her professional interest shifts to something more. She's never felt attraction like this to anyone else, but even as she grows certain she'll never be able to live without him she worries what she'll do if she ruins her blooming career and winds up on the streets.

CONTENT WARNINGS: suicidal ideation, sexual assault attempt, sexual assault (implied but off page), misogyny, some foul language, explicit sex scenes between a human woman and a non-human man, discussion of depression, depiction of depression, self-harm, anxiety, toxic family dynamics, bullying, death of a parent (not shown).

TROPES: virgin MMC, hurt/comfort, MMC with praise kink, dude in distress (FMC saves MMC), forced proximity/ isolation, fated mates (lite), dark secret, redemption, age gap (216 vs 26), slow burn.

Contents

CHAPTER ONE

Once Upon A Time

Jordan's golden-brown face was pouring sweat, his brown eyes locked on the heavy stone fists of the rogue golem as they swung for him again and again. Claire Odetima wasn't used to seeing her cousin so serious and focused. It was weird.

The mage of their group, Hereon, was quietly weaving together a containment spell that would let them tease out the location of the vulnerable molten core hidden somewhere on the golem's body. His long brown fingers plucked and fluttered through the air, leaving glowing aether trails as the spell started to take shape.

Claire was still on her questing trainer's permit and was as such stuck hanging back and "watching the pros handle it," as her cousin Jordan kept saying. She'd cleared the small town square where Jordan and Hereon had cornered the hulking creature, making sure there weren't any innocent bystanders at risk of getting trampled. She'd also sent a couple of people out to act as criers, urging the rest of the townsfolk to stay indoors until they announced the all-clear. Now all she could do was watch and try to be ready if things went sideways and their need for help outweighed the Guild's restrictions on trainee participation.

Claire hated being stuck on the sidelines like this, but until she passed her entrance exam and has a full license she simply wasn't allowed except in the direst of emergencies. Her permit allowed her to shadow, and that was really it. She idly scratched at one of the exposed strips of scalp in between her cornrow braids, suppressing the restless fidgeting that wanted to possess her limbs. The day was warm, and with nothing to do but hang back the constant streams of sweat down her back made her twitchy. She rubbed at her deep brown heart-shaped face with a restless hand, desperate to do *something*.

"That spell almost done, Herry?" Jordan gritted out, keeping a healthy distance from the golem's swinging fists as he danced around it, trying to find an opening to hack at its joints with his sword to slow it down.

"Almost, Jor. Just keep him distracted a little longer."

Jordan sighed, swaying back to avoid the golem as it took a shuffling step closer to him.

The golem let out a roar and lunged at Jordan, swinging its solid stone fists at his head with renewed fury. Jordan cursed, ducking and scrambling backward to avoid the blows, but the golem didn't let up, crowding right back into the space Jordan had made and forcing him to retreat farther and farther.

"Hurry up with that fucking spell, Herry!" Jordan called to his party member, finally managing to get his weapon up.

Golems were, by design, brainless creatures incapable of doing too much more than moving around and taking care of simple tasks. Which was why none of them were expecting this one to let out a grating, high-pitched sound like a hawk's cry, a pale green glow bathing its stone surface from within, only for that pale green luminescence to shoot forward as a wall of light into Jordan, knocking him back several feet and causing him to lose his footing.

Faster than stone should have been able to move even with the help of aether—the stuff of magic—the golem was charging *past* Jordan, heading for the homes beyond the square.

The ones full of innocent bystanders huddling in fear.

Jordan cursed again, staggering to his feet to pursue the golem. Hereon sighed, reeling in his half-done spell and joining Claire in pursuit.

The golem crashed through the house in front of it, the timber parting like wet paper in the face of the golem's size and strength. Claire heard shouts and screaming, and then the crash of the golem breaching through the opposite wall.

Since he'd been closest to the golem when it ran off Jordan was farther ahead than the other two, charging through the house to try and keep up with it. Hereon, with his long legs, was pulling ahead of Claire too, closing the distance between himself and her cousin.

As she got closer the perforated house wobbled, stone and mortar crumbling away at the edges of the massive holes.

"It's heading south!" Jordan called from the front of the pack, already on the street on the other side of the ruined house. "We've got to herd it again and get that spell on it!"

Claire had finally made it to the first hole. "What about the person in this house?" she called, seeing a woman collapsed on a pile of rubble a few feet inside.

"Leave them for now!" Jordan shouted back.

Claire flung herself to a stop, almost losing her balance on the uneven terrain. She looked at the second hole on the far side of the house, then at the unconscious woman. Her feet were moving before she'd even made a conscious decision.

Darting over and dropping to her knees, she checked for a pulse, and to see if the woman was still breathing. Claire loosed a relieved sigh when she found both. The woman was collapsed on her side, her brown hair caked with dust and splinters. Lumber and plaster continued to fall from the holes in the wall and the ceiling, raining down on Claire and the woman both as Claire's eyes darted around the wreckage.

Spotting a dining table on the far side of the ruined room, Claire surged to her feet to drag it over. She carefully wedged it against the wall above the woman to try and keep the worst of the debris off of her while Claire figured out how to move her. It wasn't a good idea to do too much until a healer had looked at her since she could have damage to her spine that moving her would make worse.

Claire bolted for the bedroom, snatching the blanket and a pillow off of the bed and returning to the living room.

A large chunk of plaster fell from the ceiling, striking Claire on the back of her head and knocking her off of her feet. She fell onto her hands and knees, scraping her skin raw. Her vision went spotty, and she had to stay there on the ground, desperately blinking to try and clear the spots away.

Claire staggered to her feet, grabbing the blanket and pillow again and returning to the woman's side. She folded the blanket in half lengthwise and tied the top two corners of the halved blanket together in a loose knot. She wedged the pillow into the cradle formed by the knot and laid the makeshift gurney on the floor beside the unconscious woman. As carefully as she could, Claire eased the woman onto the blanket, using the pillow to try and keep her head and neck still. Debris continued to rain down on them from above, the table keeping Claire's head from taking any more knocks.

Claire muttered a quick prayer to the deity Frichta for a safe path out of the crumbling house, then surged out from behind the barricade, dragging the pallet behind her by the end that wasn't knotted.

Head swimming, Claire did her best to get out of the house quickly but smoothly, kicking debris aside to keep the pallet level. They were closer to the entry hole, but the exit hole had a clearer path, so she dragged her charge that way.

As she drew close to the exit hole more plaster and large splinters of wood fell on top of Claire's head, making her wince and her eyes tear up from a mixture of pain and thick dust. The groaning from the roof became more intense, and Claire put on a burst of speed, desperate to get outside the house.

They had just gotten to the inside edge of the hole when the center of the roof caved, sending a cloud of dust and more sharp splinters their way. Claire flung the loose end of the blanket back and over the unconscious woman as best she could, taking hold of her feet through the blanket and yanking her out and around the rubble scattered on the street outside.

Coughing and wheezing, Claire forced her shuddering legs to hold out just a few more steps, finally allowing them to give out when she'd managed to drag the woman several feet past the ring of debris left by the golem when it had made the exit hole. Once they were more or less safe her whole body went limp and trembling, and she sank against the wall of a neighboring house.

"Vitrin's mercy, are you alright, miss?" another woman

called from the front of a small crowd that had gathered at the end of the street. Claire gave her a thumbs-up, coughing a few more times before sucking in a breath.

"I'm fine," she called. "But you shouldn't be out here. The danger's not passed yet, my party members are still—" but the rest was choked off by another coughing fit.

The woman from the crowd ran forward, coming to kneel by Claire's side and smacking her on the back.

"Back…" Claire choked out, "not…safe…"

"Come on, let's get you away from this mess," the stranger said kindly, pulling Claire to her feet with surprising strength. Unable to speak amidst all the coughing and hacking, Claire dug in her heels when the woman tried to lead her away and pointed at the bundle at her feet, peeling back a corner of the blanket to show the unconscious woman's pale, pinched face.

"Why that's Brekka!" the other woman gasped, looking at Claire with wide eyes. "I didn't know she was home," the stranger said quietly, almost as if she was apologizing.

The woman crouched and grabbed hold of Brekka's feet, helping Claire drag her all the way to the crowd at the end of the street. A small old woman was pushing to the front of the throng, her tawny face deeply colored and softly lined like old but well-loved leather. She hobbled to meet Claire and her helper, crouching with a loud crack to get a closer look at the injured woman.

"I'm the village healer," she barked, her fingers moving over Brekka's scalp. "You're one of the questers?"

Claire nodded, settling into a crouch herself and wiping at the dust now caked into the sweat of her face. "I'm with them, but I'm on my learner's permit still. Can I leave her with you?

I have to catch up with the rest of my party and—"

"Claire!" Jordan shouted from behind her. Standing and turning, she staggered towards where he and Hereon were running at her from the other end of the street. "Salerah's fires, where *were* you? What the fuck happened to you?" His expression was quickly sliding from worried to angry. Claire winced.

"There was someone in that house who needed help," she told him, lifting her chin. She pointed at the pile of rubble that had been a house just a few minutes ago.

"I told you to leave it, Claire," he shouted. "We needed you! That thing almost got Hereon! It could've escaped! If you're in a party then you need to *stay with the party.* Not to mention you're on your permit and I'm responsible for you *and* everything you do!"

Anger simmered hot under her skin. Jordan was taking a tone with her that she *really* did not like. He was only two years older than her, but he was treating her like a child, like she'd just wandered off instead of stopping to help someone.

Claire wrestled for control of her emotions. "I'm sorry for disappearing but I couldn't leave her, not when I could help."

"And if we wouldn't have been able to handle the golem on our own it might have killed people! Lots of people. Once those things go rogue they have the potential to do so much harm." Jordan sighed, his shoulders dropping. "Look, Claire, I get why you did it. I really do. But questing is tough stuff. You gotta be tougher. And sometimes that means…making difficult calls."

She'd heard this same speech before, dozens of times by now, from Jordan and several of her instructors from her questing preparatory classes. She understood that it was important, that it was the way things were done for a reason.

Suddenly, she was exhausted and felt all of the fight leaving her. It was done now, and she didn't regret her choice even for a moment. So she nodded, said she understood, and joined the rest of her party in finishing up the quest.

One Month Later

"Congrats on making it through the exam process, Claire," Dretta intoned, looking bored, or maybe just tired. They were shorter than Claire, and a bit more square-shaped, with pale skin and short coppery hair. Dretta was the mentor that Claire had been assigned to for her first year of questing, and according to the profile she'd been given Dretta had been a member of the Guild for fifteen years and had chosen never to rise above a C-Class, a fact which Claire found interesting. She couldn't imagine why anyone would *want* to stay at a lower level for that long.

"I'm here to answer any questions or concerns you might have about the process and what we do here," they continued, settling into their chair across from Claire at the badly nicked wooden desk. Their office was one that all C-Class mentors shared, so while it was a large room the sheer number of people crammed into it made it feel cramped. "When you're out in the field you'll start off reporting to me so that I can give you feedback and direct you on next steps." They sighed heavily, looking more tired the longer they talked. "And if you need backup, you'll get a distress beacon that'll be keyed to me, or you can send me a letter. I have a direct inbox so if you write to me I'll get it pretty quickly. If there's an emergency either I or someone else will be dispatched to help out."

Claire decided that more than anything else, Dretta looked like they needed a nap. One that would last at least a few years. Their eyes were weighed down by heavy shadows so dark they looked like bruises, their skin dull and pinched-looking.

"Any questions so far?" they asked, hiding a yawn behind their calloused palm.

Claire shook her head. At this point, if there was something she didn't know, she wouldn't know she didn't know about it unless Dretta brought it up.

"Alright," Dretta went on, slumping further back into their chair and sighing again. "Most mentors will pick out your first quest for you, but I think it's a good exercise to head over to the board room and pick your own. Plus I like to see what kind of things my mentees go for when they're given free rein. It can say a lot."

Nodding, Claire got to her feet. "Do you recommend I look for anything in particular? Or avoid anything?"

Dretta rubbed their chin, screwing up their face as they thought. "Well obviously you're limited to C-Class until you get the higher-level weapon-carry licenses," they began. "But beyond that, I'd say focus on your strengths, and be careful about private quests. Sometimes they get an attitude because they're footing the bill and it can be discouraging if you're new and still getting your feet under you." They yawned, thin lips stretching tight as their mouth opened obscenely wide. Claire thought she heard something crack. "But any of the Consortium-funded quests will be fine, they like to be nice and hands-off," Dretta continued, smoothing down their short ginger hair. "Don't pay as much, of course, but sometimes the hassle just isn't worth the bigger payday on those private quests, you know?"

Claire cocked an eyebrow, smirking. She knew a little bit about that from her family. She was painfully familiar with the entitlement of the wealthy, and how demanding and petty they could get when you didn't cooperate with their vision.

It was why her father had disowned her for questing instead of being a demure little housewife for a man of her father's choosing. It was why so much of her existence had been cold and empty before Adeela had swanned into her life as her father's housekeeper—and Claire's savior. She'd immediately adopted Claire as one of her own and had raised her and loved her when no one else had wanted to—especially not her father.

Shoving aside thoughts of her father, Claire took her leave and headed down to the basement level, where the board room was.

Really, the place should be called a *boards* room, because there were dozens of boards crowded into the space, each one keyed to a different Cillurean province and displaying the posted quests and magical anomalies needing to be investigated.

She considered the green-colored C-Level posts, pinching her bottom lip by putting her thumb and forefinger on the corners and bringing them together so that the middle bulged out. She thought her mentor was right to caution against the private boards for a new quester, if only because she didn't think she had it in her to deal with an aristocrat so soon after the mighty battle of wills she'd had against her father just to get here. She sidled up to the Kesterinian board, curious about what sorts of things had been brewing close to home.

The board was the same massive slate slab as all the others, the top edge of it reaching two feet or more beyond the top of Claire's head, with faintly-glowing scrawls crammed into every inch of space, listing the minor troubles and nuisances that the Consortium's forces didn't want to bother with. C-levels were green, of course, with B's colored blue and A's purple. Private quests had a little gold disk at the start of the posts, making them easy to avoid.

From what Claire could see, most of the quests on the board were spells gone awry—but not *too* awry, because then they'd be handled by the Consortium, the collective of powerful mages entrusted with keeping Cillurean magic safe and secure, itself. There were also lots of missing things and magical pests that needed removing, as was typical. But there was one, right at the very bottom of the board, that immediately stuck out to her. It was old, so old it was written in a different handwriting than the others, but still more curiously it had no posting date. Or, it did, but it was smudged somehow. There was no way it could have been smeared, because this was all done magically and automatically, so no hand ever actually inked anything *to* smear on the slate slabs.

A large anomaly in the woods outside of Edden, it read. *Reward: 0 gold, 0 silver, 0 copper.* Claire was surprised; she hadn't thought it was possible for even a public quest to be posted without *some* reward. No wonder it had languished on the board for so long: no details and no reward making it worth it to find Edden, wherever that was, and scour the woods looking for something that you didn't even know whether or not existed. Or what "it" even was.

But Claire couldn't look away from it. She couldn't stop

her mind from turning it over, imagining someone lost and hurting for the gods only knew how long. She wondered whether this imaginary person might still be waiting and hoping, praying for someone to come along and help them.

As she had been taught, there were little oblong indents along the left-hand side of the board beside each quest. She pressed her thumb into the one beside the old quest, causing it to flare brighter before disappearing. A badly yellowed slip of parchment fluttered into a basket near the floor, just beneath the board. On one side of the parchment was a copy of what had been written on the board, and on the other side was a map of Edden and its surrounding woods, with a large "X" marked where the anomaly had happened.

It was probably nothing, this odd little quest. But what would it hurt for her to go and check it out?

She left the board room and climbed the stairs back up to the offices to show her mentor what she'd picked. Dretta read through the scant text on the slip of parchment again and again, their eyebrows raised high in disbelief.

"Really?" they asked for the third time. "This one?"

Claire nodded, keeping her shoulders firm and her chin high. "Yes. It…appeals to me."

Dretta gave her an incredulous look then shrugged. "It's your time," they drawled, "spend it how you will." They pulled a form from one of their desk drawers and hastily filled it out and signed it, handing it to Claire. "This'll get you gear and your stipend from the shop down on the main floor," they explained. "Ordinarily the quest would come with one of these already filled out, but I guess this one must be *really* old. Some of the old timers say it used to be that you had to fund it all yourself." Dretta snorted, rolling their eyes. "The things questers used to have to put up with."

Claire thanked Dretta and stood, shaking their hand and promising to send letters regularly with updates once she was on the road.

As she made her way down to the main level she considered whether or not she should take her mentor's skepticism of her chosen quest more seriously. On the one hand, an underwhelming first quest could make it harder for her to find willing party members once she branched out into doing partied quests. Prospective group mates might see her record and think she wouldn't be able to carry her own weight, and partied quests were the best way to gain the kind of income and acclaim that would allow her to support herself doing this work. Now that she was disowned and disinherited she *had* to be able to make her own way. But on the other hand, she couldn't ignore the increasingly intense pull she was feeling toward this odd little quest. Her mind was already racing with tactics, churning away at what scenarios could be awaiting her and how she'd tackle them. Despite how boring and inconsequential it looked on paper, Claire was *excited* about this quest, and that counted for a lot in her book.

Maybe no one else in the entire Guild thought it was worth taking the trip to this town, Edden, to see just what sort of an anomaly had cropped up there, but that had never stopped Claire in the past.

"Stubborn", Adeela called her. "Pig-headed" was her father's term, but so many of her early years had been spent alone, and she'd come to know herself very well in that time. She trusted her instincts and her skills, and her instinct said that this was the one. Handing over the requisition form to the store clerk, she decided that this was indeed the path she wanted to walk. If she had to spend more time doing solos because no one wanted to group with her then so be it. She'd always been fine on her own.

When the clerk returned with a pack filled with her supplies she thanked him and made her way out to the street to hail a cab and go home.

Once she was settled into the mage engine-run single-seater carriage she poked through what the Guild had given her to inspect it. Everything was very plain and utilitarian, but of fairly sturdy make. The pack was a nice, heavy canvas reinforced with leather, with lots of pockets and straps to hang things from. Included with the pack was a waterskin, a waterproof cloak, enough jerky and hardtack to last a week or two, a coin purse with thirty silver in it for expenses, an arrest kit with paper charms and the activation paste that would allow her to subdue and round up law-breakers magically and safely without being gifted, a diviner probe for finding and tracking aether signatures, a pair of hardy boots, a distress beacon that would summon nearby questers and alert her mentor if she activated it, and a sleek new baton. Claire had a dagger she'd purchased herself as a graduation present, and Adeela had gifted her a lovely leather-bound notebook and brass pen for her to take notes with during her investigations. She'd also splurged and gotten herself a set of communicator pendants so she could contact Adeela immediately if she wanted to.

The palm-sized mirrored pendants were the height of indulgence, since getting the activator paste was both too difficult *and* expensive to make them something one could use regularly, which was why the Guild generally stuck to letters and things like the distress beacons for communications. With the aether channel mail system, one could send letters immediately to where they needed to go, so it was usually quick enough when one had to get a message out.

But she wanted to give herself the option to be able to see or hear Adeela at a moment's notice. She was a strong and capable woman, and she knew who she was. But sometimes you just needed to talk to your mom about things to get your head on straight, so she had decided the cost was worth it.

Claire had been told that Edden was a town, but that might have been too generous. With just one street that was barely more than hard-packed earth and a smattering of simple shops, it could really only be called a village. Back in Kesterin the entire place would have fit on a single city block.

But it was a welcome sight, she had to admit: it was small and simple, but it wasn't squalid, and the brightly-painted shop fronts were jarring but welcoming. People drifted about peaceably, talking and haggling and shooting her curious looks. Children were darting around playing, a small red-headed boy screaming with laughter as he chased a chicken the same coppery red as his hair. He almost collided with Claire, skidding to a stop inches from her legs.

"Hullo there," she greeted the young boy, smiling warmly. "I'm new in town and was hoping to get a room at the inn. Do you know where it is?"

The boy nodded, pointing farther along the road. Well, she supposed that only made sense.

"Thanks. I think your friend's getting away," she added, pointing to where the chicken was wandering between two of the shops. "You'd better go catch her!"

The little boy gasped. "Nellie!" he exclaimed softly, darting off without another thought for Claire.

Chuckling, she hoisted her pack higher on her sore shoulders and made her way further into Edden.

The inn was small, but that was to be expected. It was called *The Dragon's Spur*, with a hanging wooden sign swinging in the breeze painted with a creature that looked more like a cockatrice than a dragon, but the inn looked clean and inviting.

Claire threw open the door, blinking in the dark of the interior, so jarring after being out in the midday sun.

"Hello, miss!" a man called out from somewhere near the back wall, and she squinted to try and bring him into better focus. Dimly, she saw a beaming middle-aged man with thinning brown hair and ruddy cheeks. "Welcome to the *Spur*," he said warmly, wiping his hands on a rag and coming out from behind the bar he'd been tending to greet her. "What can I help you with today, then?"

"I'd like a room," she answered. "I'm not sure for how long just yet. I'm a quester," she pointed to the gleaming silver badge pinned to the strap of her pack, "and I've taken on a quest that's supposed to be around here, in the woods."

The innkeep's eyes lit up. "A quester!" he exclaimed, whistling low. "My husband Sil'll be excited to hear about that. The man loves everything to do with adventure and magecraft."

Claire dug around in her pockets until she found the old scrap of parchment with the quest details on it. "This is all the information I have on the quest currently, so if you happen to know anything else, or could point me toward someone who could help, I'd really appreciate it."

He took the parchment from her hands and studied it, mouthing the scant words to himself.

"Far as I know there's nothing out that way except an old manor that's 'sposed to be cursed. You think that could be it?"

She shrugged. "Sure, sounds quest-y enough to me. Do you happen to know anything else about it?"

He grinned, blue eyes glittering. "A bit. There's some mysterious someone guarding it, some of the tales go." The innkeep leaned in as if he was sharing a secret. "Sometimes the young bucks slip out there looking for it on a dare, but none of them have ever come away with more'n stories. It's not common anymore, more of a tradition for mine and my da's generation than this'n, but I do recall it's 'sposed to be due east of here."

"That's *very* helpful, thank you *so* much, Mister…?"

"Teran, Miss. Just Teran is fine, I don't like putting on airs just because I own a building." He chuckled, his blue eyes twinkling. "And what might I call you, if it's not too bold to ask?"

"Claire," she said, returning his smile.

"Right-o, Miss Claire. If you'll follow me, I'll get you set up in your room."

As Teran walked her through the check-in process, she came to understand that the inn may have been his business, but gossiping and telling stories was his passion. He was terribly kind, but refused to leave her alone to settle in and unpack. In the end, the only thing that saved her from being Teran's unwilling conversational partner for a *full* hour was someone calling his name from downstairs.

"Oh, that's Sil! Must be another guest. You'll have to excuse me Miss Claire, duty calls!" Then Teran was off, allowing her to sag in relief and flop onto the bed at last. At least some of the information he'd been flinging at her had been relevant to the quest. She'd learned that the tales about what resided in the manor varied, but generally it was agreed that there was someone living there, though they tended to stay hidden and out of the way, so there was no consensus on what they looked like. Some stories insisted that it wasn't a person, but a monster, a beast, with sharp claws and wicked fangs, but no one had ever been attacked. No one had ever gone missing.

Another interesting tidbit was that anything taken from the manor tended to disappear not long after the person who'd taken it had gotten back to town as if it were bespelled to return to its owner. Just how that could be useful, Claire wasn't sure. But it was intriguing.

Of all the things she had been expecting, had been preparing for during her endless two weeks of travel from Kesterin to Edden, none of them had been a haunting. Or at least, that was what it was made to seem like—whether or not ghosts were real was yet to be seen, but there was *something* haunting that manor, from what Teran had been able to tell her. Perhaps they were trapped, this mystery person who may have actually been a monster.

For not the first time, Claire wished there would have been more information in the posting on the board. Though the innkeep clearly loved his gossip and storytelling, he'd been painfully brief on talk of the mysterious manor, switching to other topics as soon as he'd answered her question, so that she had to steer him back to it more than once.

It was the damnedest thing.

Still, it was better than nothing, and in her quest to be a

professional, she made sure to record everything she'd been told in her journal. It felt like a waste of time, but sometimes you just didn't know a thing was important right away.

Once she had finished her recording she gave herself a sink bath and wrapped one of her silk scarves around her tightly-braided hair for the evening. It wasn't even close to nightfall, but she was exhausted and desperate for rest in an honest-to-gods bed after four days on horseback and two on foot.

After sleeping for nearly a dozen hours Claire awoke fresh and ready to get started on the quest properly. Without the heaviness of fatigue weighing her down and distracting her, she found she was excited to make her way out there and dig into the mystery. It was a different kind of excitement from what she'd been feeling. That had been an excitement to sink her teeth into a problem, to be able to help someone if the manor was, indeed, occupied. But as she'd gotten closer, there'd been something else fluttering in her belly, something she couldn't put a name to, that was adding a sharp edge to her enthusiasm. *Maybe it's just nerves,* she reasoned.

Claire peeled herself from bed shortly after dawn, shuffling down to the communal bathroom to relieve herself and wash up in the sink. The inn didn't have any tubs or heated plumbing, so Claire was forced to sponge-bathe out of a basin with icy-cold water. Goosebumps prickled all over her shivering skin, her nipples hardening to aching points, but she was certainly more awake for her discomfort.

Back in her room, she carefully applied her rose face

cream and spread moisturizing oil over the rest of herself, frowning at where dry skin had started to build up and give her burnished brown skin an ashy cast. She'd have to scrub at that once she got a chance to take a proper bath. The changing of the seasons always did this to her, but two weeks of hard travel certainly hadn't helped things.

Even though she'd wanted to head off into the woods as soon as she was done, she decided it would be better to hang around Edden at least one day and continue to chat up the locals and establish this as her outpost, of sorts, with Dretta. And she'd be lying if she said she wasn't also eager to send a letter off to Adeela, checking in and catching her up on what had been happening while Claire'd been on the road.

She flitted from shop to shop for several hours, striking up conversations with owners and patrons alike to try and glean anything she could about what was going on with the manor in the woods. Everyone she talked to was kind, if a bit wary of an outsider, but didn't have anything much to add beyond what the innkeep had already told her.

"My ma used to talk about there being a strange manor in the woods," the middle-aged Orcish owner of the general store had told her, her olive green arms crossed over her broad chest as she'd eyed Claire. "It was supposed to be haunted, or enchanted, I think."

"Do you know anything about the creature that lives there? Or what happened at the manor?"

The older woman shook her head, looking annoyed. "Don't sell stories," she grumbled, "I sell goods."

Claire sighed internally but decided she might as well stock up while she was here and hope it would endear her to the Orcish shopkeep. Claire never wanted to make an enemy if she could help it, and after a childhood spent misunderstood she worked hard to give others the benefit of the doubt. So as she was leaving the shop Claire offered the woman a smile and held out her hand for a handshake. "My name's Claire, by the way. It was nice to meet you. You have a lovely shop."

Something softened in the shopkeep's golden eyes. "My thanks. I'm O'brenne." She took Claire's hand and shook it with firm strength and unexpected warmth. She put her hands on her hips instead of crossing them back over her chest. "Will you be needing anything else?" O'brenne asked, the ghost of a smile twitching at the corners of her mouth.

"Not just yet. But I'm sure I'll be back!" Claire smiled again and gathered her purchases into her pack.

Continuing to make her way through town, she found that the apothecary owner was able to give a vague description of the manor's occupant, saying they were "huge and frightening" but that he only got a chance to see them once. The baker's wife corroborated that the beast of the manor was large, describing him as a wicked demon. But she, too, had been left alone. Claire supposed it bode well that so many people were able to say they'd seen the beast and lived. She was still a bit nervous, but between the accounts and the fact that the quest was C-Class, the worst of her fears were gone.

CHAPTER TWO

Pain Untold

A visitor was the last thing he'd wanted to deal with, but after nearly two hundred years, Beast should have known he wasn't ever going to get his wish.

He'd been ripped from one of his many nightmares by the breathtaking pressure in his chest that marked someone passing through the dull silver gates outside, signaling that he needed to start getting ready to meet whoever it was. He would not be able to take a breath until he obeyed the compulsion, and while Naja had made sure he could never die or take permanent harm while he was trapped here at the manor, not being able to breathe was still horrible.

He hauled himself to his strange high-ankled feet—more like dog paws really—and shuffled over the wardrobe to dress. He'd had to sew all of his clothes himself from spare linens and curtains, as Naja had apparently intended he walk around naked, but he'd gotten quite good at it over the years. Two hundred years to get it right helped, even with his large hands proving so clumsy and difficult to gentle. He wasted a lot of needles and fabric at first, but somehow he'd never run out. He wondered if that was Tully, somehow. It would also explain why he never ran out of his other craft supplies. Certainly, Naja would never have given him such gifts.

Once he was dressed in clean clothes, he headed down to the foyer to greet his latest guest, hopefully without incident. It had yet to be a smooth first meeting, but he couldn't help but hope for it.

The shadow creatures that haunted him were out in full effect today, howling and laughing at him like horrible, warped jackals with glowing eyes and human cruelty. It was so hard to tell if they were real; they felt real, looked real, but no one ever reacted to them but him. He tried not to think too long on that though, not liking what the answer might say about his sanity. Not that he wasn't aware that it was slipping, but the shadow creatures seemed like an especially bad sign, like he was near the end of what he could endure. Like maybe he was close to losing himself entirely.

He tried to take the stairs down to the first floor slowly despite the shadowy teeth nipping at his heels, to prolong the time when he was still alone. Miserable and lonely and losing his mind, but also safe, unharmed. He knew he looked terrifying—a hulking mountain of muscles and wicked teeth and claws, his short but sharply pointed horns sweeping back from his temple to a little above the points of his ears—but he tried so hard to be calm and unassuming. To not be as scary as he looked.

It never worked.

Most of the scars from these rocky starts were gone now, as part of the enchantment that kept him trapped and undying, but he still remembered every wound, and he thought it was likely that there wasn't a single part of him that hadn't been scarred at some point. Sometimes he wished the wounds would stay so that he had more proof of what was real and what was nightmare.

It was early evening now, but because it was the depths of winter—sometime in Hectrin, he thought, though keeping time had long ago fallen to the wayside—it was already pitch black outside, the only light coming from the sconces that had lit at his guest's entry. In the flickering gloom, it was hard to tell what they looked like, but he could just make out a spot of gleaming silver attached to their heavy-looking pack. His stomach sank: that was never a good sign.

Beast was still hanging back in the shadowy depths of the second floor, whose lamps he'd willed stay dark so he could hide for longer, but it was like the visitor downstairs could sense him. They drew their sword and dropped into a slight crouch, their head swiveling slowly as they searched the darkness. Beast sighed quietly, bracing himself for what was to come.

He had no weapons, and though he had sharp claws and teeth and horns, he would never use them against another person. He couldn't, thanks to Naja, but he wouldn't anyway. He'd already caused enough hurt in the world, and he'd rather suffer all this pain than put in more, even if it did mean losing his mind in the process.

He stepped gingerly into the first swaths of candlelight, putting his hands up with his palms out in supplication.

"Hello," he called down, keeping his voice as gentle as soft as he could manage. It was no easy feat, considering he thought he sounded like someone had taught a bear to speak. "I mean you no harm. Welcome to my manor, traveler."

The visitor whipped to the side to face him, their eyes wide and the tip of their sword swinging around to point directly at him. As they took him in, emerging slowly into the candlelight, their back stiffened and the sword shivered just the littlest bit in their grip.

"Stay back!" they warned, and from their voice Beast thought they might be a man. "Stay back, monster!"

He halted, still several risers up from the bottom of the winding staircase. "You have nothing to fear from me," Beast tried to soothe, keeping his hands up and his posture as relaxed as his strange physiology would allow. If his teeth weren't so unnerving he'd try a smile, but the best he could do to look friendly was to keep his eyes soft.

The visitor surged forward, the silver badge on their pack flashing in the dim lighting. Beast sucked in a breath, his whole body locking up, bracing for the inevitable. He didn't mean to close his eyes, but it was too terrible, watching the razor-sharp blade slice through the air, swinging with inexorable momentum towards his vulnerable side. He braced, hoping it would be over quickly, at least, and thanking the gods that he'd had the foresight to put on one of his least favorite outfits, the seams lacking his practiced straight, even stitches.

The blade hit him just under his ribs, cutting through his flesh and organs with wet, sickening sounds. The column of his spine stopped the momentum of the blade, preventing it from cutting him clean in half, and he was thankful for that, because it would mean less healing time. At first, there wasn't any pain, the shock too great for anything to filter from his nerve endings to his brain, but that moment was achingly short. Too soon, pain was a raging fire licking all throughout his body, stealing his breath and clenching all of his muscles, which only made the pain that much worse.

His strength fled him, and he slumped forward, his broken body falling heavily, the impact of the stairs on his horrific wound blackening his sight. If he had had breath to scream, he would have. He slid to a stop near the foot of the stairs, his blood a thick coppery reek on the air, spreading out in a hot pool around him. He could hear the visitor panting, their breaths wheezing in and out of their throat in their panic.

Beast felt his heartbeat begin to slow and weaken, his eyes open now and frozen on the twinkling chandelier high above him. He still wasn't breathing, and he knew that to the person standing over him, staring down at him with wide brown eyes, he would look dead. But he wasn't; he was still fully aware of what was going on around him, but trapped in his dead body and helpless. In time, his flesh would begin to knit together, his organs would regenerate. Nerves and tendons would re-connect, a process that was always horrible, and any broken bones would fuse themselves back together. And the whole time, his world would be frozen in heavy pain, feeling all of it and unable to do anything.

With a shuddering sigh, the visitor cleaned their blade on a part of Beast's shirt that wasn't soaked in blood and sheathed it. He felt their eyes on him for several moments, pain slicing through his body in waves, his heart and lungs still. A tentative foot prodded at his shoulder, jostling him, but when he remained still and lifeless the visitor loosed a relieved sigh and spun away. He heard the footsteps receding down the hall that led to the southern wing of the manor, and then he was alone, left like so much trash in a heap on the gleaming marble floors.

Beast didn't know how long he was stuck frozen, lying there

and in pain, but he knew it had been long enough that the visitor had combed through the manor and left, and for the setting sun to sear into his eyes from the west-facing window in the foyer several times. His blood had long since cooled and coagulated, and had begun the process of drying and flaking by the time he was healed enough to begin to feel the pain shift from *oh gods something is wrong something is very wrong this is death* to the slightly less alarming pain of healing, full of sharpness and throbbing but without that instinctual feeling of wrongness and danger. He still couldn't breathe, still didn't feel a heartbeat, but he was able to start moving his eyes the littlest bit, and he thought he felt his extremities twitching occasionally.

The shadow creatures hung back, perhaps also fooled into thinking that he was dead, but they still shuffled around at the edges, barking out harsh laughter and watching him with glowing eyes. But the buzzing tingle of Tully's touch was also never too far away, localized on his still face more than anywhere else, and somewhere beyond the sucking maw of the pain his heart was breaking for her, having to see him like this over and over and unable to do much about it.

He heard a sound like the concussion of thunder without the boom, and his heart sank. A visit from Naja was the last thing he wanted right now, which was probably why she had shown up.

"Hello, worm," she called as she strode into the foyer, snowflakes clinging to her blue cloak. "I see you've been up to no good again. How marvelous!"

She strode over to him and crouched just beyond the pool of his drying blood, studying him with her cold blue eyes, her pale skin flushed pink from the cold outside.

"This one got you good," she murmured, studying his injury. "Almost cut you clean in half."

He could say nothing, the only sign of life he was capable of the slow slide of his brown eyes over to her face.

"I'll speed up your healing this time," she announced, a razor-sharp smile spreading across her beautiful face. "So we can get you back on your feet again for your next guest."

This wasn't a mercy, he knew. Speeding up the healing only made the pain worse, more intense and traumatic, and he knew more pain, another injury, was on its way on top of that, given her phrasing. If he could have spoken, he would have wept, begging her yet again to release him, to show him the mercy of death at long last. But then she was working her spell, and his world was focused down to howling, shrieking pain. Every nerve was sharp and icy agony, and in time he found his breath again, using it to scream himself raw.

All the time he was writhing and twitching and screaming on the floor, stirring up his dried blood and his nails gouging into the marble tiles of the foyer floor Naja stood by watching him, her ice-chip eyes drinking in his suffering. She watched him with a kind of grim determination, as if she no longer enjoyed doing this but did it because she had to. He wondered sometimes if Naja even knew why she was still doing this, still tethering herself to him to punish him for what he'd done to her daughter Ingrid all those long years ago.

Eventually, the pain subsided, brought down to a dull ache in his side, an enormous silvery scar wrapping around his right side from near his navel to just alongside his spine, his gray flesh lumpy and dusky along the violent mark. His breathing evened out, his heart rate settling, and he sat up, ripping his blood-soaked shirt the rest of the way off and using it to mop the tears and ropes of snot from his face.

"Good to see you as always, Naja," he said to his jailer, his voice rasping and raw in the unnatural quiet of the manor.

"And you, worm," she said, baring her teeth in a predatory smile. "It's always so satisfying to see you cut down and in pain."

Beast didn't answer, making his way unsteadily to his feet. Now that he wasn't collapsed onto the floor the marks of his struggle were disappearing, the manor's enchantment erasing the blood and gouges from the stairs and floor as if they'd never been there, just like it always did. A part of him wished the evidence would remain for longer, so that he could at least have the reassurance that it was all really happening. His mind had gotten fractured long ago, and between the nightmares and the shadow creatures, he was having a more and more difficult time telling when he was awake, in figuring out what was real and what was in his head.

"What can I do for you, Naja?" he asked next, hunching forward to hide his naked torso from the mad fae mage.

Her predatory smile slipped, something hollow filtering into her eyes. "You can do nothing, worm," she said softly, almost gently, her gaze going distant. "You know, next week is her birthday. The third of Dima." Ah, so it was almost spring then. It didn't *really* matter what month it was, any more than it mattered what year it was, but he found that he rather enjoyed the milder weather, when he could throw the window open and soak up the sun and fresh air.

"I'm sorry, Naja." He murmured it quietly, but he knew she heard. The fae had sharp hearing, after all. "I'm so sorry." He meant it now, just like he'd meant it every other time: he was sorry he'd failed Ingrid, sorry that he'd let her get hurt, that he'd been too much of a coward to stand tall and do what was right. He was sorry that he'd caused Naja so much pain, even if she was returning it to him tenfold. He was sorry that he was like this.

Naja ignored him, eyes distant and full of longing for her lost child, gone these long years. She shuddered, her eyes snapping back into focus and searching his face.

"Your words mean nothing to me, worm. Not unless they can bring her back."

He hung his head, his shaggy crimson hair falling forward into his face, hiding him. His fingers were twisting and pulling into the fabric of his ruined shirt, her attention too heavy for him to handle. He wished with everything he had that Ingrid could come back, that he could fix the wounds of the past, but there was no going back. Time only ever marched forward.

She shook herself, scowling at him. "Get dressed. Your next guest will be here shortly," she snapped, spinning on her heel and throwing the door open. She stepped out into the gently falling snow, pulling her hood up to cover her fine white-blond hair. The door slid shut on its own, sealing him back into the manor. He strode up to the shut door, trying to lock it even though he knew it wouldn't work. None of the locks worked for him, so that anyone was free to come here and do whatever they wanted to him, to his home that was also a prison. He couldn't keep anyone out, he couldn't go past the fence that surrounded the manor and its grounds, and he couldn't even properly hide—no matter what, he had to at least introduce himself to his guests.

He sagged forward, his forehead hitting the door with a sharp *thunk*. Then he straightened, sighing and combing his hair back and between his horns with trembling fingers. After a moment of staring at the door as if it would suddenly gift him with answers, he turned and lumbered back upstairs to change and get ready for the next guest, the caustic laughter of shadows hounding him down the hall.

This one was a screamer. As soon as her pale green eyes had locked on his form she'd shrunk back from him and shrieked in horror. No silver badge this time, so Beast hoped that meant he'd be able to escape unscathed from this encounter. It was a shame that she found him so horrible, because before she'd started up with the screaming he'd been struck by how kind and lovely her face was. Quicker than lightning a fantasy of friendship and love flickered in and right back out of his mind. It was always like this.

Some of the shadows in the corners of the foyer peeled themselves away from the rest of the gloom, twisting and twitching into something like a wolf with glowing red eyes, sharp silver teeth bared in a snarl. Beast froze at the sight, his eyes locked on the creature as it stalked closer to him, ignoring the guest and coming straight for him, thick ropes of shadow-like saliva dripping from its maw. When it lunged at him, those teeth snapping closed inches from his face he flinched, tipping backwards onto his ass painfully, a whimper escaping his throat before he could choke it back down.

He hurried through a greeting for the terrified young person still standing in his foyer, scrambling back, still sitting, until his back hit a wall. He couldn't see the shadow wolf anymore, but he could hear it, snuffling and growling from just behind him, no matter where he turned. When his eyes next landed on his guest he noted that they looked almost as confused as terrified, inching further in as he tried in vain to crawl away from the creature hunting him.

Unfortunately, this young woman ran deeper into the manor rather than out the front door and back the way she came, which meant he'd probably be getting cozy in the old stables until she left. Now that he'd faced his guest the enchantment would let him hide, and he had a stash of blankets and books out there for this exact reason. He hoped she'd leave soon though; it was *cold* out there at this time of year, and there was no fireplace to keep him warm.

And of course, there were the shadow creatures—with all of the shadowy nooks and suspicious crannies in the stables, it was all but guaranteed that the creatures would pay him a visit. But what other choice did he have? The more the visitor looked at his hideous face, the more likely it would be that they'd snap and try to hurt him, and his side still ached fiercely from his last wound.

Beast slipped out into the stables, going to the stall he'd claimed as his and peeling the topmost blanket back from the little nest he'd put together among the hay and settling himself into the chill wool—wool he'd spun himself, and then painstakingly knitted, making it a comforting favorite, for all its shabbiness. He shivered, curling into a ball and using his big hands to heap straw on top of himself so he could hide more easily if the young lady happened to come through here. She was probably one of the young people from the village who seemed to come out here on a dare, to see if they could make it a whole night in the haunted manor in the woods. He and Tully were the only haunts of this cursed place, of course, but none of those young people had ever actually talked to him or asked about ghosts.

As much as he wanted someone to look upon him with kindness, he had to admit it was probably better this way. Even before his imprisonment, he was used to being alone. His parents had ignored him and left him on his own as soon as they could. None of his classmates had ever wanted to play with the dour, too-quiet little boy who only ever wanted to play strange games. No girls would look ever look at him with heat or interest, even before his transformation. And anytime someone *had* worked their way in close, what had it gotten them? Tully loved him fiercely, had been his best friend, mother, and closest confidant from the minute she'd sailed into his life as his parent's retainer mage. And now she was trapped here with him, stuck someplace just under the skin of this world and more ghost than anything. He couldn't talk to her, couldn't hear her if she spoke, couldn't even look upon her except in his memories. There was that tingling warmth that made his skin jump even as it soothed him, and that was it. He dreamed of her often, but who could say if that was really her? She had loved him, and now she was being tortured just as he was.

He squirmed deeper into the blankets, curling tight to keep every scrap of warmth he could. He sighed, closing his eyes in the hopes that he'd be able to nap. It was a way to pass the time, and he was exhausted from the healing. As he was drifting off, he felt the buzzing caress of Tully along his forehead, as if she was trying to comb his hair back with her fingers. He wished he could actually feel her rough, her cool hands, hear her husky voice warbling one of her Viskegan folk songs in his ear like she'd done so often when he was a boy. The tingling warmth wasn't as good as her really being there fully, in the flesh, but it was enough for him to slip the rest of the way into sleep.

It started off as a nightmare.

He was hiding, pressed into cold, slick stone, his hands trembling and covered in warm, sticky blood. He had been trying to talk to his family when he'd lost control of his body, watching from an obscure and ever-shifting distance outside himself as he'd mauled them. When Tully had walked in he'd fled, finding the tight stone room in the bowels of the manor-that-was-not-the-manor of his dream. He was sitting there, scared and whimpering and hoping that Tully wouldn't find him so he wouldn't have to hurt her, too, when he heard a soft noise.

He tried to press his bulk further into the little nook, but just like in real life he was massive and ungainly, and some part of him stuck out no matter what. He was desperate and whimpering, so aware of the blood on his hands that it had begun to sting.

"I don't want to hurt anyone!" he called desperately, squeezing his eyes shut. "Please, just stay away!"

But the faint padding of footsteps didn't stop, only crept closer and closer, and now he was weeping, his hands clenched into tight fists, knowing he'd be forced to hurt someone he loved again.

Something clattered across the floor, kicked by the person whose footsteps were getting so close.

"There's a lot of bones here," a feminine voice mused, and Beast could have cried with relief that it wasn't Tully, it was a stranger; he didn't know that smoky voice.

I didn't mean to, he tried to stay, but the words would not turn into sound no matter what he tried. *I didn't mean to!*

"It's alright," the voice soothed him, hands like autumn

twilight reaching for him. "I know."

It had been so long since someone had touched him with kindness and love, and though he couldn't see the person crouched in front of him, he had the impression of a warm smile, of softness and light wrapping around him.

He shuddered, tears falling in his dream, as the stranger pulled him close, wrapping him in arms that were warm and strong. The blood on his hands was gone, and he clutched at the strange dream woman, burying his face in soft and springy hair.

"It won't be much longer, now," the woman promised, her smoky voice gentle and soothing. Her arms tightened around him. "You've only got to hold on a little longer."

He whimpered, burrowing deeper into the embrace. "I don't know if I can." Somehow he knew what she meant, knew she was talking about the curse, his punishment, and how he felt closer to being lost by the day now—maybe even the hour.

"If you get any more lost I may not be able to find you," she cautioned, making Beast's heart sink into his gut. "You can do this," she promised.

Warmth like the sun cocooned them, and his hands grew desperate, clutching at her, golden light so bright around them that he couldn't see her at all now.

"You'll be alright, I'm coming for you," she promised again, the flesh in his grip going hazy, like she was dissolving away even as he tried to hold her tight.

"No," he cried, the word ripping out of him from somewhere deep in his guts. "Don't go!"

"It's only for now. Be strong for me, sweet man."

And then he was kneeling on the floor, cradling warm

mist to his chest, dry sobs ripping from his throat.

Beast awoke gasping and reluctant, his dream fading too quickly. Soon, all he could remember was bright golden light, and arms around him, holding him tight and strong. He wanted nothing more than to sink back into sleep, to rejoin that beautiful presence, but he was too keyed up now.

He lay in his musty nest, his heart hammering and sluggish in his chest. When no more memories of the dream were gifted to him and sleep refused to come back he peeked out at the dim stables, straining his ears for any sound. Certain the young woman was nowhere near him—he could hear her singing to herself somewhere far-off, possibly on the second floor—he stretched and snagged one of his books from the little shelf he kept them on. It strained his eyes something fierce to read in the two guttering lamps of the stables, but it was either that or stare at the ceiling.

CHAPTER THREE

Claire

It had taken most of the day to make her way to where Teran had indicated the manor should be, but as the sun set she finally spied the dull silver of a fence and gates through the trees.

"Salerah's fires, fucking finally," Claire muttered, equal parts annoyed and relieved to have reached her destination.

She trudged up the crunching gravel drive, well-manicured grounds caught in flashes of dwindling sunlight as she made her way to the large manor home. She'd seen no signs of the manor being inhabited yet, but she kept her silver badge front and center and kept a hand near the hilt of the dagger at her hip. Just in case.

To her surprise, the heavy front doors opened automatically on smooth, silent hinges as she reached the steps leading up to them. Claire froze, not certain what the protocol was here.

"Hello?" she called, leaning forward to try and see inside but keeping her feet planted. "Hello?" she tried again. But there was no response.

Squaring her shoulders and keeping her hand near her

dagger, Claire climbed the steps and tread over the threshold, looking around the manor's foyer, squinting in the near-dark. It was huge, and even with the gloom it was obviously grand. The air inside smelled stale, as though the place had been left closed up for too long, but from what she could see in the dim light it was still clean and well-maintained.

Claire considered that perhaps the door had been enchanted to open like that, and since enchantments could live on after their creator had passed—until whatever internal mechanisms that fueled them broke or wore out—then maybe the place was abandoned after all. Perhaps that was all this quest was: machines chugging away for a master long dead.

It was so quiet inside, like noise was not just absent, but swallowed up. How could anyone be living here?

Claire took another step inside, her eyes still straining for detail in the oppressive dark, when several wall sconces sprang to life, driving away some of the shadows. Now able to see, Claire was utterly stunned at the grandeur of the entryway: white marble tiles polished into mirrors gleamed underfoot, flowing towards the grand central stair off to her left. Rich mahogany, just as well-polished as the floor, seemed to sprout from the marble tile and flow up to the dark upper reaches with the grace of a winding river, the cobalt carpeting serving to enhance the effect. Cream wallpaper with intricately-wrought pale gold filigree covered the walls, and the polished brass sconces dripped with cut glass more brilliant than any gem Claire had ever seen. Though it was unlit, facets of similarly brilliant crystals in an enormous chandelier high above caught the light on the ground floor and twinkled like stars. Fine, utterly life-like oil paintings hung in gilded frames on the walls, and in the painting closest to her she could see a rendering of the front gates, and beyond it what must be the manor in daylight. The hand that had painted the house had managed to breathe something tight and aware into the lines of it that made her uneasy.

Still no one came to meet her, and nothing stirred.

"Hello?" she called again, her voice small and frail in the heavy emptiness. She cleared her throat and tried again, willing more strength into it this time: "Hello? Is anyone here?"

Claire held her breath, waiting. Her ears strained to hear anything beyond the roar of her blood in her ears, but she could hear nothing—even the usual night sounds were oddly absent. She took another step inside, the door swinging shut behind her, sealing her in. She tried not to panic. Every nerve was strung tight enough to break, her ears straining, listening, until—

Footsteps. Soft but heavy, and if it were not an utter silence she never would have heard them, but there they were, padding towards the grand stairs from somewhere on the floor above. Claire's heart began to thunder in her chest, her breath turning thin in her throat. What manner of thing was about to meet her? She took a step back towards the closed door on unsteady legs, stopping when she felt the knob dig into her hip, her numb fingers slipping on the leather-wrapped hilt of her dagger. *No one has ever been hurt after coming here,* she reminded herself, trying to get her breathing under control. *No one has ever gone missing.*

"Hello. Can I help you?" A deep, gruff voice asked from the murky heights of the grand stair, and Claire's eyes slid up, scanning the dark, picking out a deeper shadow than the rest, and *oh gods* but it was huge. This must be him then, the beast of the manor come to greet her, hopefully, and not rip her to shreds for trespassing. Claire gulped, palms going slick with sweat. She took a steadying breath and willed her spine to straighten. The creature—person?—hadn't attacked her, and she took that as a good sign.

This was it. Claire was no coward. And more importantly, she was not rude.

"My name is Claire Odetima, sir." Her host had sounded put out, so she opted to elaborate, hoping that explaining herself would ease things between them. "I'm from the Questing Guild. Newly minted, I have to say, so if I've missed some element of decorum here I'm sorry. Your door just opened on its own and I figured that meant I was being invited in. If you want me to go…"

"No, that's alright. It's…you're fine." she heard him clear his throat. "Do you know what I am?"

She took a shuffling step closer, her heart hammering against her ribs.

"You're some sort of beast, according to what little information I could scrounge up. Supposed to be harmless?" She hadn't meant for that last bit to be a question. It would seem her nerves were getting the better of her. She took another breath, willing her stomach to stop its sickening swoops and clenches.

She thought she heard a dark sort of chuckle drifting down from the upper floor landing. "Indeed. Harmless," her host agreed in a voice as dry and brittle as old bone. As he spoke, the shadowy figure peeled itself away from the rest of the gloom, coagulating into a vaguely human form as the beast of the manor descended the stairs.

He talked like a man, and he walked like one, but from

there the resemblance twisted and blurred. Huge gray paws, as large as a bear's but shaped like a dog's, served as his feet, complete with high ankles hovering well above the floor, and legs thick with powerful muscles that the fine black material of his pants couldn't hide. A white linen shirt and matching black waistcoat strained across a large barrel chest and thick abdomen. His arms and hands, also gray from what she could see, were more or less shaped like a human's, but just as swollen with muscle as the rest of him, and she could see the light glinting off wickedly sharp claws on each finger of the hand gliding over the polished handrail. As his face sank into view, Claire's impression was of a demon, or perhaps a gargoyle, the features harsh and oversized. Thick eyebrows the color of blood hung low over eyes that glittered darkly in the dim light, his hair a bright mop of crimson that was oddly boyish compared to the rest of him. Wicked-looking horns swept back from his temples, ending just past the points of his elfish ears. A large nose jutted from between cheekbones so sharp and stark it looked like they might burst through his granite skin. Bowed slate-colored lips were sunk in a frown, the sharp jaw completing the impression of a face made in the image of a knife.

Her pulse was thrumming fast under her skin, making her hot and chilled at the same time and causing spots to bloom at the edges of her vision, but she forced her feet to stay planted, for her scream to stay locked in her throat.

He edged closer, reaching the bottom of the stairs and standing utterly still. Now that he was close enough for her to see his eyes, she saw that they were a warm and glittering brown that spoke of loneliness, sadness, suspicion, even nerves...but no malice, no anger even, despite the frown and gruff tone. And so Claire decided to take a chance: she forced herself to relax, to smile warmly, and stepped toward him, offering her hand. He recoiled from her, even though he towered over her by at least two feet, and stared at her proffered hand.

"It's nice to meet you. As I said, my name is Claire. What might I call you, sir?" she asked.

Despite the frown dragging down the corners of her host's tight mouth, she saw surprise in his eyes. Was he surprised that she was smiling? That she was introducing herself? Had he expected her to run screaming into the night as soon as she saw him? She supposed if every other visitor he'd had was a kid from the village looking for a spook then that might very well have been the case. As he continued to stare at her, still so tense and wary despite how much warmth she was trying to show, a mad thought crossed her mind: could it be that he was *afraid* of her?

"It's alright," she murmured, keeping her hand out, "I'm not going to hurt you."

He started, like she'd reached out and slapped him, then reached for her proffered hand and shook it gently, careful of his claws. Some lingering nerves pebbled her skin with goosebumps at his touch.

"Please, no 'sir'. I am only Beast," he murmured, looking at her with some emotion she couldn't quite read. His mouth twisted and gods, was that a *blush* creeping into his face? "And—and you are welcome here, Claire," he added, and she was certain now that he was blushing.

Beast dropped her hand and stood there at the base of the stairs, his stance rigid and guarded. He kept darting looks at her face and then letting his eyes skitter off of her again just as quickly, as if he wanted to look at her but was also nervous about doing it. The silence stretched on between them, and Claire began to feel a bit hot and uncomfortable. He hadn't shown her any violence, and that was good, but just what was she supposed to do with him, now? Sweet Delenaa, but she wished she wasn't so tired. And hungry. She was disappointed in herself to realize she had been expecting him to take the reigns once she made it to the manor, and so she had no next steps prepared.

She studied her host for another moment and decided on instinct that she'd need to be casual with him. He was stiff and nervous, so she'd have to be relaxed and warm.

Taking a deep breath, she took a step closer to Beast. The sheer size of him immediately made her heart race with fear, but she did her best to choke it down. She grinned up at him and leaned in just a little.

"Sorry I just showed up unannounced like this," she offered. "There wasn't any contact information on the quest."

He nodded, one corner of his mouth twisting like he was fighting a smile. "Yes, it does that," he murmured. "Like I said, it's alright."

She cleared her throat. "Anyway, I just want you to know I have a couple of weapons on me that are for self-defense, but if that makes you uncomfortable I can leave them outside."

Her mountain of a host blinked down at her, and she wondered if maybe he hadn't understood her.

He shook himself, combing his hair back with his hand, revealing the bases of his horns at his temples. "No, you don't have to do that. But I—" he cleared his throat, his cheeks coloring "—I very much appreciate the thought." He swallowed, his throat bobbing.

She smiled again. There was something about Beast that was...sweet. He looked terrifying, especially with the shadows twisting all around him, but if he was going to be dangerous he'd had a wealth of opportunities to hurt her by now. She couldn't say that she trusted him just yet, but she wasn't really afraid of him anymore either.

"Why are you here?" he asked quietly, startling Claire from her wandering thoughts.

"Oh!" she exclaimed, pulling her pack off her back and digging through a side pocket for the printout from the quest board. "I'm here from the Questing Guild to look into this," she said, handing him the slip of paper.

He read it quickly, his bowed lips still settled into a frown, then handed it back. "Interesting," was all he said.

"Do you know what the anomaly might be? It's been impossible to get anything from the locals."

"I do, but I cannot say. I am...gagged."

Claire wanted to cry, or scream, or both. Of *course* the only person with information would be barred from talking about it by a gag enchantment. No wonder no one knew anything.

"Can you tell me what you're gagged against talking about, perchance?" she asked, hoping that there'd be *something* he could tell her.

His brow furrowed, his large clawed hand raking through his hair again. "I don't really know, actually," he admitted. "I don't think I can't talk about all that much. Certainly not what the quest might be about, but I've never actually tested it before. I haven't really been able to."

There's hope, she thought, a spark of excitement flaring in her stomach. "Well, if you're open to it I'd love to test that out with you. Not tonight, obviously," she added, waving towards the darkening windows. "Perhaps tomorrow." She looked around at the grand entryway again, looking for a sign of anyone else besides Beast. "Is it just you here, then?" she mused.

He nodded.

"Is there a place I can stay while I'm here?" she asked, her exhaustion starting to drag at her heels again. "If not I can camp outside, I suppose."

"No, I can give you a room," he assured her, looking a bit horrified at the prospect of her camping. "I can take you there now. Or…I could show you around? If you'd like."

"I'd love to have a look around," she said. She leaned in conspiratorially. "I'm incredibly nosy, absolutely love snooping and sticking my nose in things. I hope that's alright." She thought she saw the faintest whisper of a smile tugging at his lips.

"I don't mind," he rumbled.

She dipped into a sweeping bow that would have made her governesses proud. "Then lead the way, Sir Beast."

This time, he didn't correct her about the honorific.

Claire found that the longer she was in Beast's presence, the more her fear waned. Maybe it had been her fatigue getting the better of her and spooking her. He looked unusual, but he was so obviously scared of *her* that she just couldn't find it in herself to stay unsettled about him. She no longer felt the urge to run screaming from the manor, which bode well for her work.

"So how does it happen then, my staying here?" she asked, bracing her hands against her lower back to relieve some of the tension there. Since others had visited in the past, she figured there must be some sort of procedure in place.

"You'll have your own room, and can go anywhere you like in the manor or on the grounds," he said, eyeing her thoughtfully "and you can stay as long as you like. The entire manor is enchanted, cleaning and maintaining itself. Meals are automatically served in the dining room at seven, twelve, and seven. You might be able to coax snacks from the kitchen, but it can be a bit, um, temperamental. Your soaps and other toiletries will automatically be supplied as well."

She whistled low, wiggling her eyebrows up at her host's stern face. "Fancy. You might have a hard time getting rid of me," she joked, throwing in a broad wink for good measure.

His mouth quirked up on one side. "I've already told you that you can stay as long as you like."

Her first order of business was getting this giant stick in the mud to smile, she decided. "Very true. That means you can't ever claim that I'm squatting."

He loosed a startled bark of laughter, shooting an uncertain glance her way at the sound. But when he saw her smiling he hesitantly smiled back, looking flustered. It was a sweet victory.

She liked Beast, she decided. There was something about him that felt familiar somehow—like they were already halfway to being friends. He might not have agreed, but she thought underneath the nerves and the wariness he might feel the same. It kept looking like he was doing his best not to react to her, to stay serious in the face of her teasing.

"Follow me, then," he muttered, coughing once and

turning to head into the darkened hall, clogged thick with shadow in the twilight. The wall sconces flared to life as they approached, however, chasing the dark away with bright, steady candlelight.

"That's a neat enchantment," she said, pointing to the flickering candles. "Do you have to do anything to trigger that?"

He shook his head. "They will light for you, too."

He continued leading them down the hallway, candles flickering to life as they approached, until they arrived at a set of wooden double doors.

"This is the dining room," he announced, throwing the doors open wide. "Once the meal is laid out the food stays at the table for roughly forty minutes, so you do need to be somewhat punctual if you want to eat here for your meals."

They stepped over the threshold and a small but elegant dining room bloomed into being around them as the candles lit. The large wooden table was set with gleaming silverware and delicate china painted with wildflowers in peak bloom. A decanter of wine and a steaming basket of rolls were already set out at one end, at the head of the table and the place setting at the left elbow of the head. Covered dishes and tureens trailed down the center of the enormous gleaming slab of wood.

"Were you in the middle of dinner?" she asked.

"Not yet, no."

"Would you rather have dinner before showing me around?"

He studied her face, combing his hair back again. "I'm quite alright. I can give you the tour first. I *did* offer."

She shook her head, her own stomach growling as the

smell of the rolls reached her, reminding her of her long day traveling on foot with just jerky and hardtack to tide her over. "Well thank you then, for taking the time. Would you...would you mind if I joined you after you've shown me around?"

He looked surprised by her request. After a moment he smiled slightly, sharp teeth flashing white and gleaming behind his bowed slate-colored lips. "I suppose I don't mind. You're um—you're welcome to join me, that is," he stammered, color staining his sharp cheeks.

Something shifted in Claire's chest. There was something about the way of this man—large and terrifying to behold, but sweet and polite, even bashful—that intrigued her. It made her hope she would get a chance to spend time with him while she was here investigating the quest. She hoped she would be able to coax him into blushing like that more. It made something inside her...purr.

She smiled as she took a step towards him. "Well, alright then," she said, and wasn't it a bit odd that her voice sounded almost...husky, just then? She cleared her throat and met Beast's soft brown eyes again. "Where next?"

"This way," he replied, leading her out of the dining room. She noticed that he walked more slowly this time, staying close to her side instead of slightly ahead of her.

He led her down the hall, passing a closed set of doors— the other entrance to the dining room, he said—and continuing on to a large, well-furnished study smelling of oiled leather and cedar wood near the end of the hall. "It is technically mine, but I don't mind if you want to use it. I also frequent the library," he told her as he shut the door. "We'll see that next."

She nodded. "What do you usually get up to around

here?"

He paused, looking at her strangely. "Not much," he admitted. "If there are visitors in the manor I try and keep out of the way."

How lonely that was, that even when there were other people around he was still alone.

She studied the harsh profile of Beast's face, wondering what he must be thinking about at this moment. She frowned, her heart aching at the thought of so much emptiness in someone's life, remembering how cold and dreadful that kind of loneliness had been for her all those years ago.

"What if I don't want you to keep out of the way?" she asked softly.

He blinked. "Then I suppose I will have to accommodate," he said slowly, a shy grin sliding across his sharp face.

She rather liked his smile: his cheeks rounded pleasantly, and crinkles popped into the corners of his eyes and made them twinkle. There were creases that bracketed his mouth that were almost dimples, but not quite. She almost didn't notice the sharpness of his teeth, or the odd stone-gray color of his skin, when he smiled.

"I won't be interrupting your usual routine?" she asked. She had never quite gotten over how one of her governesses, Ms. Morya, had hated it when Claire or her sisters had toddled up to her when she was trying to get through her sewing, or a book, and would snap at them like a particularly vicious wild animal.

"Not at all. Or even if you are, I promise you it is a routine that could benefit from being interrupted."

She laughed. "That's good, then. Because I will absolutely be filling your days with rude interruptions while I'm here."

He paused, darting a nervous look at her. "I look forward to it," he rumbled softly, making her heart do something odd in her chest. She nodded, his eyes searching her face in a way that made her skin prickle with awareness.

The next room, the library, proved to be more of an overlarge study, but there were some floor-to-ceiling windows with armchairs snugged invitingly close that looked like they'd be a delight to curl up in in the light of the sun. Being east-facing, the windows held only velvet night now, though. Shelves stretched from floor to ceiling on the other three walls, though Claire noted that the highest shelves were bare, and the shelves that had books weren't particularly full; if she needed to do more research she'd have to leave and visit a university or a Guildhall.

Aside from the chairs by the windows, a large wood table took up the entire middle of the room, with trays and cubbies full of writing supplies down the center at regular intervals. There was another smaller desk with an inviting leather chair tucked between the long table and a freestanding shelf. It would be a nice enough place to work, Claire thought, aside from the lack of books.

As they turned to leave she spotted an odd knee-high bundle near one of the far armchairs, shrouded with a cloth. Curious, she pointed to it. "What's that?"

He turned to look where she pointed, and he combed his hair back with his hand again, looking embarrassed. "Oh, that's um…my spinning wheel."

Well now, but that *was* surprising. "Really? You spin?"

"So?" he snapped, shoulders tensing.

She winced, realizing how she must have sounded to him. She laid her hand on his arm, smiling up at him. "It's alright,

I think it's charming. I'm hopeless at it; my…friend Adeela has been trying to teach me for *ages* and it's never stuck. But I'd still like to learn. It seems so soothing."

His anger melted, replaced by embarrassment. He shifted uncomfortably, nodding. "I'd erm—I'd like to apologize. For snapping. I worry I'm very…rusty."

"Apology accepted," she assured him. "I consider it part of my job to try and understand the subjects of my quests and be patient about things like that. It's one of the things they teach us in the psychology class in prep school. Because, you know, sometimes the wounds aren't physical, right? And every wound heals differently."

He combed his hair back again, some of it tangling on the point of one horn, and he yanked it free with a curse. He darted a look at her. "It is soothing. Spinning, that is. I could…show you, if you wanted."

"Yeah, that would be great," she said, smiling warmly. "Maybe there will be something about how you do it that'll finally make it click for me." He nodded, sweeping his arm out to indicate they should move on.

The kitchens were eerie and empty, unused. It was sad to see, but with the enchantment providing all of the food the room that was usually the beating heart of a home was left cold and abandoned. She felt the urge to set up and cook something, just to bring some life and cheer to it. She wondered if Beast ever tried to cook something here. He didn't seem like the sort, but then he didn't seem like the sort to plop down in front of a spinning wheel, either. She couldn't even really picture it, all of that hulking muscle and those large clawed hands bent and bowed over a bit of fluff, patiently pinching and drafting it out to be spun into yarn. So perhaps it wasn't too much of a stretch to picture him flustered and dusted with flour, huge hands kneading bread dough.

That image did something to her. It made her feel…*melted* in a way that hadn't happened in a very long time. She mentally shook herself, cursing her weariness. It was making her feel odd.

From there they trekked upstairs, where he showed her to her room. It was plain compared to the rest of the manor, with simple white plaster walls and ash wood furniture—all of it large and fine, but understated. Sage green linens graced the sizeable bed, with matching shutters drawn over the two small windows. She was surprised when her host pointed out that she had an attached bathroom—*there* was the luxury.

"I'll see you downstairs, then? Once you've settled in?" he asked, crossing his arms over his barrel chest.

"Absolutely," she winked, reveling in the flush creeping up his neck again. Maybe it was a little childish, to try so hard to make him blush, but in her defense, seeing a towering gray demon flushing with nerves was not a sight one got to enjoy often.

With another uncomfortable nod and a furtive look in her direction he turned and stepped into the hall, closing her door behind him.

CHAPTER FOUR

Dinner

Claire had only been at the manor for a little over an hour and already she had Beast wound up and turned around, blushing and sweating like he was fourteen again. She had one of the silver badges, but she hadn't tried to kill him. She hadn't even screamed at him or tried to tie him up or anything that his dozens of guests over the years had tried to do. And he'd noticed that ever since she'd walked in the doors the shadow creatures had hidden from him, barely more than a flicker in the corner of his eye. These things were objectively good, but they were also new, and new was bad, wasn't it?

The thing about being alone for nearly two hundred years was that one got very used to a routine. It was horrible, and maddening, and bleak at times, but it was familiar and solid, and there was comfort in knowing what to expect, what to do. But now he was thrown. What was he supposed to do with a woman who—who teased and joked and smiled with him? How was he supposed to talk to her? What was he supposed to do with his *hands*?

"Did you see her, Tully?" he whispered into the still air of the manor, his heart hammering in his chest. He felt vaguely feverish, his simple linen clothes clinging to the dampness of his sweat. His mind kept replaying the moment when he'd first caught sight of Claire, sinking into the memory like a hot bath.

He'd been at the top of the stairs, fighting the compulsion to go down and greet her, because he's seen one of the silver badges on her pack and had been frozen in fear and trepidation. His wound from the last one was still tender and aching, even though it had been half a year at least since he'd sustained it. But he hadn't been able to fight the urge for long, and when his foot had come down on the creaking third step from the top she'd spun around to face the sound. He'd seen large hazel eyes and a full mouth that sat comfortably in a heart-shaped face the deep brown of ground cloves. Dark brows arched playfully over those bright eyes, so expressive and lively he had thought she must be the sort who telegraphed their every thought on their face. Her wide, delicate nose and high cheeks were just blushed; was it late enough in the summer to be cold outside? Her hair was carefully braided in rows tight against her scalp, highlighting the graceful curves of her skull and the elegant line of her neck. She was achingly, stunningly beautiful, and at the sight of her it had felt like something inside of him had clicked into place.

He felt that familiar warm tingling he associated with Tully along his right arm, but even that felt charged somehow, as if Tully was frantic as well. "Gods, but she was beautiful, and so damned *nice*. No one's ever talked to me like that. And she *touched* me. Like I was just a regular person, Tully." The buzzing against his granite-colored skin intensified, spreading onto his shoulder.

He was so agitated and distracted he nearly tripped on the stairs heading back down to the dining room, and did actually trip over his own feet in the hall outside it. He landed heavily on his knee, scraping it raw inside his pant leg, but no one had been around to see it, so really that was alright. He hauled himself to his feet, brushing himself off and combing his messy hair back with a frustrated huff. He had to get a grip on himself in the precious few minutes he was still alone.

He managed to make it to his chair and unsteadily flop into it. "Water," he barked, and a glass *thunked* softly into existence in front of his place setting. He clutched at it with sweaty, shaking hands and chugged it messily, rivulets coursing down his chin and onto his shirt. He cursed, swiping at the damp spots with his fingers. Faintly, he heard a door close upstairs, followed a breath later by the creak of the third stair from the top, and his heart jumped into his throat. She would join him soon, and he was still a certifiable mess.

He cursed again, dabbing at his shirt frantically with his napkin, all the while choking down rough breaths that were meant to be soothing. He could get a handle on himself—he *would*.

The skin of his tense shoulders began tingling, and he closed his eyes, finally able to pull in a deeper, more even breath. Tully was still here with him, supporting him. With that touch he felt her calm, felt her faith in him. He ached sharply for her, to be able to talk to her and ask her for advice, for her to wrap him up in her small but strong arms. But this was still something; it was enough.

"Thanks, Tully," he whispered, his sensitive ears picking up footsteps on the thick carpeting outside. His spine straightened, sending a twinge of pain through the scar on his right side. His pulse was still surging in his ears, but he no longer felt like he was going to peel out of his own skin. He managed to suck in another deep breath, letting it out through his nose with a faint smile when Claire walked through the open doors.

"Hello, stranger," she called cheerily, heading straight for the chair at his left.

As she sat Beast caught a whiff of her scent, vanilla and rose, and his stomach gave a little lurch like he'd fallen from a high place. He had never smelled something so delicious and entrancing before in his life.

She smiled at him warmly, her lips looking so velvet-soft and full it sent a shiver down his spine, his reeling thoughts swirling around what it would feel like to kiss those lips, to bury his face in her throat and breathe deep of that intoxicating scent.

Oh, she was saying something—he hadn't been paying attention. He wrestled away his lovely thoughts of lovely Claire and how lovely she'd feel in his arms, redirecting his attention to what she was saying with a mighty effort. As distracted as he was by her...everything, really, he also was swept up in a burning desire to know her, to know everything about her and figure out what had made her choose kindness when no one else had before.

"...pretty sick of jerky, I've got to say. If I never see it again, I think it'll be too soon."

Ah, food. A very safe subject. He cast about for something to say, his mind still tangled from her nearness, from the sweetness of her scent wrapped around him.

"While you are here you needn't have any jerky at all," he

said, feeling awkward. "Do you have a preference for dinner?"

She plucked a still-warm roll from the basket between them and nibbled on it delicately. "I don't know. What do you usually have?"

He shrugged. "Meat? I like meat." Food was a safe topic of conversation, but it was proving difficult to make it interesting. It felt important, that Claire find him interesting. What if she got bored with him and started being cold, or got angry with him? That might be worse than if she'd come into the manor swinging.

"Just meat? Like a pile of meat heaped on your plate?" she asked, brow arched and a ghost of a smile teasing at her lips.

"Sometimes."

She laughed, the sound bright and glittering in the evening air. "I want to see this," she declared, sitting back in her chair and gesturing for him to continue. "Pretend I'm not here. Get what you'd usually get, and I'll steal some if it looks good."

He combed his hair back with his fingers, uncomfortable with the attention being all on him. He cleared his throat. "Chicken," he rasped, peeking at her out of the corner of his eye.

An herby rotisserie chicken blinked onto the table, along with roasted carrots and something green and garlicky. The covered platters that had been on the table disappeared at the same moment, back to the aether they'd come from.

"That's interesting," she mused, shifting closer to the steaming food. "You only asked for chicken but it gave you sides, too. Is that normal?

He shook his head. "The enchantment keys into the needs

of guests, though I'm not sure how. It must have picked up on you and adjusted." He ran his fingers through his hair again. "Is this alright? Do you like it?"

She nodded, smiling and reaching for the platter of carrots. "Oh yes, it's wonderful. I mean, it's not jerky, right?"

Claire had changed into a clean shirt, this one white and more form-fitting, and he found himself admiring the obvious flex of muscle in her arms as she lifted platters and served herself food. She was perhaps a bit above average height for a woman, but solid in a way that spoke of strength. She curved appealingly in all the best places, but the way she moved—precise, easy, graceful—revealed those curves were not all softness. In comparison Beast felt clumsy and hulking; for all that he was packed with muscle, he never used it, and suspected he hadn't wasted away over the long years only because Naja wanted him to look monstrous. But even if he worked at his physical fitness he suspected he'd never be able to move like Claire—his parts didn't fit together well, being a product of Naja's cruel imagination rather than nature. He always felt unstable and top-heavy, his limbs prone to tangling and his sharp claws and horns catching on things as soon as he stopped paying attention.

"You're not eating?" she asked, noticing his empty plate.

He felt heat crawl up his neck. "It's…not pretty, when I eat. My teeth aren't suited to chewing in the usual sense. It gets messy."

"You should eat," she insisted. "I don't mind. I promise you I'm used to worse. When I was on my training permit I studied under my cousin Jordan and that…was a lot." She leaned in, putting a hand to her mouth as if sharing a secret, "He thought washing your hands after using the bathroom was *optional*."

He chuckled, still feeling bashful. But in the end his hunger won out, and he snatched up the platter of chicken, ripping the bird in half lengthwise with his hands and plopping one half onto his plate. "I always wash my hands," he added helpfully, eyeing his guest as he replaced the now half-empty platter onto the table.

She threw her head back, laughing. "Gods, I hope so!"

"I should have cut that with a knife, shouldn't I?" He was so rusty, so unused to having to perform in front of another person. Dimly, he realized that her response to his tearing an animal carcass in half had been amusement instead of horror or disgust, and that was promising, right?

"No, I don't mind. I feel like maybe I *should*, but I did tell you to pretend I wasn't here," she grinned.

He smiled back, nerves eating away at his appetite. But as he watched Claire take more food—including the leg from the other half of the chicken—he realized that for all that he was deeply out of his element, for the first time in centuries he was spending a quiet, domestic moment with someone. No one was screaming, or crying, or bleeding, and it was as wonderful as it was strange.

They lapsed into silence while they ate, but it was unlike any silence that he had ever experienced before. It wasn't the hungry, sucking silence of the manor. It wasn't the tense, brittle silence of someone getting tired of him. It was comfortable, companionable, easy. It felt...warm.

The weight of food in his belly started to cut the edge off of his nerves, letting his heart rate settle and the sweat begin to dry. He even managed to strike up a new conversation.

"I hope your journey from Edden wasn't too difficult," he

commented, darting a quick look at her face from the corner of his eye.

She shrugged, chewing her bite of carrot. "It's a lot of walking, but it's not a bad walk, all things considered. When I was doing my shadowing with Jordan we wound up in a bog for the better part of a week and *that*," she jabbed her fork in his direction, the piece of food she had speared on it threatening to fall onto the table, "was rough traveling. By the end of the first day I was filthy, covered in bites, and all but begging for the sweet release of death." She shook her head, giving a theatrical shudder at the memory. "In comparison to *that*, the hike from Edden was nothing. But I suppose I am still tired, and it's making me a bit quiet."

He nodded, musing. "A difficult thing is no less difficult just because something else might have been more difficult, once." When he dared a glance at her face, she looked surprised. He cleared his throat, idly tearing the remainder of his chicken into small bits as he struggled to come up with something else. "You um…you needn't apologize for quiet. I'm quite used to it, really. And even quiet company is better than none."

She looked at him with those bright, bewitching eyes of hers, considering him for so long he felt a fresh blush creep up his face. "You're absolutely right, Beast. I suppose I'm just too used to being around people who can't stand silence and make it everyone else's problem." She grinned, spearing more food onto her fork. "I think we're going to get along well," she declared, flashing him another smile before digging back into her meal.

CHAPTER FIVE

Dreams

Claire was bone-tired and aching all over from walking all day—which had really just been one leg of a journey that had taken nearly two weeks even with having a mage car the first few days. All she wanted, now that her belly was full, was a bath and to collapse into the sweet oblivion of sleep.

The dust of the road and days' worth of sweat were caked into her hair, but with how she was feeling she knew she'd never be able to manage a full soak without falling asleep. There wound up being hot water in the taps, a fact which had her groaning in relief and re-thinking the "quick" part of her bath. The private bathroom really was beyond luxurious, and she found herself thinking of home, of the extravagant grandeur of her father's estate...and how it had been just as lonely and cold as Beast's enchanted manor. And there, they had had no excuse—they had *chosen* to be cold to her, to be cruel, and then didn't seem to understand why she wanted to distance herself from the lot of them.

There'd been one last blowout before Claire had left to go on this quest. Her father, Draseus Odetima, had met her at the front door, his hands clasped behind his back and his thick mustache quivering with anger.

"You really won't see reason, Claire? You are completely determined to scorn your legacy and shame me?"

She had sighed and spun to face him, tossing her pack to the floor and settling her hands on her hips.

"How am I shaming you?" she'd snapped. "You've yet to explain how your youngest daughter devoting herself to the protection and care of others is shameful."

His sparse brows had creased, brown eyes flashing with anger. "How is it something to be proud of that you're spitting in the face of tradition? Gransen's Mercantiles has been in my family for four generations—"

"And it is still in the family."

He'd closed his eyes and looked to the ceiling as if beseeching the gods for strength. "That is not the *point,* young lady. The point is that part of our success has been because of our unimpeachable pedigree. We have ancestors who were *kings.* And now you want to go gallivanting all over Cillure like you were raised in a hovel? Do you have any idea how that makes us look? Have you thought of that at *all*?"

She had wanted to scream and claw at his smug face. "Yes. I've spent most of my life until recently thinking about that. Have *you* thought about how ill-suited I am to that path? How miserable I would have been? And how would *that* be good for the business?" The tracks of this argument had been well-worn at that point, and before Draseus had been able to wheel out his next retort—usually some nonsense about familial duty—Claire had snatched her pack back up and strapped it on firmly. "I am going, Father. I will be gone for quite some time, and travel is always dangerous; is this really how you want us to part? On another fight?"

His face had gone shuttered and cold, something hard making his gaze cut into her like a knife. "No, I didn't want that, Claire. You are my youngest daughter but I can no longer dismiss this behavior as the folly of youth." His shoulders had straightened, his chin lifting until he'd been looking down his nose at her. "I wish all the best for you, my dear, but I cannot allow you back here. I will not suffer this disrespect anymore."

She'd been floored, stunned to silence. A part of her hadn't thought he'd ever actually do this. "You—you're kicking me out?"

He nodded. "And I will be removing you from all of the family accounts, and from my will. Should you see the error of your ways I may be convinced to welcome you back but, well, this is quite a deep wound that you will have to mend."

All the breath had fled her lungs, and she'd thought she might throw up, but her voice had been steady when she'd finally responded. "Alright, then. Goodbye, Father."

Remembering that terrible exchange, she snorted and shook her head, picking up a bar of soap from the little table of toiletries beside the claw foot tub, scrubbing herself clean with the cotton cloth provided. It was no use lingering on it, seeing as how her father would only let her back in if she groveled and did what he said, and she had no intention of groveling. Not anymore. It was painful, to think that her broken relationship with her father might never heal now, that he'd die, or she'd die, with all of this bad blood between them…but it wasn't her fault, not really. Adeela had told her again and again that love wasn't supposed to come with strings attached.

By the time she was done, her eyes were so heavy she dried herself off and got dressed in her nightclothes with her eyes closed, only opening them a crack to make sure she didn't trip or walk into something on the way to the bed. She collapsed onto the plush mattress, whining to the empty room when she had to thrash around in order to free the blankets from underneath herself.

Usually when she was in a new place sleep resisted her, slipping away and staying shallow, until she'd been in a place long enough for it to be comfortable. But this night, she fell asleep instantly and stayed asleep all night.

But it was not a restful sleep.

Her dreams that night were vivid. *Too* vivid.

One moment she was just snugging herself into her bed, the next she was walking around the manor, caught tight in the snare of a dream. She peered around herself, realizing she was back on the first floor, outside of the library she'd been shown on the tour. There was a bright light spilling onto the carpet from the half-open door, and she found herself blinking rapidly to try and see through it.

She didn't remember walking through the door, but she was in the library now, watching her awkward host haul an armful of books from one end of the library to the other, looking very tense and nervous.

"What are you doing?" she asked, her voice echoing strangely in the dream.

Beast pursed his lips and furrowed his brow as if stumped. "I've got to clean these," he rumbled, dropping the armload onto the floor in a cloud of dust. He stalked back over to the other side of the library, wrapping his long and thickly-muscled arms around another pile of books and returning to where he'd dumped the first batch.

"Shouldn't you be more careful with those?" she asked, feeling her own brow furrow.

"Oh yes, you can't be too careful." He repeated the process until there was a large crumpled pile of books. Then he began removing his clothing, as if it were the most natural thing in the world.

He waved his hand at her in a *come on* motion. "You're going to get messy in those."

She looked down at her clothes, which, sure enough, were already smudged with sooty debris. "Oh, shit," she cursed, hurrying to take off her own clothes before the mess got any worse. When she'd finished the discarded clothes simply disappeared. "That was a good call," she told him, nodding.

She crossed her arms under her breasts, plumping them and hoping he would notice, but he was absorbed in his task: digging through the haphazard pile in front of him, looking for something. She cocked her head, curious as to what he was doing.

"It's here somewhere," he mused, digging. "You've got to get it at the source or it'll just keep coming back."

"What is it? What are you looking for?"

"You'll see—ah *ha!*" he pulled an enormous, wriggling beetle from under a particularly heavy and dusty-looking volume, causing a geyser of thick black ooze to start erupting, covering the books. He rolled the beetle into a ball, making it look like a pill bug, and tossed it into a basket she hadn't noticed was off to the side.

"Isn't that bad? We're supposed to be cleaning those," she said in a panicked whisper.

He rose, clapping his hands together. "This is how you

clean them. It dries as soap. Have you never done this before?"

She was embarrassed to admit that she hadn't. She shrugged.

Something about that simple motion made her keenly aware of how naked she was; her breasts took on a distinct weight, peaking in air that had gone chill, and for the first time she recognized that Beast was also nude, and very close. The dream shifted, and then their bare bodies were *much* closer. Her mouth went dry as she took him in. He was just as massive in her dream, maybe even more so: he towered over her, his gray skin rippling over taut, well-shaped muscle. He still had his claws, his fangs, his odd high-ankled feet, his horns that swept elegantly back from his hairline, but he'd grown a thick tail and leathery wings, as if her sleeping mind wanted to complete his resemblance to a gargoyle.

But it wasn't his tail or his wings that held her attention; her eyes were drawn to his cock, rock-hard and throbbing before her, bobbing gently in time with his pulse. It was darker gray than the rest of him, the head the same slate shade as his lips, and flushed an almost purple color at the base. The thatch of curls his thick member sprouted from was just a shade darker than the unnatural red of the hair on his head.

"I didn't say you could look at that," he rasped, taking himself in his hand and pumping his huge fist up and down the stunning length of himself.

"You didn't say I *couldn't* look," she shot back, angry at this demon-man for getting snippy with her. She was also upset that he had immediately started touching himself, without giving her a chance to play. Or, better yet, before touching her.

She slapped his hand away from his swollen member, her sex clenching as she watched moisture bead and drip from the slit at the head. She stepped closer, wrapping her fingers around him at the base and squeezing. He moaned, throwing his head back, his tail coming around to slither its way up her legs.

A gasp that slid into a moan of her own burst from her as the thick prehensile tail began stroking along her slit, teasing at the sensitive flesh and making heat gather low in her belly. Her fist began to pick up speed, her wrist twisting at the head, making him roar and fling out his wings.

"You can't win this," he growled, his tail slipping past her now-sopping folds and beginning to work itself inside of her. Claire bit her lip, grinding her hips down, meeting the thrusts of it with her own movements and creating more of that delicious friction. His hand reached out for her, his fingers finding her clit and rubbing it between the knuckles of his curled fingers, keeping his deadly claws well away from her delicate flesh.

She gasped again, her knees going weak at the sensation, but they were floating in the air now, Beast's wings still flung out around them, and even though the sensation was blissful, was better than anything she'd ever managed with a partner or alone, it wasn't *enough*, and she wanted to cry out with the frustration of being just *there*, and nowhere near it at the same time.

She increased the tightness of her hands on his cock, pumping faster and making him jump and shudder, and as the mounting pleasure painted itself onto Beast's expression Claire felt her own orgasm inch closer, and so in the way of dreams, she knew that her orgasm and his were interlinked, and redoubled her efforts.

They panted and surged against each other, both moaning and groping wildly from atop their cushion of air, Claire bringing out every trick she knew to push him closer and closer until, at last, the wave of pleasure broke for them both, and they came together with a cry that sounded more like a roar.

It was the most intense orgasm she had ever experienced, and it tore her from sleep, making her whole body convulse with wave after wave of pleasure, the epicenter her pulsing cunt. She lay in the strange bed, gasping and sweaty, sure that she could just hear an echo of Beast's final horrified cry from her dream: "The books!" Weak sunlight was seeping in from around the shutters; it was morning already.

As her body eased down from its high, she groaned and rubbed her hands down her face.

"Well, I guess I won't be able to look Beast in the face at all today," she muttered, her fingers delving tentatively between her thighs, where she was damp with her release and so sensitive she jumped. She sighed again, wondering why it was that the sleeping brain felt the need to provide sexy dreams about people you felt no attraction to in the daylight. Then she threw off the covers and stumbled into the bathroom to pee and clean herself up.

It was probably best not to study that dream too closely. It certainly wasn't the first time something like this had happened, and even if it was uncomfortable it was normal enough, right?

But no matter what she tried to get it out of her mind it refused to stop reviving the dream, lingering in it, until she felt like she might go mad.

A Light in the Dark

CHAPTER SIX

By the Light of Day

Beast hadn't intended to hide from Claire the next morning, had even been so excited at the prospect of spending more time with her that he'd hardly slept. But sometime in that vague time between midnight and dawn, he'd begun to worry. He'd begun to wonder: what if it was a fluke? What if, in the light of day, everything changed? It hadn't helped that as those doubts had crept in his phantoms had too, as if sensing his weakness. The shadows in his room had started darting all over, glowing red eyes watching him from the deepest shadows. He'd heard dark laughter, distant and taunting, culminating in screams that may have been his own. By that time, he'd lost a lot of awareness of himself.

With such a dark night, how could he not have a difficult morning?

Angry buzzing flared all over him, sharpening his unrest, but his fear of confronting what he'd felt last night in the light of day was far stronger.

"I know what you want Tully, and it's not going to happen," Beast grumbled after a particularly intense round of tingling assaulted his back, which was turned resolutely to the door of his bedroom. He'd sat himself in his oversized desk chair roughly an hour ago and had refused to so much as consider getting up, much to Tully's chagrin.

He imagined Tully fuming at his stubbornness, calling him all sorts of nasty things in Viske, her native tongue, but staying resolutely at his side. She was as stubborn as he was, a fact that she had loved to claim was proof that no matter whose blood flowed in his veins, *Tully* was his mother.

"Last night was a fluke, *madjem*," Beast admitted softly, his eyes locked on a far corner of his room, memories of the gods-cursed howls from the long night echoing in his ears. The insistent sensation on his arm eased, growing slower and more soothing. His large clawed hands wrung together in his lap, his eyes squeezing shut to try and will away the things in the dark that haunted him. They made him feel small and so afraid, and made it seem all but certain that in the light of day Claire would no longer see him as a person, would no longer treat him with warmth and kindness.

He couldn't get Claire's face out of his mind, couldn't stop catching phantom whiffs of her intoxicating scent in his nose. The way she'd smiled at him, laughed with him, *joked* with him jockeyed for space in his mind with the shadows and horrors. He started to cling to those memories, to the feeling that she might already consider herself his friend, and he had to admit that he felt a bit better when he did. The howls trailed off into growls, the shades paling, and the tingling feel of Tully's incorporeal hands growing stronger and warmer.

But still he hid. Even with the shadows reduced to almost nothing, he couldn't get up out of his chair and face things.

It was almost noon when he decided the manor had been still and quiet for long enough that he felt secure slipping out of his room. His sensitive pointed ears detected movement behind the door of Claire's room, and he released a slow breath as he eased down the hall and towards the stairs. Despite his care, he managed to land wrong on the third step down, causing it to creak softly. He winced, freezing in place and holding his breath, waiting to see if he heard her moving to her door. But it remained quiet and still, the only sounds his heart in his ears and paper shuffling behind the closed bedroom door. *Thank the gods.* He continued his slow creep, taking extra care now, and made his way to the kitchen for a snack. He figured he'd get a bite and then snatch a book to read from the library. There was one he'd just found tucked away on a high shelf, *Sanity's Requiem,* by his favorite author Garnette Mason, that looked like it would be a good one.

Beast was terribly addicted to romance novels, and the raunchier the better. He had been locked up at just sixteen, and had never had a chance to so much as court someone, let alone to fall in love or have any kind of sex. And with the echoing loneliness that had been his childhood, there was nothing more appealing to him than a whirlwind romance. He yearned to find someone who would prove that they cared for him and wanted to take care of him and would treat his heart like the fragile thing that it was. He wanted true love, soul-deep and powerful. He wanted a best friend who he could lavish with attention and pleasure. He knew he'd have a lot of learning to do, but he would be all too happy to learn, if his partner was fine with teaching.

He bet Claire would be a good teacher.

The thought made him tingle and flush all over, his pants growing tight in a way he was very glad no one was around to see. He grunted as he adjusted himself, then hurried along.

He managed to slink into the kitchens and convince an apple and some cheese to materialize. The enchantment that provided supplies tended to be stubborn with him, and over time he'd become convinced it must be because of Tully's meddling that he was able to get any creature comforts at all. Naja certainly wouldn't have been concerned with whether or not Beast was comfortable and entertained, but Tully would. And she'd be clever and powerful enough to twist Naja's own enchantment out from under her and hide her tracks to boot. There was no other reason for it, or how it had escaped Naja's notice during her regular check-ins.

His stomach contented, he made his silent, careful way back down the hall to the library to snag his book and slip back into his room. He hadn't heard any stirring yet coming from the upper floor, but he didn't want to risk hanging around only for Claire to decide to make use of the library.

He wanted to see her again, of course. He thought maybe he wanted another of her warm smiles more than he wanted his next breath. Which was why he *couldn't* see her again if he could help it.

He found his book, cradling it to his chest reverently, but found his feet unwilling to move just yet. He was absorbed in thoughts of glittering hazel eyes and soft smiles, his whole chest aching with the need to seek her out, to bask in her warm presence. He was so absorbed in those thoughts, in fact, that he failed to note the gentle click of a door sliding carefully shut, the pad of feet creeping along carpet. It wasn't until Claire stepped on that same creaking step that had almost caught him out that he snapped back to reality with a soft curse. Could he risk trying to make it out to the stables? The kitchen door wasn't far, and from there it was just a few yards to the stable doors.

He remained frozen and unable to decide for too long, and before he knew it he heard her crossing the foyer's marble tiles; she'd see him for sure if he left now. He broke out in a cold sweat, his pulse thudding through his body, his mind desperately combing through his options.

You could go out and meet her, the boldest part of himself considered. *Maybe last night wasn't a one-off and she'll still want to talk and be friendly.*

As her footsteps began to pad along the hall outside the library he decided to play at nonchalance: he'd sit and pretend to read in his favorite armchair by the window and hope that she wasn't heading to the library. The door was only open a crack, and unless she came in she'd never see him all the way over by the windows. And it wasn't like this was a particularly well-stocked library; what were the chances that she'd be coming in here? The dining room was much more likely, considering it was close to lunch.

He hurried over to his chair, carefully scooting his covered spinning wheel to the side, his book clutched so hard in his damp hands his claws were digging into the thick leather and making holes. He had just sat down and thrown the book open to a random page when the door swung open tentatively, revealing a tense but still warmly smiling Claire, just standing there in the hall as if she weren't the stuff of dreams. He kept his head bowed, pretending to be engrossed in his book, when really every nerve in his body was arcing towards her like iron to a lodestone. He watched her out of the corner of his eye, unable to stop himself. And dying to know, afraid to know—would she still look on him with kindness in the daylight?

As she crept in past the threshold, clearly intent on entering the room and joining him, he lifted his head and pretended to have just noticed her, nodding at her in a polite greeting.

She looked a little nervous, he thought, her smooth brown face tense, but a warm smile still played at the corners of her full mouth.

"Hullo, Beast," she called, swanning over to stand beside him. "Are you busy this morning?"

His grip on the book tightened. "No, not at all. What can I help you with?" Sweat began pooling under his arms and at the small of his back.

"I thought it might be fun to hang out together. Try and get to know each other a bit so I'm not just some stranger crawling all over your house."

Well now—that was surprising.

"Hang…out?" he repeated slowly, her odd phrasing catching him off guard.

"Yeah, you know: spend some time together. Be casual. Talk. Maybe get up to something fun. Hanging out." She cocked an eyebrow at him, smirking.

"Oh, yes, that makes sense. I've just never heard it said like that before."

"Really?" she said thoughtfully, pinching her lip. The look she leveled at him was thoughtful. "Interesting. Must be a Kesterin thing."

CHAPTER SEVEN

Deep Dive

It took Claire more time than she wanted to admit to get her body under control after waking up from that dream, her skin twitching and over-sensitive for what felt like hours. She hoped Beast wasn't wondering where she was while she was holed up in her room trying to ignore her arousal.

And failing at it—she'd found the urge to touch herself impossible to ignore when she'd slipped into the tub to bathe, her fingers swirling in desperate circles around her swollen and throbbing clit, her legs twitching hard enough that water almost spilled over the sides. But with another release and a bath she'd finally managed to get the worst of it out of her system. She still hadn't been quite ready to look him in the eye and be professional, so she'd dressed and sat down at her little desk to make her notes and ruminate on what her approach should be for this quest instead of going down to breakfast. She'd immediately dismissed the possibility that Beast was here guarding something. Which meant he was trapped at the manor. Since she was ungifted, her options for getting him out weren't going to be straightforward, but sometimes magic didn't work like it was supposed to, and a sort of back door could present itself to those who looked for it. And she was determined to look for it.

Once she'd finally gotten her courage she went searching for him, starting in the library, and lo and behold, there he was, sitting in one of the armchairs near the large bay windows, reading. It might have been her imagination, but his relaxed posture had seemed forced, his shoulders a bit stiff and his eyes motionless on the book in his lap.

And then there was his awkwardness over her greeting, almost like he, too, had been avoiding her out of embarrassment. And there was something about his confusion over her use of the phrase "hang out" that was niggling at the back of her mind. It reminded her of how his accent was a little off, and how the way he spoke sounded more formal than she was expecting. Was it a symptom of being alone so much, or something else? She'd have to set that aside for now; after all, she'd come here for a reason.

She took the seat beside him, smoothing her pants over her legs and smiling. "What book is it that you've got there?" she asked.

To her surprise, color flooded his face, and he looked so uncomfortable she thought he might hurt himself. "I-it's nothing. Silly, really."

"Oh. Do you like it at least?"

He shrugged, sliding the closed book across his lap and wedging it between his far leg and the side of the chair. *Alright then,* Claire thought, trying not to giggle. *Must be embarrassing.*

Her curiosity was piqued, but she was trying to put him at ease, to make him comfortable with her presence so that he would let her help him. Until she figured out more about what was going on Beast was her one and only lead, her only source of information, and she had to make sure that avenue stayed open.

"Do you like reading?" she asked, her eyes sweeping over the sparsely populated shelves.

"It's a good way to spend time," he hedged. "I like it well enough." He seemed warier today, as if something had happened overnight that had soured him on her.

She nodded and stood, striding over to the bookshelves and running her slim brown fingers along the spines of the books, noting that they were all spotlessly clean. She couldn't help but think of her strange dream, and how frantic they'd both been to clean the books, which made heat creep up her neck when her mind slid to what else she'd been frantic to do in that cursed dream. She shook herself and forced her focus back on the here and now.

Most of the books were in excellent condition, as if they were still fairly new. She plucked one from the shelf at random and flipped to the front matter page. She was surprised to find that the publication date was listed as being 3 AW (After the War), which was the current era. She did the mental math—since the current year was 230 AW that made the book 227 years old, though it didn't look nearly that old. She flipped through the pages idly, not really paying attention to the words.

"Do you prefer spinning then, most of the time?" she asked as she replaced the book and took another even more pristine one from the shelf.

"It depends on my mood. Sometimes I have no patience for it." *Published 16 AW, Cremling Brothers Press,* she read on the front matter page for this new book. "But I do like doing things with my hands, making things," he added, and Claire was pulled from her musings by his latest comment.

"Ah, a crafter." To look at him, you'd never suspect that this hulking gray monster was someone so sweet and almost boring. In the full light of the sun he looked even more unsettling than he had last night, the pewter gray of his skin shocking, especially against the equally unnatural red of his hair. His claws and mouthful of sharp teeth were more obvious, and he was wearing all black today, the overall effect sinister. "What can you make besides yarn?"

He shrugged, flushing. "I figured out how to sew." He coughed and stuttered a bit, and she thought that might have been his gag enchantment stopping him from saying something. "Finding clothes that fit me is a challenge otherwise," he finally managed.

She chuckled, nodding her understanding. "I get that. It probably doesn't seem like it would be a problem, but you would not *believe* how long I had to look to find a seamstress who could tailor my clothes the way I like them. In Kesterin the fashion is for women to look pretty and helpless and getting them to give me simple, comfortable, and durable was *hard*." She sighed, putting the book back and grabbing an old-looking one from the shelf.

"What does 'pretty and helpless' look like?" he asked. "I'm afraid I can't quite picture it." *Published 347 AFL, Boros Limited*, this book read, and that was *really* shocking. A book from a whole other era was…unexpected. AFL—After the Flood—was the previous era, and had lasted 392 years. And even more surprising was that the book in her hands only looked old, rather than ancient, at two hundred and seventy-five years old.

"Oh, you know," she said slowly, replacing the old book and moving onto another bookshelf to continue her perusal. "Large heavy skirts, corsets, high-heeled shoes, lots of silks and satins and ribbons. Things you can't even really go for a long walk in."

Beast huffed a laugh from behind her. "And you don't like that?"

She shrugged. "Every now and again, sure. But all the time? No thank you, I'd rather run around in rags." *Published 22 AW, Herrings and Soche,* this next book read. She replaced it and grabbed another that looked old. "Would you say your interests mostly run towards textiles then?" she asked over her shoulder.

"For the most part. Every now and again though I'll, um, try to draw a bit."

She beamed at him over her shoulder. "That's so exciting, I'd love to see your art sometime!" *Published 365 AFL, Boros Limited.* The loose confetti fluttering around at the back of her mind was starting to glob together and turn into an actual idea.

He's been here for a long *time,* she realized. She'd have to comb through the books more thoroughly at some point, but the fact that the newest book she'd found was from two hundred and eight years ago was telling. Especially when he'd also mentioned that the manor cleaned and maintained itself; naturally two hundred-year-old books would look like new if they were being magically protected.

Realizing Beast still hadn't responded she turned, putting the book back. She was surprised to see him looking flustered and uncomfortable again. "You okay?" she asked, returning to the chair next to his.

He coughed, combing his hair back from his face and mussing it. "Y-yes. I just—um. I don't show anyone my drawings. Sorry."

Her lips pulled up in a gentle smile. "No worries. You can have your privacy."

He pursed his lips and nodded, avoiding her eyes.

"So have you been stuck here awhile then?" she tried, curious now that she'd noticed the dates on the books.

Beast shook his head. "I cannot say."

Right, so he can't give me any specifics on time, she noted.

"Do you like it here?" she tried next.

The laugh he loosed was dry and sarcastic. "No, I can't say that I do."

"What would you say your least favorite part of it is?"

He blinked, brows lowering. "The…quiet," he said after a few heartbeats. Her heart clenched.

"In some ways, too much quiet is worse than too much noise," she offered gently. She grinned at him. "I think *my* least favorite part of the manor is how remote it is," she quipped, trying to lighten the mood. "Why would anyone decide to build a home here in the middle of the forest, with no roads leading here? There's not even a road *near* here. It's madness!"

He huffed a laugh, his eyes going less cold and distant as they met hers. "They should have consulted you when they built it."

"Absolutely they should have." She tilted her head back to take in the towering ceiling and the elaborate motifs that had been painted all over it. "It's lovely though, despite being too hard to get to and too quiet. Is it yours?"

He was quiet, and she returned her gaze to his. He looked

uncertain, his only response a shrug. *That should have been a yes or no question,* she mused.

She decided to change tacks. "My father owns a mercantile business," she told him. Maybe it would encourage him to share a similar detail about his parents, or whoever it was that owned this place, if she talked about something similar first. "His home is about this large, and not too far off from being as lonely."

"You...don't live with your father? Are you married, then?" he asked, color staining his cheeks again.

Claire snorted. "No, I'm not married. Or engaged. Or seeing someone. It's kind of rough out there," she barked a laugh, shaking her head. "I guess I don't really live anywhere anymore. Me and my father had a bit of a...falling out. I'm not close with my family." She cringed inwardly, realizing she was falling into her bad habit of getting too familiar with people too soon.

"Oh. I apologize if I was prying.."

She waved her hand dismissively. "You're fine! If anything I'm over-sharing." She laughed. "I don't let it bother me anymore, that distance with my family. Sometimes you just don't mesh with the family you're born into, right? Sometimes you've got to *make* your family. And honestly, I found a family that was plenty amazing.

"When I was, I don't know, ten? Twelve? My father needed a new head of house and hired a woman named Adeela. And right away she saw how lonely and sad I was and adopted me, made it her mission in life to pour so much love into me that I'd burst. I'm closer to her girls than I ever was with my actual sisters, I love them all to pieces. Adeela's retired now but we still talk all the time. But if you hear me talking about my mom, that's who I mean. My natural mother died giving birth to me."

"I'm so sorry."

She smiled sadly. "Thank you. I wish I could have known her, and I'm sorry that my older sisters had to lose their mother, but I can only know her through paintings and stories. It's…a different kind of loss."

He nodded, combing his fingers through his hair some more. She was finding that she rather liked seeing how mussed he looked after a few swipes, several tendrils inevitably wrapping around his horns and getting stuck. It was…cute. "I…have someone similar," he told her after a moment. He shifted in his seat, his knees drifting apart from the tight clench he'd been maintaining the entire time she'd been in the library. It drew her attention to the delicious thickness of his thighs in a way that caused an echo of her dream to flit through the back of her mind. She squeezed her own thighs together against the sudden throb in her sex. *NOT the time for that, you perv*, she hissed at herself. "Her name was Tully. She also worked for my parents, like your Adeela. She said I was the saddest and quietest child she'd ever seen. She lived for making me laugh and smile."

"You miss her," Claire said softly, her heart clenching again.

"Yes." He swallowed, his huge hands clasping together and dropping to his lap. "My parents didn't like having me around too much, but Tully wanted me to get to know the family business, so she made a point of taking me out on their business trips from time to time.

"We went to the shipyard once, when I was a boy. I remember being awed by just how *big* they all were, and that we owned them and used them to get things that people needed from all over Cillure. That made me proud. There was one that was especially large, with three masts, and all these oars poking out the side like little legs, that especially captivated me. I asked Tully what it was called, that ship, and she'd said—" Beast coughed and sputtered, his hand coming up to cover his mouth. "Erm, it was named after me. I later found out it wasn't, but Tully was always trying to make me feel special like that." *Apparently, his name is forbidden information. Interesting.*

"She sounds so special. I'm sorry you lost her."

His smile was strange. "In some ways I feel like she's still with me."

She was about to ask him more about Tully when something else slid into place in her mind. *Hold on, no engines on the ships,* she realized with a jolt. *That means they were old enough to still be moved entirely by wind- and manpower.* Mage engines had been the standard on vehicles for *ages* now. Especially for the wealthy, which Beast's family had clearly been. She dug through the faint memories she had of her history classes. Mage engines had been invented a little over a hundred years ago, she wanted to say around the 110's? It had been a while since those classes, and she'd never had much enthusiasm for history. But it made her think her observation about the books hadn't been a coincidence. *Sweet Delenaa, he's been here for—*

"You've been here for more than a century," she breathed. *Shit.* She hadn't meant to say that out loud.

He didn't respond, but the way he stiffened said plenty. Her heart stuttered in her chest, mind balking at the enormous, aching weight of that many years of loneliness.

"How are you not completely mad?" she asked him, incredulous. She wanted to crawl out of her skin just *thinking* about it.

He smiled sadly. "A very reasonable question. But the answer is that I don't know that I'm not. My time here has marked me. I'm not the man I once was, though some might say that that's for the best."

She wondered if that meant she should be scared of him. She watched him for a moment, how he untangled his hands from the nervous knot that had been twitching in his lap to rake through his hair. How those hands then landed on the arms of his chair, sliding against the brocade fabric, making loud rasping noises. If he was dangerous, he was hiding it better than she'd ever seen.

She'd always had a knack for spotting bad people. Vanessa, her oldest sister, had even said that as a baby Claire would only cry for the meanest of the nurses tasked with her care. As she'd grown up she'd been able to avoid the worst of the bullies in her classes because she just *knew*, deep in her gut, who they were. And even beyond that, in her experience dangerous people didn't want you to know they were dangerous. They swore up and down that there was nothing wrong, that you had nothing to worry about, and if they slipped and you saw the monster anyway they tried their best to convince you it was your fault, or that you were in some way mistaken. Nothing about him had set off her alarm bells, and if that filthy dream was any indication then her subconscious even seemed to *approve* of him.

For not the first time, Claire wondered what was going on here. *An anomaly in the woods outside of Edden.* That was all she knew for certain. It was such an odd little quest, but it was also completely dull: the only person in the entire manor was Beast, and he was harmless and up to exactly nothing. The manor and its grounds were grand and well-equipped, but aside from the enchantments it was all very ordinary so far. She'd done research on the surrounding area at the Guildhall before making her way to the village of Edden, and there were no landmarks or places of power nearby, there wasn't anything historically important about the area, and now that she was here there didn't seem to be anything significant being kept in the vicinity. She'd still do a sweep with her diviner to see if it could pick up anything besides Beast and the manor's enchantments, but she was confident it would reveal nothing.

She looked up and met his eyes again. He had been watching her closely, following her fingers as she'd fiddled with her clothes, the seat, her hair, while her mind had wandered. He looked away once he noticed she'd caught him, color spotting his high sharp cheekbones. She couldn't help the smile that pulled at her lips.

"What do people usually do when they get here?" she asked. "There's not much to do, right? So what do they get up to?"

He unclasped his hands and ruffled the hair at the back of his head. "Honestly? I don't know. They avoid me unless— um, they avoid me."

She quirked a brow. "What? What were you going to say?"

His knees squeezed together again, his hands trapped between them. "Nothing."

She cocked her eyebrow and tucked her chin in, doing her best to mimic Adeela's Look—it always worked to get Claire to spill the beans.

He huffed and grumbled, squirming in his seat. He sighed heavily and rolled his eyes. "It's—gods, it's embarrassing. But sometimes…they fight me. So even if they don't avoid me I avoid them."

She blinked. "Fight you?"

He nodded, still finger-combing his hair nervously. "Yes. People don't tend to like me. Sometimes they *really* don't like me." He shrugged, trying to look unbothered. Her stomach dropped. There was something about the way he was saying that that set off alarm bells in her head.

"Did they…did they *hurt* you, Beast?"

His eyes shuttered, his posture stiffening back up. "Does it matter? " he snapped.

She blinked, taken aback by this sudden shift. His tone got her hackles up, but she resisted the impulse to snap back at him. If it hadn't been clear already it was more than clear now that she was dealing with someone who was traumatized. She had to tread carefully and be patient with him.

"Alright, I can respect that you don't want to talk about it," she told him, wincing internally when she caught the sharp edge to her voice. She took a breath to relax.

He was silent, his hand frozen in his hair, avoiding her eyes. When he spoke, it was to say something she hadn't been expecting. "While I am here, I can come to no permanent harm," he said softly. "And I cannot die." *He's just as frozen in time as all the rest of it,* she thought. "So it really doesn't matter."

She frowned, her hands clenching into fists. "How can you say that about yourself?" she breathed. "I don't care if you couldn't even feel it, that was still an awful thing that happened to you. And it *shouldn't* have happened." His throat bobbed, but the corner of his mouth quirked up.

He was close to two feet taller than her, outweighed her by at least fifty pounds of pure muscle, and his claws and teeth could shred her to ribbons without a thought. But Claire knew a delicate soul when she saw it. Like called to like.

His mouth twitched in a wry smile and something shifted in his eyes, locking her out. "You don't know what you're talking about," he told her heavily, his big body curling back in on itself. "I deserve it. I deserve to be here."

She cocked her head, considering. "Interesting response. You really believe you should be at the mercy of others?"

His face fell, eyes going distant. He nodded, the movement stiff.

She frowned. So he was definitely here being punished, then. And whatever he'd done, it was bad enough—or he had been made to *think* it was bad enough—that he felt he deserved to be hurt. That he deserved untold years of loneliness. That he deserved to be stripped of absolutely everything.

If he was being punished, then the Consortium needed to hear about how he was being treated. There were rules in place for these sorts of things, rules against solitary confinement and other forms of cruelty. There should have been a reference to his disciplinary records with his quest information, but maybe the age of the quest was to blame for that, too. She'd have to look into it.

"Well, we'll just have to agree to disagree then," she said, frowning at his sullen expression. He was practically pouting, and it made her want to slap him upside the head and wrap him up in a bear hug at the same time. *Why does he make me feel so gods-damned confused?*

She resisted the urge to groan and leave him to his sulk. *Traumatized,* she reminded herself. *He needs patience and empathy.*

"So has it been nothing but a parade of assholes through here?" she asked him casually, crossing her arms over her chest and cocking an eyebrow at him.

"Yes," he grumbled, his hands clasped tight together and wriggling in his lap.

"No one wanted to be your friend, huh? How would you like it if I said I wanted to be your friend?"

"I might say you were a fool," he murmured. He only met her eyes for a moment, but she saw something odd in that brief flash.

She sighed. "Do you really have to be rude to me?" She was starting to feel tired more than angry at his sour attitude. She just wanted them to be friendly.

His mouth twisted into a scowl, his large nose wrinkling in disgust. But then he closed his eyes, and when he opened them and looked at her something had softened.

"I do not. I'm sorry, Claire. You cannot really mean to call me friend after just a day though, surely."

"Apology accepted," she said, shrugging. "Maybe we just promise to be nice to each other and see what happens, hmm?"

He grinned, flashing those sharp teeth at her. "Alright. Can't do anything but try, I suppose."

Before she could respond, a loud gurgle rent the silence, and Beast's eyes snapped over to her. She laughed, her hand going to her stomach. She craned her neck to look at the clock over the doorway and saw they were missing lunch. "Sweet Delenaa, the time really got away from me. Join me for lunch?" she asked her quiet companion, hauling herself to her feet and holding her hand out to help him up, too.

The smile that spread slow and shy on Beast's ugly gray face warmed her spirit. *He's not really ugly,* she corrected herself, *just...unusual. But there's a certain appeal there.* Or was that her dream talking again?

When he took her hand, his grip was so gentle and hesitant, his hand so warm and solid, that she decided she rather liked holding it. He hauled himself to his feet and dropped her hand, but it felt like perhaps he hesitated, just a little.

She smiled up at him and led the way out to the dining room.

CHAPTER EIGHT

The World Beyond

Beast had earned this fate, no matter what Claire thought.

He had failed Ingrid. He'd let her get hurt over and over again. He'd…he'd *killed* her. He deserved this, and he couldn't let himself forget no matter *how* dazzled he was by a pretty face and a kind heart. She meant well, he knew that, but she didn't know what she was talking about. *He* did.

But he *was* dazzled, of course. Every time he caught sight of her the breath fled his lungs and his stomach started doing uncomfortable flips, like he was nervous, but not quite *just* that. Whenever she drifted close to him he felt compelled to drift still closer, to feel her satiny soft skin, her heat. When she'd offered him her hand to help him from his seat he'd been so shocked he'd given it to her. Her hand was so small and delicate compared to his, but she'd been able to help him to his feet easily, her grip strong and sure. The contact had hit him like a bolt of lightning, snaking down his spine and setting his hair on edge. He hadn't wanted to let go of her, even if he'd also been awkward and skittish about it.

Once in the dining room, he wrestled his thoughts to focus

on the here and now; he didn't want to upset her with his brooding. The large platter of sandwiches—and slices of an orange melon he couldn't name—laid out on the long table for them had his stomach rumbling.

"Ooh, that looks good!" she exclaimed, sliding into the same seat she'd used last night at dinner—the one at his left side. Despite his seconds-old promise to start distancing himself from her, he warmed at the sight. At how easily and naturally she sat beside him.

He shook his head, glad she wasn't looking at him to wonder why. "It does," he agreed faintly, not quite able to keep all traces of his sourness from his voice. But it was slight, so perhaps she wouldn't notice—

"Are you alright?" she asked gently, her sharp, expressive brows slamming together in concern.

He cursed inwardly. She was entirely too perceptive. "I'm fine," he lied, taking his own seat.

"Liar," she insisted, her eyes narrowing. "Something's bothering you, and since I'm the only one here I'm forced to conclude I did something. So spit it out."

He blinked, wondering if she was reading his mind. Part of him wanted to come clean—well, as clean as he could with the gag restricting what he could say—because he thought she'd earned that from him, his honesty. But a much larger and louder part wanted to pull into his shell and protect her, in his way, from all of his nonsense.

"It's nothing. I'm fine," he snapped, wincing inwardly at how harsh his tone had been. He hadn't meant that. "Let's just have lunch, alright?" He swiped a sandwich off of the platter and ripped off a big mouthful before she could keep peppering him with questions, trying to force him to open up.

And for what? She wasn't going to be able to help him, he was being locked up here on purpose. He should really just send her away, get rid of her and be done with it.

Claire was glaring at him, her lips pursed, watching him eat. Then she sighed, taking a sandwich of her own and several of the melon slices. "Alright, grumpy pants. You don't want to talk, that's fine. But you're just hurting yourself. You leave a wound to fester and it's never going to heal."

His brows lowered as he swallowed the huge bite of sandwich at last. What did this woman, this stranger, know of wounds? They said time was supposed to heal them all, but he'd had nothing *but* time and here he was, still miserable with them. She thought that just because she had a fancy badge and had taken some classes that she could actually *help* someone like him? It was laughable.

You leave a wound to fester and it's never going to heal, she'd said. It kept looping through his mind, stabbing at him, making him think about things he didn't want to think about. How did someone even heal wounds like that, anyway? How did you heal something you couldn't see, couldn't touch or smell?

"I'll probably begin combing over the manor with my diviner in the next day or two. It's going to take forever, between the size of this place and how much interference I'll be getting from you and the manor."

He grit his teeth. She'd *just* said she was fine with not talking. "Do whatever you want," he snapped at her. "I don't even know what a diviner is, so have at it."

A tightening of her mouth was the only thing that revealed that his tone had bothered her. The rest of her face was carefully neutral. "A diviner is a device used to track and sort aether signatures. To detect magic and find hidden things." She bit her lip, hard enough that he was worried she might draw blood. "Why don't you want me to help you?" she blurted, her neck darkening in a faint flush. "Half the time it seems like you want my help and the other half you don't, and you want me to leave. So what's going on?"

He took another huge bite of food so that he wouldn't have to reply yet. The answer was that she shouldn't be helping him, that the quest she'd pulled up about this place must have been an error, because he was *supposed* to be here. Naja had made it very clear that he needed to be punished, so here he was.

Darting a look at Claire, he was surprised to find concern painted on her face instead of the anger and resentment he'd been expecting. Even with him being an asshole, she was still kind. It made something crack open deep in his chest that snuffed out his anger as quickly as it had flared.

"I just...I know we don't know each other very well, but I do deserve to be here," he admitted quietly before he realized he even meant to speak. "And it's...hard to hear you say otherwise."

He kept his eyes fixed on his plate now, his claws beginning to shred the hem of his shirt out of sight beneath the table. He wanted to look at her, to reassure her he was telling the truth now if nothing else, but his eyes felt so *heavy*. All he could do was close them and steel himself for what would come next. She'd likely resist, given how kind she was, would try and soothe him with empty platitudes and hollow assurances.

"Alright," she said softly. "You would know best, between the two of us. But can I suggest something?"

He opened his eyes, peeking up at her, shocked despite himself. She was impossible for him to pin down. It frustrated him. "You can," he rumbled, tensing against what she might say.

"Maybe this mage had a good reason to chuck you in here and throw away the key," she allowed, her eyes flaming and bright like a beacon in the dark he couldn't look away from, "but is it not also possible that you can change? That you can grow past the person who deserved this and leave him behind? That you can learn from whatever you did and challenge yourself to do better, to *be* better? Because from what I've seen, you're not a bad person. I know what it's like to hate yourself for something you did a long time ago, and I know how *good* it feels to realize that that doesn't have to define you."

Tears threatened, stinging fiercely. Most of him dismissed her words and called them idealistic foolishness, insisted people weren't capable of re-writing themselves like that, that *he* wasn't capable of it—

But something deep inside himself wondered. He'd just told her that he wasn't the same man he'd once been. He'd been talking about his mental stability, which had long been nonexistent, but maybe there was a chance she was right. That he didn't deserve this.

But he didn't know if he had it in him to fight against his chains again. It was so much: so much energy, so much pain, so much humiliation when he failed. He didn't think he had it in him anymore.

But I wouldn't be alone this time, that gentle voice insisted. Because *she* was here. And she had vowed to save him. He just had to trust her.

Could he do that? Could he trust her?

He suppressed a shudder, feeling stretched taut with his uncertainty. He wasn't sure if she was waiting for an answer from him; he was too much of a coward to look at her, his attention once more fixed firmly back on the table.

"Just think about it, okay?" she said softly, her fingers brushing against his arm.

He nodded, reaching out for his half-eaten sandwich to occupy his hands, to fill his mouth with something so he wouldn't have to risk speaking. He couldn't seem to stop the glance he flicked at Claire, eyes darting over like it was a reflex. She was smiling at him, the gesture so warm, so *knowing*, that it took his breath away. How was she not mad at him? How was she able to sit there smiling at him like he hadn't just spent the last hour being a bastard?

He ripped an enormous bite from his food, trying to breathe around the thundering of his heart against his ribs. His mouthful tasted like ash and was fast growing tacky with how dry his mouth was, and he hoped he wouldn't start choking on the damned sandwich, of all things.

She's here to save me. And there was a chance he was worth saving. Something thick and heavy inside of him started to crack open, chasing away the last of his dark mood.

"You know, you're right—we do still barely know each other," she said, startling him out of his spiraling thoughts and almost making him choke after all. "So let's fix that. I've been asking a lot about you so how about you ask me some questions now? Whatever you want to know."

I want to know everything.

He forced down the thick wad of food, casting desperately for what sorts of questions people asked each other to get to know one another. "I don't know," he sputtered, his face flaming hot. "Erm—what made you get into questing?"

She smiled warmly. "I really like helping people. But I don't have any gift to practice magecraft and no stomach for healing. So this is the way I've chosen to contribute positively to society." She bit her lip, hesitating for just a moment. "I had a difficult time growing up," she admitted, her voice going quieter, smaller. "And it made me determined to protect people from being hurt like that. It made me want to do some real good for the world. My father wants me to join my sisters and their husbands in carrying on the family business and climbing higher in Kersterinian high society, but that's not me."

It suited her, he decided. She was so calm, so soothing, that for her to have lived her life tethered to a merchant would have been a crime. "If I ever get out of here I think I'd like to help people as well," he offered, his voice slipping closer to a whisper, as if in speaking his dreams too loud he might invoke the wrath of the gods. "Maybe even a healer. I've had to patch myself up a few times after—" he coughed. "Well, you know. And I think I'd be good at doing it professionally."

She beamed at him. "I think that's an excellent plan. And if you join the Guild you'll already have a sponsor for your shadowing hours. Because obviously, I'm going to have to insist you shadow me."

"You'll be sick of me long before then," he said, stinging with the truth of that. But he smiled and tried to make it seem like he was just joking.

She glared at him, frowning in an exaggerated way that had him wanting to laugh. "Your training starts now," she declared, picking up her neglected food and taking a big bite.

"A quester is kind to themself," she declared, swallowing her food with an uncomfortable-sounding gulp. "So every time you're mean to yourself I'm writing you up."

He couldn't help the laughter that burst out. "If you're going to be that strict then maybe I'll find someone else to shadow."

She gasped, clutching at the front of her tunic as if it were a string of pearls. "How *could* you? After I taught you everything I knew!" She grinned, dropping her hand and reaching across the gap between their seats to swat at his arm gently. "You're very funny. What a good joke, thinking you'll be able to get rid of me that easily."

They both broke out in laughter, their food mostly forgotten as conversation began to flow between them more easily. Something between them had melted, somehow, and that feeling he had had of comfortable recognition bloomed, until he was relaxed enough to tease her back.

"I'm not saying you *are* a grandpa," she teased as they'd talked about his crafty hobbies and love of quiet. "I'm just saying that you have a lot in common with the average grandparent."

"Like you're one to talk, Odetima!" he scoffed, suppressing a grin. "You were just telling me how much you like knitting and reading. I've been on my own for a while, but last I checked twenty-somethings were supposed to be flitting about town enjoying parties and socializing."

She snorted, flinging a piece of crust from her forgotten sandwich at his chest. "I did that too! I just didn't like it. Too many people my age—" she snapped her lips closed, realizing what she was saying.

"No, go on. Say it. Finish that sentence," he goaded,

grinning like mad and having more fun than he could ever remember having before.

She sighed heavily, rolling her hazel eyes. "Too many people my age are interested in different things. Sillier things. So I never feel like I can talk to them."

"So you're an old soul."

"Yes, those words have been used to describe me in the past. What about it, old man?"

"You have no room to talk, calling me an old man."

"Rude!" she laughed, throwing her head back. "Agree to disagree," she grinned. "But if you ever start a sentence with 'kids today' I am never going to let you hear the end of it."

"Respect your elders," he shot back, gladly taking the lump of crust that was thrown at his face.

"I liked it better when you were too afraid to talk to me," she grumbled, before giving in to the smile twitching up the corners of her mouth.

CHAPTER NINE

Spinning Lessons

The next morning Claire once again headed to the library to try and talk with Beast, her freshly combed-out curls drifting freely about her shoulders. Her arms were a bit sore from spending close to two hours painstakingly picking the braids apart, combing her hair out, and moisturizing it, but she'd had the cornrows for over a month and it had been overdue.

When she swanned into the library that morning she was mildly surprised to see him parked in front of his spinning wheel, a basket of wool the same warm brown as his eyes in a basket at his feet and looking the most relaxed she'd seen him yet. It was one thing to know he did something so…domestic, but it was another thing entirely to see him actually *do* it.

"Hullo, Beast," she greeted him, plopping down into the armchair she'd used yesterday.

"Good morning, Claire," he mumbled, his shoulders stiffening just a bit. Was he nervous again? They'd gotten so far towards getting comfortable yesterday.

"I'm not here to interrupt," she assured him. "Please, pretend I'm not here."

He grunted, his eyes locked on the wool in his lap.

She opened her notebook, skimming over her notes like she hadn't been doing exactly that since yesterday. She'd spent several hours last night making notes about what she'd learned during their conversations that afternoon, what she'd seen in the books, and trying to work out her next move. When sleep had eluded her, she'd even crept down to the library, poking through more of the books for their publication dates. She'd yet to find anything newer than 30 AW.

"In the interest of full disclosure, I am probably going to bother you," she teased, leaning towards him. "But I wanted to give you the opportunity to think I wouldn't."

He stiffened, his shoulders tightening up near his pointed ears, before barking a surprised laugh. "Well, alright then," he chuckled, his body relaxing visibly. He was quiet for a moment, and she was content to watch him work. "I like you here," he admitted eventually, his voice going tight as more color crept up his gray neck. "You're good company." The look he threw at her was furtive, a little panicked.

She smiled, her stomach swooping deliciously. Flashes of her dream from the first night played at the back of her mind, making her heat and clench.

Too aware of her body and wanting a distraction, she changed tack. "You make that look so easy. Are you showing off on purpose?"

He chuckled. "I've been doing it a while. Everyone's first time looks like a mess. I've just had the time to bury my shame out where they'll never find the bodies."

She laughed, glad he was back to joking with her. "You didn't keep your early work?"

He grinned, shaking his head. "No, but I should have. I regret it now. It would be fun to compare them, see just how far I've come."

"What do you do with all the yarn you spin?"

"I tried knitting, but my hands struggle with the long needles. I kept snapping them from gripping too hard. So now I just…stockpile it. There's a storage room upstairs with several full trunks."

Claire whistled low. "Maybe we trade. You teach me to spin, I teach you to knit. I have a scarf project with me that has my nice metal needles. You shouldn't be able to just snap those."

"They have *metal* needles now?" he gaped.

She nodded, laughing. "There's also a new craft technique that uses just one hook and you only work one stitch on it at a time. Adeela was gushing about it the last time I saw her, but her tools were still on order so she couldn't show me. She saw it at a craft show she went to without me."

He gaped at her in delight and disbelief. "Now *that* I would love to get out of here to go see." She laughed—of all the things to capture his attention it would be *that. Mage engines? Ho hum. Automatic mail? Boring. A new type of needlecraft? He loses his mind.* "I think a trade sounds great," he said, combing his hair back and grinning at her sheepishly. "Thank you, Claire."

She beamed at him, excited. He smiled back, shy and hesitant but warm. She couldn't help noticing how his eyes glowed with honeyed sparks in the sunlight, or the way his curious gray skin rippled with the shift of the prominent muscles along his bare forearms. "Did you mean it when you said you'd try teaching me?" she asked.

"Of course. When were you thinking of sitting down with me to do it?"

"Why don't you walk me through what you're doing now," she prompted, scooting her armchair closer to his.

"How much do you already know? So I can use the appropriate terms."

She pinched her lip, thinking back to those failed lessons with Adeela nearly a decade ago. "Uh…I know that what you're spinning is 'wool'."

He chuckled. "Good start. What else?"

"You draft the wool out to get it thinner. And uh…you have bobbins? And there's the wheel, obviously. With a very naughty bit called the orifice."

He laughed loudly at that one, and she decided she wanted to tease those kinds of laughs out of him all the time. "It's not naughty, it's just this bit here," he said, stopping the wheel and tapping on the thin tube the spun yarn was disappearing into at the front. "And this is the bobbin, which sits on the flyer," he tapped the spool the yarn was slowly winding onto, the stilled flyer looking like a pair of thin wings on either side of the bobbin. "It seems like you know all the big important things, so that's quite good. What got you all tripped up before?"

"Everything else," she admitted. She was good at memorizing things, but her body often struggled when it came to coordination, and there had always been something about spinning that tripped her up over and over no matter what she had tried with Adeela. It was also why she was only a C-Class; she could build the muscle to handle heavier weapons, but the muscle *memory* was an entirely different matter.

"Do you want to take over? Show me what you can do?" he asked, gesturing at the stilled wheel.

"I can, but when I mess that project up you have to promise not to murder me."

He smiled, sharp teeth flashing through slate-colored lips. She should have found it unsettling, but his eyes were so bright it only made her flutter. "I promise. Come, sit."

They swapped seats, Claire feeling extremely self-conscious as she settled in front of the wheel. She was sweating, she realized, her fingers trembling. It was ludicrous, of course, being so nervous, but she hated to underperform. She just couldn't shake it, the feeling that if she wasn't better than good then she was less than acceptable.

She took a deep breath, letting it out slowly through pursed lips, and darted a quick look over at Beast sitting beside her, leaning over the arm of his chair to better see what she was doing. "You've got this," he assured her, smiling gently. "I believe in you, Claire."

And for some reason, that made her throat knot painfully with emotion. She managed a smile, and then picked up the lump of wool he'd let dangle and smoothed it out flat onto her thigh. She carefully placed her foot on the treadle, just barely tapping it and watching the footman slide up slowly. She pushed her foot all the way down and was disappointed that the wheel didn't seem to want to move very fast at all.

"Try pushing the wheel with your hand to get it going— away from you, to keep it in the same direction I was going, there you go— then picking up the rhythm with your foot. Watch how the treadle moves when you rotate the wheel, try and mimic that."

She nodded, doing as he suggested. The wool in her loose

grip was immediately yanked away from her, slipping into the orifice and snagging on the flyer hooks.

And so it began.

Beast was an excellent teacher, gently coaxing her to keep trying, to slow down and try this or that to force her body and brain to line up better, but after an hour she was still no closer to spinning wool into anything resembling yarn. If it didn't break suddenly it yanked itself right out of her hands, and no matter how she tried to feel out the tempo she should be pumping the treadle it staunchly refused to turn the wheel more than a handful of rotations.

After the singles broke yet again she made a violent, frustrated sound in her throat and threw the sweat-damp wad of wool roving down by her feet, standing up and trying not to scream. "I can't do this," she announced, hanging her head and wiping her hands on her pants. "You're a great teacher and I really appreciate your trying, but I think it's hopeless."

His somber gray face twisted with disappointment. "I still think you could get it," he offered, hauling his enormous body up and retaking the seat she'd abandoned. "But you're definitely too frustrated to continue right now. It's too bad I don't have a drop spindle or something. Those can be a lot more beginner-friendly."

She nodded, then huffed back into her seat, feeling sullen. Maybe getting back to work would be helpful. She opened her notebook, which she'd abandoned on the floor next to her chair, flipping through her notes so far.

"It pains me to do so, but I have to admit that the asshole who trapped you here must really know their stuff," she mused, watching his massive hands work. "you've been here for a long time and all the enchantments still work."

He was conspicuously silent, playing at drafting with entirely too much concentration. Her eyes narrowed.

"What?"

He shrugged, eyes darting to her face and then just as quickly away again.

"Do you not like it when I talk about them? The mage?" She leaned across the gap between their chairs and put a hand on his forearm, forcing him to look at her, even if it was only for a moment. "Seriously, Beast—if you don't like it, tell me. I don't want to upset you but if you don't tell me I'm not going to know."

"It's not that," he muttered. "I don't even know if the gag will let me tell you."

"Do you want to try?" she asked softly, squeezing his arm in a way she hoped was soothing.

He pursed his firm lips into a hard line, grabbing the wheel and stopping it. "She comes back," he admitted, his eyes snapping to hers, full of a tension she couldn't name. "The enchantments do break down, so she comes back and does maintenance. It's always a surprise when she visits." At the look on her face, he hastily added, "But she's never come when a guest's here."

She realized her mouth had fallen open and was hanging slack; she snapped it closed and blinked, holding his intense eye contact.

"Beast that…that's *huge*. Vitrin's mercy, I can't believe she left that for you to be able to say!"

His thick brows drew together. "It's…good? Does that help?"

She nodded, scooting even closer and gripping his arm with both of her hands, now trembling with excitement from what she'd just learned. "My sweet Beast, this is *fantastic*. You've been here for what I've already estimated is at least a hundred years. You haven't died or aged because of the enchantment. But there's only one way for a mage to be able to live that long without losing any of their power or potency.

"Your mage is *fae*, Beast. That's what that tells me. And there's not that many fae left alive at all, and the number that's female and a gifted mage has to be even smaller, so it narrows things a *lot* in terms of finding her. But even if I don't figure out who the mage is, knowing she's fae helps me narrow my strategy. Because the fae have always operated under very strict rules, very rigid hierarchies. The way their magic works is unique to them and has specific counters because it, too, has a lot of rules and hierarchies built into it. And if I know the rules, I can play the game." She felt a wide grin spreading across her flushed face. Her whole body was buzzing with excitement.

This might have been the break she was hoping for, the clue that would get her feet back on a path. She lept from her seat to throw her arms around his neck in a brief but very firm hug. She took her seat again quickly, face flaming hot and feeling more than a little flustered. But she couldn't tear her eyes away from the expressive bow of his mouth, at the way his bottom lip, so much fuller than the top, pouted out in a way that made her want to sink her teeth into it and lick it. Claire smoothed her clothes down and tucked a loose curl behind her ear with a casualness she didn't actually feel. "Do you have any books on the fae in this little library of yours?" she asked, finally tearing her eyes away from his face and feeling a bit breathless. She hadn't yet spotted one she could remember in her perusals.

He cleared his throat, pulling the arm she had been holding closer against his big body. "Yes, though it's mostly folklore, I think. My father liked to collect them, said it made him feel closer to his distant fae ancestors."

"Do you mind helping me find them?"

"Not at all," he said, looking a little dazed still.

She smiled. "That's so weird that you have fae ancestors too, because my birth mother was supposed to have some. My father says she was a quarter fae but that seems unlikely, based on what little I know about it."

"It's not common," he agreed, his fingers back to their mesmerizing rhythm of pinching and drawing. "Did your parents make an unnecessarily big deal out of it, too?"

"*Yes!*" she cried, her hands fluttering in agitation around her face. "And Sweet Delenaa was it embarrassing. My father would take *every* gods-damned opportunity to bring it up at parties. 'Oh hello Mrs. Crasmussan,'" she said, imitating her father's deep but nasally voice, making Beast laugh, "'what a lovely party. Almost as lovely as my three part-fae daughters. How are you liking the weather lately? I'd prefer it if it was less sunny. Fae heritage in the family and all that.'" She started giggling, remembering how she and her sisters would groan in unison whenever Draseus would do it too often in one night. It made her ache a little for her distant family.

Beast was laughing alongside her, his spinning wheel still. "Vitrin's mercy, *yes* it was exactly like that. When did they all agree that that was so impressive? It doesn't make any sense to me. Once you're anything less than half the bloodline is too diluted for you to get the interesting fae traits, like long life or guaranteed mates, or heightened senses. But they'd go and bring it up any chance they got to like it was a personal achievement." He shook his head, huffing another laugh.

"What always got me was that my father was the one who was always bragging about it when the fae came from my mother's side. All he did was purposely marry a woman who had the right pedigree and get her pregnant three times." Her voice had taken on a bitter edge, even to her own ears. She took a deep breath and let it sigh out of her, trying to cool the anger that had flared when she thought about her father and his social climbing. It always got to her, because she knew it was why her mother had died.

She saw him watching her out of the corner of her eye. He pursed his lips, one of his hands reaching up to comb through his hair a few times. He cleared his throat nervously.

"Are…you okay, Claire?"

She sucked in another breath and smiled. "Yeah, I'm fine. Sorry, I was just thinking about something."

"Is it part of your tragic backstory?"

She laughed. "My *what?*"

He shrugged, his cheeks coloring. "You know, your tragic backstory. In all the adventure novels the hero always has one."

She laughed again, this time flinging herself back in her chair and clapping her hands. "You have been reading too many damn books, my friend!" she howled, swiping tears from the corners of her eyes. "Although thank you for finally admitting that I'm your hero."

He snorted, his neck flushed and splotchy. "Don't read too much into that, Odetima. I never said *that*." He started laughing with her though.

After a moment, once she'd calmed down, he cleared his throat and looked at her again. "But in all seriousness, if something's bothering you, I hope—um. I'm here to listen."

She was stunned that he'd offer. Just yesterday he'd been standoffish and close to biting her head off, and now he was opening up to her, and offering her his friendship. She felt humbled by how much trust he was putting in her so soon after her arrival.

Being locked up all on his own for so many years could have easily made him cold and cruel. But deep down he seemed sensitive, kind, and thoughtful. He was perhaps delicate, and a little too rigid at times, but that really just made it *very* fun to tease and joke with him. And when it worked, it felt...*right*. As if this gentle tumble towards each other was meant to happen.

Something inside herself was pulling her to let him in deeper, to show him more. It was like some force inside herself was loosening her lips and pushing the words out before she could stop them.

"As you know, my mother died giving birth to me," she began, "and I'm the youngest of three girls. My father was devastated that I had killed his wife and hadn't even had the decency to be a boy." She laughed wryly. *Tragic backstory, indeed.* "And my older sisters hated me for killing their mother. I'm told I look a lot like her, which just made it worse. So they weren't kind to me. My sisters hurt me, stole my things, told lies about me to get me in trouble, played cruel tricks on me...really whatever they could think of. And our father ignored us, for the most part, but especially me. I wasn't even a good girl, sweet and demure like my sisters, to make up for all the other ways I disappointed him."

Something tickled her cheek, and Claire was surprised to find her fingers damp when she brushed them against her face. She was crying.

Hesitantly, Beast reached across the space between them and patted her arm, lingering against her bicep before sliding his warm, rough hand down her arm to clasp her hand. She sucked in a breath, skin tingling and hot in the wake of his touch, but the comfort she felt from that one gesture was so full and immediate it was beautiful. It was beautiful, that something as simple as his hand on hers made her aches gentler and dried her tears. She shot Beast a watery smile and pressed on.

"Anyway, my mother's pregnancy with Danielle—she's the middle child—was difficult. The healers told her she shouldn't have anymore. But father…he insisted. He believes in the one god, in the importance of legacy, and the current law in Kesterin is that titles and wealth are passed down from father to son. So he pushed her, and pushed her, until she gave in and got pregnant with me.

"Adeela wasn't working for my family yet, but she was working for another family that visited often, as their lady's maid. It was all over town, how sick my mom looked. And when I was born, there was nothing the healers could do. Something happened to her brain, I think, and even gifted healers can't fix that." She still wasn't sure why she'd decided to tell him all this, but it felt right.

"So anytime I think too much about my father, and how much he loves trying to get ahead in life it makes me…sad. And angry. Because he did that, and because he let my sisters blame me for it for so long."

"I can see why you and he are not close," he murmured, his hand still warm and rough on hers. She managed a watery laugh. "And thank you for sharing with me. For trusting me." He smiled softly, releasing her hand and going back to his spinning. "If you manage to free me after all, I'd be happy to fight him for you."

She laughed again, the mental image of huge, hulking Beast coming after her father, making his thick mustache quiver in fear, barreling through her brain. "I thought you said you weren't dangerous," she teased.

"I'm only dangerous to people who are cruel to those I care about," he rumbled, blushing and making her melt.

CHAPTER TEN

Divinations

As much as Claire was burning to head back to Edden to reach out to Dretta, she decided it was best to do the divining first. She *may* have been avoiding it, knowing it would be time-consuming and tedious, but for a quest like Beast's it was essential, and Dretta would probably ask her about it.

"Just to give you a warning, I'm going to be starting my divining today," she announced at breakfast the morning after her disastrous attempt at spinning. "It's part of the investigation process so I'm obligated to get it done."

He nodded, tearing a chunk off of a ham steak and chewing thoughtfully. "Alright. Do whatever you need, Claire." He fidgeted a bit, avoiding her eyes. "Does this mean you'll need me to stay away?"

"Not at all," she reassured him, smiling at him when he darted a look at her face. "In fact, if you want to you're free to tag along. I shouldn't need to concentrate unless I find something, so it's not like you'd be a distraction."

"You won't go crazy if I follow you around all day?"

She snorted. "You're good company." She echoed his

words from yesterday on purpose.

He tore off another bite of the ham. "If you're sure you don't mind, then I think it would be interesting to see a professional quester at work," he told her once he'd swallowed his huge mouthful.

They finished their meal, then Claire darted off to snag her gear. The diviner was a spiffy bit of tech, she had to admit, even if using it was about as interesting as watching paint dry. It was a box, about the size of her face, made of brass, with several dials and switches on its face and two short antennae on its front. It allowed the user to track and measure aether signatures and sniff out hidden magicks. It required a lot of calibration in cases like Beast's, because he and the manor itself would each have a signature that would need to be filtered out. Otherwise, the diviner would never stop reporting findings. It was much easier to operate and carry than the complex rods and wires that were previously used, but that didn't stop it from being dull as dirt.

They met in the foyer. "I've got to calibrate the damn thing first," she explained. "It's just going to be me fiddling with it for forever."

He nodded, standing with his arms clasped behind his back, seemingly content to just sit tight while she did what she needed. *Well, alright then,* she thought, a little surprised that he was sticking around for this. If the positions were reversed she probably wouldn't have.

Her fingers skittered over the face of the diviner, tweaking knobs and spinning dials until she honed in on first Beast's aetherwave frequency, then the manor's. Then she set the values into a face on the side that collected exclusions. It was still fascinating to her that two objects enchanted by the same mage would still have wildly different energy signatures like that. She knew it had something to do with the way that aether interacted with different kinds of matter—both that of the mage and the object of enchantment—but the math behind it was positively inscrutable to her.

"Alright, that's it for calibration," she announced at last. "I think I'll start with the first floor of the manor." While it was a nice break for her scalp to have her hair loose it had started getting in her way almost immediately, so she tied her hair up into a pouf on the top of her head. She resolved to put her hair back into braids that night once she'd finished with the diviner. "If you get bored feel free to abandon me and do something more interesting," she teased as she began sweeping the diviner over the foyer.

"I'll keep that in mind," he rumbled, following her. "I *am* a very busy man, lots of meetings to get to."

"Smartass," she called over to him, grinning.

It was a positively endless march of hours getting through the first floor. Every nook and cranny had to be scanned, and it had to be done somewhat slowly to ensure the readings were accurate. Once she'd settled into it Beast went quiet, and towards the three-hour mark she was too bored to let him maintain his stoic silence.

"I thought you were going to keep me company," she smirked, cocking an eyebrow. "Distract me from how boring this is, please."

He grinned, shrugging. "I forgot to mention it, but I'm very boring. So it's more like if you entertain yourself I'll watch and try to help out." She squawked, then burst out laughing. He'd been alone a lot, had suffered through trauma, and if that made it hard for him to reach out and start conversations then she was alright with that.

"So the people who've been here before, what did they come here for?" she asked idly, sweeping the diviner slowly over the north wall of the library.

"I'm not sure. Some came to steal, but I don't think it worked. The things they took have all wound up returning. I think some others might have come on some sort of dare, and seemed to think the manor was haunted." he was quiet for a moment, and when she shot a look at him over her shoulder his lips were pressed together in a hard line.

"What is it?" she asked, lowering the diviner and turning to face him.

His face immediately shuttered. "Nothing."

"Seems like something," she said slowly, putting one hand on her hip.

He avoided looking at her, his eyes locked on the floor instead. She pursed her lips and turned back around to continue her sweep. "Well, obviously you don't *have* to tell me. You don't owe me your secrets. But for what it's worth, I want to be your friend, and a part of that is trusting your friends with your hurts because they can make them better." It was something that was far easier said than done, and Claire knew that. But she figured it couldn't hurt anything to remind him of it.

He was silent behind her for so long she thought he'd never speak. "That silver badge on your pack…what is that for?"

She paused again, surprised by the question. "It's proof that I'm a registered member of the Questing Guild," she explained. "So that people who might need me, or need to work with me, can identify me." He nodded, avoiding her eyes. "Why do you ask?" she murmured, her stomach tensing.

He was silent for a while longer. "I...I think some of them might have been questers," he admitted at last, his voice barely more than a whisper. She felt her eyes bug out with how wide they went. "And they...they all tried to hurt me. Took one look at me and—well."

Her fingers grew cold and numb around the diviner. "Other questers?" she asked, her voice so high and far away it didn't even sound like hers.

"I-I think so. They had the same badge as you, at least."

The diviner fell to the floor with a crash, slipping from Claire's unfeeling fingers. She winced, but left it where it had fallen, crossing the distance between her and Beast and looking up into his face. "Other questers were here...and they *hurt you*?" she cried.

He shrugged. "Yes? They could have been impersonating a quester though, I suppose."

"Oh, Beast..." she breathed, her hands trembling as they came up to cover her mouth in horror.

If others had been here before, then all of them had failed, or else the quest wouldn't have been back on the board for Claire to accept. Though usually there were reports filed when that happened, to help the next quester who would try to take it. And the fact that they had seen him and all of them had tried to kill him before thinking to help was beyond disgusting to her.

His tension and fear made a lot more sense now.

"How can I make it right?" she asked quietly, her hands reaching out to take his automatically. She squeezed his huge hands tight, noting the fingers were a little cold, making her squeeze tighter. "What can I do?"

He blinked down at her. "Do?"

"Do you remember their names? Or even better, their badge numbers? The provinces they came from? I could pass that on to my mentor, see if they can sniff them out and find a way to make them accountable. Or, I don't know—would you like a hug? Sometimes hugs help."

He blushed fiercely, his hands going clammy in hers. "No, that's alright. It was a long time ago, now." He squeezed her hands back, though he seemed reluctant to look her in the eye. "And—and I'm sure they thought they were doing the right thing. I know how I look, and, well…"

She frowned. "No, don't you dare. They just charged into a situation they knew nothing about and decided to stab first and ask questions later! I don't care what you look like; unless you provoked them, were hostile towards them, there was no excuse."

He gently pulled his hands free and took a half step back from her. She gave him his space and went back to the diviner to continue her sweep. "You don't need to protect them, Beast," she said quietly as she went over the last section of the north wall. "You can get upset with them, with how they treated you."

"I know how I look, Claire," he repeated, voice stern. "It's alright."

She spun back around to look at him. "You're not a monster! You are kind and gentle and you *did not deserve that!*" She huffed out a breath, closing her eyes and trying to calm herself. "I know I just got here, and maybe I'm out of line saying this, but you should be mad that you were treated like that. You should be *furious.* We only just met and I know

I am."

He blushed, combing his hair back. "Why? I mean, like you said, you barely know me. Why does it upset you so much?"

Well now, wasn't that a good question. But she didn't think she was ready to answer it just yet. "Why *doesn't* it upset *you*?" she countered.

He looked at her for a moment, frowning, then sat on the floor, bending his knees and resting his elbows on his bent legs. "You know why," he grumbled.

She rolled her eyes, setting the diviner on an empty stretch of the bookshelves and squatting beside him on the floor. "Yeah, you think you deserve it. And I think you don't, so we're at an impasse." She put her hand on his shoulder, rubbing it just a little. "But I think even if you did something that needed to be punished, that doesn't mean you deserve *all* punishment. You don't deserve everyone in the whole world turning on you and trying to hurt you."

She gave his shoulder one last squeeze, then got to her feet and got back to work.

The north wall was finished and the east wall—which was mostly windows, making it a bit easier to check—was almost done when she heard shuffling behind her. "You think they'd get in trouble, for what they did?" he asked her quietly.

"Yeah, I do. There's rules about engaging a hostile, the first one being that you have to reasonably establish that a subject is, in fact, hostile."

More silence. Then, so quietly she wasn't even certain she'd heard it: "Thank you."

She turned to look at him again. He was still on the floor, though he'd shifted to face her. "What for?"

"For…being mad. For me."

Sweet Delenaa, he was breaking her heart. "Alright, that's it," she snapped, putting her diviner on the armchair. "Unless you say no I'm coming in for a hug."

He looked shocked, his brown eyes wide, but he didn't say no.

She knelt on the floor next to him and threw her arms around his neck, giving him a brief but fierce hug. He sat frozen and tense, not touching her, but when she pulled away he was smiling and blushing furiously. She smiled back, her heart doing acrobatics in her chest. She really did love his smile, sharp teeth and all.

Surging to her feet and returning to the diviner, she once again got to work. She heard Beast get up and make his way over to her, asking a few timid questions about what she was doing. Their conversation was halting at first, and a little awkward, but before she knew it they were talking like old friends, deep-diving into topics, joking and laughing.

Once she had finished checking over the library she called it a day. To her surprised delight Beast tagged along with her on her divining sweeps all four days that she picked over the manor, keeping her entertained and making the task far less awful than it could have been. She was heartbroken when he declined to join her for her sweeps of the grounds, but she couldn't blame him for bowing out. Still, those final two days were lonely and difficult for her to get through.

As she'd suspected, nothing unusual showed up on the diviner. It was just Beast alone in his enchanted manor, with nothing to guard, nothing to protect, nothing he was hiding. And she couldn't stop wondering just what was going on at this gods-forsaken place.

CHAPTER ELEVEN

Edden

"Would it hurt anything for me to pop into town for a few days and come back?" Claire asked at breakfast once she'd finished her divining. It was time to check in with Dretta, maybe see what they recommended her next course of action should be, especially what she could do to try and find this fae mage. If they were an elder fae then even the Consortium might not have a record, which would make this yet another dead end, but it was best to take things one at a time. And if it also gave her a chance to check for mail from Adeela…well, that was just a nice bonus.

Beast's brow furrowed. He shook his head, a look like dread stealing across his features. "No, you are not a prisoner here. You can…leave whenever you want."

"I know," she smiled gently, "I meant it more like if I leave will there be anything that stops me from coming back. Enchantment-wise."

He shrugged. "I don't think so, but I have no way of knowing. No one's ever tried to come back." It made her heart clench. He was so lonely.

"Well then, I suppose we can test it, and if the

enchantment stops me then I'll have to burn this place to the ground or figure out some other way to carry you off," she joked, hoping she could make it so, if it came to it. She wondered if it was worth risking not being able to come back, but it could be valuable, to have that bit of data: it was a perplexing piece of the puzzle, the ease with which everyone except Beast was able to come and go as they pleased. And she really did want to talk some things out with Dretta.

When she looked back up into his face, she was startled by the intensity of the emotion in his gaze. She couldn't quite read it, but it seemed something like desperation, or fear. "Are you alright?" she asked, her hand reaching out to him without thinking.

He grinned, combing claws back through his mop of crimson hair. "Yes, I'm fine. You should go, take care of your business. I'm just tired. Didn't sleep well last night."

"Alright," she hedged, unconvinced but deciding it was worth it to go, if only for the hope that some progress might be made on the quest. "Then I'll leave tomorrow at first light. I can't imagine it will even take me half of a week to get there and back. Can I get you anything while I'm in town?"

He shook his head, his shoulders slumping in a way that made her ache.

And that was that—but why did it feel like she was betraying him by leaving him behind? She would come back to him, after all. No matter what, she would come back.

She would sooner pull every fingernail off her own hands than betray her sweet, gentle new friend. It would be fine. *He* would be fine.

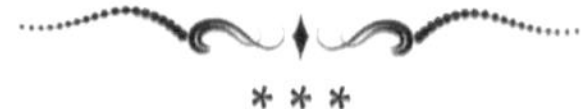

* * *

It was late enough in the summer that when Claire hoisted her pack onto her back and stepped out into the gray dawn Vitrin's kiss had begun to creep into the air, making her shiver. She had a full day of walking ahead of her, and soon enough she would be yearning for this early-morning chill, she knew. Though Vitrin was beginning to capture the nights, Salerah still held tight to the days, and from the damp she suspected it would be hot *and* muggy today, which would be hell on her hair. She'd done some simple two-strand twists the day before and had pulled them back into a bundle at the back of her head, but all of her baby hairs and flyaways were going to frizz up and stick to her face in the way that drove her crazy.

She urged her sluggish muscles to move faster, increasing her pace. If she managed to keep it brisk she should reach the little village by late afternoon. With how remote Edden was she was confident she'd be able to get a day or two of lodging at *The Dragon's Spur*, but if the rooms were all taken she'd have to camp in the woods or try and convince a stranger to let her sleep in their barn.

Despite the rising heat and cloying moisture slowing her, she did wind up making good time, arriving in Edden as the sun was just beginning to dip towards the horizon.

"I smell like a dead horse, but I gods-damned made it," she groaned as she spied the apothecary that marked the edge of town. Seeing her goal in sight infused her legs with a little more strength, a little more energy, and she managed to get to the *Spur* and rent a room just as the sun was dipping below the tree line. Teran remembered her from when she'd first arrived two weeks ago.

"Made it to the manor alright, Miss Claire?" he asked as

he helped her with her pack—a gesture that was entirely unnecessary but which he insisted on.

"Oh yes, it was due east just like you said," she replied with a warm smile for the kind middle-aged man.

"And are the stories true? Does a wild beast live there? Or a wicked mage? Or is it abandoned? Serra—that's the healer's boy—says it's likely moldering away off in the forest, and the legends is just idle talk."

"There is a beast, but he's not wild. He's very…kind. And polite. He's trapped there but it's all very mysterious. It's no wonder there's so many rumors around town about it."

"A polite beast?" Teran set her pack down by her bed and rubbed at his chin, making stubble rasp. "Does he talk, then?"

She nodded, crossing her arms over her chest.

"My husband'll like to hear that one. He loves hearing about the weirding ways of magework, and if that's not magecraft I'll eat my best boots. Are you done with your questing then, to be back with us so soon?"

It was all coming back to her now, slow to boil up through her fatigue: this one was *very* chatty. "No, I just came to town to take care of a couple of things. I'll be heading back out there in a day or two." She feigned a yawn and unfolded her arms, planting her hands on her hips. "Well, I have to say it's been quite a long day for me, Teran. So thank you *so* much for your help, but I think I'd like to head to bed now."

"Of course, my apologies for keeping you, Miss Claire! My husband's always saying I talk so much I probably won't even stop once I'm dead," Teran said with a chuckle, inclining his head and making an exit. "If you need anything else just holler. G'night!"

"Goodnight, thanks!"

At last she was alone, loosing a massive sigh of relief. She liked Teran, but she really was completely exhausted. She vaguely recalled meeting his husband the first time she was here, and in the way of such things he'd been a much more quiet and reserved person.

The room felt bare and tiny after the finery of the manor, but the inn was clean and neat, and now that Teran had left, quiet. She was completely exhausted, weaving and half-asleep on her feet, and only managed to shirk her boots and outermost clothes before wrapping her hair up in her silk scarf and flopping onto the thin but fresh-smelling straw mattress.

An hour later she was still awake, furious that she couldn't find sleep despite her exhaustion. Every time she was close, her muscles loosening and her breathing leveling out, Beast's face would flash through her mind, riling her up. She couldn't get how upset he'd looked at the idea of her leaving out of her head. It had made her want to pull him into her arms again, to hold him until he felt the truth of her promise that she'd come back. And wasn't *that* just the oddest thing? It went beyond her natural instinct to comfort and soothe, to someplace so deep inside her she was scared to see it creeping out when she was supposed to be working.

But there was just something about him. He'd been cranky at first, sure, but knowing what she did now, how could he *not* be on edge with a new person? All things considered, he'd actually opened up to her and come to trust her remarkably fast. And now he was funny, and sweet, and a kind of vulnerable that brought all of her protective instincts roaring to life. And if she was being honest with herself—here, in the dark and by herself, miles from anyone she knew—she had started finding him to be rather handsome. His features weren't beautiful in the classical sense, but the more she looked at them the more she liked them. And his *body*—sweet Delenaa, he was exactly her type. Wide shoulders, a broad chest, thick with muscle but with a nice layer of softness over the top of it all to cuddle into and grab onto. And those *hands*. She'd always had such a weakness for hands, of all things, and his were a work of art, the fingers long and thick yet graceful, delicately veined on the back, and with a wrist that was defined without being too bony. In the quiet she started to heat, thinking about those hands caressing her flesh, running through her hair, hefting her up against him—

No, no this was *bad*. She needed to keep her head on straight. If she was going to let herself get distracted like this then she might as well go back to Kesterin and give up her badge now. She'd only just begun her career, and if she couldn't keep it together and do her job then she had no business doing it. And she'd worked too hard for too long to just give it all up. She'd given up so much to be here, created such deep rifts with her father and her sisters by insisting on this.

This quest had to go well. She couldn't afford too many setbacks, with the safety net of her father and his money ripped away now. She could always turn to Adeela or one of her daughters—Cat and Aubrey—if it was an emergency, but with Adeela retired and Aubrey's medical bills from transitioning she didn't want to have to do that if she could avoid it.

And it was a matter of pride, too. Her father had scoffed and rolled his eyes at everything she'd ever been passionate about, and now that she was putting her money where her mouth was failure just wasn't an option. So as much as Beast was lighting her up and making her feel sweet and steamy things, she couldn't give in to it. She had to stay professional and level-headed about this, and do her best to solve the quest and save Beast.

A thin strip of sunshine seared into Claire's eyes and woke her early the next morning. While she felt stiff and sore she was also surprisingly clear-headed and alert, given the restless night she'd had. It was very early, she thought, but she knew she'd never get back to sleep, so she decided to start her day.

Snatching the provided basin off the bureau, she shuffled across the hall to the communal bathroom and saw to her needs. Teran and his husband had sprung for indoor plumbing and a toilet, but there wasn't a bathtub (hence the basin) so she filled it with water from the sink and returned to her room for a sponge bath.

The manor with its heated indoor plumbing had spoiled her, and she found washing up with the ice-cold water at the inn to be miserable. By the time she was done her skin ached and pebbled, but it finished waking her up and encouraged her to move quickly. She changed into her spare clothes and left her dirty laundry in a bag by her door for the laundry service she'd splurged on.

She was eager to get on with things and start heading back to the manor. She wasn't looking forward to having to make that long walk again so soon, but she did miss her new friend something fierce. She kept seeing things that she thought he'd like, or thinking about something she'd have liked his input on. She wondered if he'd like a small town like

Edden, or if he'd prefer a bustling city like her hometown of Kesterin better. She smiled, imagining how Beast would take Teran's relentless barrage of conversation; the poor man would probably be too bashful and polite to be able to bow out and wind up trapped forever. She thought he might hate that more than being trapped at the manor.

She decided to start her errands by reaching out to Dretta about how she might discover the identity of Beast's fae mage. She'd likely have to submit an official request for Consortium registration records, but there may be other, more obscure paths that Claire didn't know about as a fresh inductee that Dretta would, with their years of experience. She sat at the tiny round table tucked into the corner of her room and carefully penned a query to her mentor, outlining the little bit of progress she'd managed to make in these first two weeks.

After a few minutes of consideration, she also penned an inquiry for the records office of the Guildhall, requesting any reports that may have been filed for Beast's quest. If other questers really had been there then surely there must be *something*. And she really wanted to try and find those bastards and make them answer for what they did.

Finished with her notes and feeling wound too tight, she stomped out of her room and down the stairs. She could smell breakfast cooking in the kitchens, but she decided she was too restless to wait for it to be served, charging out the door and into the cool early morning.

No one was open for business just yet, but there were some folk up and tending to the day's chores. She figured she could wander a bit while she waited for the shops she needed to open up for the day. She really just needed to get out under the open sky and *move*.

In the end, she walked a slow loop around the outskirts of Edden, admiring the bounty of the forest and thinking more about Beast. There was a particular warmth to the way he looked at her sometimes that would sweep through her like a wave, lighting her up and making her feel taut and tingly. It made her think of the scandalous dream she'd had her first night at the manor. She shook her head, realizing that the dream may have been prescient more than anything else. She wasn't the sort of person who was attracted to other people immediately. But whenever she was around Beast she found her body drifting close to his, her skin tingling with the urge to touch him. It had only been a couple of weeks and she was already feeling things for him that should have taken months to bloom.

A part of her had wondered if it was the forced proximity of being the only two people around for miles, but even now that there was distance, her thoughts clung to him. A part of her *yearned* for him, and that really scared her.

It was a sobering train of thought. Being friendly was alright, especially with how traumatized he clearly was. His trusting her and opening up to her had been directly responsible for the breakthrough she'd had, even if it was small. Like last night, she resolved to force him from her mind, to create the professional distance she should have maintained from the start. What was wrong with her, that she'd let it get like this?

After finishing her loop around Edden she thought the sun was high enough now that at least the post office should be open. She turned back and made her way to the center of town.

Sure enough, the post office was open, the clerk stationed

at the front desk looking very put-upon. The clerk sat hunched forward, her elbows planted on her desk and her chin resting on her palms.

"Can I help you?" the clerk intoned, voice as dull as her eyes.

"Yes, I have a couple of letters to post and wanted to see if I might have gotten any mail. I'm a non-resident." Her bright smile and cheery tone of voice seemed to go completely unnoticed.

"Name?"

"Claire Odetima."

The clerk snatched the sealed letters from Claire's hand then slid out of her chair, shuffling to the back. Claire had only seen the back of a post office once, but it had been fascinating to see the brass tubes that deposited mail all over Cillure. The complex system of aether channels that connected the tubes, allowing the specialized cylinders to travel leagues of distance in a few hours without chance of being intercepted, had been a revolutionary invention. It was awe-inspiring, what mages could come up with, and the speedy mail system was an invention—along with mage engines and water filtration—that Claire was especially grateful for.

After several long minutes, the dour clerk returned, holding a letter with Claire's name printed on it in Adeela's looping hand. Her heart lifted at the sight, excited for that taste of home. The clerk handed it over and grunted at Claire's thanks. She turned and left, eager to get through the rest of her errands. Despite the almost overwhelming urge to tear into the precious letter, she made herself stuff it into her pants pocket so she could read it in privacy later.

Continuing down the only road in Edden, she stopped to

see if the general store was open yet. She had hoped to snag a fresh waterskin to replace the one from the Guild, which had gotten damaged on the road, as well as a few other odds and ends she was running low on.

By a stroke of luck, the general store was just opening as she approached the bright blue door. She thought that was one of the more charming aspects of Edden: the buildings were simple constructions, but everyone had taken the time to paint the fronts with bright splashes of color, and even if some had started to fade and peel the overall effect was still vibrant and endearing. The general store was blue with yellow trim around the windows and along the baseboard inside, and was one of the more freshly painted storefronts.

O'brenne, the middle-aged Orcish woman whose small tusks twisted her otherwise handsome face into an unpleasant frown, grunted a welcome at Claire as she came in.

"Good morning, O'brenne," she called with a small wave.

"Good morning, lass. Can't say I recall your name, though I know your face well enough."

"Claire," she offered. "I'm looking to stock up on some travel supplies," she paused, hesitating before blurting, "but was wondering if you might have a drop spindle for sale as well." She wasn't *terribly* excited to learn how to spin, but it was a useful skill. Really though, it was the thought of how proud he'd be if she managed it, how he'd no doubt light up at her and gift her with one of his bright, full smiles, those warm brown eyes shining, that had her looking to bring one back with her. It was a good thing for one friend to do with another.

"Spindle?" O'brenne scratched at one olive-green cheek with her short black claws. "I don't, no. But Felda might have a spare she can part with. You know where she is?" Claire shook her head, and O'brenne gave her directions to the woman's cottage.

She managed to convince the surly Orcish shopkeeper to engage in a little pleasant small talk with her, then thanked O'brenne for her help and left to seek out Felda. She followed the directions she'd gotten from the shopkeeper to a small house with pleasantly gaudy pink and purple paint.

Slinging her bag with her purchases from the general store higher up onto her shoulder, she knocked on the front door. No sounds trickled out from within, but after a moment the door swung open and a shapely woman in an airy magenta wool sweater and plain tan skirt peered up at her, her short chestnut-colored hair artfully mussed.

"Oh, good morning," Claire chirped, "I hope I'm not intruding! My name is Claire, and O'brenne said you might have a drop spindle you'd be willing to sell me."

"Did she now? I think I might. What size whorl were you looking for? I might not have a drop spindle with a small whorl but I have a support spindle that spins rather fine."

"Erm," Claire wished desperately that Beast were here to translate. "I'm not sure…something for beginners?"

Felda nodded, the barest smile twitching at the corner of her mouth, and turned to go back into her house, waving Claire in to follow her.

Inside, the fiber artist's home was just as bright and boisterous as it was outside; Felda clearly had a fondness for color, especially pink, as every surface was a riot of brightness. But for all that there was a bit of chaos to the cozy cottage's decor, the overall impression was joyful and vibrant. It made the space feel well-loved and alive with the spirit of the woman who lived there.

Felda indicated Claire should have a seat in a wooden chair painted with an intricate mural, then retreated to the back room, presumably to try and find the spindle. Claire continued to admire the little house, trying to drink in all of the delightful little details. She thought Beast would love this place.

After a few moments, Felda returned, spindle in hand. "This one was what I trained my son on, it should serve well for a beginner."

"Oh, yes that seems perfect! How much were you thinking for it?"

Felda shrugged, the airy fabric of her sweater floating gracefully around her full figure. "Not getting much use now, so I think I could part with it for four silver."

She tallied her remaining coin in her head. Four silver seemed like a fair enough price based on what little she knew of these things, but it would take a hefty bite out of her remaining funds.

She was about to tell Felda no thank you and make her exit, when an image flitted through her mind of how Beast would smile when she showed it to him. How those darling little sharp teeth would be bared, his eyes crinkling and sparkling. He'd probably blush, or run his fingers through his hair, and suddenly she couldn't leave it behind. She wanted that smile. She might even have *needed* it.

She nodded, pulling her purse out from where it had been tucked into her shirt and fishing out the four silver pieces. Felda took them and thanked her, then scrounged for a spare rag and some twine to wrap the spindle up for her.

"You have someone to show you how to use it, dear?"

Felda asked as she carefully wrapped the spindle.

"Yes, a um…a friend. He tried to show me how to use his wheel but it was too much for me. He didn't have a spindle but thought that would suit me better for learning."

Felda nodded, offering Claire a small smile as she handed the bundle over. "Well, I hope you enjoy it. I'd love to see anything you happen to make from it next time you're in town," she said warmly.

Touched, Claire thanked her again and headed back to the inn to drop off her purchases and tear into the letter from Adeela. Dee was always so full of love and gentle advice, and Claire couldn't have asked for a better mother than her if she'd tried, even if thinking such things felt disloyal to her birth mother. But Adeela liked to say that Claire's mother had sent her to the Odetima house, knowing how much Claire was hurting, how much she needed someone to love her and care for her. And maybe she had. Maybe it had been *rorto*, a return to balance, sent from her mother. She liked the idea of that.

The walk back to the inn was uneventful, but an odd sensation prickled along the back of her neck, feeling very much as if she were being watched. She went on the alert, her own gaze sweeping the thin crowd and looking for who might be causing her unease. She couldn't pinpoint any one person staring at her harder than the others, but she did note that several people peered at her curiously as she passed.

Hopefully what she was feeling was nothing more than the small town interest in strangers; even so, she made sure to watch herself and stay on alert. It was better to be paranoid about nothing than to wind up in trouble. Her self-defense instructor, Caldus Love, had been very adamant about that.

And her experiences as a woman had only solidified that belief: it was always better to be too careful.

Unsettled, she wound her way carefully back to the inn, ensuring she wasn't followed before slipping into the inn's warm common room. A few patrons had trickled in while she'd been gone, eating an early lunch and chatting amicably with each other. She'd been out longer than she realized and had apparently missed breakfast, but lunch smelled nice: a stew of some sort and fresh brown bread. She felt too on edge to mingle, so she asked for food to be sent up to her room, then headed upstairs herself to dump her purchases and soothe herself with Adeela's letter.

A kitchen boy knocked on her door with her lunch just after she'd managed to get her boots off and de-mucked. She took the tray from him with a heartfelt thanks and a tip of a few coppers, then set her meal on her desk and carefully sliced open her precious letter.

My dear sweet girl, the letter began, bringing tears to her eyes:

I hope this letter finds you well. I've been worried sick about you this whole time you've been on the road, though I know I shouldn't. I've seen you send plenty of bullies home in tears, the gods know, and that was when you were still a little thing! I'm sure with your fancy academy training you're untouchable now. But mothers worry anyway.

Catalina's met a sweet young man down at the bookshop, and we're all rooting for this one to stick! He's such a calm, quiet young man and you know all too well why we call Catalina our Wild Cat. Someone sweet and easy-going would be good for her.

Aubrey's having her final session with a medical artificer for her transition, and we're all so excited for her! We'll miss you something fierce at her new birth party, but she knows you'll be there in spirit.

Your sisters and your father are doing well, last I'd checked in on them. He's mighty bent out of shape about your leaving, but he'll just have to deal with it. I know he's your father, and the gods know I'm grateful for the work he gave me, since it led me to you, but I can't help it that he makes me madder than a cat in a bath.

We all miss you so, so much, but we also hope you're having lots of grand adventures and changing lives with that big, beautiful heart of yours. Can't wait to hear back from you, baby girl.

All my love,
Adeela

It was exactly what Claire had needed to soothe the prickles and snags in her soul. Tears fell freely from her eyes, her heart both aching and full to bursting at the same time. Missing Adeela was really the only homesickness that she was dealing with, but it was hitting her hard.

Part of her desire to find success on this quest was tied up with making Adeela proud. Dee had done so much for Claire since she had come into her life, and what better way to show she appreciated it than to become a success? She could imagine all too easily how disappointed Dee'd be if Claire showed up back home penniless and begging for help, disgraced because she'd failed to succeed on her first-ever quest. No matter what she was feeling for Beast, she couldn't let that happen.

She read the letter through twice more, digging into her meal as she did so, then started drafting a response. She'd make another trip to the post office once she'd finished eating to see if Dretta had gotten back to her yet, as well as drop this new letter off for Adeela. It meant she'd get two from Claire in the same day, but she wouldn't mind.

Sure enough, the clerk had a letter from Dretta to hand off to her, their print large and blocky but neat on the crisp white envelope, the Guild emblem printed prominently in one corner. This time she didn't bother taking the letter back to her room.

> *Good to hear from you again, Claire. I'm surprised you're still chugging away at it with nearly two weeks of no progress. I'd've expected to hear from you sooner if it was giving you so many problems.*

Claire swallowed. Dretta wasn't phrasing it like it was bad, but she couldn't help but feel like she was failing to live up to her mentor's expectations. Were they implying she was wasting her time? That she should give up and come home? That she was taking too long or behind some sort of schedule? Or was it meant to encourage her to reach out sooner when she got stuck?

> *I've submitted an inquiry to the Consortium on your behalf. They tend to drag their asses on quester req's, but I've worked with them enough that they won't just shuffle me to the bottom of the pile over and over. I'll keep you posted on what they come back with.*
>
> *I agree with you that there's something about this one that smells fishy. Beyond trying to discover the mage's identity I think you're on the right track with the subject of the quest. Getting him to talk to you has already been fruitful so while we wait on replies just keep poking around. Just because nothing showed up on the diviner doesn't mean nothing's hidden, right? A diviner won't pick up on stuff stashed away the old-fashioned way.*
>
> *If there's any other way I can help just send me a line. Good luck, Odetima.*
> *—Dretta*

She folded the letter and tucked it into her pocket, nodding at the clerk on her way out. It was good to know that something, at least, was in motion, but she couldn't help but feel like she was falling behind and failing. She should have thought of looking for things being hidden by non-magical means, and the way Dretta had drawn so much attention to how much time had passed was sitting sour in her stomach. She could believe that Dretta hadn't meant it as a chastisement, but it felt like that anyway. Maybe because *she* knew, even if Dretta didn't, that the reason for it was because she'd been so distracted by getting to know Beast. Letting herself feel… attraction for him, and then handling that attraction unprofessionally.

The temptation was to swear him off completely, but even Dretta had agreed that continuing to talk to him and get her to open up would be her best course of action for the immediate future, which meant she'd have to jump back in there and keep herself separate from him at the same time. And she'd bought that spindle, and would need him to show her unless she just stashed it away until she got back to Kesterin.

The whole thing was leaving her feeling prickly. Why did she have to meet someone like him while she was working? Where had he been for the last ten years while she'd been going on endless bad dates, being courted by pretentious, selfish pricks who wouldn't know what a clit was if they got hit over the head with one? She sighed. What was done was done and there was no use wishing it could have been different. She'd just have to do better once she was back tomorrow. Now that her business was done she'd leave with the dawn—meaning that by this time tomorrow she'd be back at the manor, putting her resolutions to the test.

CHAPTER TWELVE

The Cold Gray

Beast's send-off for Claire had been reserved and polite but earnest, and he'd been rather proud of how well he'd kept it together. She'd never guessed that panic and dread were sucking at his heels even as she'd gathered her things and headed back to Edden. But once she was out the door, he'd let his control fall away.

From his vantage point on the upper floor's balcony window, he watched her head down to the dull silver gates. He couldn't help but admire how the early morning sun gilded her deep brown skin and made it glow. She'd done her hair in twisted braids sometime yesterday and pulled them back into a bundle at the back of her head for her journey. Her hips swung smoothly as her powerful legs ate up the distance. She'd make good time if she kept that up, and would make it to Edden well before nightfall. He felt better seeing how quickly she traveled, knowing it would mean she got to safety that much faster. It was generally safe around these parts, and Claire was a trained member of the Guild, so he knew the danger was minimal, but it wasn't in his nature to remain calm and collected and rational when he had perfectly realistic worst-case scenarios to obsess over instead. He knew that she was capable and strong—he'd seen her doing her morning exercises, she was a lethal thing of *beauty* with that baton of hers—but he also knew accidents happened, and sometimes people left and never came back.

Sometimes it was because they chose not to.

"She'll be back," he whispered, Claire's form finally slipping beyond his line of sight. "She said she would be. She'll be back. She promised."

A tingling buzz swept over his shoulder, lingering and intensifying as if a hand was trying to soothe him.

How can you be so sure? A dark voice like smoke hissed in his ear. *You're disgusting and pathetic. She's so relieved to be away from you.* He thought he saw something skitter away down a hall out of the corner of his eye, but when he turned to look there was nothing there. His stomach sank. He'd hoped he'd have more time before the darkness came for him.

He decided he had to do something to try and beat back the darkness. The only problem was that nothing seemed right. When he tried spinning he only managed a few minutes before he had to put it back, seething that he kept breaking the singles whenever he heard teeth snapping by his ear or claws scrabbling on marble. He picked up his book only to find that reading about romance made him think about Claire, which only encouraged the voice he was trying so hard to block out.

He found some relief towards the afternoon by deciding to comb through the manor looking for more fae literature for Claire when she came back.

She's not coming back, you fucking idiot.

He shook his head, refusing to acknowledge that. She

would come back. He'd only known her for a little under two weeks but she wasn't the sort to lie.

Unless she was trying to be nice and spare your feelings. Unless she was afraid of what you'd do to her if she told the truth.

No, none of that. Absolutely not. She was his friend. She wouldn't abandon him.

Everyone else has. Not even your own parents wanted you. You are the worst kind of filth, and the world would be much better with you gone. Growling, low and furious, trickled into his ears, making his hair stand on end, and he thought he might have even felt hot breath stirring his hair.

It was time for a nap, he thought, wiping the dust caking his hands onto his pants. He hadn't slept well last night or the night before, and it wasn't like he had anything better to do. Sometimes naps settled him, smoothed out the worst of the barbs in his head. Maybe with some sleep, the darkness would back off and give him some room to breathe.

But this one was not a good nap. He was haunted by unsettling dreams of being lost, of searching, of failing to reach something in time. He awakened near sunset damp with sweat and more irritable than before. But underneath that, he felt it: the darkness, hungry, undeniable, relentless, circling like a hawk before the dive.

Naturally, that was when Naja decided to check up on him again.

"You were getting awfully cozy with this one, worm. She's lasted much longer," she sneered from his bedroom desk chair. Usually, she didn't visit him in his bedroom like this, but whenever she did it unsettled him even more than usual. He probably wouldn't be able to sleep here for several days, now that she'd been here.

"This one is nice," he hedged, avoiding her pale blue eyes.

"She is." Naja stood and crept closer, her hand reaching up to wrap around one of the posts of his four-post bed. "What did you do differently this time?" she asked, her keen eyes trying to flay him.

He was confused, sleep still clinging. Different? To his knowledge, he'd done nothing different, and he told her as much.

She snorted. "You had to have done *something*. She's not —" Naja pressed her lips into a hard line, stopping herself from saying what she was planning on saying. "Why is she here?" she asked instead.

He told her about the quest but left out what he'd told Claire that had helped her figure things out. He didn't want Naja to hunt her down, to hurt her. No one else should have to pay for his sins, especially not Claire.

Naja sighed, rolling her eyes and taking a seat near his feet on the bed. "Vitrin's mercy, that Guild is such a thorn in my side. I need to figure out how to keep you off of their board entirely," she mused, turning thoughtful. "Making it uninteresting and repellent only goes so far, there's always *some* that try anyway. As you've seen."

His eyebrows flew up in surprise as he realized what she was saying. The quest that Claire had come here for was *him*. He didn't know how, or why the circumstances of his imprisonment were an anomaly, but something about him, or this place, had triggered the quest's existence. And that also meant that those others with the silver badges likely *had* been questers.

He was speaking before he could stop himself. "Why do

they always try to hurt me when they come here, Naja?" He froze, his wide eyes darting over to her lovely face. She gave him a sweet smile that failed to warm her eyes.

"Because they see your true nature, worm. They see you for the monster you are, and they take action accordingly. Why else?" Growls and manic laughter assaulted him from all sides.

A monster.

You're a monster, worm.

He hung his head, drawing his knees up to his chest and wrapping his arms around them. When next he looked up Naja was gone, probably off repairing an enchantment or torturing a small animal, or whatever she did when she wasn't haunting him.

Shaken now, he sighed heavily, his claws digging painfully into his scalp with the force of his hands combing back his hair. The growling was back and even stronger than before, and now he saw thick shadows and glowing red eyes circling around the edges of his room, prowling around him like whatever it was was looking for an in, a way to sink its teeth into him and rip him to shreds. He squeezed his eyes shut, fear taking hold. What were these creatures that stalked him from the darkness?

The growling dragged on and on, growing deeper and more furious. His breaths began to hitch and grow shallow, his hands alternating between more painful combing and pressing hard into his eyes. He thought he felt the hot breath of the shadow creature trickling over his neck, his face, making him shiver and squirm, but he kept his eyes tightly closed, trying to will it away. Distantly, he realized he was losing his control, knew he should force deeper breaths, he should leave this gods-damned room —

A high-pitched whine started up in his throat, and he tried to choke it off, he really did, but it was like someone else had slipped into his skin and was keeping him cut off from his own body. He couldn't stop it, nor could he stop the slice of his claws through his skin as his grip tightened and dug deep, leaving burning trails on his face, along his scalp, up and down his limbs. The whine grew, bubbling louder, and he curled up into a tight ball on his side, chest heaving with his quick breaths. The air in his lungs grew thinner and thinner, his arms tightening around himself.

There were no words, no thoughts. There was only the gut-wrenching feeling of *bad*, of *wrong*, pain and terror twisting together and feeding into each other. He imagined himself screaming, over and over, his throat ripping raw and his lungs aching from being emptied past comfort, imagined that that would actually help. His breaths became gasping, giving way to sobs, and then his awareness fled entirely. If he was conscious of anything, it was so dim, so far away, that it might as well have been happening to someone else.

He didn't remember growing tired or falling asleep. One oblivion was simply traded for another.

And that was that: all he managed to do for the next two days was lie in his bed, hiding from the wolves, praying to all of the gods for the mercy of death, for this nightmare to finally end and give him peace. Howls and snarls echoed throughout the manor, following him no matter what room he went to, the hot rancid breath of shadow creatures always at his back.

This is your life now, worm, the dark voices hissed. *You will never be free. You will never see Claire again.*

The one blessing was that he didn't have to see Naja again, and Tully's warm, tingling touch was never too far away. He might have eaten, though if he hadn't it wouldn't really hurt him, and he made sure to at least scrub his skin clean in a sink bath every day. Normally he wouldn't have bothered, but he held the tiniest, most delicate kernel of hope that Claire would return, and if she did he wanted to be presentable for her. But even those fast wipe-downs with a rag took him hours to prepare for. He had to sift through his energy stores all day to find enough to manage just that. And they were such endless days.

But then—

One moment he was lost in the gray ache, wishing he could end it, craving oblivion more than he craved Claire's smile, her joyous belly-laughs, because he was certain she had only ever been a beautiful dream; the next he was bolting upright and out of bed.

The pressure in his chest. The entry wards.

Claire.

He tore himself from his bed, his vision going black and starred at the edges, his legs unsteady and cramping, but he ignored it, fumbled past it to his wardrobe to put on fresh clothes. The hounds that had been nipping at his heels for three days slunk into a corner, going quiet, as he hurried to get ready. Thank the gods he'd kept bathing; his hair was a snarled, greasy mess but he didn't stink, and he could easily throw his hair up into a knot to hide the worst of it.

The wounds from his claws had scabbed over, but were still healing and tugged painfully when he moved his face certain ways. He *definitely* couldn't tell her what had happened there.

Dressed, he hurled himself from his room and raced down the hall, down the stairs, and into the foyer, his chest heaving and tight. He slid on the polished marble, almost tumbling to the floor, but managed to keep his feet. He had no thoughts in his head beyond Claire's name, repeated over and over in a silent, feverish chant.

It was the first time in his long confinement that he hadn't had to be compelled by the enchantment to greet a guest.

The door swung open and there she was, outlined in golden late-afternoon sun. Sweat dewed her face, making her dark skin sparkle. There was something tense and guarded about her expression, a tension that he wasn't used to seeing around her mouth, and his stomach knotted at the sight. Had something changed? Had being around normal people made it hard for her to stomach being around him?

Her eyes met his, taking him in, and then the stiffness faded, her posture loosening as she beamed at him. "Hey, you," she called, flinging her pack from her back and stretching her arms above her head until something cracked loudly.

She crossed the short distance to where he stood, then crooked a finger at him, indicating he should bend forward. He obliged, curious about what she could want, and to his eternal surprise, she wrapped her arms around his neck in a hug. Her body pressed tight up against his, the swells of her breasts flattening against his chest, her delicious rose and vanilla smell mixed up with the musk of her sweat and making his whole body throb. He was so shocked all he could manage was an awkward pat on the back in return.

As she pulled away one of her delicate fingers traced the edge of the healing scratches, that small touch making his cock thicken against his leg.

"What happened here?" she asked gently, her black brows lowering in concern.

"Oh, just an accident. I need to trim my claws soon, they're getting too long," he supplied, ruffling the hair at the back of his head. He was glad most of the wounds were hidden under his hair and clothes. That would have been a very uncomfortable conversation to have with her.

"Yeah, I'd say so!" She pulled away completely, returning to her pack and hefting it onto one shoulder again. "So how are you?" she asked, "What did I miss?"

His face heated. "Not much," he muttered, clasping his hands together behind his back to hide their trembling. A dark chuckle flitted through the air, but Claire didn't seem to hear it. "I tried looking for more fae literature for you, but haven't had any luck so far."

"That's sweet of you, you didn't need to do that," she said, scrubbing her face with a hand and grimacing at the damp left on her palm. "It was a pretty uneventful trip for me. It's a sweet little town though. Everyone I've met so far has been great."

He nodded, following along as she made her way upstairs. He was barely listening to what she was saying, truth be told, because he found himself mesmerized by the warmth and light of her expressions, the spark and fissure of her light brown eyes as they met his, setting something deep in his belly ablaze. He got lost in studying the contours of her face, the way it animated with what she was saying…instead of listening to *what* she was saying. But he tried. He wanted to hear all about what she had done.

He was just distracted by how badly he wanted to pull her

into his arms. Distracted by how he wanted to crush her to his chest, to breathe her scent in deep, and never let her go.

"…and then I picked something up I can't wait to show you. I hope you'll help me with it," she was saying as they reached the top of the stairs.

That got him to stop mooning and pay attention. "What is it?"

"It's a surprise," she winked, opening her bedroom door. "I'll show you after dinner. I'm going to have a bath in the meantime though, get some of this travel filth off of me. I *stink*."

He chuckled, grinning and feeling lighter than he had all week. "Hardly. We should all be so lucky to be so radiant after a day of travel." He coughed, feeling a blush creep up his neck. Was that weird for him to have said? It felt like it. "I will see you at dinner, then," he finished awkwardly, forcing himself to move away from her door with an oh-so-casual wave when all he really wanted was to twine himself around her like an enormous snake and hold on for dear life. It was like he had been slowly suffocating, only for air to pump back into his lungs with heady sweetness, and he wanted to do nothing more than breathe her deep into his starving lungs.

Lost in thought, he wandered back to his room, deciding that if Claire was bathing he should as well; now that she was back he was disgusted by his state. He was an adult; it was shameful that he let himself get so bad just because she went into town for a few days. He should be able to take care of himself. What would he do when she went home for good?

He took his bath, painstakingly combing the snarls out of his wild mop of hair and getting himself clean. Some of the scratches were re-opened by the force of his scrubbing, staining the water pink. But by the time he was toweled off and ready to get dressed the bleeding had stopped. He still wore dark clothes to hide it if they did start up again.

By the time he made it downstairs into the dining room, the sun had dipped below the horizon, a chill shivering in the air. He took his usual seat at the head of the table, waiting anxiously for Claire to join him. He found he was ravenous, his days of barely eating catching up to him. He was also very curious about what she could have possibly gotten in town that she'd want to show him. But really, what thrilled him most was that she had been thinking about him while she was away. He wasn't sure that that had ever happened before. It usually seemed like people only thought about him while he was there in their presence. But she had seen *something*, whatever it might have been, and thought to herself, "Beast needs to see this." And then she'd come back to him when she hadn't needed to.

She hadn't abandoned him. She'd *come back*.

The full force of that hit him then, stunning him and knocking the air from his lungs.

She had left *and then come back*. And she had *hugged* him when she saw him. No one except Tully had ever been so excited to see him that they'd done that.

Steps padded outside the door and the ephemeral beauty herself drifted into the room, looking decidedly less wilted than she had before. She had a long bundle tucked under one arm, about as long as her forearm and somewhat flared at one end. He was curious about what she would have gotten to show him, but all he really wanted was to drink in her presence. To remind himself that she was real. His fingers itched with the urge to reach out and touch her, to hold her.

Despite his hunger, he found that he couldn't manage to pay much attention to dinner. It was some sort of roast and a side he didn't bother touching but that Claire dug into with relish.

"Sweet Delenaa, I missed this food," she sighed, closing her eyes in rapture as she chewed. "Don't tell Sil I said this but stew gets old so fast. That's the chef at the inn in Edden, I don't know why I thought you'd know who that was." She giggled, rolling her eyes at herself. "Sweet Delenaa, I'm goofy tonight, sorry. I wish I could bring you with me, the walk is so lonely and boring." She paused, pearly teeth worrying at her plump rosy-brown lip. "Anyway. I was able to relay what I've learned to Dretta and they're helping me get in touch with the proper channels at the Consortium, so I'm hopeful we'll be able to make some real progress soon on your quest. I don't know about you, but I'm *very* excited about that. Are you excited?"

Her good spirits were infectious, the darkness peeling back more and more the longer he sat with her. He couldn't even hear the growling anymore. He chuckled, nodding. He wondered if he could tell her about what Naja had said to him during her brief visit, but as soon as he opened his mouth his throat closed off, making him choke; that would be a no, then.

She joked and teased as they ate, drawing him out and thawing the last of the chill loneliness from his bones. She was the one who had left, but with her here beside him like this, sharing a meal and warm companionship, he found himself feeling like *he* was the one who had come home.

The meal done and the dishes cleared, she clapped her hands and snatched her parcel up, her delicate fingers picking apart the knotted twine to unwrap it. "Now, it's nothing fancy," she warned him, "and possibly I'm the only one who's going to be excited about it. But something tells me you'll like it."

He nodded, mesmerized by the way her hazel eyes sparkled with excitement. It didn't take long for her to work the knots loose, and then she was carefully unwrapping her prize.

"Ta-da!" she cried, holding up the bared object.

It was a drop spindle. It was a bit rough and plain, but it looked well-balanced and was a good size for beginners, the whorl small enough to get a good amount of twist in per spin but not so small it would get away from her. He melted at the sight.

"I remembered what you had said about how a spindle might be better for me to learn on, so while I was in town I asked around and found someone who could sell me a spare. But I'll still need you to show me how to use it, if you don't mind," she said, her expression full of hope. As if he would refuse her anything.

"I'd love to," he murmured, his heart aching with feeling.

"You're the best!" she exclaimed, reaching out and squeezing his arm. "Let's do it tomorrow though. I'm too tired tonight."

"Certainly. Will you be off to bed, then?"

Her mouth twisted as she considered. "I don't know. Are you going to bed?"

He shook his head. "I'm not tired just yet. But I haven't been traveling all day."

"Well, what are you planning on doing? Maybe I'll tag along."

His heart clenched again. "I might read in the library for a bit."

"Sure!" she surged to her feet, re-wrapping her spindle. "Is it a good book? Maybe you could read it to me."

His spine stiffened. He was in the middle of an absolutely filthy romance novel, a fact which he was determined to hide from Claire at all costs. But there was another, tamer book about a quester going on an adventure that he had been meaning to read that he could start, that he could read with her. "I have one you might enjoy. I'd—I'd be happy to read it to you."

"Then it's a date," she declared, slipping her arm through his and gesturing with her wrapped spindle like a scepter for him to lead the way.

He was suddenly very sweaty.

CHAPTER THIRTEEN

Garnette Mason

Claire's whole trip back from Edden she'd been steeling herself against getting overly familiar with Beast when she saw him. She'd told herself, on no uncertain terms, that she would install a professional level of distance. She'd pack up her confusing feelings for him and tuck them away. She swore to herself that this time she'd refrain from touching him needlessly, that she'd stop drifting close just to catch a whiff of his warm, sweet scent.

And then she'd seen him and it had all gone out the window. She hadn't been able to resist throwing her arms around his gray neck and taking a deep breath of his delicious smell as soon as she saw him. The adorable little topknot he'd been sporting, which showed off the delicate points of his ears and the thick column of his throat, had made her weak in the knees. And then there was the way he'd looked at her as he'd met her at the door, as if he had never seen anything more perfect than her dirty, sweaty face.

Now she was walking arm-in-arm with him to the library, leaning subtly closer to the hot bulk of his body. It was like as soon as she saw him all sense fled her, some other version of herself that was a shameless flirt taking over and insisting on getting as close as possible. Once dinner was over she hadn't been able to walk away, to say goodnight and return to her cold, lonely room.

Her arm tightened around his, her free hand coming up to pet his firm bicep, reassuring herself that she really was back, that the wards hadn't locked her out, that he'd been more or less alright without her. She'd tried not to dwell on it, but she had been worried that she'd get locked out. Of course, the fact that she hadn't been meant now she'd have to figure out *why*, on top of all the other strange mysteries circling this place.

He cleared his throat, and she thought he might have leaned, just the barest amount, into her embrace. "Do you, um, like adventure stories?" he asked, his voice a little strained.

She should ease up on the poor man, let him catch his breath before she started getting this cozy. But much as she tried, she couldn't quite manage to loosen her grip and lean away. "Yeah, they're alright. But my favorites are romances."

He turned his serious gray face to look down at her, a smile gently tugging on his firm slate lips. His free hand came up to comb his hair back in that nervous gesture she was growing so fond of. She loved how deliciously mussed he looked after a couple of swipes of those big clawed hands. Plus his horns looked so dashing, sweeping back from his temples like that. "You like romances?" he asked shyly.

She grinned. "Oh yes. I have a hard time finding authors that I like but I'm such a sucker for a good romance. Two star-crossed lovers destined to be together, overcoming the odds, fighting to be together with everything they've got—what's not to like?" Her face grew flushed as she confessed, "It's what

I fantasize about finding for myself."

He was silent for a few heartbeats. "I also dream of that," he admitted, his voice barely above a whisper. He cleared his throat. "Do you…have you ever read Garnette Mason's books?" When she looked up at him he was avoiding her eyes, his whole face flushed.

She shook her head, dropping his arm so they could take their seats in the armchairs in front of the now-dark bay windows of the library. Dissatisfied with the distance between the two chairs, Claire stood and shoved hers closer with a firm bump of her hip. She couldn't help the flare of pleasure when she noticed how he watched her, those soft brown eyes liquid and hot in the dim candlelight of the library.

"She's probably my favorite romance author," he continued, his voice tight. She was surprised that a man would admit to even reading romances, let alone to having read enough of them to have favorites. It made him that much more endearing, and it was a fact about him that piqued her curiosity. Even if he was reluctant to admit that he liked such books, he was still admitting to it, and that really did something for her.

She flushed with heat, picturing how consuming romance literature might inform his approach to a relationship. She could picture him very earnest, intense, sweet, gentle yet passionate…and it was thrilling, to let herself picture, just for a moment, what those huge warm hands would feel like trailing over her skin, his face lowering slowly to hers, mouth slanting

—

She clenched her hands into tight fists, letting her nails dig into her palms. She mentally shook herself, second-guessing her decision to avoid bed. *Down, girl,* she hissed to herself silently. She absolutely *had* to get a grip on herself if this was going to work.

"Would you let me borrow one?" she asked, forcing her focus back to the present and away from her steamy thoughts. In the dim light, his features were thrown into higher relief, swathing his face in shadow, but it also softened some of the harsher planes of his face, making his mouth look softer, his large nose proud and graceful instead of jutting. She couldn't take her eyes off of him.

"Uh…if you want, sure. But they're um—a little…adult? If something like that bothers you," he muttered, avoiding her eyes again and ducking his head so the scarlet waves of his hair flopped forward into his face.

The last of her control fled, her whole body going tingly at his sweet shyness. He was going to make her *combust*, truly. "The spice is what makes it so nice," she teased, pitching her voice low and leaning towards him like they were sharing a secret.

He made a strangled noise that sounded like part cough, part squeak. She bit her lip, thinking perhaps she had pushed things a bit too far. "Sorry, I'll behave," she promised, patting his forearm reassuringly.

"Thank you," he choked out, voice rough. "Vitrin's mercy, you just got back. Give me a minute, Odetima."

She laughed, throwing her head back. "Oh, of course, I'm sorry. I forgot I was dealing with someone extremely old."

He scoffed, trying his best to stifle a grin. "You're back on this already? How does such a tiny person fit that much audacity inside them?"

"Excuse you!" she cried, reaching across to smack at his arm. "Why are you so hell-bent on calling me tiny? I'm the

tallest in my family! I can lift over a hundred pounds and can carry almost two hundred on my back. *No one* would call me small!"

"That's rude, calling me no one."

She started laughing again, slumping against the arm of her chair. "Being rude is pointing out that the reason you think I'm small is because your old man eyes don't work anymore. And that compared to you most oxen are petite. Which I'm *not* saying, because I'm not rude. Just as examples."

They both collapsed into laughter, the books all but forgotten.

Once they'd calmed down, Beast got up and retrieved some slim books from the higher shelves and handed them to her.

He said they were his two favorite Garnette Mason books. "This one, *Heart of Winter*, is about a woman who gets trapped in a world of eternal winter and falls in love with one of the locals when seeking his people's aid, and this other one, *Fireblood*, is about a woman who is caught by a fire drake and discovers that he and the others who have been terrorizing her town are actually being ravaged by a terrible illness that makes them violent, and so she gets wrapped up in trying to help them." They didn't sound like any romances she'd ever read before, but she couldn't deny they sounded fantastic. It was like romance wrapped up with adventure, and that really appealed to her.

Published 19 AW, Montgomery and Assoc., one read on the front matter. *Published 20 AW, Montgomery and Assoc.,* said the other. They were among the newer books in the library, but they were still old. Maybe that was why she'd never heard of Garnette Mason before.

They talked a bit about what they liked and didn't like in romances, and books in general, and then the cozy warmth of the library and of the little bubble that they'd cocooned themselves into as they'd shared and laughed, worked its way into her. She drifted closer and closer to his big body, caught in the pull of his warm brown eyes and the way his cheek creased with his smiles, and she was alarmed to feel herself cracking open, unwinding the bindings around her heart that kept it so secret and safe. She felt the need, suddenly burning and urgent, to make him understand why she wanted to be able to love freely, to have the easy intimacy featured in her favorite novels.

"I've not had very many real relationships," she admitted quietly, tracing the embossed lettering on the cover of the book in her lap. "I can't even count the number of times I've met someone, thought they were wonderful, only for it to have been…a lie, I guess. They wanted my body so they made themselves into who they thought I wanted in order to get it. And then once they'd gotten what they wanted they just…left."

She heard him swallow, and she peeked up through her lashes to watch his thick throat work. "That's…gods, that's so awful, Claire. I'm sorry."

She smiled wryly, meeting his burning gaze for just a moment before retreating to look at her hands in her lap again. "I should know better by now, really," she admitted. "But I just…can't stop hoping, I guess. That it'll finally be real. You know?"

He was silent. "No one has ever approached me…like that," he said softly. "But I understand the hope. How sometimes you have to—to cling to it, even when it feels foolish, because it also lets you know that you're still going, still…"

"…alive," she whispered, her throat tight and thick with emotion.

She studied his face, feeling something click into place in her chest. He met her gaze and offered her a shy smile, sending her pulse skittering faster. She'd never felt this kind of a connection to another person before. And suddenly, it was scaring her. Terrifying her, because of how real and intense and *deep* it felt. It was hitting her all at once, so sharp and sweet, and it was too much, and what in all the fires of Salerah was she *doing*—

"I think I've bothered you enough for the night," she sputtered, shooting to her feet and clutching her borrowed books tight to her chest. "I'll just—I'm going to head to bed, I think."

"Oh," he said softly, looking confused and a little crestfallen. "Of course. You've had a long day, you should rest."

She nodded, turning on her heel and striding to the open doors.

She paused at the threshold, however, and turned to look back at him. He looked so dejected, his shoulders bowed, and she felt ashamed by her sudden retreat. Vitrin's mercy, but what was *wrong* with her lately?

"Good night, Beast," she murmured.

He smiled at her, perking up a little and digging her guilt in deeper. "Good night," he rumbled.

And before she could think it about it too much and second guess herself, she blew him a kiss and slipped out into the dark, chill hall, scurrying to her room.

CHAPTER FOURTEEN

Ensnared

Beast didn't want to say that Claire was hopeless, but when they'd sat in the library and she'd managed to do exactly no successful spinning after more than an hour, he'd toyed with the idea of using the phrase. Her bitter frustration had been hard to see, and he'd done his best to encourage her, to soothe the sting of failure and give her hope for the future. But he hadn't thought that it was even remotely possible that she'd actually try it again, let alone take his advice and hunt down a drop spindle. But here they were.

Digging through his stash of fiber, he chose a tougher wool this time around with a lovely crimp, his thinking being that it should spin easily for her, even with her...issues. He could no longer recall exactly what the name of the sheep breed had been that the wool had come from, but he knew it was from the far north of Cillure, where Vitrin's breath never stopped flowing over the dry mountain peaks and frozen lakes. It was a very warm wool, but scratchy against the skin. Luckily first spins were saved for the memories, not to actually be used.

Assuming, of course, that this lesson wound up more

successful than the last and she *had* any yarn to show for it at the end.

While he was looking for fiber for Claire, he paused at one of the trunks he had all his finished yarn stashed away in. He hesitated, running his hand along the top, mind churning, before he opened the lid and dug through it for two particular skeins. Then he took the bundle of items downstairs to meet her.

He made it back down to the library first, fidgeting in his seat as he waited for her. He wanted a cool head, to be able to calmly demonstrate how to use a drop spindle, but he was just so…worked up. He kept thinking about that hug, about how she'd clung to his arm and blown him a kiss goodnight. It made his skin feel taut and oversensitive, and it was a struggle to keep his thickening shaft from being obvious.

Get it together, you idiot, he silently cursed himself, willing his pulse to ease, for his skin to cool, for his blood to settle anywhere else in his body besides his damned cock.

He heard the creak of the stair that announced someone heading down, and he prayed to the gods for control of his body. He took several deep breaths, hoping it would be enough to cool him down in the few seconds he still had.

Claire strode confidently through the door, her wrapped spindle clutched to her chest like a baby. "Sorry it took me so long!" she trilled, breezing over to him.

She plopped down beside him in her armchair with a huff. The impact made her breasts jump and jiggle beneath the loose fabric of her shirt, undoing all of his hard work in calming himself down. But he refused to stare, refused to give into his baser instincts and sit there drinking her down like a greedy lecher.

She carefully unwrapped the bundle in her lap, moving as if it would shatter like brittle glass. He found himself smiling, his chest warming with something softer than lust. She was so precious, his Claire.

No, not mine. Except as a friend, she will never be mine. He heard cackling, the sound distant and muffled. Eyes flashed in his peripheral vision. He shook himself, returning his attention to Claire.

Once the spindle sat revealed in her lap, she sat there staring at it, her fingers lightly stroking the edge of the whorl. She turned to him, her twist braids swaying to frame her rich brown face prettily. "So what do I do now?" she asked, picking it up by the shaft and wielding it like a club.

He flinched back from the hook at the end of the spindle, which had come a little too close to his face for comfort, and plucked it gently from her fingers. "I'll get it started for you this time, so you can just focus on getting the movements of the spin itself down."

He tied some scrap yarn he'd brought down from his room to the shaft just under the whorl so that a loop was hanging off rather than a line, just like Tully had shown him all those long years ago. He was relieved to find that his hands seemed to remember what his mind had let go fuzzy, quickly maneuvering around the drop spindle as if his last time using one hadn't been more than two centuries ago. He brought the free end of the loop up and around the side of the whorl, slotting it into the notch that had been cut there to catch the yarn and keep it from sliding around the circumference of the whorl; that would stabilize the whole process and help the spindle stay level. To finish setting it up, he continued the path of the yarn up into the hook at the top, passing it through the eye.

"It's called a drop spindle," he began to explain, "but the way I was taught to use it at first doesn't involve dropping it."

She chuckled. "Thank the gods. But I bet you I'm going to wind up dropping it a whole bunch anyway. I'm utterly useless with this stuff."

He frowned at her. "That's my friend you're slandering. Please be nicer to her," he scolded, laying the spindle in his lap to snatch up a handful of wool from the bundle he'd brought down. When he looked back up she was blinking at him, looking shocked. When their eyes met her expression softened, color creeping into her cheeks.

"Yes, sir," she murmured, smiling at him gently. He nodded, smiling back.

"Now that that's sorted out, here's your lesson, Claire: spin and park." He drafted out a bit of the wool and passed it through the free end of the loop, twirling the spindle counter-clockwise with his fingers to twist the wool into the beginnings of a singles. "Pinch your fingers together where the spun stuff ends to keep the twist there. Then once you've got it going like this, all you do is spin it—" he set the shaft of the spindle against the outside of his right thigh, then rolled it towards his knee with the palm of his hand, going slow so she could see what he was doing, then again at the speed he actually needed. When he got to his knee, he let it hang freely, the momentum he'd built carrying it through several more rotations. "—then you park it between your thighs," and here he felt his own face flame, thinking about how shapely and strong hers were, and how a part of him envied the spindle for being able to spend so much time wedged between all that glorious flesh in the near future, "and then use your free hand to draft the wool out, loosening the pinch in your other fingers to let the twist travel up the drafted bits." It was always so satisfying, watching the fibers compress and settle into place, as if they'd always meant to be yarn, and he was just allowing nature to take its course. He loved the faint snap against the pads of his fingers, the tiniest crunch of the fibers melding together, locking in place.

He finished letting the twist he'd gathered move into the wool, then wound the length of singles he'd just created onto the shaft. He handed it over to Claire with a smile. "Make sure you wind the singles on evenly or you'll get a lot of wobbles. But I think you've got this," he assured her.

She pursed her lips, looking doubtful, but she nodded and took the spindle, pinching the spinning just above where his fingers were to keep the twist locked in place. She stared at the tool in her hands for a moment with a tension that would have been more at home had she been asked to hold a viper, but after a moment she let out a heavy breath and squared her shoulders.

"Alright. Here goes nothing."

Her movements were halting and slow, her hands uncertain on the whorl as she tried to wrap her head around which direction to spin.

"Hip to knee," he interjected gently.

She nodded, doing her best to mimic him. And to his utter delight, she managed it: the amount of twist she got in was low, but it was a solid spin and she didn't drop it, flip it up into her face, or break the yarn, and that was a triumph. A grin started curling the corners of her mouth, light dancing in her hazel eyes. She wedged the shaft of the spindle between her thighs, drafted the wool out, and slid her pinched fingers up, making several inches of singles.

She shrieked, stomping her feet on the floor and scaring Beast so much he almost fell off his chair.

"I did it! Oh, sweet Delenaa, I *did it!*" she whooped, bouncing in her seat and beaming at what she'd done. "You're a *genius*, Beast. You've done the impossible! Dee's going to be so proud." She turned her face up to him, her happiness so bright and sparkling in her face, and he found himself suddenly struggling to keep his hands in his lap, to stop himself from reaching for her brown heart-shaped face, cupping it in his massive gray hands so that he could capture her mouth in a kiss.

He cleared his throat, leaning away from her to try and kill the urge. "I told you you could do it," he choked out, his eyes frozen on her lips. "All I did was give you another option. You had it in you all along."

She beamed at him again, then returned her attention to her work, leaving him feeling curiously bereft. He could almost *feel* the kiss. And to know it would never happen was making something go cold and jagged in his gut. He could feel the first brushes of the chill fingers of his darkness curling around his heart, whispering dark things in his ear, dragging him down into the bog. But he fought it; even if he couldn't kiss Claire, couldn't hold her or touch her like he wanted to so very desperately, he was still bringing her joy. It was *Beast* who had brought such light to her face. And even though she would likely never return his romantic feelings, she still clearly cared about him. She called him "friend" with all the warmth and affection that word deserved.

"I'm almost done with this bit of wool. How do you add more?" her question snapped him out of his reverie, making him start just a bit. He smiled at her, feeling his face heat.

"It's actually quite simple. Here, let me show you…"

For the next hour, Claire spun excitedly, beaming at the rough and bumpy yarn she was making slowly but surely.

"I still can't believe I'm doing this," she told him as she drafted out some more wool. She'd almost finished what he'd brought down. He couldn't help the wide warm smile that seemed to be stuck on his face.

"I can. Sometimes you just have to look at a thing sideways to see it."

She looked over at him. "What does that mean?"

He shrugged. "Tully said it all the time. I think it's like… like maybe sometimes you just need a new perspective on things to be able to tackle them properly."

She nodded slowly, something he couldn't read slipping into her warm hazel eyes. "I think I might be done for now," she said suddenly, handing the spindle to him. "I should really start reading all those books you've found me on the fae. Get some actual work done." She looked a little forlorn as she said it, and he wanted to protest, to tell her that she didn't need to do any of that, that she could just stay here with him and do this every day. The manor would take care of all their needs, and even if it couldn't Edden wasn't very far away. He didn't know what he'd do about Naja, but for one burning moment he thought it would work, that he'd do whatever it took to *make* it work. He couldn't go back to the way he'd lived before Claire, not now that he'd had a taste of what it was like to have a friend, to have someone who understood him, keeping him company, making him laugh, sharing their warmth.

"I—I have something for you," he blurted as he showed

her how to put the spindle away so the project would stay intact. "It's nothing, it's silly, but I saw it and I thought…I thought of you." Her eyes widened in surprise, her eyebrows hiking up towards her hairline.

"You didn't have to do that, Beast." Her smoky voice was soft and sweet.

He shrugged, his face too hot, as he grabbed the two skeins of yarn he'd grabbed from the trunk in the storage room. They were the most beautiful thing he'd ever made, a pale cerulean blue blend of aerlanis and silk he'd gotten as a gift eons ago. The blend had the sheen and drape of silk but was strong and warm thanks to the added aerlanis wool. He knew the color would look stunning against her warm brown complexion, and the luxurious texture was no less than she deserved. He handed them to her with trembling hands, his heart in his throat.

She gasped when her eyes settled on his gift. "Sweet Delenaa, Beast…they're stunning. I-I can't accept something that nice."

He shook his head, thrusting them at her again. "Please take them. I want you to have them. I haven't used them yet in all this time, so I'm not going to suddenly decide to now."

She lifted them from his outstretched hands, squishing the skeins in her hands before bringing them to her face and nuzzling them against her cheek with a moan that made his cock twitch. "Holy gods, it's so *soft*. Are you absolutely sure you want me to have these? It's the nicest yarn I've ever seen. Where did you even get this?"

He flushed, pleased she liked it. "I spun it. The fiber was a gift from Tully for my fifteenth birthday. And yes, I'm completely sure I want you to have them. It would—it would make me really happy," he finished in a near whisper, his hand combing furiously through his hair.

"Oh, Beast," she murmured, looking at him with so much tenderness it made him ache. Then she was standing up, placing the skeins on her seat, her arms wrapping around his neck, holding him close against her and rocking from side to side gently. He was so much taller than her that even though he was sitting she didn't have to lean over all that much to do it. Unlike when she'd hugged him yesterday, his arms came up to wrap around her right away, looping around her slim waist and clinging tight. He took deep, greedy lungfuls of her scent, trying to memorize the shape of her, how warm and soft her body was pressed against him.

It was over far too quickly, Claire pulling back gently but not quite breaking the contact yet. Her light brown eyes blazed hot, searing into him and making his heart beat faster and faster. He swallowed, noticing that her eyes tracked the movement in his throat before settling on his mouth for a long moment. It took all of his willpower to stop himself from swaying closer to her, to test and see what she'd do if he started closing the distance between their faces. She bit her lip, her eyes tearing from his mouth. She leaned back in, to the side, and he thought she would go back to holding him, but instead her velvet-soft lips pressed to his cheek, lingering in a gentle kiss. The tip of her nose nuzzled at his cheekbone for the briefest moment, and he shuddered, his hands tightening against her back. She pulled back once more, stepping out of the cradle of his arms this time, her pupils blown wide and her cheeks flushed with color.

"Thank you," she murmured, her voice deeper than usual. All he could manage was a small nod.

Claire was starting to think that it was actually impossible for her to put professional distance between her and Beast. Every time she resolved to do it, he'd do something sweet, opening himself up to her in a way that was so achingly tender that she couldn't stop herself from letting her walls down. Knowing what he'd been through, it seemed cruel to deny him like that when he took a chance and let himself be vulnerable with her.

She hadn't meant to kiss him when he'd given her that gift. But she couldn't even really say she regretted it. His cheek had been surprisingly smooth and soft, the texture of his skin more plump and bouncy than she had been expecting, making her wonder how he'd feel about her gently sinking her teeth into him. He was so…*meaty*, and now that she'd had that one little wisp of a taste she was hungry for more, to get her mouth all over the rest of him.

She was in her bathroom, washing up before lunch, and as her thoughts kept getting steamier she clutched the edge of the sink, hanging her head and sighing deep. Vitrin's mercy, what was *wrong* with her? She'd never been one to—to *lust* after someone like this. To yearn and ache and strain for someone without being able to control herself.

Maybe she should just leave. Pack her bags and go back to Edden, or better yet all the way back to Kesterin and give up on the quest entirely. She needed to get her head on straight and stop messing around. She wasn't here to fall for Beast, she was here to do a gods-damned job. If she couldn't handle this one then the best thing to do would be to try again with a new quest. It was heartless, but everyone was always telling her to harden herself, to be more willing to make the hard choices. And there had been that line in Dretta's letter, about hanging around at the manor without any progress. What if it *had* been an admonishment?

It didn't matter that the thought of leaving him made her whole chest hurt, she told herself.

She allowed herself to wonder, just for a moment, what would happen if she gave in to her feelings. They were both consenting adults, and as long as she was transparent about everything the Guild wouldn't care beyond that. It wasn't so long ago that the Guild moonlighted as a matchmaking agency, people putting out quests just to meet Guild members in the hopes of romancing them. But it wasn't really about getting in trouble.

Got nothing to do but wait around right now, part of her insisted quietly. True: it would take several days before either the Consortium or the Guild would finish digging through their records to find the information she'd requested. *But I could have stayed in Edden instead of coming back.* Also true, but it was a lot cheaper to stay at the manor, though she was fairly certain Teran was cutting her a hefty deal on the room rates. She's set those wheels in motion, and she should at least stay until she knew for sure it was nothing but dead ends.

She could just picture the look on her father's face if he found out she was with someone that looked like Beast. There was no way she'd ever get back in his good graces and repair her relationship with her father and sisters. She couldn't even say for certain that Adeela would be okay with being presented with someone like Beast, no matter how much she loved Claire. She'd mentioned him in her most recent letter though, a part of her trying to soften her up and prepare her for…for what?

She twisted the cold water on viciously, splashing her face and trying to get ahold of herself. She was *not* going to pursue something romantic with Beast. She was going to be a gods-damned professional and focus on the quest. She took a deep breath, squaring her shoulders, before heading down for lunch.

After lunch, they went back to the library so that Claire could start looking through the books he'd managed to find in his little collection on the fae. Most of it was folklore, but there were a couple of old volumes on genealogy that might have something more concrete she could use. He offered to help her look, and despite herself, she found herself agreeing easily. She loved reading but hated doing research, most of the time, an irony that was not lost on her. And it would be an excuse to linger near Beast, to absorb his warm, solid presence and let it calm her.

Just because she wasn't going to let herself pursue something romantic with him didn't mean she couldn't still be his friend and enjoy being with him. Plus, he *needed* her.

"You know, Beast," she mused, her eyes drifting from the ancient volume of fae folklore spread on her lap for likely the fifteenth time in as many minutes and letting it slam shut, "I think today could be a nice day to go for a walk around the grounds." Reading endless tales about fated mates and the instant soul-searing attraction it roused in them when they met was making her feel cranky, forcing her mind back to her own unrequited attraction again and again.

He lifted his gaze from his own book, blinking rapidly to wrangle her into focus. He looked over his shoulder to the sunny late summer day beyond the window at his back.

"Yes, I suppose it looks nice enough," he agreed. "But I'm fine in here, I think."

Her stomach sank. "Really?" She flashed a wide grin and fluttered her eyelashes at him. "Come on, it hasn't been sunny in *ages* and you never leave the manor. It'll be a nice change of pace!"

"You should go then, don't let me hold you back," he replied, shrugging and re-settling himself in his seat. There was something about the set of his broad shoulders that spoke of discomfort. *Curious.*

She bit her lip, considering. She *did* want to go outside. Her skin was practically screaming for sun, her heart aching for the smells of these last lingering days of summer, for the feel of a warm breeze on her face, twining through her hair. Who knew how many more lovely days like this they'd get before the bitter bite of winter swallowed it all? But while being alone had never bothered her, she didn't want to go alone this time. An image had kept flashing through her mind as she read stories about summer feasts and galas, of Beast walking beside her in the gardens, laughing, the sun flaming his crimson locks and the breeze playing with the short downy hairs that hadn't made it into the messy topknot he was sporting. She wondered if his granite-colored skin might not glitter like granite in the sun. The image grew brighter and more powerful in her mind, and it was suddenly hard to breathe.

"I don't want to go alone," she responded, hating the hint of a whine in her voice. She swallowed, then blurted: "I want to go with you." She wanted to see him having fun, being free. Well—as free as he *could* be, anyway.

He stilled, his eyes still locked on the book. He sat there, quiet, for a heartbeat, and she found herself standing, and putting her book aside, and preparing to leave, with a forced lightness that felt very heavy.

"Alright then," she heard him say quietly as she was turning for the door. She spun around to face him again, not even trying to stop her smile.

They had both dressed casually that morning, in loose linen pants and shirts, and given the warmth of the day they opted not to change, merely switching from house slippers to boots, in her case, since Beast never bothered with shoes, before setting out across the front lawn.

Neat flower beds and intricately shaped topiaries hugged the sides of the manor, trailing away to merge with the wilder flora of the general grounds. Stone benches interrupted the piles of greenery along the rough path that wound through the most obviously manicured bits of the impressive gardens. She wished she knew more about what was growing all around her, but if you couldn't eat it or die from it she hadn't bothered to learn about it. But even so, she could still appreciate that it looked nice and smelled even better. Butterflies and bees flitted and hummed throughout the flowers, working hard in the silky late-summer heat.

Beside her, Beast was silent, his eyes downcast and hidden by the sweep of his thick red lashes. She found herself studying his face covertly, at the jutting blade of his nose, the sharp cut of his jaw, the high sharp points of his elfish ears. He looked sad, she thought, or perhaps just intensely pensive. She forced herself to look away before he caught her staring.

"So why do I never see you out here?" she asked.

He shrugged, shoving his hands into his trouser pockets.

"Don't like it."

"Can I ask why?"

He hesitated, his mouth twisting. She thought he would refuse, he was quiet so long.

"It's because I can't leave," he said quietly, darting a quick glance at her face before returning to his scrutiny of the ground. "Being outside, knowing that I can go no farther...it bothers me. If I'm inside the manor, then the walls keep me penned in, but it's a kind of comfort, to know that there is more beyond, even if it is just the grounds. But out here...there's nothing else. These are my bounds."

Her chest ached at his words. She imagined what it must be like, stuck here for the gods only knew how long, with nothing and no one beyond the rare visitor. It was so immediately awful it took her breath away. It was like the loneliness of her childhood but bloomed up to unthinkable proportions.

She took a steadying breath, then cautiously reached out and took his hand, threading their fingers together and squeezing gently.

He straightened, looking surprised.

"I can't even imagine how awful that is," she murmured, "and if you want to go back in I completely understand; we can go."

He shook his head, soft brown eyes meeting hers. "You couldn't have known, it's alright. It's actually not so bad, with you here." Color crept up his neck, and he cleared his throat nervously.

She beamed at him. "You just needed a big strong quester to make you feel safe, huh?" she teased, squeezing his hand again and grinning up at him. The smile he turned on her took her breath away.

"Yes, I suppose I did," he rumbled.

She was starting to think that one of Beast's biggest problems was that he didn't know how to have fun. He had things that he enjoyed, but having fun was different: it was bigger, louder, and you had to cut something loose to have it. So while she had him out here, she was going to try and get him to have *fun*.

"Let's play a game," she suggested, swinging their joined hands together.

He drew up, thick brows arching in surprise. "A game? What game?"

She shrugged, bouncing on the balls of her feet. "I don't know. What do you have?"

"Nothing. No one in the history of this manor has ever played a game."

She snorted at his joke—or at least, she *hoped* it was a joke —then frowned, looking around them as if a ball or a bat or a net might appear and save her idea. And then she remembered one of her favorites from her physical fitness licensing course—a simple exercise, and one that didn't really require any equipment. "Let's play capture the flag!"

"Really?" he asked, and she held her breath, hoping he'd be interested. "Don't we need more people?"

"Ideally," she allowed, "but I think we can make it work. It'll just be a real dirty game, lots of cheating. To make up for there being just the two of us."

He laughed, the sound deep and faintly rasping. "Why would we need to cheat? How do you cheat at capture the flag?"

"To keep it interesting, of course." She grinned wickedly,

delighting in the smile he returned right back at her. "The way I learned it, there was no tackling and you had to put the flag someplace reasonable, out in the open, to make sure your defensive teammates were getting good practice in. So we put our flags anywhere we please. And you will get no mercy from me, dear Beast. I suggest you pray to your gods now."

"I can't tackle you, I'd probably squash you," he objected, his own grin spreading across his lips and making her knees feel distinctly liquid.

"You're just scared, old man," she taunted, dropping his hand and striding over to a plume of delicate red blossoms the same shade of red as Beast's hair and snapping two of the flowers free. "These will be our flags. We'll take a minute to hide them somewhere on the grounds, then the game is on."

"How are we dividing the area? Whose territory is where?"

She pinched her lip, eyes roving over the expanse of greenery in front of her. She twisted to look behind her as well, considering.

"Hm…maybe we say everything behind me is my territory and the rest is you?" She pointed to the red rose bushes on either side of the path where they were standing. "That can be the dividing line."

He nodded. "What sorts of places are off-limits for hiding spots?"

She laughed. "You're thinking too much!" she called as she jogged off back towards the manor, considering whether any of the topiary or statues they'd passed on the way out might make good hiding spots.

He laughed again, shaking his head. Then he, too, was off. She tried not to notice the way the muscles of his legs flexed and jumped, or the way the wind flattened his shirt against his torso, emphasizing the broad heft of him. And she especially tried to ignore the way the sight of him light and laughing and free made her ache in a way which was absolutely not friendly.

After a few seconds of scouting, she spotted a small fountain with a cherub emptying a pail at its center, with enough of a gap between the water line and the side of the pail to wedge the flower in. Then she snapped around, jogging back in the direction that she'd left Beast.

She kept herself low, knees soft, moving slow and smooth, leaning on her training to keep herself as silent as possible. It might have been just a casual game, but she never turned down a chance to show off. Her heart hammered in her chest, her ears straining above the buzz of insects for the sounds of breathing or footsteps. She crept around in ever-widening circles, eyes roving constantly for a flash of fiery red hair, of gray skin.

She had made her way over to a small copse of young maples, still no sign of him, when she heard the creak of wood overhead. She froze, ears straining, her eyes shooting into the leafy canopy above her. She didn't see him, but she heard the unmistakable sound of someone trying—and failing—to hold in laughter.

"I hear you, you coward!" she called, turning in a slow circle, "come out and fight me!"

She heard him laughing in earnest now, no longer trying to hide it.

"How did you even manage to get up into these trees, anyway?" she called, "you are *gigantic*, there's no way these little things can support all that weight!"

More rustling and creaking sounded above her and to the right, and after a moment Beast's feet sank into view, his sharp back claws digging into the tree bark, muscles bunching visibly in his powerful thighs and broad back as he lowered to the ground. "You said cheating was fine. I cheated gravity, obviously," he declared, clapping his hands clean on his black linen pants and grinning broadly.

"Show off," she grumbled, eyeing the tree he'd come out of. Beast crouched, spreading his arms and watching her as she circled closer to the tree.

"You're not going to get that flower, Odetima," he taunted, keeping himself between her and the tree.

"You should have hidden it better if you didn't want me getting it, old man," she fake-sneered back, shaking her limbs loose and crouching again. She thought she could probably manage to get around him; he was big, and obviously strong, but Claire was quick, and hard to keep hold of. And Beast was a homebody, she reminded herself—despite all that muscle he wouldn't have nearly the athletic skill of her classmates, and even they had struggled to keep up with her and keep their grips during grapples. She was so slippery that her instructor, Caldus Love, had taken to calling her Trout by the time she graduated.

It was relatively simple, to come at the tree from one direction, then pull back and feint the other way. His grasping hands closed on empty air, and then she was leaping, hands wrapping around her chosen bough. She wasn't acrobatic enough to have swung herself up onto the branch with her momentum, but she did manage to bring her feet up to finish hauling herself up onto the branch.

"Ha!" she crowed, beaming down at Beast, who wasn't

even trying to catch her anymore. He was just standing there, his hands on his hips and chest heaving slightly against the dove-gray linen of his shirt. A smile of his own flashed up at her, making her heart jump in her chest.

"You still have to find it up there," he said, stepping closer to her perch.

"You should just give up now, old man," she called over her shoulder, reaching up for the next branch. "I can practically taste the victory already—" but as her hand groped along the rough wood, searching for a good grip, something stung her palm, the shock and sharp stab of pain causing her to overbalance and tip backward. Her hand injured now, Claire couldn't correct the trajectory of her body, and she slid from the branch, plummeting towards the ground. Her tunic sleeve caught on a thin branch, ripping it open.

"Claire!"

She braced, her eyes squeezed shut, hoping she wouldn't suffer a broken bone when she hit the ground, but Beast proved much faster than she had thought he'd be. He caught her, if a bit clumsily, his arms snagging her around the middle, driving the breath from her lungs and making her grunt. Her left arm was pinned to her side, but her right—the injured one—landed on his shoulder, and her face was level with his.

His brown eyes were sparking with alarm, the dappled sunlight bringing out golden flecks from around his fear-wide pupils. Their faces were so close she could feel the warm puff of his breaths on her cheeks, and she realized, in a daze, that if she leaned forward just a few inches she could kiss him. His warm, sweet smell was wrapped all around her, making her dizzy, and every point of contact between them had gone hot and tingling. She blinked, pulling in a ragged, shuddering breath.

"Are you alright?" he asked gently, setting her on the ground. She immediately missed his heat.

"Something stung me," she murmured, holding her injured palm with her uninjured hand. Her palm was already red and swelling, a bead of blood oozing from a mounded puncture near the center.

"Can I see?" he asked, and she held out her hand. He took it gently, leaning close to look at it. "Definitely looks like a sting. I'm going to squeeze it a little to check for a stinger, alright?" She nodded, her lips pursing as she held in a grunt of pain when he did as promised. "I'm sorry, I'm sorry," he breathed in a chant as he worked.

"No stinger," he concluded, releasing her hand. She wished, just a little, that he had held on a bit longer.

"Good," she managed shakily. "You really would be a great healer," she added with a trembling smile.

He beamed at her. "Thank you, I'm glad you think so. We should, um, go back inside, get your hand cleaned up. Are you alright to walk? Do you need a moment?"

She shook her head; her whole arm was starting to throb, but her legs felt steady. "If this were a tournament game you'd have been disqualified for using insect warfare," she joked, wanting to lighten the mood, to move them past this moment where she still felt his strong arms wrapped around her, felt her lips tingling just from imagining how it would feel to kiss him. "I think inside is a good idea," she conceded.

Soon they were passing the fountain she'd hidden her own flower-flag in. She put her uninjured hand on Beast's arm to stop him and trotted over to retrieve it. She returned to his side and held it out to him with a flourish, bowing.

"For you," she announced, "for saving me from danger and certain death. Even if it was your fault in the first place."

He took the flower gently, twirling it between his thumb and forefinger before tucking it behind his ear. "Does it suit me?" he asked.

"You look beautiful," she assured him, whipping around as she realized what she'd said. Heat flooded her face. She hurried on ahead, afraid to look back. Had he realized what she'd said? What would he even think?

"I have thread and needles, if you need them," he said, clearing his throat. "For your sleeve."

Claire sighed, lifting her uninjured hand, which was the arm with the torn sleeve. "Yeah, I guess I do. I love this shirt, it's a shame I've ruined it." She lowered her arm again. "I'm a terrible seamstress."

He looked at her thoughtfully. "I could sew it up for you, then." He blushed, combing his hair back. "I'm pretty good at it. And that way you can keep working. If you wanted to."

She smiled up at him, admiring how sweet he looked with a flower tucked behind his ear, blushing and smiling bashfully. "That would be so great, thanks."

He nodded, shifting subtly closer to her as they walked, making her heart hammer in her throat.

CHAPTER FIFTEEN

A Visitor

Claire had only been back from Edden for three days when things were upset once again.

They had been sitting in companionable silence in the library, Beast reading—well, re-reading, really—a Garnette Mason novel in the late afternoon sun pouring in from the bay windows, while she slogged through *Fae Genealogies of Eastern Cillure* from her armchair. She was bored to tears reading it, her eyes sliding over to the windows, to the titles of the books on the shelves, to Beast tucked into his chair and his face slipping into different expressions as he read. She found herself running a finger along the nearly invisible seam of where he'd mended the sleeve of her emerald-colored tunic as she watched him, feeling such warmth for the man it threatened to take her breath away.

The only time she was genuinely engaged by the book in her lap was the brief thrill she'd had at finding a chapter on her mother's family. According to the chapter, Claire and her sisters were only one-sixteenth fae at best, likely even less than that, but even if her father knew that she doubted it would slow down how often he brought it up.

Unlike the folklore, she thought the *Genealogies* was at least mildly helpful: it made note of when a fae bloodline produced a gifted member, allowing her to start a list of names to look deeper into later. It wasn't much to go on, but even though the fae were a magical race, they weren't able to do magecraft all that often, all-told, just like she had thought. It was good information. But sweet Delenaa was it *dull*.

She lifted her head from her reading, her neck protesting loudly at her poor posture, and opened her mouth to ask Beast if he'd like to join her for a snack when he jerked violently in his armchair, book slipping from his hands. He cursed, smoothing the pages that had gotten bent and snapping it shut. He rose, tossing the book onto his vacated chair and turning to her, confusion lowering his heavy brows.

"Someone's here."

Her eyebrows shot up. "Really? Why?" she asked.

He shrugged, running a hand through his hair and leaving it charmingly disheveled. "When someone enters the grounds, I'm alerted. I don't know who it is or what their business is, only that they're here." Right, of course.

She stood in a rush. "I'll go with you."

He pursed his lips, considering as he walked towards the door. "Best not," he decided as he reached the doorway. "If it's trouble I don't want you getting hurt."

She snorted. "I'm the one with combat training, old man. *I* would be protecting *you* from things going bad."

He grinned, ruffling his mop of hair again. "I know. But you are my guest here and I would be a terrible host if I let you charge in and risk yourself under my roof."

"But I'm offering, I want to help if I can," she insisted,

frowning.

"Humor me?" he asked as her frown deepened into a scowl. "If I need help I'll start screaming. The signal will be 'Please Claire I was a very silly idiot please please please save me'."

She couldn't help but snort with laughter. "Nice try, but you've told me what people tend to do to you," she insisted, getting to her feet and crossing her arms. "So you can either let me come with you or get mad at me for coming anyway."

He frowned, clearly wrestling with that, before nodding and stepping out of the room. "Alright, you stubborn goat. Let's go see who it is, then."

Claire dashed up to her room to grab her baton, followed closely by Beast, and slipped it through her belt loop. Then they descended the stairs to greet the mystery visitor. "I bet it's just someone from the village," she mused, trying to lighten the mood. "I've been there talking about it twice now and I bet it's drummed up interest." He nodded, looking grumpy.

They arrived at the foyer just as the front door was swinging itself open, revealing the form of a young man about Claire's age, hand raised and fisted as if he'd been about to knock. He leaned forward, eyes roving over the finery of the entryway. He hadn't spotted them yet, but she noted with some interest that he hadn't called out. Instead, he was creeping slowly over the threshold, his slight form hunched and tense, one hand resting on the hilt of the dagger at his hip.

"Greetings," Beast called, startling the man and forcing his eyes over to the two of them at last. He froze, eyes sliding slowly over to snag on Beast. "Welcome to my manor," Beast continued, keeping his voice soft and even. He was back to being the timid, closed-off creature he'd been when she'd first met him, which made her ache with sadness and grief. She put her hand on the handle of her baton, keeping her muscles loose but her senses on alert.

"Stay the fuck away from me!" the young man shouted, drawing his dagger and holding it out towards Beast with a hint of a tremble. Beast halted at once, keeping his hands up, and Claire stepped forward, angling her body so she was a little in front of her companion.

"Easy there, friend," Claire called out, "we're not going to hurt you. We're just saying hello." She edged closer, hoping Beast would stay where he was while she tried to de-escalate the situation.

The person in front of her looked to be around her age and was handsome in a bland sort of way that young men born to privilege tended to cultivate. His pale sand complexion and dark brown hair made his greenish veins stand out. Steel gray eyes took in his surroundings, eventually landing on her in a way that unsettled her. There was a distinct interest that flared in his eyes. He smiled and she couldn't help but note that the smile didn't quite reach those gray eyes. He was a few inches taller than her, and slim.

"It's alright," Beast had tried from over her shoulder. "I'm not going to hurt you. You're in no danger here, I swear it."

The young man stayed tense and on edge, the tip of his dagger dipping but staying out and pointed at Beast. "What are you even supposed to be?" he snarled. "You're a scary fucker."

"His name is Beast, and he lives here," Claire cut in, her hackles raising. Beast had told her that people were usually hostile towards him, but it was still jarring seeing it. She supposed she could understand being nervous about him, but violent? Without any cause? "I'm Claire, I'm a quester with the Guild trying to help him."

The young man tore his eyes from Beast to look at her more thoroughly, the slow sweep of his eyes over her body familiar in its hunger and no less uncomfortable for it. "Kiernan," he offered, lifting his chin in a sort of greeting. "Nice to meet you, Claire."

She considered herself a patient person, but Kiernan's casual rudeness towards Beast was really bothering her. "So what brings you to the manor, Kiernan?" she asked, letting the sharp edge in her voice happen.

"I heard you and O'brenne talking about this place when you were last in town. Thought it would be an interesting… opportunity." His eyes roved over her again, making her uneasy. She thought she might have heard a very low growl coming from Beast, still behind her.

"Well, I hope you find what you're looking for," she ground out, struggling to keep herself polite. "Are you staying the night?"

He nodded, flashing her a smile he probably thought was charming. Claire turned to Beast, schooling her expression as best she could. "Do we have a room for him?" she asked her stiff companion.

"We do," he growled, his hands clenched tight at his sides. "Follow me."

Beast led them all upstairs, Claire still keeping herself between Kiernan and her friend. He had stopped being aggressive, but she didn't trust him not to hurt Beast anyway, not when he was also giving her looks bordering on predatory.

They showed him to a room—one right across the hall from Beast's bedroom, she noted, and far away from her own—and then let him know they'd be in the library getting some work done if he needed them.

Back in her chair, she tried her best to focus back on *Genealogies*, but her already slim attention span was completely snapped now, and all she could do was sit and judder her knees, her gaze sliding over to Beast, back in his own armchair, again and again.

"Is it usually like that? When someone shows up?" she asked at last, unable to stay quiet any longer.

"No," he rumbled, his smile dark and wry. "Usually it's much worse."

Claire's breath caught in her throat. She reached out and put her hand on his knee, needing to have some kind of contact with him, anchoring herself to him so that no one could tear him away. "Vitrin's mercy. I know you've told me before, but seeing it, feeling how—how *angry* he was that you were there was…"

"Yes." He let out a breath slowly, then hesitantly reached out and covered her hand with his, not quite holding it, but close enough to make her heart sing with light.

Of course, that was the moment when Kiernan chose to make his appearance, slinking through the library door. When he saw them holding hands his expression darkened, going stormy. For a brief flash he was sneering at them, looking disgusted and horrified, and Claire was ashamed that she snatched her hand back and stood, turning to face Kiernan. *That's how people would look at us*, she realized with a sinking feeling. *How people would react if we were together.*

"So, how can we help you?" Claire asked, crossing her arms over her chest and doing her best not to dwell on such dark thoughts.

Kiernan shrugged, his eyes darting around the library now. "Just wanted to check it out. More interesting than being back in Edden, you know?"

She nodded, a smile quirking her lips. "Yeah, that's true. You're from Edden, then?"

He nodded, his eyes roving back over her body and stoking her anger. Why was this guy having such a hard time keeping his eyes on her damn face? It was a *nice* face.

"Well, don't let us get in your way, we were just getting some work done," she trilled, turning back to Beast before she lost her cool and snapped. "Join me at the table?" she asked him, her earlier shame dissolving in the heat of her fury. Who the fuck did Kiernan think he was, looking at them so judgmentally for holding hands while he brazenly ogled her to within an inch of her life? She didn't really *need* an excuse to touch Beast more—if anything she needed more excuses to *stop* touching him—but she might up the ante around Kiernan just to put him in his place. Beast looked up at her, startled, then smiled shyly and stood, following her to the long wooden work table.

Something like relief swept through her as his enormous form settled into one of the large wooden chairs across from her, between her and the door, his presence like a balm that chased away the unease left skittering over her skin. He opened his book, carefully flipping through the pages with his claws to find his spot. Kiernan watched them with a sour expression twisting his handsome face, then turned and started wandering around the library.

When he was a little ways away from them Claire leaned in close to Beast, whispering, "How can you be so—so *cavalier* about this? You saw how he looked at you; why not kick him out?"

He shrugged, one finger running along the edges of the pages, making them flutter gently. "I can't change what will happen," he said quietly. "He'll either try to hurt me or he won't. He'll either be cruel or he won't. Nothing that I've ever done has changed that."

She studied his face, her eyes tracing along the sharp cut of his cheekbones to his proud and jutting nose, so much more appealing to her than Kiernan's stale handsomeness. "So why do you let people stay here?" she pressed. "Why let them in to hurt you?"

"I…have no say in it."

"It's part of your enchantment? That you have to let just anyone come into your home and stay there no matter what they're up to?"

He nodded, fluttering the book's pages again.

"But that's…insane. And it doesn't make sense. Why would your mage do that?"

"I thought that was what you were trying to figure out," he muttered, shooting her a sly smile. "You're not much of a quester if I just hand you everything."

She rolled her eyes and slapped at his hand. "Alright, smartass. Very funny. You're right, I guess it's just another weird piece of this confusing puzzle." She thought for a moment. "Can *I* kick people out?" she asked.

His eyebrows shot up. "You're really trying to take charge here, huh?"

"For your own protection, civilian."

"Of course. Not because you just really like being bossy."

She smacked his hand again. "You're lucky I like you so much," she muttered, grinning down at her own book.

After a moment of hesitation, his fingers stopped playing with the page edges of his book and crept across the table to clasp her hand.

"I've got you," he murmured, the heat in his gaze curling around her heart. "If he makes you uncomfortable, then I'll stay with you. If you want to get rid of him, I won't stop you. I trust your instincts."

She melted, heat flooding her chest and pooling low in her belly. How had he known? How had he realized she was so deeply unsettled when she hadn't even really known it was there? She swallowed, squeezing his hand and rubbing her thumb against his large knuckles. She hoped he wasn't planning on pulling away that hand—it felt so good to hold it, so soothing, even if it was so large she could barely grip it. "Never. You're just as stuck with me, old man," she croaked.

"*Ouch!* You just can't help yourself, can you?"

She grinned. "I'm sorry, it's a compulsion. I'll behave." She sighed. "And I'm tempted to tell him to get out of here. But he's probably just someone from the village curious about the haunted manor now that I'm out here poking around it. I'm probably just…overreacting."

He nodded, combing his hair back with his free hand. The way the crimson waves slipped through his fingers to bounce against his tall gray forehead made something spark low in her gut. She was acutely aware of how long their hands had been clasped together on the table…and that neither of them seemed inclined to change that. Her heart started pounding against her ribs. "Maybe," he allowed, looking at her, "but like I said, I trust your instincts."

"We should probably get to work," she said slowly, noting that Kiernan was edging closer again, looking at the books on the shelves. "Keep up appearances."

Beast grinned, squeezing her hand. "You're so pushy, Odetima."

"But I do it out of love, my friend," Claire said, every muscle in her body clenching when she realized what she'd said.

By the gods, she thought, breaking out in a sweat and her face going flaming hot. *What a fucking slip.*

Panic began to creep like ice along her veins, somehow making her sweating even worse. She wasn't ready for these kinds of thoughts, wasn't ready to face that question. It was bad enough just calling it attraction. The idea that it could be more, that it was—

She gently pulled her hand free and surged to her feet, forcing a nonchalant smile. "I think I'm going to grab a snack from the kitchens," she blurted, feeling guilty at the puzzlement that flashed across his face at her sudden retreat.

"Oh. Alright. Do you want company?" he asked, closing his now-empty hand into a fist and drawing it toward his chest.

She should have said no, that it was alright, that she would see him in a few hours for dinner, but the hurt written on the sharp planes of his face broke her resolve. *It's not his fault I'm freaking out*, Claire reasoned, *he doesn't deserve this.*

"Of course," she said, smiling at him. "Sorry if I'm a bit strange. Kiernan just has me feeling jumpy and out-of-sorts."

He smiled back. "You don't need to apologize. I understand."

She only felt worse. *Curse* him for being so sweet and understanding. At least he didn't seem to have picked up on the whole "love" thing—she was probably just letting her nerves get to her for nothing.

CHAPTER SIXTEEN

Breaking Through

Claire had said that she loved him. Beast was still reeling from it, unable to believe he'd heard her correctly. Though even if he had, she probably meant it in a friendly way.

But she'd also held his hand. The memory of the slide of her thumb on his skin was still sending liquid heat to his belly. How had such a small bit of contact felt so *big*?

But then right after she'd said it something had changed, her face falling and something like fear entering her eyes. And then she'd pulled away.

Maybe she didn't want him to get the wrong impression. She knew how lonely he was; she probably thought he'd take something like that and run with it.

And if that was the case, she wasn't wrong. Was that not, at this very minute, what he was doing? *You're reading too much into it, you idiot,* he scolded himself. She was just a friend to him. A really, really good friend.

But he knew that when he was in bed alone tonight, in the dark and the silence, he'd imagine that sweet moment when the wrong words had slipped past her lips. That he'd fantasize about what would have happened beyond it if she hadn't meant it in a friendly way. If she'd let go of his hand to join him on his side of the table. If she'd have slid into his lap, looping her arms around his neck, her soft lips parted and inching closer to his as her eyes fluttered closed—

But that was just a fantasy. And one that was wildly inappropriate to be having while the subject of his fantasies was walking beside him, blissfully unaware of where his thoughts had turned. Unaware of what was happening in his pants while he thought of the soft curves of her body pressed against him—

Naja really was right about him. He wasn't any better than Tollem and Deven. He was the same kind of monster, at his core. Though he might have allowed that he was probably better than Kiernan. The way that that man had stared at Claire, like he was trying to bore holes into her clothes and snap her up in his hungry jaws, had made him *furious*. Simple appreciation for her beauty he could understand, but what he'd seen in Kiernan's gray eyes was dangerous. He'd seen it plenty of times in Tollem and Deven's eyes, back then.

But as angry as he'd been at the objectifying way Kiernan looked at Claire, it was nothing compared to the helplessness he'd felt when he'd realized just how little he could protect her.

He prayed that Kiernan wouldn't be trouble. If it were just himself it wouldn't have mattered how dangerous and untrustworthy Kiernan was. But with Claire here it was a different story: she was precious, gentle, deserving of nothing but kindness and respect. If Kiernan tried to do anything to her...well. Beast was not a violent person, but the idea of seeing Claire scared, or gods forbid in pain, unleashed something primal and hot inside him that made him want to shred things and spill blood. But knowing Naja, there was no way he'd be able to act on that. She wanted him declawed and powerless. But he was big, and Kiernan didn't know any of that, so if he at least stayed close to her that might be enough.

Please, let it be enough.

The kitchen was still and quiet when he and Claire stepped in, nothing out of place and everything tidy and neat, as it always was.

"Are you hungry for anything in particular?" she asked, drifting towards the heavy woodblock island she had come to prefer making her food requests from.

He shrugged. "I'm not hungry, really. I'll steal a little of whatever you have."

She scoffed. "You've got some nerve!"

"What?"

"Everyone knows it's extremely rude to steal food from a hungry woman. And dangerous."

"I've been promised that if my life is in danger my wonderful friend Claire will swoop in and save me like the delicate creature that I am," he threw back at her, smirking.

Her eyes narrowed in a smoldering glare that was ruined by her lips twitching up in a smile. "You're treading on thin ice, sir."

"Because I'm being so charming you can't handle it?" he teased, fluttering his eyelashes.

She muttered something he didn't quite catch, then sighed heavily and asked for a plate of chocolate chip cookies, making him smile warmly. He'd never heard of them before Claire started requesting them, but they'd quickly become a favorite. They often shared a plate in the evenings when they sat in the library and took turns reading to each other.

The plate materialized in front of Claire on the island counter with a delicate clatter. She grabbed the plate and tipped her chin towards the door. "Back to the library?" she asked, snatching a cookie off the plate and taking a large bite.

"Sounds good," he agreed, snagging a cookie of his own, despite her frustrated huff. "I don't know if I'll be able to get any more reading done, but maybe some spinning would be nice."

She swallowed her mouthful, her pink tongue darting out to lick crumbs from the corner of her mouth, setting his whole chest on fire at the sight. He swallowed thickly. "You still owe me another spinning lesson on the spindle, you know. Maybe after we finish the cookies you can take me through it?" she asked, exiting the kitchen and retracing their route back to the library.

"Of course. I'm sorry for not remembering sooner," he returned, feeling self-conscious now. Seeing that little flash of tongue gliding along her full rosy-brown lips had unsettled him, making him too aware of his body.

"It's alright," she assured him, smiling. "Have another cookie, I can't eat this whole plate by myself."

"It doesn't upset you?"

"What, the cookie or the forgetting?"

"...both?"

"Neither. I was just teasing you, sw—silly man."

He wondered what she'd almost called him just then, but he obliged and took a cookie. "You're done trying to hoard them, then?" he teased as he nibbled.

"You wore me down with your heartfelt declarations of friendship," she grumbled, shoving the library door open with her hip. "Besides, how could I resist that face, you shameless

—Oh, hello again, Kiernan."

His spine stiffened immediately. Kiernan had as much freedom to roam around the manor as anyone else did, of course, but it still felt like an intrusion. It still felt like Kiernan was pushing in somewhere he wasn't wanted by staying in the library.

But what if Claire wants him here? Maybe she'll enjoy being able to look at an attractive face for once.

He shoved down his jealousy and attempted a warm smile. "Yes, hello again, Kiernan," he managed.

Kiernan all but ignored Beast, turning a beaming smile on Claire as she eased into the room. "Hey, Claire. Got yourself a snack?" Kiernan asked from his perch in the armchair that Beast had always considered his, a fact which made him bristle all over again.

"Yep. Cookies. We decided to grab them before settling into our work this evening."

"What kind of work?"

Claire moved stiffly to the work table, setting the plate down and pulling out the chair that would put her back to Kiernan. Beast headed to the other side, wanting to keep an eye on the newcomer. "I'm a quester, if you'll recall, and I'm trying to help Beast. He's part of a quest that's basically ancient at this point. So if you'll excuse us…"

"That's interesting; I wouldn't have expected it."

Annoyance twisted Claire's face and she met Beast's gaze with wide, rage-filled eyes. But she managed to school her expression before turning to face Kiernan. "And why is that?" she ground out.

Apparently unaware of Claire's anger, Kiernan smiled and leaned forward, resting his elbows on his knees. "Just because you're a beautiful woman. It seems like most pro questers are men, and what women I have seen have been…homely, I suppose."

Though he could only see her face in profile, there was no mistaking Claire's rage. She pressed her lips into a firm line, a muscle in her jaw ticking with strain. "Look, you just met me. It's kind of soon to be a sexist prick, don't you think?" she snapped. Beast wondered if he should say something, too.

Kiernan held up his hands in supplication. "Whoa, whoa! I didn't mean to offend, I was just pointing out what I've seen."

"And how many pro questers have you seen, exactly?"

"A few," he hedged.

"Well as I said, I'm an actual professional in this field. I just graduated with my license and our class was a pretty even gender split. We're going to be getting to work now, please don't interrupt."

"Salerah's fires, sorry. I didn't mean to offend," Kiernan muttered, having the decency to at least look embarrassed.

Claire ignored him, turning to face Beast again and snatching another cookie off the plate and snapping off a furious mouthful. He smiled at her and took another cookie of his own, leaving just three more on the plate.

"What will we be working on today?" he asked gently, sliding his knee closer to tap hers under the table, hoping to calm her with that small gesture.

She smiled up at him, some of the tension easing from her shoulders as her eyes met his. "I've been wondering some things about your quest, and I know the gag makes it hard for you to talk about it, but sometimes you can come at a question sideways and get more than you'd think."

He nodded, sucking a bit of melted chocolate off the pad

of his thumb. Claire watched him do it with an intense look in her eyes he couldn't place. It made his heart surge. "Alright, I'm willing to give it a shot if you are," he allowed, grabbing another cookie and nudging the plate with the last two on it towards Claire, letting her know he was done.

"Is this what you guys get up to all day?" Kiernan asked, slumped into the armchair, and Beast saw a guilty look flash across Claire's face.

"It varies," she said, turning to look Kiernan in the eyes. "Right now I feel like I need more information, so that's what I'm trying to do by talking to Beast. But a little while ago I spent an entire week going over the place with my tools." She bit her lip. "What uh…what do you do, Kiernan?"

He shrugged. "I'm on break from school. I'm going to Whittley College in Citrine to study politics. My old man wants me to follow in his footsteps. He's the mayor in Edden."

Claire nodded, nibbling at another of her cookies. "That's nice, going into the family business." She popped the rest of the confection into her mouth and dusted the crumbs from her fingers. "Anyway, so we're just going to—"

"Have you been working this quest long?" Kiernan interrupted.

"A few weeks. Maybe three? If you want you can grab a book off the shelf while we work, so you're not just sitting there…"

Kiernan waved his hand dismissively. "Nah, I'm not much of a reader. Would it bother you if I watched you work?"

Beast saw her fingers clench into a fist on the table. "No, that's fine," she managed to say without a hint of her annoyance.

Claire's eyes darted all over the table, searching for

something. Brow furrowing, she ducked her head under and scooted her chair out to look under it.

Without a word, Beast rose and strode over to the unoccupied armchair, where the satchel she kept her journal full of notes was resting. He snatched it up and made his way back to her. He handed Claire her supplies with a flourish, bowing low. "Madam quester," he rumbled, smirking at her.

Claire inclined her head, her expression haughty and queenly. "Sir Beast," she returned.

Beast heard Kiernan snort in his chair behind them, and a surge of pride made him feel warm. He might have been ugly, but he could make Claire smile, make her laugh. He could make her feel safe, and that was worth at least as much as a pretty face. He straightened and resumed his seat across from her, folding his hands in his lap while she pulled out her notes and got organized.

Claire clicked her tongue several times, reading through what she'd already written. "Alright, here we go. The quest didn't say anything about your being here as a punishment but it's pretty obvious that that's what's going on, so can you tell me anything about that? Case number, any of the Consortium officials involved, who your judge was. Anything about your hearing or trial would be helpful too, so I can pinpoint where the anomaly comes in."

His brow furrowed. "My…hearing?"

Claire snorted. "Yeah, the one your mage arranged to determine your sentencing. Where they would have gotten clearance for punishing you by keeping you here for whatever it is you did."

"I—" but he couldn't say it, that he hadn't had a hearing, he'd never seen any Consortium officials. He was gagged against it.

Claire's sharp hazel gaze shot up to meet his. "Did you have a hearing?"

His every muscle locked, preventing him from answering. But Claire had seen the gag kick in enough by now to recognize what was happening.

"Vitrin's mercy," she breathed, awe and anger warring for control of her lovely face. "You *didn't* have one, did you? Gods above and below Beast—you're here illegally! That mage doesn't want anyone to know what you did or who you are because it would implicate them. They'd be arrested and disbarred from practicing magecraft ever again. You and this whole gods-damned manor are what the anomaly is." She sagged back in her chair, her hazel eyes wide and round. "This is *huge!*"

He had to admit he was a little confused. "There are laws for situations like mine?"

She nodded. "Old laws, too. As old as the Consortium, maybe older. The law allows for magical punishments occurring outside of the official judicial systems of local governances, especially for non-violent and victimless crimes, but there still has to be a hearing to determine the appropriateness of the punishment to the crime, to verify that private punishment is valid in the first place. Namely, they have to establish that there was a punishable offense, and then prove that whatever it was doesn't need to get escalated to an actual court.

"So if your mage stashed you away in here without that hearing happening then I might be able to get you out *soon*. I'll have to go back to the Guildhall in Kesterin, report to my superiors and get them to open an official inquiry. This could be *it*, Beast!"

"Whoa, did you just figure it out?" Kiernan whistled low from his seat in the armchair. "Guess I got here at the right time."

As Claire turned around to answer Kiernan, Beast's awareness began to slide away from him. The thought of Claire leaving him again so soon after returning, of her going all the way to Kesterin, filled him with a blind and howling panic. Hulking shadows loomed at the corner of his vision, his skin crawling like he was covered in bugs, millions of them that he couldn't quite see. Howls and laughter fought for dominance in his skull, making his ears ring. It felt like the world was tilting and sliding around him, and he might have been starting to slip sideways out of his chair.

Claire called his name, surging from her own chair and catching his shoulder before he could fall to the floor. The ringing in his ears kept him from hearing what she was saying, but he could hear her talking from what seemed like far away. He could feel her small, warm hands squeezing his arms and combing his hair back to look in his dazed eyes. "…are you sick?" he heard, finally able to focus. He squeezed his eyes shut, willing it all to go away, for the monsters to leave him alone, but they didn't leave, they just tucked themselves into the corners.

"Do you need me to get anything?" Kiernan asked, half out of his chair now and watching them closely.

Claire leaned closer, looking closely at his eyes and frowning. "How about some water?" Kiernan nodded, slipping out of the room and leaving them alone.

He wasn't sure how he could say that being ripped away from her would be more horrible than any of the two hundred years he'd spent stuck at this manor. That just the idea of never seeing her again made him feel like he was dying. Maybe he was—without Claire, what hope did he have to cling to this last shred of himself that he'd managed to hang onto all this time? She was all the hope he had left in the world, and without her, he…he was scared. So scared. He didn't want to lose himself, didn't want to die, not really. "Do you have to go?" he found himself asking, cursing his cowardly heart.

"Go? Go where?"

"Kesterin."

"Oh, no I don't *have* to go, I suppose. I could send reports from Edden, it'll just take much longer that way." Her voice dropped low, concern filling her soft hazel eyes. "Do you not want me to leave? Is that what this is about?"

He stayed silent, his eyes closed tight against the shame of his weakness.

Rose and vanilla drifted in, sheathing him in warmth and softness, and then he felt arms wrapping around his neck, squeezing him tight but not choking. His awareness sharpened in a breath, the shadows and the tickle of bugs on his skin fading away as he homed in on Claire pressed tightly against him. He wrapped his own arms around her back, pulling her in closer, his nose full of the sweet warm smell of her hair.

"I won't go if you don't want me to," she murmured. "I'm here to protect you and keep you safe, sweet man."

Sweet man. He felt his throat go thick with tears, she said that with such tenderness and warmth. There was something about that phrase that felt familiar, as if he'd heard it a long time ago, but he was distracted by his sensitive ears picking up on Kiernan's steps outside.

He wondered when he'd stop falling in love with Claire. When would he find the limit of how much love could fit inside himself? Or would it always be this way: her working her way deeper inside him and filling him up, showing him against his will that there was more to him, that *he* was more, and making it so that everything he was, everything he had, was served by no greater purpose than in loving her. Claire was the blood in his veins, the air in his lungs, the light in his dark, and he hoped that someday he could be worthy of her. Even if she never returned his feelings he thought that just this, this closeness, this friendship, was a treasure beyond anything. He wanted to be better for her. He *needed* to be better. Because it was what she deserved.

"You scared me, old man," she admonished him quietly as she pulled back from their embrace. "Thought you were having a heart attack," she smirked, but the worry pulling at her features showed the truth of her concern.

"So uh…he's okay?" Kiernan asked, handing over the glass of water before sitting back in his chair the begin cleaning under his nails with his dagger. "You hug all your clients like that?" he asked, his steel eyes going hard with something Beast couldn't name.

Claire stiffened. "Actually, quest subjects are almost never the clients," she said, her tone going a little cool. "And Beast is also my friend, and last I'd checked hugging friends was totally legal."

Kiernan smirked as he flicked dirt from the tip of the blade onto the floor. "Sure, yeah, I guess you're right. It's just pretty strange to see someone just…hug a monster like that, like it's nothing."

"Well, he's not a monster," Claire snapped, returning to her seat, "so maybe that'll clear up some of your confusion."

Kiernan pursed his lips, considering something that Beast couldn't guess, then shrugged carelessly. "Guess it does." He stood, sheathing his dagger. "When was dinner again?" he asked.

"Seven," Claire and Beast answered together, shooting grins at each other. Kiernan nodded, then left them alone in the library.

CHAPTER SEVENTEEN

Thin Ice

Claire was relieved that Kiernan kept to his room the rest of the day. When he did finally make an appearance it was to join them for dinner.

She was seated at her usual spot beside Beast when Kiernan strolled in, selecting the seat across from Claire and throwing her another one of those cold smiles that didn't reach his eyes.

"Hello again, Claire," he said, ignoring Beast at her side.

"Hello again to you too, Kiernan," she managed, wary. Was he trying to snub Beast, or had it been a misstep? He'd helped when Beast hadn't felt well, and he'd been less creepy, so she was hoping that he was calming down.

Kiernan began helping himself to food, heaping roast lamb and potatoes onto his plate and pouring himself a generous glass of wine. "How long have you been here?" he asked her as he dug in.

"Just a few minutes."

"No, I meant at the manor."

At least he was sticking to inoffensive small talk now, but she could have sworn she'd already told him that earlier in the library "A little under three weeks, but I did pop back to Edden for a few days at one point. As you know," she answered slowly, watching Kiernan carefully.

He shook his head, sawing at his food. "That long with just this guy for company?" He jabbed his dirty knife in Beast's direction, shaking his head and looking vaguely disgusted. "That has to have been tough for you." Ah, so he was going to be a bastard.

Claire's hands clenched into fists, rage sweeping through her in a wildfire. "What the fuck is wrong with you? Beast has been nothing but a good host to you and we have both made it clear that those kinds of comments are unwelcome. Beast is my *friend* and *your* host and you will address him with respect or you will *leave*."

Kiernan blinked up at her, cold rage seeping into his flat gray eyes. His neck flushed red, but she didn't think it was embarrassment; he'd gone too hard around the edges, the barest hint of a sneer on his lips. But he managed to coach his expression and set down his silverware to put his palms up in supplication. "You're right, that was rude of me," he said, smiling stiffly. "My apologies. It was just a joke, I swear. A poor one, obviously. But just a joke."

She didn't believe him for a second. She'd seen a lot of his type growing up in the viper's nest of Kestrinian aristocracy—entitled little assholes who thought they were clever saying whatever hateful thing they wanted to if they laughed it off and called it a joke after. He'd been a little rude earlier, but something had changed while he'd been by himself, making him downright nasty.

She could feel the stiff tension rolling off of Beast to her right. She darted a look over at him, and when their eyes met he shook his head "no" in the barest hint of movement. Fine, he didn't want to make a scene, so she'd leave it at that. But she hadn't let it go. And now her desire to see Kiernan gone was stronger than ever.

Kiernan finished off his first glass of wine and poured himself another, shaking his head, "Wow, you've been here for three weeks and haven't made any progress? Do these things usually take that long?"

Bristling, Claire clenched her teeth and sucked in a breath. "Sometimes," she ground out, not wanting to admit that she didn't know. "But I did just have that breakthrough earlier today, so it's looking up."

Kiernan leveled a smug look at Beast. "Maybe it's a lost cause," he mused, darting a look of contempt over at Beast. "I could keep you company on your way back to Edden. I think if you got to know me you'd find we have a lot in common."

Beast tensed at her side, his fingers digging into the arm of his chair hard enough the wood groaned softly. Disgust writhed in Claire's gut, obliterating the scraps of her appetite. She felt stuck, unsure how to respond. "Sorry, not interested. I don't think this quest is a lost cause and I'd much rather stay here." She didn't even try to keep the hard edge out of her voice.

Kiernan chuckled, his steel eyes glazing as the wine began taking effect. "I don't bite," he assured her. "I'm just trying to be friendly."

Claire snorted, her rage and disgust joined by impressed disbelief at this particular idiot's audacity. Did he really not realize how he was coming off? Or was it a ploy—he was very careful to say things that sounded plausibly inoffensive, so that he could deny he meant it badly when he was confronted. It wouldn't be the first time she'd encountered this tactic. She leaned to her right, settling closer to Beast and letting her knee brush against his, sharing in his strength and offering him her comfort. Poor Beast looked like he might snap and turn violent—a feat she had until now thought impossible—and she knew that was the last thing this situation needed. Even if Claire would have absolutely *loved* to see it.

Kiernan snatched up the bottle of wine, pouring his third glass. Beast frowned, and when Kiernan next took his eyes from the near-empty bottle it vanished from the table. She frowned; had Beast done that? He hadn't seemed to have any gift before now.

Taking another healthy swig of his wine, Kiernan leered at her from across the table, his gaze lingering on her mouth, her chest. Claire frowned, crossing her arms to obscure his view. Her face flared with heat, rage and disgust battling in her roiling stomach. "So, Claire," Kiernan began, his words beginning to slur—was it the wine already taking effect? Or was it possible Kiernan had brought his own drink and begun in his room before joining them? It would explain the intense shift in his behavior. "Do you have a man in your life?" he asked, his gaze continuing to slither over her.

"I don't see how that's any of your business," she ground out.

Kiernan's teeth flashed. "So sensitive," he purred, "I guess that means no, huh? You're far too tense to have a man back home taking care of y—"

Beast slammed his massive hand on the table, startling them both and sending the little roasted potatoes rolling off of the edge of Claire's plate. *"That is enough,"* Beast said with deadly quiet, flaying Kiernan with his eyes. "You will stop asking such prying questions and treat the lady with the respect she is due or you will *leave*."

Kiernan, apparently shameless, feigned confusion. "What did I do? I was just trying to get to know my new friend Claire, here—"

"You are making her uncomfortable," Beast growled.

"Claire isn't saying anything to me, maybe you need to let the lady speak for hers—"

"Oh no, you absolutely have been," Claire interjected smoothly, willing her voice to stay firm despite the panic that she hated was clawing its way up her throat. "Is that clear enough for you?"

Kiernan sneered, his eyes sliding back and forth between Beast and Claire, his fingers tightening on the cup of his goblet. "Alright," he ground out. "Just relax. Taking everything so gods-damned seriously." He took another gulp of wine.

Claire pushed her food around on her plate, her stomach too knotted up to eat. She hated the situation, and she had no idea what to do about it. Had they been too dismissive of Kiernan? Had they been rude first? She ran through all of their interactions so far and it distressed her that she couldn't say for sure one way or the other. She hadn't meant to be rude. But there was just something about Kiernan that rubbed her the wrong way.

Maybe she should sleep in Beast's room tonight. The thought made heat flood her face and made her stomach flutter, but she also wondered if she'd be able to sleep otherwise.

Kiernan gulped down the remainder of his glass of wine,

then shoved back from the table and stormed out of the dining room. They heard every one of his heavy stomping steps all the way back upstairs to his room. Naturally, he slammed the door.

Claire put her silverware down on her half-full plate and pushed back from the table.

"I think I need some fresh air," she announced as she threw her napkin onto the table beside her plate. "I'm going to go for a quick walk around the grounds."

Beast blinked up at her, his heavy brows pulled low over his eyes. He still looked furious, a scowl twisting those slate lips. "Would you like company?" he asked.

Normally she would, but right now…solitude felt much more appropriate. She shook her head, her twist braids loose and brushing against her cheeks. "No, but thank you." He nodded, something in his eyes shuttering.

Claire slipped out of the dining room and headed upstairs to grab her cloak and her baton before slipping out the front door and taking a deep lungful of the crisp evening air. She went down the front steps and began to follow the paved pathway that would eventually converge with the gravel drive. She wanted a nice long walk but didn't want to have to stumble around in the dark without a lamp or a landmark, so she planned to follow the driveway to the gate, then walk along the inside of the gate to give herself a nice long route that she couldn't easily stray from.

As the soothing murmur of leaves in the wind and night insects worked at the snarled threads of her anxiety, her mind tumbled around what was happening. Kiernan's arrival had certainly shaken things up, but in the dark, by herself, she could admit that it hadn't been entirely his fault that things were sour. He made her uneasy, and she thought that she was right to keep him at arm's length, but she also resented him. Because he'd come here and forced her to acknowledge some things that she'd been able to hide from when it was just her and Beast.

She was not doing a good job with the quest. She should have left and headed back to Kesterin to dig into Consortium records, to query the providential judiciary offices about any punishments that fit with what Beast was being subjected to so that they could get to the bottom of things and get him out if he really was here illegally. At the absolute *least* she should be going back to Edden to send another letter to Dretta.

But she hadn't. Because she hadn't wanted to leave Beast again so soon after coming back. She told herself that it was because he'd had such a strong reaction to her leaving, that he needed her here. She sighed deeply, her fingers trailing along the cold metal slats of the gate, a barely-there gleam of silver in the light of the half-moon. But that wasn't it, not really.

The truth was that she was developing feelings for Beast. She couldn't seem to stop touching him, couldn't stop thinking about him, teasing him, talking to him about anything and everything *but* the quest. She woke up in the morning thinking about what she'd get up to with him, she dressed and put herself together based on what she thought would catch his eye. And when her mind wandered during her workouts she found herself fantasizing about freeing him and keeping him with her. She imagined what it would be like to take him all over Cillure, showing him the wonders the world had to offer, watching awe and happiness spread across his face. Her dreams were filled with strong gray arms and sharp-toothed smiles, and she didn't think she could keep ignoring it. Not just because the feelings were bubbling up hotter and brighter by the day, but because it was keeping her from doing her job.

She'd finished walking along the southern perimeter of the fence, turning left at the corner to continue along the eastern side—which followed the back side of the manor. She sighed, wishing Adeela was here for her to talk through her feelings with. She just felt so…confused. Were her feelings even appropriate? It wasn't technically forbidden for questers to form attachments with the subjects of their quests, but consent had to be unimpeachable. She worried there was a possibility that Beast would feel pressure to accept her advances because she was rescuing him. Or just because she was the first person to show him kindness in a very long time.

On the other hand, it did feel like he was interested in her as well. As often as she reached for him he reached for her. He was opening up to her so much, being so tender and sweet with her. Sometimes she caught him looking at her with a gleam of hunger in those soft brown eyes, spearing her with heat, and every time it happened she let herself imagine, even just for a moment, that he'd act on it. That his control would snap and he'd reach for her, pull her close, run his big hands all over her body and bury his broad face in her throat. Thinking about it now made her sex clench so hard she gasped and paused.

Once she'd gotten her breath back she continued walking alongside the fence, her left hand scrubbing down her face. By all of Salerah's fury, she had it bad.

Maybe if she just went back in there and fucked him she'd be able to get it out of her system and get her head on straight again. Not that that ever seemed to work when people did it, but maybe this time?

She shook her head, sighing again. No, she couldn't just sleep with someone and pretend that was all that there was to it. By virtue of the fact that she wanted to have sex with him, she knew it was already too late to avoid getting her heart involved. That was just how attraction worked for her.

So then what was she supposed to do? Tell Beast she wanted him and was falling for him? Just put her heart out on a platter like that for him to tear to pieces if he wanted to? Adeela would probably spear her with one of her *are you serious?* looks and tell Claire that yes, that was exactly what she should do. Either way, she'd at least have a way forward. She wouldn't be stuck in this horrible limbo.

She squeezed her eyes shut, taking another deep breath of the biting early-autumn evening air. She was almost at the turn that would take her along the northern wall of the manor, and her mind felt just as overfull as it had when she'd stepped out.

She was about to cut her walk short and head inside to hide in her room when she heard a twig snap loudly behind her.

CHAPTER EIGHTEEN

Through the Ice

Claire froze, a chill slithering down her spine and snapping it straight. The sound had been loud, a big twig snapped under a heavy weight. Her mind immediately went to night cats. Huge and smoke-gray, they were exclusively nocturnal animals that prowled the forests of northeastern Cillure. Four feet tall at the shoulder and over four hundred pounds of clawed muscle, no one would want to encounter one all alone with just a baton for protection, but here she was. She cycled through the tips she'd gotten in her survivalist class: stay near a fire (too late for that one), don't try to run, and get up into a tree. They weren't good climbers and preferred to ambush their prey from the ground. That was probably her best bet.

Claire spun, her eyes searching desperately for a climbable tree. But her eyes picked out a pale face edging closer to her in the faint moonlight. She gritted her teeth, her hand curling tight around the handle of her baton. She thumbed the button that extended it but kept it concealed under her cloak. It was possible that he'd come out here seeking the same things she had: space and fresh air. But Caldus Love's voice flitted through the back of her mind: *"You can apologize for being paranoid, Trout. Can't say the same if you're dead. So keep that head on a swivel and pay attention to your gut."*

"Hello, Kiernan," she called out, her hackles raising when he froze instead of greeting her back. After a moment he seemed to shake himself loose and resumed walking towards her.

"Claire," he returned once he'd gotten within a few feet of her. "I see you had the same idea as me. Great minds think alike, eh?"

"Guess so." Once he'd pulled up beside her she kept walking, watching him closely out of the corner of her eye. They continued in silence for some time.

"So uh—about dinner," Kiernan said at last, angling his head to look at her face. "I didn't mean to make you uncomfortable. Guess I had a little too much wine and said more than I should have."

"I'm not interested in you, Kiernan. I know you're interested in me but I just don't return it. And taking it out on Beast isn't fair."

Kiernan stepped closer to her, crowding her closer against the fence on her right side. "Yeah, I got the message. But you can't honestly tell me you'd rather have *him*, right? He's disgusting, he's terrifying."

"Who said it was between the two of you? Maybe I just want to focus on doing my job. Maybe I *do* have someone back home. Maybe I don't want anyone. You don't know me." She tried to make that last bit gentler.

Kiernan grabbed her left arm tight and squeezed. "I have been *trying* to be nice to you, bitch." The sour reek of alcohol on his breath washed over her face and made her want to gag.

"All I wanted was to tell you how pretty you are, how you drive me crazy with that body. I'd be good for you, Claire. I'd make you feel good. But no, you're too good for me or some shit. You think you're too good for everyone, I bet." He yanked on her arm, pulling her closer to his body. With his other arm, he grabbed her shoulder and spun her to face him fully, his head dipping closer to her mouth. "Why won't you at least give me a fucking shot, huh?"

Before she could pull away his mouth was on hers, their lips mashed painfully together. One of his hands came up to palm her breast, squeezing it to the point of pain. She put her hands up and shoved him back as hard as she could.

"Don't *touch* me!" she cried, her baton coming up between them and enforcing the distance she'd created. "You don't *ever* get to touch me like that! Or any other way! So turn around and go back inside before you get hurt."

He scoffed, taking a half step forward so that the baton was pressing into his belly. "What are you going to do to stop me? Hit me with this little stick?" Was he serious? Did he not realize how much damage a weapon like this could do? Or did he think she was bluffing, and that he was calling that bluff? Either way, he was very wrong, and in for a world of hurt if he came for her again.

Moving faster than she was expecting, he managed to dodge around the extended baton and get a hold of her again, his rank mouth descending once again. He didn't bother disarming her, and she was going to make him regret that. She tightened her grip on the baton, pressed between them from how he'd grabbed her, then lifted her foot and brought it crashing down on his instep.

Kiernan's mouth tore away from hers, a howl of pain and

fury ripping from his throat. His hands loosened on her arms, and she was able to pull free and get behind him.

"Fucking *bitch!*" he screamed, twisting around and lunging for her.

She spun on her heel, dodging his clumsy attack, and brought her baton down on one of his shoulders as he stumbled past her. The blow dropped him to one of his knees and made him snarl. "What the fuck is wrong with you, you crazy bitch?"

Saying nothing, Claire grabbed one of his wrists and twisted his arm up and behind his back, making him yelp. "Get up," she instructed, tucking her baton into her belt with her other hand. "We're going to go inside, you're going to grab your things, and you're going to leave."

"Are you crazy? There's fucking night cats out there. You want to kill me then just do it now."

Claire's searching fingers found the hilt of Kiernan's dagger. She pulled it free and shoved it through her belt. "If you build a fire or climb a tree you'll be fine. You should be much more concerned about getting out of here before I arrest you for sexual assault and attempted battery."

He was quiet, his feet uncertain on the uneven ground in the dark as they marched towards the kitchen door—which was the closest way into the manor from where he'd attacked her. "You…can do that? Arrest me?"

She snorted. "I absolutely can. And no matter what, a Guild arrest goes on your record, follows you around for the rest of your life. So if you have *any* sense of self-preservation you'll do what I say and get out of here and never come back. Do we have an understanding, Kiernan?"

He nodded stiffly. "Can you let my arm go? That shit

hurts. I promise I won't run."

"Good to know. But you'll get your arm and your dagger back once we're back in the manor."

CHAPTER NINETEEN

Drowning

Beast was worried that he'd done something wrong. Claire had stormed out so abruptly, turning down his offer for company, and she'd been out there for what must have been close to an hour already.

He could have sworn he heard her come back in at one point, but he must have been imagining the creak of the front door hinges, because no one had been there when he'd poked his head out.

He'd been frozen in place at the dinner table ever since. This happened, sometimes, when he felt overwhelmed: he just froze, his body and brain both locked up tight and unable to move onto some form of action until the situation had passed completely.

"Maybe she's finally gotten tired of me," he mused aloud, his chest going cold and aching at the thought.

Warm, gentle tingling cupped the back of his head. He sighed and tilted his head back until it thunked against the high back. The twin gouge marks that had gradually worn into the wood over the years from his horns digging into it were still there, oddly enough, reminding him of how things wound up whenever he touched them.

He was considering just letting his big body slide to the floor, the woven rug looking unusually inviting, when he heard the kitchen door fly open and slam into the brick wall. He bolted to his feet, his heart racing with alarm. He jogged quickly out of the dining room and down the hall, his long strangely-shaped legs allowing him to eat up the distance quickly.

He could hear voices now too, male and female. He reached the kitchen, ducking into the doorway and drawing up suddenly at what he found.

Claire was shoving a red-faced Kiernan in front of her, one of his arms twisted behind his back and caught tight in her grip. Her other arm was gripping her baton. Fury twisted her features, but instead of making her ugly her rage only made her beauty gleam brighter, the added hard edge taking his breath away.

He managed to gather his senses. "What's going on? What happened?"

"Kiernan is leaving," she spat, her pale brown eyes darting over to his face and softening. "Can you take him and escort him back to his room to gather his things?"

He went cold at the look in her eyes. He swallowed, then nodded and took hold of Kiernan's arm. Claire released him, shoving him slightly towards Beast. Hazel met warm brown, searing into him, holding onto his gaze with a kind of desperation that scared him, before she turned away and strode out of the kitchen. He tugged on Kiernan's arm, urging him forward and causing the smaller man to curse and start fighting his grasp. It was a losing battle though; Beast was much larger and stronger, and was perfectly capable of simply picking Kiernan up like a sack of potatoes and carrying him the whole way if he wanted.

Once they made it upstairs Kiernan's struggles ceased, but it was only so he could get enough breath to start tearing into Beast with his words.

"My father is going to hear about this, you creepy fuck," he spat—literally—into Beast's face. "He won't stand for his son being disrespected by an uppity bitch and a gods-damned mon—" Beast yanked on the arm in his grasp, his fingers tightening until Kiernan gasped in pain. He bent down and snarled in Kiernan's handsome face, gone slack with alarm.

"Insult me all you want," he growled, baring his mouthful of sharp teeth, "but you will *not* say a single cruel thing about Claire. You will address her with respect or I will make you *bleed.*" Beast was panting, his pulse throbbing through his whole body as the urge to rip and tear through pale flesh grew almost impossible to ignore. The creatures that haunted him were howling for it, their glowing eyes hinted at in flashes in the deepest shadows.

He'd grabbed the front of Kiernan's shirt and held it tightly in his fist, dragging him slightly closer. It was only the thought that Claire wouldn't like it, would be disappointed to find Kiernan ripped to shreds at Beast's hands, that stopped him from giving into the wild, rasping voices urging him to maim. "I am no fool, Kiernan. I can imagine what you have done, and believe me when I say you should be singing her praises for sparing your wretched life. If it were up to me these walls would be painted with your guts." Kiernan had begun shaking and had gone bone-white as Beast had loomed closer and closer, fury mounting so hot that he'd begun to drool with his bloodlust.

He straightened, wiping his mouth with a sleeve, and continued dragging Kiernan down the hall to retrieve his things.

"What in the name of the gods does she see in you?" Kiernan muttered as they reached the doors of his room.

Beast threw open the heavy wood door, shoving Kiernan in ahead of him and closing the door again behind him. He crossed his arms and leaned back against the closed door, watching Kiernan gather his things back into his pack. Every movement was accentuated by grumbling and angry looks sent Beast's way, but he didn't care. He'd meant it: Kiernan could say whatever he pleased about Beast; he'd long since stopped caring.

"Never should have fucking bothered," Kiernan was muttering now, and something about his phrasing sparked something in Beast's brain. He went stiff against the door, heat and chill sliding through his body.

"You came here for her," Beast ground out. "You came here to pursue her."

A flash of panic entered Kiernan's gray eyes, but he straightened and lifted his chin. "So? She's a beautiful woman. Of course I'd want to take a shot at her."

Beast's teeth ground together painfully. "If you were interested in her, why not talk to her in the village?" His brows lowered, another growl rumbling up from deep inside his chest. "Instead you followed her quietly, stalking after her like a hungry night cat, hoping to catch her alone and vulnerable." The way that Kiernan had acted when he'd first arrived, staying quiet like he was trying to sneak into the manor undetected, flashed through his mind. He couldn't help the snarl that tore from his throat. This—this *creature* was just like Tollem and Deven had been. "Finish gathering your things and leave this place."

"I-it wasn't like that," Kiernan tried to insist, but his voice lacked conviction. "I was just trying to get my courage up."

Beast said nothing, leveling a hard stare at him. Kiernan swallowed, adam's apple bobbing, before he huffed and shrugged. "Whatever, asshole," he muttered, throwing one last item in his pack and tying it closed.

Beast wrenched the door open, shoving Kiernan out ahead of him. He took his arm and guided him back downstairs, where he saw Claire was waiting for them by the door, something small cradled carefully in her hands.

"You are to leave the manor and the grounds immediately," she intoned. "Do you understand?"

Kiernan nodded, scowling and digging his fingers into the straps of his pack. "Can I get my dagger back now?"

Claire pulled it from her belt loop, flipping it and handing it back to him handle-first with practiced ease. Kiernan snatched it, shoving it into its sheath. As he approached the waiting open door Claire took a step forward and pressed whatever was in her hands onto Kiernan's chest, making him start with a yelp.

"What the fuck did you just put on me?" he snapped, trying to bat away her hand but missing.

She scowled at him. "I lied. This is an arrest charm." She smiled at him coldly. "Only a judiciary official can remove it, and you will be compelled to seek one out. I believe the nearest office is in Citrine so you've got a bit of a walk ahead of you. But don't worry—you'll have the freedom to gather provisions and rest along the way."

Kiernan's face contorted with rage. "You *bitch*!" he

howled, his face darkening. "I should—"

Beast's hand shot out to grab Kiernan roughly by his scruff, freezing the furious younger man. The curse prevented him from throwing Kiernan out the door, but he didn't want him leaving just yet anyway. "I warned you, Kiernan," he growled, anger giving way to fear in the other man's gray eyes. "You will apologize to Claire for your rudeness, and moreso for the harm you have done to her by putting your hands where they weren't wanted."

Kiernan swallowed, eyes darting between Beast and Claire.

"I-I didn't even really do anything!" he protested. "You're blowing this out of proportion!"

Beast's fingers tightened against the feverish skin of Kiernan's nape, making him wince. "Honesty is the better tact, here."

Kiernan swallowed again, eyes flashing, before sliding away from Beast's face and settling on the floor by Claire's booted feet. "Fine, whatever. I'm sorry, okay?"

Beast squeezed again. "For what?"

Kiernan shot him a look. "For—for calling her names and…the other stuff."

Beast growled, muscles bunching with the urge to spill blood, but Claire's smooth smoky voice cut through the red haze.

"Enough, just let him go, Beast. I'd like to see the last of him."

He frowned, giving one last squeeze with his fingers, letting his claws dig into the tender flesh, before dropping his hand and stepping away for Kiernan to stand beside Claire. Without another word Kiernan was spinning on his heel and scrambling out the manor's door and into the night.

As soon as the door was closed and locked Claire sagged back against it, closing her eyes and letting out a shaky breath. Her deep brown skin had a grayish tinge to it he didn't like, hard lines bracketing her mouth and eyes. After a minute a violent shudder wracked her body, and to his horror tears leaked from her closed eyes, her lower lip wobbling. She sagged to the floor, curling in on herself, her knees bent and hugged tight against her chest.

It was instinct that pulled him to her side, something so much deeper than thought that had him falling to his knees and wrapping her up in his arms. For a breath she was stiff in his embrace, and he was worried he'd overstepped, but then she was unfolding, blooming into him and clinging as she shook and cried.

Her strong arms wrapped around his waist, squeezing tight, and his own arms tightened around her back, one curling so he could cup the back of her head. She burrowed her face into his chest, the feeling so right and perfect he almost started crying himself. He nuzzled the side of his face into the top of her head, taking a deep breath of her rose and vanilla scent. His other arm started stroking along her spine, the way she was gasping and shuddering against him cracking his ribs wide open.

"I've got you," he murmured, sitting and crossing his legs so he could pull her into his lap. "He's gone, you're safe now. I've got you."

Warm wetness soaked into his shirt, and he pulled her in tighter, wishing he could take her hurt from her, make it so that she never had reason to cry ever again. It was absolutely wrecking him, seeing his bright beautiful sun clogged with shadow and rain.

I should have been there. I should have protected her. He went cold, knowing that if he'd been there to protect her then Kiernan never would have tried anything. He should have kept a better eye on him, should never have let him out of his sight to make sure he left Claire alone. And instead what had he been doing?—just sitting on his ass, moping in the dining room about nothing. He'd failed her, this beautiful woman crying into his chest and making his heart feel like it was splitting into a hundred brittle shards.

He hadn't learned a thing from what had happened with Ingrid. He was still a coward, still unable to get over himself to protect those who needed him.

It was a while before Claire started to calm down, her body going limp and sinking into his. She sat sideways on one of his thighs, her head resting on his shoulder and her arms still loosely clasped around his waist.

"Is this okay? That I'm…touching you?" He went cold, realizing just how badly he might have overstepped her boundaries.

"Don't you dare let go," she grumbled into his shoulder, her arms tightening around his waist. "If I didn't want you near me your nose would be broken right now." He snorted; he absolutely believed her.

"Sorry for freaking out on you like that," she murmured, her voice thick and broken from her tears. "I don't know where that came from."

He squeezed her against him. "What in the world do you mean? I can't think of a more reasonable response to whatever it was he put you through." She hadn't said, and he didn't expect her to, but it was clear that Kiernan had done something awful—awful enough that she'd had grounds to arrest him.

She was quiet for a moment, still but soft in his arms. "He grabbed me. K-kissed me. Grabbed my breast—" she shuddered, her fingers tightening to ball his shirt up in her fists. "I knew he was up to something. I should have been more careful, I should have—"

"Stop that," he murmured firmly, his heart aching for her. "His actions are *not* your responsibility. You went for a walk, Claire. Even if you had been stark naked it would still not be your fault. Kiernan had no right to touch you."

She sniffled, burrowing her face closer against his shoulder. "Logically, I know that. But I guess some habits die hard." The dejection in her voice physically pained him.

"What do you mean?"

She shrugged against him. "I don't know. You hear your whole life that the bad things that happen to you are all your fault and you tend to believe it. Even once you grow up and you learn better, a part of you still believes it."

His breath fled his lungs. He pulled her closer, laying his cheek against the top of her head, wishing he could be enough to protect her, to keep the evils of the world from touching her. "I'm so sorry, Claire. For everything you've been through, for someone lying to you and telling you you deserved it, for not being there for you when you needed me...all of it. More, even."

She gave a watery laugh. "You goof." Her hands stopped clutching at his shirt and smoothed along his side instead, leaving tingling in their wake. "You don't have anything to apologize for. You've been amazing." Gods, but he wanted to kiss her. It was so wrong, and so inappropriate in that moment, but he was burning for it, aching for that closeness with her. "But I appreciate it anyway," she added softly.

"I'm not usually a hugger," she said quietly after a while, one of her arms sliding around to rest against his stomach, "but I just feel so safe with you…" Her fingers stroked lightly over his abs, making heat pool low in his belly.

She shouldn't feel safe with me. That's how people get hurt, trusting me. But that wasn't what she needed right now. "How are you feeling?" he asked her, unable to stop himself from rubbing his cheek against the top of her head again.

"Better," she allowed with a wry bark of laughter. "I can't believe I let him get the drop on me like that. I'm lucky he was so drunk and stupid."

"Very stupid," he grinned. "I'm glad you're alright. What…what can I do to help, Claire? I-I'll do anything for you."

She tilted her head back, her gaze sliding up to settle on his face, a look in her eyes he couldn't read. He held perfectly still, frozen by her sudden intensity. Her eyes slid down his face, settling on his mouth. She sucked in a breath, her chest flaring closer to him, and he thought she might have leaned further into him.

"You really mean that, don't you?" she mused. "You'd do anything for me. You'd take care of me. You *are* taking care of me. I'm literally sitting in your lap and you've done nothing but hold me and try to soothe me." Her eyes searched his face, one of her hands sliding up to his chest, pressing firmly between his pectorals.

He swallowed hard, nodding, because there was no way he could manage to say anything coherent in that moment. His body had finally noticed her closeness, and despite his best efforts his cock was thickening and twitching against his thigh. *Please, by all the gods, let her not feel that.* The backs of her thighs were perilously close to it from her seat on his leg, but they weren't touching him directly.

Her fingers dug into his shirt again, her eyes going heavy-lidded, and now she did shift, her weight coming down harder on her legs so could get leverage to inch higher. He froze, not even breathing, as he waited to see what she did next. He felt her brush against his aching shaft as she moved, and though he tried his best he couldn't suppress the way it surged against her, as if it was trying to get closer to her, to press tighter against her soft warm flesh, and he saw on her face when she felt it.

She stilled in his lap, her eyes snapping open and going wide. Color crept into her cheeks and then she was springing to her feet, stepping over his other leg and putting some distance between them. He scrambled to get to his feet as well, cold dread warring with hot shame.

"I'm really tired," she blurted, avoiding his eyes. "I-I think I'm going to go to bed."

He wanted to apologize and reassure her, to remind her he'd never do anything to hurt her, but his tongue felt like it was stuck to the roof of his mouth. He could only watch helplessly as she retreated to her room.

Well, that was that then. If he'd thought there was a chance she was attracted to him there was his proof that she wasn't. She'd been so repulsed by him that she'd had to flee.

It's for the best, he told himself, his chest aching and his heart low in his stomach as despair began to take root. She wasn't safe with him. He couldn't protect her, couldn't even control himself around her. He was just a hideous, worthless coward, and his dreams of being able to love her had only ever been that: dreams.

Dark cackling and howls followed him all the way to his bedroom.

CHAPTER TWENTY

Burning

Claire didn't blame Beast for getting an erection while she'd been sitting there wriggling and cuddling in his lap—who wouldn't respond to that? But she'd fled like it terrified her anyway. She'd been about to kiss him when she felt that hard, thick bar against the backs of her thighs, and it had made her go half out of her mind with lust. He'd just been so *big*.

It only made sense: Beast was a very large person in general, so why wouldn't he be big everywhere? But she'd been more surprised by the hard throb between her thighs, by how she'd immediately started getting wet thinking about reaching for him, squeezing him through his pants and watching him unravel. She'd been blasted with arousal so intense it had taken her breath away as her mind had conjured what was waiting for her on the other side of that fabric, how it would feel in her hands, on her tongue, pumping in and out of her.

It was so wrong on so many levels, not the least of which was that she'd just been attacked not more than an hour ago, yet here she was practically throwing herself at Beast. Had it been a stress response? Maybe it was just her body's way of trying to relieve its tension and self-soothe? She's never been interested in sex as a coping mechanism before, though.

She'd had to flee, to try and get a hold of herself. But she'd felt bad about it almost as soon as she'd made it back to her room. She'd avoided looking at him as she'd hurried away, but she'd still managed to catch sight of his dejected expression, at the shame and embarrassment plain on his face. She hadn't wanted him to feel bad about himself, about his body's natural reaction—especially when it was a reaction that a small part of herself had been aching for—but she hadn't been able to stop, to say anything.

What a fucking night, she'd thought as she'd stripped naked and slipped into the bath. She'd been stretched so thin and tense by Kiernan and his unwanted advances, and then thrown for a loop as she'd been forced to reckon with not just her feelings, but how those feelings we affecting her work and career. And now—now *this,* whatever this was.

Claire had never been the sort let her romantic feelings get in the way of what she needed to do in the past, so what was so special about now? Why was Beast so different? It was like something inside her was desperate to connect with him, to slip him into her skin and absorb him into her very bones, and the more she fought it the harder it pushed back. She'd never felt attraction like that before, and its intensity scared her.

She lay in the bath for a long time, her mind turning over what had happened with Beast and what a mess she'd made of things. It was better than thinking about Kiernan and how badly that could have gone for her if he'd been less drunk or more determined and aggressive. Her stomach hollowed out and went sour, and the intense vulnerability that had sent her spiraling into tears, that had made it so easy to fold herself into Beast's arms, came crashing back.

This had been the first time she'd really needed to use her combat training, and it had been every bit as terrifying as Caldus Love had said it would be. She hadn't frozen, thank the gods, but she hadn't been prepared for how rattled she'd be having to use her hands to harm someone. Yes, he'd had it coming, and yes, it had been to protect herself, but it was still a knowledge that was having trouble settling comfortably inside her.

And then to cry like that after…it had to have been the adrenaline crash. She hadn't cried like that in front of someone for years and years now. But her feelings for Beast were so different from what she was used to that she wasn't even embarrassed about that part. It had been the most natural thing in the world to fling her arms around his solid bulk and bury her face in his broad chest, letting the thump of his heartbeat soothe her. It didn't bother her knowing he'd seen her crying, because she knew he understood, that he wouldn't see it as a show of weakness.

The water was cold and Claire was a pruned mess by the time she dragged herself out of the bath and into her nightdress. She didn't have a clock in her bedroom, but she thought it was very late from the position of the moon in the sky. She sighed, closing the shutters and shuffling carefully to bed. She'd get some sleep, let herself rest and process, and then she'd apologize tomorrow for how rude she'd been. He deserved to know he hadn't done anything wrong, that it wasn't like he'd been rubbing himself all over her; in fact, she was pretty sure he'd tried to angle himself *away* from her, now that she was thinking about it. She tied her hair up into its silk scarf and lay down, hoping her churning thoughts wouldn't keep her awake all night.

After a restless night spent agonizing over what Claire should do about Beast and her feelings for him, she wasn't ready to face the man in question and pretend to have a normal meal together, but she did want to be an adult about this. To be professional. She threw on her loose beige outfit then steeled herself and went down to the dining room.

Only, Beast wasn't there. According to the clock in the hall it wasn't even half past seven, and the room looked untouched, which told her she hadn't missed him. She settled in to wait, apprehension tensing her stomach and dulling her appetite. He wasn't avoiding her…was he?

She finished her meal in silence, the clinking of her silverware against the china deafening in the heavy quiet. As much as she'd been dreading having to face him after her embarrassing reaction, she found that not seeing him was far worse. Her mind quickly spiraled out of her control, concocting horrible and insidious scenarios to explain his absence.

Once she'd swallowed the last bite of food from her plate she flung her silverware down and surged to her feet. She'd find him, and apologize for being so rude. Like a gods-damned adult.

The library and study empty—which she'd figured would be the case, but she'd needed to check anyway—Claire charged up the stairs and down the hall to stand outside Beast's closed bedroom door. Raising her fist, she knocked as hard as she could, determined to be heard no matter what he was doing.

When he didn't respond she knocked again, the sound echoing in the cryptic quiet of the manor.

"Beast!" she called, knocking yet again. "I know you're in there. I'd like to talk to you, can you let me in?" She held her breath, straining for even the tiniest sound from inside the room. When she heard nothing she frowned, pressing her palm flat against the heavy wood. "Beast?" Still, nothing.

She frowned, her brows bunching together in concern. "If you don't answer me I'm going to come in. I need to make sure you're alright!" She pounded on the door again, frustration making her hit the wood so hard her skin stung.

As her hand wrapped around the ornate metal handle, she heard a shuffle and sigh from within. The doorknob felt like it was quivering and buzzing against her palm. Was it nerves? "I'm fine," he called out, his voice sounding wan and hoarse even with the door muffling it. "So just leave me the hell alone already."

Claire blinked, rearing back. "You don't sound alright," she pressed. "Please, I just want to come in for a minute to talk about—"

"*I said leave me the fuck alone!*" he roared, making Claire's gut twist. "Are you stupid? Leave. Me. A. *Lone.*"

It felt like she'd been slapped, her breath trickling from slack lips as tears threatened at the backs of her eyes. He'd *never* spoken like this before, not to her, not to Kiernan, not even when talking about the mage who'd imprisoned him. It hollowed her out and made her cold inside. She bit her lip, begging it to stop wobbling, then spun on her heel and retreated.

She made it to her bedroom before the tears started, her

heart breaking open all over again at his furious rejection. Had she hurt his feelings that badly? Was he even upset about last night, or had something else happened?

After a moment of self-pitying, her despair ran itself out, replaced by hot fury.

Claire was angry.

Why couldn't he get over himself and come out and talk to her like an adult? Had she not proved she was reasonable and understanding? Had they not already had difficult conversations and helped each other weather them? It was the height of immaturity for him to lock himself in his room and throw a fit, insulting her when she came to check up on him like, like—like some sort of *brat*. She surged to her feet, seething. He had some nerve doing this to her, and right after she'd been through something difficult and scary *just* the night before! She began pacing her small room, her limbs trembling with her mounting anger.

He was being selfish and pulling away because he didn't want to have a conversation with her. He was pulling away because he didn't want to deal with her, or deal with his feelings, or whatever it was keeping him locked up in his room.

She could let him pull away from her, she supposed. She could do what he seemed to want and leave him alone, go back to Kesterin and finish up the quest from there. It was the better professional move, and it would serve him right for treating her like this. But that didn't sit right with her; she wanted him to know her rage, to know the pain he'd caused her, and to feel bad about it. But beyond that, she couldn't quite give up on Beast yet, even if that made her as much of a fool as him.

But right now she wasn't just mad, she was *furious*. Her bruised heart demanded vengeance, and so she resolved to give him what he wanted and leave him alone. If he wanted to hide in his room and ignore her then she'd just ignore him right back. It was unprofessional for her to sink to his level, but then things hadn't been purely professional between them for a while now.

Her body craved activity, something that would act as a release for all the tension thrumming through her. It was much later in the day than she would normally exercise, but the idea of getting sweaty and pushing her muscles to the point of exhaustion sounded too good to pass up.

She pulled her hair up into a bundle at the top of her head and tied her sweatband around her hairline. She grabbed her gear then headed outside to the little field she'd taken to doing her training in.

Caldus Love had given her a routine she could easily do to keep herself at a base fitness level, mostly things that utilized her own body weight and that used more than one muscle group at a time. It was simple to make it more challenging when it got too easy, which was also an excellent fit for her. All Claire had to do was add more repetitions per set, increase her pace, decrease her rests between sets, and it would be a whole new workout without her having to try and navigate her body through confusing new motions.

That afternoon Claire did all of it, as fast as she could do it. By the end of an hour she was completely soaked in sweat, her throat raw and burning and even a little tight. Her heartbeat pounded through her, so hard and so fast she could *see* it, her sight throbbing with her pulse. She could barely keep her dagger in her grip, between the sweat and the weakness of her exhausted muscles. But it had been what she needed.

Not only was the tension of her fury gone, but her exercise had bolstered her spirits and helped her work through some of her lingering feelings from Kiernan's attack. It was good to lay claim to her own body like this, to work at shaping it to her will, to make it stronger and faster than it already was. Claire was a capable woman, and even with being caught off guard and unprepared in the dark she'd managed to take care of herself. She wasn't invincible, but her workout had helped remind her that she was strong, that she was damn hard to take down. And that soothed her.

Claire put her hands on her hips and admired the sunset blazing across the sky. She took deep, hungry breaths of the cooling air, her heart feeling settled in her chest. She was starting to figure out where what had happened with Kiernan fit into her, where it could live inside her without hurting her anymore. She closed her eyes, letting her awareness sink into the world around her: the calls of birds and insects, the scents on the breeze, the way the wind stirred her baby hairs and lapped against her sweat-damp skin. She tilted her face into the heavy gold of the setting sun, luxuriating in the warmth of it. When she opened her eyes she saw that some of the sky had gone the same shade of shocking crimson as Beast's hair.

Claire's heart sank in her chest. She missed her quiet friend, despite everything. She hated that things between them were like this. Had he pushed her away because he was ashamed? Because he was hurt and didn't know what to do with it? It didn't excuse his behavior, but it did make her want to go back in there and try talking to him again.

She sighed, gathering her things to head back inside. The

temperature was dropping now, and she wanted to get into the bath and soak away the grime of the day.

When she closed the great front door behind her, she made sure it slammed loud, so that Beast would know she'd come back. For better or worse, she was still with him.

"You'll have to try harder than that to get rid of me," she muttered as she passed the hall that led to his room. "You moody bastard," she added.

A strange tingling started trailing over her arm, making her skin jump and shiver. Claire shook her hand out, wondering what in the world could be causing it. Luckily it was brief.

Once she was back in her room she stripped off her sweat-damp clothes and let them fall into a soggy heap on her bathroom floor. She drew her bath, pouring a liberal splash of her favorite lavender-infused bath salts into the steamy water to help her relax. It was likely almost dinner time, and while she was confident that Beast still wouldn't make an appearance, she wanted to make sure she was calm and centered just in case he did. She didn't want things to break any more than they already had.

As frustrated as she was with Beast's behavior, she couldn't help sympathizing with him too. So much of her early life had been lonely and miserable, and it had definitely stunted her and made her lash out and avoid intimacy. Adeela had saved Claire from that darkness and given her her life back, and slowly but surely she had grown determined to live it, and to live it for *herself*. She ignored the matches her father was constantly trying to make between her and the sons of his business contacts. She'd insisted on going all the way with her schooling, and once she'd discovered what she wanted to do with her life, she'd taken on more schooling and worked so, so hard to make it happen.

Joining the Guild and becoming a professional quester might have been the final nail in the coffin of Claire's relationship with her father, but as she'd gained some distance from him and his constant attempts to make her feel bad for her choices, she'd become more and more certain that this was right, that this was where she was meant to be. Meeting Beast had only solidified her belief that she was meant to help others, that like Adeela she could swoop in and be a guiding light for souls trapped in the darkness. She could be strong for the weak, brave for the fearful, warmth for the cold.

She sighed, hauling herself out of the bath and drying herself off with one of the fluffy towels provided by the manor. She pulled on clean clothes and headed down to the dining room. She wasn't sure what time it was, but it seemed like it should be close to dinnertime. She both hoped and dreaded she'd see Beast in there, even if he was slouched into his chair and sulking.

It was too much to hope for; he wasn't there, the table laden with platters that no one was around to enjoy but her. She spun on her heel and stomped back upstairs, making her way to his bedroom again.

The door was still shut tight, and at the sight of that heavy slab of wood standing in her way she saw red.

She pounded on the door, her exhausted muscles keeping her from putting as much power into it as she'd wanted.

"Open up the damn door, you big baby!" she called out. "We are both adults and we are capable of having an adult conversation!"

Nothing by silence greeted her words, and she snorted.

Fine, if he wanted to be like that then she'd just keep yelling at him through the door.

"Look, I'm sorry okay? For last night. I shouldn't have just run off like that when all it was was—was a normal bodily function. It was just a reaction and I shouldn't have been so rude about it. And I'm sorry if the way I acted hurt you." Silence continued to weigh heavily against her ears, making her pulse overloud. That tingling, buzzing feeling was back, this time on her hands and making her fingers twitch and jump. She shook her hands out absently, straining to hear anything from the other side of the door.

"Please don't shut me out," she said, more softly now. After a pause, she whispered: "I don't want to lose you."

She waited long minutes, her forehead leaning against the door. Her stomach was quivering with nerves. What if he was hurt in there? What if she never saw him again because he locked himself away in his room? She'd almost preferred him yelling at her and being nasty; at least that way she knew he was okay.

"Please, just talk to me," she tried one more time, pressing her palms into the door. "I...I miss you. I'd like to talk."

She waited for several more minutes and had just pushed away from the door to head down to dinner when she heard a creak on the other side of the door. She froze, her heart skittering in her chest with a flush of hope. But the door stayed firmly shut, keeping her out.

At least I know he's alive and well enough to walk around, she thought with a sigh, giving up and going back downstairs to try and choke down some dinner.

CHAPTER TWENTY-ONE
Mending

"You will really let that *stroga nazsam* win, *maya boichik*?" Beast started, shocked to hear Tully's warbling voice. He blinked around at where he was, only to see it was…nowhere. Or at least, he couldn't pin down any details about where he was supposed to be; everything was oddly blurred and shadowed. He grunted, settling back into whatever he was sitting on.

"I'm dreaming," he announced, trying to find Tully's face, to at least see his mother this way.

She scoffed. "Certainly, sweet one. But this does not mean you shouldn't listen to me. When have I ever steered you wrong, hm?" He twisted, trying to see behind him, but all he could see was shadowy nothing.

"Well, never. But you're gone, *madjem*. Probably dead. It's been two hundred years."

"Not dead. I promise this, *maya boichik*." He felt the warm buzzing against his left side that often crept over him while he was awake. "I don't have much time, so I need you to listen carefully. Can you do this?"

It was an odd dream he was having, very different from any other dream he could remember, but he figured he might as well enjoy it. "Alright. I can do that."

"Good. You have been so brave, and so strong, my love. I hope you know this." The tingling settled on his left hand, and if he concentrated he almost felt like he could feel the weight of her hand on his. "But the time for strength is just beginning. You cannot keep hiding from Claire. You must do the very scary thing and open yourself up to her. You must *trust* her."

His brow furrowed. "Why?" He paused. "She's not interested in me, *madjem*," he added more quietly.

Tully sighed. "She is as stubborn as you, *maya seza*. But she cares for you, I promise this." The tingling moved, stroking up and down his arm slowly. "If you do not take a chance, then nothing will change. This is safe, I know. And your life has made safe the most attractive thing. But I want to see you *happy*, and that will only come with change and risk. That *mala crujzta* had no right, doing this to you, and Claire… I think she can help you. She can undo the crimes that have been done at this place. She *sees* you, my love. She sees you when no one else has been able to, and I think this is how she is able to help you. Something about her gets around the curse, or perhaps cuts through it. I'm not sure what it is, but she is not gifted, so it cannot be too many things."

He remained silent, absently reaching with his right hand to grab at the hand he could almost feel holding onto his left. Shockingly, he actually *did* feel her hand, though he couldn't see it.

"Time runs thin, my dear. Can you tell me what it is that keeps you hidden away from her? I think you need to talk this out before I go."

He pursed his lips, holding tighter to her invisible hand. "I —it's stupid."

"Never," she insisted fiercely, the buzzing against his skin intensifying. "Tell me, please."

He had to force the words out, even though this was Tully, this was the woman who'd loved him and raised him without a drop of her blood in his veins. And it was a dream anyway. "Because she got hurt, ma. I failed to protect her and she got hurt because of it. Everyone who I care about gets hurt because I'm too weak and scared to protect them."

She was quiet for a moment, considering his words. "No."

He scoffed. "What do you mean, 'no'? No what?"

"Not everyone you care about gets hurt. I am not hurt! Your parents were never hurt. None of your parent's staff were hurt. This is a lie that *crujzta* Naja has told you that you have made into a truth. But it is not.

"And I do not think you are weak just because you are not a natural-born protector. Some people are not made to be a shield. Some people are made to be...like a cozy hearth. Warmth, comforting, a place of safety. Claire protected herself, yes? She did not need someone to protect her. She herself is all the shield she needs. But she did need someone to hold her through her tears, and that you did beautifully, my dear."

He blushed, remembering how *that* had ended. "I ruined that too," he muttered.

"Pah! Ruined nothing! She was just pounding on your door demanding to talk to you. That is not the behavior of someone who considers what is between you ruined." The tingling warmth slipped out from under his hand and started tingling along his scalp, making him shiver. "She is scared, in her own way, I think, of the feelings she has for you. She is very patient and kind, but she is still human and unsure of herself. But nothing is ruined. If you take my excellent advice and find your courage, I *know*, with everything I have, that you will find happiness with her." Tully's voice had begun to weaken, the sensation of her touch going dull and quiet.

"Let yourself love her, *maya boichik*," she whispered, her voice sounding so distant now. "And let her love you." He groped in the thickening dark for her, desperate to keep her close, to keep talking to her. He had so many questions for her, so many things he still needed to know.

"Tully? *Madjem?*" he called, trying to stand, trying to move at all, but his body was so heavy he couldn't even twitch, and then he couldn't even make a noise. He struggled against it, desperate to cry out for her again and draw her close.

He awoke with a strangled yelp, his whole body jerking violently. He'd known it was a dream, but discovering it really had been still upset him. It had felt so *real*. She had felt so *close*. Tears gathered, but he took a deep breath and managed to hold them back. He'd done enough crying lately.

It was odd that Tully had appeared in his dreams just to give him a pep talk. Usually his dreams weren't that kind to him. Part of him wanted to believe that somehow, Tully had really visited him. That she'd figured out some way to get to him to tell him something important.

He flung off his tangled blankets, sending several pillows from the nest he slept with flying across the room, and lay flat on his back in the chill early morning air, replaying his dream inside his head. It was all nonsense, of course. What was all that about shields and hearths? How could his dream version of Tully possibly know what Claire was feeling? Tully had been a powerful mage, but she'd never been a mind-reader. She'd never had precognition. She *couldn't* know. And, he reminded himself, it had all been a dream anyway.

But the longer he turned it over, the more he wondered: what if it hadn't been all in his head? What if Tully really *had* managed to slip into his dream to give him that bit of motherly advice? What then?

For starters, it meant he needed to get out of bed and get himself cleaned up and down to breakfast. It meant he couldn't spend yet another day in his room, not eating. It meant he'd have to go down there and talk to Claire about his feelings, about what was happening between the two of them. It meant he had to admit, even if just for a moment, that something *was* happening between them, that it wasn't all him this time. It meant he needed to adjust how he looked at himself and what he'd done. He'd have to rethink how he fit into the world.

He groaned, digging the heels of his hands into his eyes. Oh, that was all? He just had to rebuild himself from the ground up? Yes, that was *so* easy, Tully really knew how to ease him into a project. But the more he thought about it…the more he thought that maybe the reason he hated the sound of it was that he knew it was true. He *was* way too gods-damn old to be running and hiding from Claire just because she was making him feel things that were scaring him. She herself wasn't what he was scared of; she'd only ever been warm and kind. It had always been his reactions, his feelings, that had set him off. He let himself consider, just for a moment, what it would look like for him to go down there and sit down with her. What was the worst thing that could happen?

Nothing. The worst thing that could happen was that he tried talking to her, opened up to her, and she shut him out and walked away. But if he *didn't* go down there, then the same thing would happen, it would just be him who had retreated instead of her. Clarity arched through him, stealing his breath: the end result was the same, and if he did nothing he'd just torture himself over what might have been if he had tried. He would agonize over it for the rest of his long days.

He surged upright, swinging his feet over the edge of the bed and striding over to the bathroom.

"Alright, Tully," he muttered, "I'll do it."

On some level, Beast knew that this was good for him, that his being forced to confront his demons—rather than just ignoring them like he had been—would allow that which was festering inside him to drain and heal. But that didn't stop it from being painful and frightening.

Forcing himself to do the right thing had become unavoidable, but there was nothing stopping him from getting in a good grump about it while he was still alone in his room. His morning routine wound up very dramatic because of it: there wasn't a single moment where he wasn't sighing or grumbling or grousing, no sentence spoken without swearing, no object which was treated with care or consideration. He'd get it all out of his system, then go down to breakfast to face what he'd done like an adult and apologize for it.

Usually when he got like this, the creatures that shadowed him grew more bold, more vicious, but they were blessedly quiet today, as if they could sense his bad mood and wanted to leave him to it. There were growls, and distant snarls, and dark corners didn't look empty when he spotted one, but all in all, it was easy to ignore, and that, at least, was something he was thankful for.

He was tempted to wear all black to telegraph his mood, but even as he reached for his black trousers he wondered: was that *really* what he wanted to say to Claire? That he was in a bad mood because she had made him accountable and insisted on openness? That seemed…childish. He released the black fabric and went for the chocolate brown pair instead, pairing it with a dove-gray tunic.

Not quite ready but out of reasons to delay, he lumbered down to the dining room for breakfast. According to the clock in his room, he was a bit late, but he couldn't bring himself to hurry. He was just so gods-damned *scared*.

"There you are," Claire called as soon as he'd crossed the threshold, "I was wondering if you'd actually join me or if you'd keep hiding from me," she said, her tone just a little icy. It hurt, but he deserved that.

"I came down, alright?" he snapped, wincing at how much like a petulant child he sounded.

She arched an eyebrow at him, tucking in her chin and spearing him with a look that made him feel like a little boy again. He dropped into his seat, letting his hair fall into his face so he could use it as a buffer.

Claire sighed, pushing back from the table and standing. She walked over to stand beside his chair, and he braced for her fury, for the lecture, for hearing again how much he had disappointed her.

Strong arms and a soft cloud of roses and vanilla wrapped

around him, startling him.

"I'm not going to hurt you, you idiot," she said into his hair, squeezing him tight. "I just want us to understand each other."

"What's there to understand?" he spat, still sounding distinctly bratty. "I'm a terrible monster who hurt the only person who's ever been kind to me because I'm a coward."

She squeezed him again. "Is that really what it was?" she asked quietly, pulling away to look at him in the eye.

Under the strength of her honey-brown gaze, he squirmed, fighting to get the words out. "No," he finally admitted in a near whisper. "I was…" but he couldn't finish it, couldn't let that see the light of day. It was too much of himself to give.

"You were what, Beast?" she asked gently, pulling her chair over to sit closer beside him. She wrenched his tightly clasped hands apart and took one to hold it. "You were what?" she repeated.

Could he admit it? Could he slice into himself that deep to show her what dwelled there? He wasn't even sure that he himself fully understood it. It had been hidden for so long that he might have purposely lost it, because looking at it was so painful.

"I was scared," he whispered, squeezing his eyes shut.

"What were you scared of?" she asked, just as quietly.

He thought for a moment. "Of history repeating itself. Of…you seeing who I really am and leaving me. I-I've never had a real friend before. So I guess I'm scared of losing that."

"So you thought you'd get ahead of things and be the one to pull away?"

He nodded. He'd told himself that he needed to push

Claire away for her own good, because he wasn't the kind of person she needed in her life. But hiding under that, deep inside him, there'd been that fear. That she'd wake up one day and be disgusted by him, and throw him away like everyone else had. And he wouldn't have even blamed her for it.

"I understand," she said, squeezing his hand in both of hers. "The gods know I've done the same thing. But here's the truth of it: when you push people away you trade the possibility of things falling apart for a certainty. If you cut me out of your life then I'm gone. And I…I don't want to *be* gone. Pushing me away hurt me, but this is still where I'd rather be."

Tears threatened, much to his shame, as he slowly absorbed her words. It was hard to hear, that he'd hurt her. He knew he had, of course, but it was different, hearing her say it. But more than that, his emotions were running high because it sounded like Tully had been right, in his dream: Claire really did care for him. She wasn't mad about how his body had reacted to her closeness—she'd already said that yesterday—she was upset that he'd locked her out and been cruel to her.

Was he safe with her?

"I'm so, so sorry, Claire," he moaned, her face blurring and fading with the tears that were on the cusp of falling. "I'm sorry I did that to you. I didn't mean what I said, I hope you believe me."

"Sweet man," Claire murmured, standing to hold him once more, and that was his undoing: the tears fell now, his chest feeling like it was cracking open, like it was peeling itself raw from the inside out. He couldn't help but tally all the ways he'd wronged her, this beautiful shining light of a person, and ask himself why she still wanted to be his friend. But maybe that was part of his problem: he needed to stop counting all the ways it didn't work and start appreciating all the ways it *did*.

He clung to her, steeping himself in her warmth and her heady scent. But he couldn't get the question out of his head: "Why are you so nice to me? Why haven't you abandoned me like all the rest? The gods know I've given you plenty of reason."

"I guess that's a good question," she murmured into his hair, one of her hands rubbing a soothing path against his back. "And I don't have a good answer for you. I just feel drawn to you, like…like you belong in my life. And like you need me. You're a good person under all the scars." She pulled back, meeting his eyes. "So I'm sorry for freaking out on you before, and I promise it wasn't because of you. It was… something else. With me."

He nodded, snatching a napkin from the table and mopping his face. "All is forgiven," he rasped. "If you forgive me for being rude and shutting you out."

She nodded, smiling slightly. "I do. Friends?"

He nodded back, a small smile of his own breaking through. "Of course."

Claire squeezed his shoulders and nodded once. "Good man." She retook her seat and resumed eating, and he took her lead and tucked into some bacon and sausage.

"How are you?" he asked after too much quiet had sat between them.

She paused, her fork in midair. "I'm…alright. Kind of tense. Kind of paranoid that he'll come back and I'll have to get more forceful." She paused, pinching her lip. "Is it bad that I'm not worried about whether or not he made it back alright?"

He grinned hesitantly. "If it makes you feel any better, I actively hope he got mauled by a night cat."

She grinned, chuckling mildly. "So violent." She searched his face, her eyes boring into him in a way that made him squirm. She reached out and grabbed his hand, holding it tight. "I'm so glad you came out to talk to me," she said in a hoarse rush. "I...I don't know what I would have done if I'd lost you." He thought he saw tears gathering in the bright amber of her eyes, but she blinked and it was gone, her face once again smooth and calm.

"I think if I would have actually managed to push you away I would have regretted it the rest of my life," he whispered, feeling faint with the raw openness of his admission. "So I am also very glad."

"Yeah," she responded softly, a wobbly smile slipping onto her face. Something shifted in the next moment, her eyes going wide and unsettled. Her smooth brown brow furrowed, her smile slipping. "Yeah," she repeated.

CHAPTER TWENTY-TWO
Healing

Apparently, not even enchanted food was completely safe from the threat of food poisoning. Something from breakfast had decided to turn sour on Claire, and it had been an absolutely miserable two hours of trying to manage her body wringing every drop of itself out.

She missed Adeela fiercely, missed the warm roughness of her chapped hands rubbing Claire's back and smoothing the sweat-damp baby hairs away from her feverish face whenever she'd been sick. She moaned, aching in every bone, chills wracking her body so hard her teeth clacked together, and no one to care for her. She was alone in her bedroom with her heaving stomach and her roiling thoughts.

It gave her plenty of time to think about how at breakfast Beast had said something that had cut her to the bone: that if he'd let himself push her away he'd regret it for the rest of his life. It was making her wonder about her own feelings. It was the smart thing to keep him at arms' length, to maintain a professional distance from him—or at least, that was what she'd been telling herself.

She tried to look at it objectively: as a woman in a field

that was diversifying but still somewhat male-dominated, she had to be more competitive than her male peers. She knew her father and sisters would think something was seriously wrong with her if she went to all the trouble of becoming a quester just to come back from her first quest with a monstrous new companion—that she was romantically involved with, no less. She could picture their horror and disgust so clearly. They'd think she was foolish, that she'd lost her mind.

Those weren't things that Claire was worried about for their own sake. It hit her like a bolt of lightning as her stomach gurgled ominously and a twinge of pain rippled through her middle: she was denying her feelings because she was afraid of what other people would think of the situation. She was taking longer than she'd expected to work her way through the quest, but objectively, it wasn't because she was distracted by Beast so much as it was because the quest was strange and old. Lots of people got involved with the subjects of their quests, and she knew she could still do her job even if she gave in to her feelings. So what if other people might think she couldn't?—all she had to do was get through the work anyway to prove them wrong.

She was disgusted by the fact that she was letting her family's disapproval factor into the decision. Of all the people whose opinions she should let sway her in her life choices, why was she giving so much power to the three people who had hurt her and abandoned her the most? If she was being objective, Adeela and her daughters, Cat and Aubrey, would barely bat an eye, so long as he was a good person and took care of Claire. *They* just wanted her to be happy.

Claire pursed her lips against another wave of nausea,

willing her gorge to settle, as her thoughts continued to tumble through her. She'd have to think more on it when she was feeling better and had a clear head. There was always a chance that feeling ill was affecting her judgment.

A loud knock on her door startled her, making her tender guts cramp. "Claire? Are you alright in there? You didn't come down for lunch."

She swallowed, wiping at her sweaty face with her trembling hand. Her fingers were already aching from the fever. "I'm sick, Beast. Food poisoning, I think."

There was a pause. "That can happen?" he asked incredulously. "It's enchanted, though."

She laughed weakly. "I thought the same thing," she croaked, wincing at the burning ache in her throat.

"Can I get you anything?" he asked after another pause. "Can I…come in? I'd like to help. I don't like the idea of you all alone, And—and no one should have to be alone and have to take care of themselves when they're sick."

Maybe it would be good to let him in, to scare him away with the mess in her room. He'd already pulled away once, after all. Her heart ached at the thought of it, but that ache was the point, was it not? Better to lose him now when it was just an ache, she thought with some bitterness, than when it would tear her apart. And she *was* tired and desperate for company.

And a small voice, so deep inside and so whisper-quiet she couldn't even really hear it, insisted he wouldn't run, not again. And that when he didn't, it would mean that she would have to stop her own maddening retreat.

"It's so bad, Beast," she croaked, lifting herself onto an elbow. "You can't even imagine how bad I smell."

"I don't care, I want to help. I'm sure it's not even all that bad."

She groaned. "You'll never be able to look at me the same if you come in here," she warned.

"I very much doubt that," he rumbled softly from the other side of her door, and her heart clenched with want. She wanted to say yes, she wanted to lay her aching, burning eyes on his beautiful gray face, let herself sink into his soft brown gaze. She wanted to bury her face into his chest again, wrap her arms around his solid bulk, wanted him to hold her close and tight. She wanted Beast with every fiber of her being, sickness be damned.

She hesitated for one more moment before groaning and hauling herself up into a sitting position, stiff muscles and tender joints protesting.

"Alright, but I did warn you. I tried to protect you!" she called through the door. "Come in."

The door burst open, slamming into the wall and no doubt leaving a mark in the white plaster as he strode in, towels and a bucket slung on one arm. His eyes roved over her room, taking note of the defiled basin beside her bed, the rumpled bedding, the soiled clothes heaped onto her desk chair. His eyes settled on her lying at the center of the rat's nest of her bed, soaked in sweat and the stink of vomit. Shame flared hot in her face, curving her spine and limbs inward to try and fold herself so small she blinked out of existence.

"It's not the worst thing I've ever seen," he said, grinning. "You wear vomit well, Claire."

She groaned, rolling onto her back and dragging a pillow onto her face to hide. He laughed again and gently tugged the pillow away, setting it down next to her head.

Beast set the bucket on the floor and pulled a chair up to her bedside. He soaked one of the towels in the bucket of water and rung out the excess, mopping gently at her hot face. The cool water was bliss, washing away sweat and dried spit and chasing away the worst heat of the fever. She wanted to cry at the relief, at the thrumming of her skin at Beast's tenderness, his nearness. She had a sudden wild urge to reach out and snatch his hand, to hold onto him tightly and never let go.

Well, why couldn't she?

The scariest part had been letting him in; now that he was here, steady and calm and sweet as he ever was, getting straight down to the task of caring for her without hesitation, her shame and nerves were sliding away. She was watching him closely for any twitch or tick that would spell out disgust, but she couldn't see anything but tender caring. As she watched his face, he even seemed *happy* to be here, as if her sick room was the only place he wanted to be in all the world. Her heart raced, her illness having nothing to do with the ache that settled in her chest. Would it be so wrong to turn to him for comfort? He re-wet the towel and dabbed at her neck, combing the wet stringy baby hairs back from her face, taking the utmost care not to graze her with a claw.

Weak and hazy though she was, it was such a simple thing to catch one of his massive hands in her two small ones. He froze, staring at his hand wrapped by hers, holding the damp towel. She closed her eyes and breathed deeply through her nose, hating the ache that throbbed in her joints.

"Thank you for helping me," she murmured, squeezing his hand even though it hurt her fingers. He took the damp towel from the hand she held and returned it to the bucket with his free hand. She opened her eyes to drink in his face. There was a certain harsh beauty to the sharp jut of his high cheekbones, the thick prominence of his brows, the expressive bow of his mouth. But it was his eyes that she always landed on, and in the light from the fireplace and the heat of her fever they glowed like amber, like honey pouring into her with such sweetness and fire.

"I'm glad you let me in," he said roughly. "I wanted to respect your privacy but I was afraid you were dying." Smirking, he added, "From the sounds and the smells it seems like you already have."

She moaned theatrically, taking back one of her hands to clutch at her chest. "Shame on you, picking on your poor, sick Claire," she rasped, grinning.

He smiled, his sharp teeth glittering in the firelight, and dabbed at her face and neck again with the cool towel. "My apologies ma'am, I guess they'll have to tack on more to my sentence." He paused, brows furrowing. "I...I've never taken care of a sick person before. Is this alright?"

She nodded. "Yes it's lovely, it feels *so* nice." As the water sizzled into her skin she became aware of how thick and pasty and sour her mouth was, how red hot her throat burned. "I am very thirsty though. Could I have some water to drink?"

"I've forgotten a cup. I'll be right back. Don't die, and don't lock me out."

She nodded, aching for him to return as soon as he'd left. The heat of the fever was burning away the last of the walls she had built against her feelings, and she was glad for it. She was so tired of fighting them.

He returned a moment later, cup and pitcher at the ready. Hesitantly, he reached under her shoulders and lifted her up to drink. Every nerve thrilled at his touch, electricity sparking along her skin and humming in her chest.

After she had drained the cup he laid her back down gently, straightening the hem of her nightgown and fixing the sheets and blankets still wadded up all over the bed, then pulled them over her. The feverish chills had vanished for a moment when he first came in, but they were slinking back into her body and knocking her bones together violently.

He leaned over and gingerly lifted the nearly-full basin of sick and carried it to the bathroom, where he dumped it into the toilet and flushed it with a loud rattle of the chain. She heard water running, too tired to scrounge up horror at what he had just seen. He was back a moment later with the newly cleaned basin, setting it on her nightstand within easy reach if she needed it.

"There you are," he said, giving her feet a satisfied pat through the thick layers of blanket. "Do you need anything else?"

She considered. "Can you stay?" she licked her dry, cracked lips. "I missed you."

"You missed me?" He asked quietly, lowering himself into his chair.

"Of course," she said, smiling and reaching for his hand again. "I miss you any time I'm not with you. Even—even if I'm also too proud to let you see me like this."

He cleared his throat and squeezed her hand. "Well, thank you I—I miss you as well."

She smiled again, charmed by his awkwardness and deciding that since the walls were down she was going to enjoy it and be frank, be bold. "You make me very happy, Beast. I've never known another person who understands me so well. You're the first person I feel I can be myself wi—"

Oh no, please no—

She couldn't stop it, barely managing to twist to the side in time as she vomited up thick orange bile right into Beast's lap. She hoped that the illness would actually kill her, now.

"Oh gods I'm so sorry, I'm so sorry oh—oh no, and you had *just* cleaned the basin—"

She burst into tears, covering her face with her hands and burning with shame. She felt so stupid, trying to charm him in her condition—what had she been *thinking*?

He made a soft, soothing sound in his throat, one large hand clasping her shoulder and squeezing gently. "It's alright Claire—really it's fine, please don't be upset."

"I'm so embarrassed, I can't believe—"

"You're sick, and I don't care. Look it's not even that much, I've already cleaned it up."

Sure enough, when she cracked an eye open and peeked at him from between her fingers there was only a damp spot on his linen breeches to show for the hellish embarrassment coiling in her belly. She lowered her hands from her face, but found she couldn't quite meet his eye.

"If you want to go running now I wouldn't blame you. No one wants to spend their free time getting puked on by someone who smells like a dead animal," she said quietly, trying to lighten the mood despite her heavy shame.

"Are we not friends?" he asked gently, reaching out to rub her arm after a moment of hesitation.

She chanced a quick glance at his face—earnest, open, concerned, and not a hint of disgust—and that filled her with something she couldn't name. She nodded, a single tear squeezing out of her hot, gritty eye and soaking into the pillow beneath her cheek. "Of course," she croaked.

"Then you're going to have to throw up on me a great deal more than that to get rid of me," he said, smiling down at her with that gentle twist of his lips that she loved so much.

"Actually," he continued, refilling her water glass and handing it to her, "I think throwing up on me means that we're *best* friends now."

And then she was laughing, the sound a dry rasp that had her stomach muscles protesting, but it felt good anyway, and it felt *right*. It felt like this was what life was meant to be, laughing with Beast when everything else was trying to drag her down.

"I don't think I've ever had a best friend before," she admitted, taking the glass and drinking carefully. "When we get out of here we'll have to find a jeweler to craft us matching bracelets. And obviously you'll be hosting the slumber parties, but I can be in charge of snacks or entertainment if you want."

He grinned at her, something warm flickering to life in his eyes. "Why stop at bracelets? If we're each other's first-ever best friends then we should really do it up." He leaned forward and tucked her blankets in tighter around her shivering body. "That looked like it was all bile that time, so whatever it is must be almost out of your system now," he said. "How do you feel?"

In answer, a violent shudder wracked her body, and she was suddenly ice-cold. She rolled onto her side and tugged the blankets higher over herself, leaving the barest circle free for her face. "Cold," she moaned.

He stood up, eyes darting around her small room. He walked over to the wardrobe, yanking open the doors and rifling through its contents. He found a small afghan tucked at the back and brought it over, draping it across her legs and feet. She continued shivering, the spasms sending pain knifing through her already abused muscles. She couldn't help but whimper, trying to curl into an even tighter ball to salvage any warmth she could. Beast continued stomping around the room, likely looking for more blankets. But then she had an idea that made her shudder for an entirely different reason.

"N-no m-more blank-kets," she ground out. "C-can you lie n-next t-to me? L-lend me s-some of your heat-t? You're l-like a gods-d-damned f-furnace, I b-bet."

He froze, staring at her. She tried her best not to look like she was scheming. She *may* have played up her shivering, just a little, to try and coax him close.

I'm just a poor sick girl, Beast. C'mon, get in the bed.

Hesitantly, he came around to the other side of the bed, the one she had her back to.

"Are you sure?"

"Please."

The mattress sagged under his weight, the solid oak of the bed frame complaining slightly. She held still now, resisting the urge to roll down the slope of the mattress into his side. She felt like she was trying not to startle a wild animal. She risked a look over her shoulder and saw that he was just barely sitting on the edge, looking incredibly stiff and uncomfortable, mouth pressed into a tense line.

"You're still very far away," she chided, rolling over to face him clumsily. "I'm so cold, Beast."

"I don't want to be improper."

"Then don't be. Please come here and warm me, little furnace man."

He hesitated for another moment, then slid his legs onto the bed and joined her under the covers.

Still shuddering, she held her breath as he settled next to her and lay on his side, peering into her face with a raw intensity that rocked through her. She tried her best to hold still. *Don't want the deer to bolt.*

Satisfied he had at least committed to not running for the immediate future, she squirmed up close, sighing as his impressive body heat started seeping into her.

At first he was still and tense beside her, like a deliciously warm statue in her bed, but as she settled against him he began to relax, his arm coming around to rest on her waist.

"Thank you, that's lovely," she murmured, wriggling still closer. She could hear the great bellows of his lungs, could even feel his heartbeat against her forehead, she was so close to him.

"Is that better?" he asked, his hand tentatively rubbing her back in comforting strokes.

She nodded against his chest. "Gods yes, you're *so* warm. I should have you do this all the time."

He chuckled, relaxing a little more. "You'd never be able to afford my rate."

"You would *charge* me?" she scoffed. "I thought we were friends."

"We are, but you'd have to be an awfully good friend to get these goods for free."

"Cruel man, absolutely heartless. You'll have no one but yourself to blame if I hogtie you and hold you prisoner here."

He laughed again, the sound vibrating through Claire, too. The shivering had calmed by now as his impressive body heat beat back the fever, slowly breaking it.

She groaned as she realized she wasn't wearing her head scarf.

He stiffened against her, his hands pausing in their soothing paths. "What's wrong?"

She sighed. "It's nothing. I just forgot to put my silk scarf on my hair. It protects it while I sleep. But I should be fine skipping it just the one night."

"Where is it?"

"I keep it hanging up in the bathroom. You don't mind grabbing it?"

"Not at all," he scoffed, easing out from under the covers and padding back over to the bathroom. He emerged a moment later with her favorite scarf held gingerly in his hands: the burnished copper one that was almost crimson. She took it gratefully, and he helped her to sit up. She wrapped it around her hair carefully, tying a simple knot on the top of her head.

"Alright, now I'm ready," she groaned, easing herself back onto her side. Exhaustion began to drag at her, her eyes refusing to stay open for one more aching minute.

As consciousness slipped from her limp fingers, she whispered, "Please don't leave. I need you." Hopefully he would listen and stay with her even once she was asleep.

The sleep that claimed her was heavy and thick, vivid dreams holding her hostage but never lingering for more than a moment, the churning images strong but impossible to catch. She only woke once in the night, her breath catching in her throat when she realized Beast was still with her, now sleeping as well. She craned her neck back to admire his face in the light of the fire burned down to embers.

He was beautiful. The harsh and unexpected lines were

still there, but in sleep he was so delicate, so tender, that her heart ached with want for him. His lips were parted slightly, his dark red eyelashes laying gently against his gray cheeks. A lock of hair lay against his forehead between his horns, and she simply could not stop herself from brushing it back gently. He twitched and snorted, but didn't wake. She smiled, eyelids turning leaden once more, and she snugged herself back up against his chest and obeyed her body's demand for sleep. The last thing she knew before she slipped back into unconsciousness was his arms tightening around her.

When she awoke again to morning light streaming into her bedroom window he was gone, the smell of him on her sheets the only proof that he had been there at all.

CHAPTER TWENTY-THREE

Hunger

Beast felt shivery and light when he awoke early the next morning in Claire's bed, with her curled snugly into his chest, feeling like she'd been made to fit exactly there. His morning erection ached painfully at the closeness of her, at the way her body molded against his, the warmth of her skin setting his on fire.

He swallowed, tempted to pull her in tighter, to draw her in as close as he could without hurting her, but decided against it. He didn't want to take more than she wanted to give.

Of course, he hoped that she'd want to give more. She had been getting very comfortable with him lately, especially with touch. It seemed like she was finding any excuse to lay her hands on him, to sit close against him, to lean in. Which he had noticed because every time it happened he felt faint; both from the intoxication of her closeness and the way blood tended to rush away from his brain and into his pants.

Though he couldn't stop his self-doubt from rushing in. His history told him she shouldn't find him desirable. He was a monster. He was ugly. He was a coward, weak, moody.

They'd only *just* begun repairing the damage he'd done when he abandoned her. What could someone who was pure light and softness want from him? What, by all the gods, could she possibly be *attracted* to in him?

But he pushed those thoughts away, deciding to revel in the moment, drinking in her scent and the soft warm weight of her pressed against him. He thought he could get drunk just from this, from the rush he was feeling at this intimacy that she had gifted him. How had other men been in this position, with Claire soft and warm and vulnerable in their bed, in their arms, and decided to just toss her away? He didn't consider himself all that bright, but at least he wasn't *that* stupid. He was cherishing it, relishing in it, and he thought that if this was something he had even a slim chance of getting to experience for the rest of his days, he'd fight tooth and nail to get it.

He loved her. There was no other word for what was happening inside him. His chest felt like it was cracking wide open, leaving his heart a raw and bleeding gift for her, if only she'd take it. He loved her sly teasing, her sweet smiles, her fanatic support, her dedication, her intelligence. He loved the way she pinched her bottom lip when she was thinking deeply, he loved how patient she was with him, and how excited she got about things that interested her. He loved her roses and vanilla scent, the way her deep brown skin caught the light and sparkled with it. He loved...everything. He let his arms tighten around her briefly, making her sigh softly and nuzzle her face closer into his chest.

Judging from the quality of the ring of light around the shutters, it must have been not long after dawn, and even with her illness he thought it likely that she'd wake soon. She was a devoted early riser. He sighed, easing his arms away from her pliant body, an ache settling in his chest at her absence. As he broke the contact she frowned in her sleep and moaned, but stayed asleep. He loosed his held breath and eased out from under the covers and off the edge of the bed. Satisfied she was still fully asleep, he crept out of the room and closed her door.

As he made his way back to his own room, he considered what it might be like to find himself in a relationship with Claire. He liked to think that if given the chance, he'd have quite a lot to give to a partner. He hadn't been reading all those romances idly. He'd been taking careful note of the sorts of things the heroines in those novels liked. Obviously, in real life it would be different, but there were certain constants that seemed worth trying at least once. Like using his mouth on her. Like licking and sucking at the sensitive bud of her clit. Like using his hands and lips all over her body, finding those places that made her shiver and moan. Surely that was at least a good place to start, even if Claire's personal preferences leaned elsewhere.

He couldn't stop himself from imagining what she'd taste like, what she'd smell like. It was making his cock even more uncomfortably hard and throbbing, and he paused in the hall to slump against the wall and squeeze himself to try and alleviate the ache. It didn't help much, but it was enough relief to make it to his room.

He slipped into his bedroom, closing and locking the door firmly behind him. "I need to be alone, Tully," he murmured, and a moment later he felt the tingle of her presence passing him, trailing out into the hall. He sighed, leaning his head back against the door, then began tearing at his clothes.

As he was pulling his shirt off over his head, the scent of

roses and vanilla swept over him, and he realized with a thrill that her scent had seeped into it while they'd slept. He wadded up the fabric and pressed it into his face, groaning as he inhaled deep. He fumbled at the clasps of his pants, his hands trembling with the urgency of his need.

Naked, he strode over to his bed and lay down, clutching at the Claire-soaked shirt like it was a lifeline. He flopped onto his back and draped the shirt over his face so that every breath would be full of roses and sweetness. They'd been so close together that he thought he could detect a hint of her personal scent, the intoxicating note that was all Claire and indescribable.

With nearly two hundred years of practice, Beast could stroke himself to completion in less than a minute, but today he wanted to savor it. He wanted to go slow and coax himself to his peak, revel in her smell and the fantasy playing behind his eyes for as long as possible. He wanted to imagine that it was her hands on him, that her scent was coming from the source instead of his wadded-up shirt.

He let himself get close, only to back away from the precipice at the last minute, again and again, until the swollen head of him was weeping precum and pleasure was streaking through him with so much intensity he had to purse his lips to stop from crying out. When he finally let himself come it was with a shuddering gasp and a moan that carried her name. His orgasm roiled through him, snapping his spine straight and making his legs clench so hard they jumped up off the bed and almost cramped. It seemed like the hot ropes of his release would never stop, leaving him helpless but to lie there and try his best to breathe through it. At last, he was spent, the only sounds in his room the bellows of his lungs and the thunder of his heartbeat in his ears.

He sat up slowly, using his shirt to mop himself up. Once he was clean he combed his hair back from his face with his fingers and sighed. He'd managed to alleviate the ache in his groin, but that had done nothing to ease his hunger for Claire. Nothing would, of course, except the woman herself.

He took a deep shuddering breath, steadying himself enough to haul himself to his feet and over to the bathroom to wash.

As Beast had suspected, Claire was exactly on time for their usual breakfast at seven. She looked more wan and wrung out than usual, her braids tucked away into a fresh scarf and circles hanging heavily under her eyes, but she was still so stunning she took his breath away. She smiled at him warmly as she walked in, her steps heavy and stiff.

"Good morning, bestie," she called, her voice croaking at the end. "I hope you haven't decided to kick me out after the horrors of last night."

He blinked, struggling to recall what it was she was referring to. "Oh, because you vomited on me?"

She sighed dramatically and sagged forward, covering her face with her hands. "Do you have to just *say* it like that?" she moaned.

"It didn't bother me, truly." *It didn't stop me from touching myself to the thought of you this morning for even a second*, he thought, heat creeping up his neck. "Like you said, it was a bonding experience. It allowed me to…really see what fuels you."

She peeked at him from between her fingers. "Did you really just make a puke joke?" she asked wryly.

"Well, someone had to," he muttered, reaching for the plate of bacon that had materialized on the table. "And I didn't hear you taking on that responsibility."

She dropped her hands and threw her head back, laughing. "You see, that's what I love about you, Beast," she chuckled, completely unaware that her words had struck him like a bolt of lightning. "You know just what to say to make me laugh and feel better." She wrinkled her nose at the proteins on the table, instead reaching for some toast and a dish of berries.

"How are you feeling this morning?" he asked, his concern for her rising to the top once again.

"Better," she allowed, taking a big drink of water. "But still recovering. I feel like I got trampled by a herd of aerlani. *Definitely* food poisoning." She picked up a slice of strawberry and placed it delicately on her pink tongue, the sight sending heat scattering over Beast's skin.

"That's excellent, I'm relieved to hear it." He combed his clean hand—the one he hadn't been using to eat—through his hair, torn between bringing up what had happened last night and ignoring it. On the one hand, maybe she regretted it in the light of day, now that the fever had passed; but on the other, maybe she didn't. Maybe she had even…enjoyed it, like he had. "I hope I was able to be of help," he said, testing the waters.

A slow, wicked smile bloomed on her face. He gulped. "Oh yes, you were *very* helpful. I've never slept so well." She bit her lip, picking at her toast for a moment. "I don't know if I could afford your rates, but I'm tempted to hire you on full-time for that."

A dim ringing began in his ears, accompanied by a frantic tingling along his shoulders. He swallowed again, his mouth utterly dry. Had he heard her correctly? Was that…was that *flirting*?

Sweet Delenaa, that might have been flirting.

In that crucial moment, his mind went blank. He had no idea what he should say, what he even *could* say, and he felt lightheaded and sweaty at the monumental amount of energy he was expending in trying to wrap his head around it.

"I've thought about it, and for you, I think I could do it for free," he heard himself say, to his complete and utter shock. Aside from the faint wheezing *that* could have been flirting, too.

She grinned, propping her elbows on the table and cradling her chin in her clasped hands. "Don't tease me now, I'll actually take you up on that," she purred, her hazel eyes sparking.

He swallowed, desperate to scrounge up even a drop of moisture. He lunged for his water glass with trembling hands, almost knocking it over, and gulped down several mouthfuls, managing to almost choke on it by the end. "Alright," he rasped in between coughs, his face completely on fire by the feel of it.

Claire giggled, biting her lip again. "Well, then it's settled. You're hired as my official bed-warmer," she said smoothly, leaning closer to him as if he wasn't currently sputtering and choking, his eyes running from the strain of ejecting the water from his lungs so that he could breathe again.

Perhaps she was still feverish. Because the alternative, that she was actually attracted to him, was interested in some sort of relationship with him, was so absurd, so far-fetched, that it couldn't be true. That situation was ludicrous. It was *impossible*.

He was tempted to snap at her, to tell her to stop teasing him like this. He wanted to beg for her mercy because his love for her was overwhelming, barely kept at bay by his need to make her comfortable, and he didn't think he could handle her teasing him about it.

He wished for not the first time that he could actually talk to Tully, to get her advice. *Was* he imagining things with Claire, or did it seem as genuine as his wildest hopes and dreams were pleading for it to be? Was flirting back the right move? He was staggering in the mire he'd suddenly found himself in. But in the end his hope won out, if only by a hair.

"Excellent," he ground out, deciding to hell with it; if it was a cruel prank then he'd just have to find a way to scrape the shards of himself back together, after. If it was real, then it would be worth the risk. "Just let me know when to start."

She grinned at him, winking. "I think I'd like you to start as soon as possible. Tonight?" At his weak nod she grinned again, biting her lip in a way that made his cock twitch against his leg, then dropped her hands and resumed her meal.

Beast found that his appetite had quite abandoned him.

CHAPTER TWENTY-FOUR

The Plunge

It had been a long day of sexual tension and cautious flirting with Beast, and by the time dinner was over Claire was more than ready to take things further. Every time she looked over at him she found herself staring at the powerful column of his throat and wanting to lick down the tendons and nibble at his pulse point. She was constantly mesmerized by the expressiveness of his bowed lips, by how sweet and soft they looked. She wanted to bury herself in his chest again, the memory of doing just that leaving her aroused and needy off and on all day.

She knew she should be preparing to make a trip to Edden, that she needed to check for updates, but her thoughts were hopelessly snagged on brown eyes warm enough to melt, on silky crimson waves and bashful smiles sparkling with sharp teeth.

Now that she had allowed herself to acknowledge her feelings for Beast, it seemed there was no escaping them. She'd realized that the whole point of breaking away from her father and going into questing was to make herself happy. She had wanted to do something for herself, to do something that was important and just for her, for the first time in her life. She'd spent so many years trying and failing to make other people happy, but here she was denying her own happiness all over again just to satisfy what other people expected of her.

She'd thought that once she started on this path that that was it, she'd just naturally make all of the best choices and live authentically. But she hadn't missed her chance yet for this happiness. She was confident now that her feelings were returned, and there was nothing to do but make her move.

It was after dinner, and they'd decided to retire to the study with their glasses of wine to chat on the cozy little couch there beside the fire. Though she'd been nursing the same singular glass of wine all night, her head was filled with a buzzing rush, and she found herself fading away from Beast's words as he spoke. She was lost in the way his lips moved, sharp white teeth flashing. She swam in the gilded brown of his eyes, soft like velvet yet bright with stars from the firelight in front of them. The way his red hair caught fire in the dim light—sparkling with golds and crimsons and russets and flowing softly around his angular face—kept her mesmerized. The swooping curve of his horns looked especially dashing to her, drawing her attention to the delicate points of his ears.

Before she could second guess herself she was reaching out, her hand glowing like a cooling ember in the firelight, catching a curling lock of his silky hair between fingers that were humming and hot, and tucking it behind one delicious ear. He had stopped talking, his mouth gaping open slightly as she raised her hand, and when the pad of her finger glanced over the peak of his ear he had closed his eyes and shivered.

She could no longer remember a single thing that they had been talking about. It couldn't have been important, not compared to the thrumming energy strung between them, so tense and taut that her skin was skittering with fire as the whole world faded beyond the man sitting beside her.

He was staring at her, barely breathing, his wineglass dangling from limp fingers and in danger of spilling. She plucked it from him, depositing it and her own glass onto a side table. She turned to face him, the very air around them buzzing and shimmering. She reached out and took his recently emptied hand, his throat bobbing and eyes burning into hers.

"Does this bother you?" she asked, throat tight.

He shook his head, swallowing again, hard enough for Claire to hear it. His hand was so large compared to hers, his skin hot. A smile curled languidly onto her lips, boldness taking hold and setting her well and truly aflame.

She slid closer, closing the distance so that she was pressed up against his side, her head tilting back to keep her eyes locked onto his. This close, her eyeline only came up to his chest, and the smell of him was all around her, that warm sweet scent that was only Beast, that she would have been able to find in a crowd, that settled deep in her chest every time she breathed it in. It was the most alluring thing she'd ever smelled, and she knew she'd never get enough of it.

"Claire…" he croaked out, something sparking deep in his eyes as she brought her hand up to cup his cheek. He closed his eyes, leaning into her touch, twisting so that his body was angled to face her fully now. His breathing became uneven, his brow furrowing as he opened his eyes to look at her again. He looked so hopeful, and so scared. Her heart clenched, understanding. Her thumb stroked the jutting plane of his cheekbone, and she wrenched her other arm from where it was pinned between them, cupping his whole face in her hands now.

"Can I kiss you?" she asked softly, wanting to know that he was right there with her, that he wanted this too, that what she was seeing in his eyes was real. The air was so hot now, buzzing frantically over her skin, making her blood sizzle in her veins. He had gone still, rigid, as if bracing for disaster. She held his gaze, still stroking his face, hoping that he wanted this too.

"Yes," he whispered, and that was all she needed.

She pulled his face down to hers, and he came easily, eagerly, to meet her, their breaths mingling into shared heat as her lips finally, agonizingly, found his.

His kiss was the sweetest thing she had ever tasted.

For all his hard lines and jagged edges, at his core Beast was all softness, and it was that softness she feasted on in his kiss. She suspected he would be clumsy, awkward even, and she hadn't been quite sure how they'd manage his sharp teeth, but if the kiss began as something halting and cautious, he settled into it quickly enough, picking up on her rhythms and matching them on instinct.

Claire clambered up onto her knees to kneel beside him on the couch, allowing him to straighten out of the hunch she'd pulled him into, and her arms wrapped around his neck. She pressed her body into his and a low sound escaped him that flooded her with heat and hunger. She pulled her lips away from his and began trailing kisses over his cheeks, up to his brows, down the side of his face to his jaw, worshipping the sharp beauty of him with her lips. She heard him gasp, his arms coming up to encircle her finally, clinging desperately to her back, as she turned her attentions to his neck. One of her hands brushed his hair out of the way, and when her lips pressed to the sensitive spot under his ear the sound he made was all animal—and it shot straight to her core, making her shudder and clench on nothing. She teased at him with her tongue and her teeth, keeping gentle but firm pressure, and he squeezed her tight against him, the faint prickle of claws at her back and the desperate gasps of his breaths in her ear goading her on.

She broke away from his neck and settled again on his face. As their mouths crashed together once more she ran her fingers through his hair, combing it back from his face between his horns, raking her fingers against his scalp, and she felt him shiver again. She wondered dimly how long it had been since anyone had touched him—held him, kissed him, *loved* him. All she knew was that it was too long, so many yawning empty years that he had endured, in pain but unwilling to let himself break and grow bitter. A wave of feeling surged in her chest, and she willed herself to melt into him so that he would never have to be alone again, so that she might soak up some of that chill loneliness and take it away from him. If they were one then they could shoulder the ache together, and suddenly it was all she ever wanted.

She traced his bottom lip with her tongue, teasing at it gently with her teeth, and her hands began to wander, drifting down his neck, to his shoulders, his chest, trailing down to his stomach—

He broke away, panting, something like fear in his eyes. She froze, her heart stuttering in her chest. "Too much?" she asked, taking her hand off his stomach and resting it back on his shoulder instead.

A look crossed his face that she couldn't quite read, and he looked away from her, eyes settling on the fire in the hearth. He sank into the couch, putting distance between them but not breaking away from her. She sat on her feet, studying his face.

"What's going on in there?" she asked gently, finger-combing his tousled mane back into place. He was silent, staring at the flames, and Claire felt him slipping away into his darkness, pulled away by a riptide she'd created. She lifted herself up again, kissing his cheek.

"Oh no you don't," she murmured, kissing an eyebrow, "you're not allowed," she kissed his forehead, "to shut me out," his chin, "so talk," and she punctuated the last by kissing the tip of his nose. He blinked, his gaze sliding to her at last, and she raised her eyebrows in silent admonishment. "But I'm sorry I made you uncomfortable," she continued gently, "I hope you know you can tell me when it's too much."

He frowned, shaking his head. "It's not supposed to be too much," he growled angrily.

She snorted. "Says who?"

He sagged, avoiding her gaze. "I don't even deserve you," he said, his voice rough and barely above a whisper. "Why should I let myself get nervous about a little…touching? I should be thankful for everything that you'd give me."

She took a deep breath, her heart clenching. "It's not a matter of deserving, Beast. I like you. I *want* you. And I *need* you to be comfortable." She wrapped her arms around his neck, pulling him against her again. He hesitated for just a moment, then sank into her and tucked his face into her neck, his hot breath tickling her sensitive skin. "Sweet man," she murmured, "always tell me what you need."

"I've never done this before," he admitted softly.

"Haven't done what before? Kissing?" He grunted, she assumed in confirmation.

She pulled back, meeting his eyes once more. He looked ragged, uncertain, still so full of doubt. So she sought out his lips once again. This time she was soft, gentle, slow. She luxuriated in the velvet softness of his lips on hers, pressing kisses from one corner of his mouth to the other. His hands began rubbing up and down her back, curling over her shoulders, and she felt like she could purr under that firm caress. A different kind of heat was flooding her limbs, and she leaned her forehead against his, their breaths tangling in the air between them.

"We go at whatever pace you're comfortable with," she assured him, combing her fingers through his hair again just for the thrill of the silky locks slipping through her fingers. "I just want to be with you. I don't care what we do or don't do. I just…I just want to love you. Can you let me do that?"

His eyes widened, going glassy, and at the sight Claire cried out in dismay.

"Oh no, gods Beast please don't cry, I didn't mean to upset you, I'm sorry—"

"No, it's alright. Please, Claire, it's…it's good, I think. Don't worry," he reassured her, rubbing her arms. He chuckled wryly, swiping a knuckle under one eye. "I've made this such a romantic experience," he said dryly.

She groaned and leaned in to kiss him again, nuzzling her nose against his. "What did I just say? Let. Me. Love. You," she repeated, punctuating each word with another little kiss.

"I'm going to start screaming if you don't."

"How bad will this screaming be? Because I don't know if I can promise anything."

"*Beast!*" she groaned, gently smacking his chest.

He grinned briefly, but sobered up between one breath and the next. He sighed heavily, cupping her face hesitantly and rubbing her cheek with his thumb. "I've had *hrk* — " he choked, clearly trying to say something his gag was suppressing, "…a very long time to think of myself as one way. It's going to take time for me to change. But I promise I'll try. I trust you. I…I love you, Claire."

She couldn't help the smile that broke wide over her face. "You really do? Since when?"

He returned her smile shyly. "Since I first saw you, I think." He combed his fingers through his hair, looking a bit sheepish. "And I've been thinking a lot about what you said, about how I can make myself into the person I want to be. And I want to be better, do better. Because for the first time in my whole cursed life…I feel like I *can* be. Because of you."

She squealed and threw her arms back around his neck to pull him into a tight hug. "You are so sweet and precious I want to scream all over again."

"You do a lot of screaming when your emotions run high, I'm realizing," he said, his voice muffled by her hair.

"You'll learn to love it," she assured him, easing up on her death grip.

He pulled back and kissed her gently. "I already do."

She melted into him, her heart so full of love it ached. What had she been so scared of? Why had she waited so long to make her move? This was beautiful, and so *right*, as if it was truly ordained by the gods. As if it was a gift from the gods. No—as if it was a manifestation of the gods themselves, a holy force of nature that made a kind of sense out of the chaos of existence.

She opened her eyes, meeting Beast's smoldering mahogany gaze, so filled with hunger and want it took her breath away. For her, this fire burned—for her, and only her. And, most dizzyingly, she wanted this fire, wanted those flames licking over her skin, setting her ablaze. She wanted to burn to ash in his fire and be remade, like a glorious phoenix, as something whole and unmarred by the cold and the loneliness of her old life. She wanted to burn so hot with him that they both melted, melded, became something new and powerful and great. Together.

For the first time in her life, Claire had a person who made her believe in a "together". Who made her feel balanced and wonderful, just the way she was. Here, at last, was the other half of her scale, the counterweight that leveled out all of the sorrow, the anger, the pain that had been so much of her life up until now. *This* was the beauty of *rorto*.

As she searched his gaze, afraid of what she might find but needing to know everything, to see it all for herself, his hands came up and cupped her face, his thumbs stroking her cheeks, and she sighed, the soft warmth of his touch an answer to a question she hadn't realized she'd been asking. She knew he was scared, knew that she was scared too, but it was nothing, this fear of what might come next, when the larger and more horrible fear was that they would let this go. That they might let slip away this thing that shone hot and golden-bright between them. For the first time in her life, Claire felt like she was finally, rapturously, enough.

It was hard to say how much time passed with them

wrapped around each other on the little sofa, trading sweet words and even sweeter kisses, but when she yawned so hard her jaw cracked they agreed it was time to go to sleep. She was more than a little tempted to invite him back into her room, just like she'd promised she would, but with his earlier skittishness about physical intimacy, she thought it might be best to let him have some alone time to process. She knew herself well enough to know she'd never be able to keep her hands off of him if he joined her in her bed.

So it was safer to go their separate ways for the night, to reflect and calm down and sort it all out. But it was the most magical night Claire had ever experienced, and she was loathe to end it.

CHAPTER TWENTY-FIVE

Reeling

Beast had agreed with Claire that it was long past time for bed, but the truth was that he couldn't be farther from sleep. He was on fire, his nerves wound tight and hot under his shivery skin. Some of it was likely Tully, ecstatic for him and wanting to share in his joy, but some of it was just the maelstrom of his feelings growing so big and wild his body was having trouble holding them all.

He was beyond happy, of course. He didn't think he'd ever have another memory more beautiful than the feel of Claire's soft lips on him, her vanilla and roses smell sunk deep in his lungs, the breathy sounds she'd made as they'd kissed. It was better than any fantasy his virgin mind could have conjured, so wonderful it made him ache.

So naturally he was also terrified and in despair. Now he had something too precious to lose, and his life had been riddled with loss so far. There was a chance that Claire *would* free him from this place, and if that happened...what then? Would she still want him if she found out what he'd done? Would she still care for him away from the manor? What if all she was feeling was due to their forced proximity here? He didn't have much to offer someone as capable and independent as she was, and he knew it. But she knew it too, surely, and still she'd said she wanted him. That—sweet Delenaa, that she *loved* him. His heart was pounding so hard that he was having trouble taking deep enough breaths.

As quickly as his chest had filled with light and hope, it filled with a bitter slash of insecurity. She *had* had wine at dinner. And he'd been so skittish and nervous, making an absolute fool of himself just because she'd touched him. He couldn't help the doubt and despair that began trickling in, souring his mood and making him deflate. Only, there was something Claire had said that kept coming back to him, and he thought of it now: *Even if there are bad things in there, you have it totally within your power to change those things. To cut out the stuff that you don't like and shape yourself into the person you want to be.*

He was tired of feeling like he was a bad person, like he was undeserving. If Naja wouldn't let him die, then maybe she'd just have to accept him changing.

He stood and hauled his heavy body into the bathroom, the wall sconces fluttering to life all around him. He stood before the mirror mounted above the large sink and vanity, studying his face. He hadn't ever been handsome, even before the transformation, but he was hard to look at now. *What does she see in me?* He tried to find it, was desperate to see what she did when she looked at him. But it was no use: all he could see what the same monstrous face he'd been staring at for two hundred long years.

"Doesn't matter what you see, you fool," he spat, forcing his eyes to meet with his reflection's. It was unexpectedly difficult. "She *sees* you, and she likes what she sees. So you'll just have to accept it and try your gods-damned hardest to be the best version of yourself that you can be. You talk to her, you put her first, you treat yourself better so you can give her everything you've got." He swallowed, shocked to find tears prickling in his eyes. "You can't let the darkness win," he whispered, his eyes boring into themselves through the glass with an intensity that had him feeling overfull. "She's decided she wants you, and she deserves the best you've got."

And a small part inside him, so deeply tucked away he didn't recognize it as a part of himself, wanted to shun the darkness for his own sake. It had held him in its jaws for so long, and he was tired of being its victim. The darkness *was* Beast—on some level, he knew that. And if the darkness came from himself, then surely he could do *something* to make it less powerful.

He sighed, shuffling over to his bath and twisting on the taps. A soak in the tub seemed like it might be what he needed to soothe his mind and body and find rest. Once the water was deep enough he stripped his rumpled clothing off, the chill air making his gray skin pebble and shiver. He hurried across the icy flagstones and slipped into the warm embrace of the bath. He slid down until his chin was at the water level, thinking.

Claire was the most beautiful person he'd ever met. But it was her light, her kindness, her bright intelligence that drew him like a moth to a flame. Her determination and sense of rightness were what he aspired to, and as he sat in his tub, the water slowly cooling as he pondered, he decided that he was going to try. He was going to challenge the darkness when it slithered in to try and tear him down. He would remake himself, as Claire had urged him, into the kind of man he wanted to be.

And he would let her in. He'd give all of himself to her from here on out: mind, body, and soul. He'd give her his best. He'd try and heal himself, if only to give her more. He *wanted* to let her in, he realized with a shock. He wanted to share everything with her, as much as it scared him. But it was a good kind of scared, he thought: the fear that comes from change, from striking out into the unknown.

He rose from the lukewarm water and toweled himself off, his mind spinning back to earlier in the evening. *She* kissed *me*, he thought incredulously, a grin splitting his face. He dressed for bed quickly, yawning in between bouts of giddy smiling.

He threw himself in bed, limbs heavy and eyelids already sliding closed. He yawned again, hard enough to feel twinges in his neck, and snuggled deep into his nest of pillows, hugging one against his chest. He'd never slept as well as he had when she'd been sick and asked him to share her bed, and now when he hugged his sleep pillow—a habit he'd developed as a young child and never grown out of—he imagined it was her pulled tight against him. *Maybe she'll share my bed with me,* he thought dreamily, consciousness finally slipping away. *Maybe she'll want to do more than kiss. Maybe she'll want to...* He was asleep before he knew it.

CHAPTER TWENTY-SIX

Breakfast

It was like any other morning, on the surface: Claire had woken up, she'd gotten cleaned up and presentable, and soon she would make her way down to the dining room for breakfast. She awoke slowly, languidly, admiring how the late summer morning had a hint of a chill to it, the sunlight beginning to develop the burnished undertones of autumn.

But it was not like every other morning, because last night she had kissed Beast. They had admitted their feelings for each other, and so the whole world had been remade. She could not stop remembering the smell of him, the taste of him, her lips tingling with the phantoms of their kisses. Her mind snagged on every second of it, demanding to relive it again and again. And she let it, because the most important thing that had happened last night was that she had stopped caring, had stopped fighting. She was officially Going For It, and the only thing that would stop her now was if he had changed his mind and no longer wanted this.

She wanted to hurry down to breakfast, to fly down the stairs into what she hoped would be Beast's open arms, but her compulsion to look her best won out—however slightly—

and she sat in front of her vanity ensuring that she looked too delectable for him to want to resist her charms. He had a maddening masochistic streak, and she knew he might push her away just because he thought he didn't deserve her, or thought she deserved better, or some similar nonsense. You didn't enter into a relationship necessarily as your best self, but there was nothing stopping you from *becoming* your best self, putting in the work to become what your partner might need, and she wanted so, so badly to dive into that sort of self-discovery with him. He'd said last night that he was ready to do that work, but there was always the chance that he'd scare himself in the light of day.

She pulled her twist braids into a tidy bundle at the crown of her head, coaxing the loose baby hairs into ringlets with some water and a deft twist of her slim fingers. She admired how they framed her heart-shaped face, bouncing against her temples and cheeks as she cocked her head from side to side. She unscrewed the cap of her face cream, inhaling the heady perfume of roses deep into her lungs, then dabbed it on and admired how the sheen of the cream made her deep brown skin glitter in the morning light. She dipped into her precious wine-red cosmetic stain, applying a faint blush to her lips and cheeks.

Satisfied with her reflection, she sprang to her feet and smoothed the lingering wrinkles from her simple but curve-hugging sapphire blue blouse and loose black trousers. She made her way swiftly down to the dining room, her heart hammering wildly in her chest and her palms slick with nervous sweat as she neared her target.

The heavy doors to the dining room were already thrown open wide, she saw as she approached, meaning Beast was likely already inside, and it took a surprising amount of self-control to avoid jogging the rest of the way. She had never felt this sort of uncontrollable fission before, had never craved another person quite like this. And it scared her as much as it thrilled her.

As she turned into the room itself and saw him sitting at the table, hunched into his chair and his whole body jiggling slightly with the force of his knee bouncing, it was like her whole body was finally able to relax. She let a breath loose with a sigh and felt a smile break wide across her face.

"Good morning, Beast."

An answering smile bloomed on his face, and she thought she might float with how her heart soared. "Good morning, Claire," he returned gently.

Her usual chair was pulled out and waiting for her, but she stepped past it, coming to stand next to Beast's chair instead.

"Could you scoot back a bit?" she asked.

Confused, he nonetheless obliged, pushing back from the table a few inches.

"A bit more, please."

Now there was about a foot of space between his knees and the table, and Claire wedged herself in, forcing his knees apart a little more, and sat herself down on one of his massive thighs.

"Hello," she said sweetly.

His throat worked but only a choked sound came out. He cleared his throat and tried again.

"Hello," he managed tightly. She giggled—actually *giggled*, she couldn't believe it—and leaned close to kiss his cheek. He smelled faintly of shave cream and soap, and underneath that the warm sweetness that was his smell, that always wound its way deep into her body and made her glow every time she caught even a hint of it. She wanted to lean into the sturdy warmth of his body, to melt into him completely, but she noted how stiff and still he was holding himself and forced herself to lean back and look him in the eyes.

And those eyes—those eyes of his were molten, piercing, shooting deep into the core of her, setting her well and truly alight. Those eyes took her breath away, made her feel stripped and raw and so deliciously warm. She bit her lip, trying to loosen the grip his eyes had on her, and took a shuddering breath to steady herself. But beneath the naked heat of his gaze she realized she saw fear, and uncertainty, and her heart ached for him.

"So about last night," she said huskily, keeping her seat on his lap but also keeping her hands neutrally clasped in her own lap.

He nodded, his expression going guarded. She wanted to kiss him again, to chase away that fear, that hesitancy, but she knew it was better to clear the air than ignore it.

"How do you feel about what happened?" she asked softly, her hands tensing together as her heart began racing for another reason: what if he regretted it? What if she had made him uncomfortable?

They were quiet for a moment, looking deep into each others' eyes, questioning, hoping, searching.

"I liked it," he rumbled, his arm slipping from the arm of his chair to creep onto her hip, making her skin buzz. "A lot," he whispered.

"Me too," she whispered back, allowing herself to slide a

little closer to his firm torso. His hand tightened on her hip and slid up to wrap around her waist a little.

"But I worry it was a mistake," he added, his face pained. Her stomach dropped, her throat going tight. But if he didn't want this, then why pull her closer? Why not ask her to get up?

She swallowed, her brows drawing down in concern. "Why do you say that?" she managed quietly.

"Because you deserve so much better than me," he murmured, tucking a loose curl behind her ear with his free hand. She leaned into his touch, closing her eyes briefly.

But then she met his gaze, so full of want and anguish, and snorted a laugh. "I knew you'd say that," she sighed, bringing her arms up to loop around his neck. Beast opened his mouth to protest but she pressed a finger to his lips, stopping him in his tracks.

She cupped his face in her hands and he closed his eyes, brows drawing together with emotion. "All I'm concerned with right now is if you want this," she continued, her voice barely above a whisper. "Because I do."

He swallowed again, his eyes brightening and going glossy. A single tear fell, trailing down one of his gray cheeks. Claire caught it on one of her thumbs, brushing it away. She held her breath, waiting for him to say something. Hoping.

"I want this," he breathed. "I want you."

She sighed, feeling like her veins were filled with light, as his other arm came up to curl across her back and pull her close against him. Her arms wrapped tight around his neck, her face angling up—for he was just so massive that even sitting on his lap he was still marginally taller—so that their lips met again at last.

Sweet fire swept through her, burning away her doubts, her hesitation, her fear of his rejection. There was only the rightness of the feeling of his mouth, his arms, of their bodies fitting together like they were made for each other. There was only the smell of him wrapping around her as tightly as his arms, there was only the small groan that escaped him as their kiss deepened, her mouth opening to let his tongue in to explore her, to taste her as she was tasting him. She was wary of his teeth, so sharp she knew she had to be careful, but he was helping her, guiding her with the angle of his jaw and with how he was holding his own tongue, and she found she was never in danger of hurting herself, not really, because he'd never allow it.

They burst apart, panting, her head spinning deliciously from lack of air, from the power of his body pressed against hers. It was like magic, a force like nature itself, as if every moment of her life had been tumbling her towards this, towards Beast. He ducked his head and leaned his forehead against hers, still breathing heavily.

"Claire," he breathed, and it was like a plea, like a prayer, and she kissed him again, but gently, softly.

"Beast," she sighed in answer, her fingers squeezing the nape of his neck gently.

They sat like that for several minutes, breathing in each other's air, nuzzling each other's faces, trading soft kisses back and forth, the whole room feeling hot and buzzing all around them.

But then something shifted in him, as if he had finally decided to accept this completely, accept her word, accept that he could go for this, be with her. Something that he had been holding back broke through its barrier, and then he was surging all around her, his mouth trailing kisses like sweet fire along her jaw, down the curve of her throat, the gentle scrape of his teeth setting her ablaze, making heat begin to pool in her core. She tilted her head, giving him better access, her breaths growing short and panting as his hands, his lips, his tongue stoked a raging fire inside her.

She wasn't a virgin by any means, but this kind of blazing heat was new to her. Here, in his arms, melting under his attentions, was the first time she'd experienced arousal so intense it *ached.* Her other lovers had been more preoccupied with their own pleasure, with consuming her beauty, whereas Beast, despite the hint of inexperience, was…well, he was *worshipping* her. And she knew that this wasn't enough, this kissing, this touching. She wanted *more.* Her sex had never been so slick and achy before in her life.

She panted and moaned, digging her hands into his hair and holding him at the hollow of her throat as his tongue lavished her skin. "I need more, Beast," she gasped, her fingers sliding free of his hair and moving to her shirt buttons, locking her eyes with his as she undid the top button. His throat worked again, his smoldering eyes drifting down to follow the path of her fingers. She bit her lip as she undid another two buttons, then slowly, teasingly, dragged the fabric apart, revealing the swells of her breasts, firmly encased in her brassiere.

For now.

She finished unbuttoning her blouse. As the fabric slipped off her shoulders and fluttered to the floor he groaned, his expression at once pained and rapt. "You are…stunning," he breathed, his hands tightening on her hips. He licked his lips, then groaned again, lowering his face to her neck. He began kissing a licking trail from her collarbones down to the cleft of her cleavage, his hands stroking up her sides, tickling her ribs deliciously. She shivered as his tongue dipped into her cleavage to lick slowly up the valley. "Sweet Delenaa, you smell so good, Claire. You *taste* so good." He nipped gently at the top of her breast and she gasped, her hands tangling in his hair again. "What do I do here? What do you like?" he asked, his voice rough and husky and going straight to her aching pussy.

She reached back and undid the clasp of her bra, letting it, too, fall to the floor. "Touch my breasts, squeeze them a little. The nipples are sensitive, and the undersides. You can use your mouth," she panted, unable to stop herself from reaching up to grab herself, pinching her nipples with a moan.

Beast practically slapped her hands away, he was so eager to take over. When his huge warm hands palmed her breasts they both moaned, her head falling back at the wave of pleasure that rolled through her from that one touch. "Gods above and below but you are so *soft*, Claire. How are you so soft?" But before she could even wonder whether or not he actually wanted an answer his head was dipping, his mouth descending on the hard peaks of her nipples, and every thought fled her. There was no room for words around that heady heat, the pleasure cutting through her like a knife, making her sex clench on nothing. She began rocking her hips against his powerful thigh, suddenly desperate for friction on her swollen, sopping folds. His mouth left her one breast with a soft *pop* that had no business being as erotic as it was, only for him to switch to her other breast to give it equal attention.

She began to whine softly, the motion of her hips getting more frantic as her need continued to build. He sat up, his hands taking over where his mouth had left off, his rough palms rolling over her sensitized flesh, his fingers pinching the dusky peaks gently. "What do you need, Claire?" he asked huskily, kissing her.

"It might be too much for you," she hedged, uncertainty seeping in at the edges. He'd gotten uncomfortable last night when her hand had drifted towards his cock, and she didn't want to make him feel that again, no matter how needy she was.

He pulled back slightly, enough to look in her eyes. His brow furrowed briefly, as if he was confused, or maybe thinking, and then his slate lips peeled back from his sharp teeth in a delighted grin. His eyes dipped to where her hips were still rocking, the movement completely out of her control now, and she realized with a start that her panties felt completely soaked. Could he feel the wetness? Had it seeped into his pants? Her cheeks flamed at the thought.

"I think I know what you need, sweetness," he murmured. She swallowed, her mouth suddenly dry. "Can I taste you, Claire?" he asked, his mouth descending on hers once more, stealing her breath. His taste, his smell, his *heat* was all around her, and still it wasn't enough. She needed more. Where had this confident man been hiding? Beast had always held an inexplicable attraction for her, but this was the first time she'd ever seen him *sexy*, and it was doing things to her, making her utterly wild and desperate. She gently broke the kiss, nuzzling her nose against his.

"Yes, Beast," she gasped, "Taste me."

She hadn't even gotten the words all the way out before he

was lifting her in his massive arms, plucking her from his lap like it was nothing, and setting her on her feet. A swipe of his arm had plates and cutlery sliding over the table and crashing to the floor. She squeaked when the steel band of his arms came around her again, lifting her and placing her on the edge of the table. He kissed her again, his tongue an invasion that she welcomed, angling her head, her whole body, to take him in as deeply as she could. She was lost in him, soaring like she never had before in her life.

He broke their kiss with a groan, leaning his forehead against hers and panting. "You are the most incredible thing I've ever experienced," he said, kissing her nose gently. She smiled, her hands gripping his shoulders tight. "I've never done any of this before, so if I do something you don't like, or you need me to do something different, please tell me."

She nodded, language proving too much for her fried synapses.

He slowly worked his way back down her body, nipping gently at her breasts when he passed them, kissing and licking his way down her with torturous slowness. When he got to her trousers he undid the ties slowly, carefully, the fiber artist in him no doubt refusing to damage fabric unnecessarily. But it would have been obscene and delicious if he would have shredded them off of her with his teeth and claws, she thought.

The drawstring undone, he placed another kiss to the soft roll of flesh on her lower stomach just above the waistband, his mouth so sweet, so reverent, that she didn't feel even the ghost of self-consciousness about it. She leaned back, settling onto her elbows, then lifted her hips, helping him slide the waistband of her pants down and off her body. Before long her legs were bare, and his eyes locked on the sopping fabric plastered to the juncture of her thighs. He sat in his chair once more with a thump, looking dazed. "Seven hells, Claire. Is all that for me?" he asked, scooting forward and guiding her legs up and over his shoulders. She bit her lip, nodding.

"All for you," she whispered, undulating her hips in front of his face, arcing closer to that hot mouth of his.

He shuddered, closing his eyes for a moment, and she worried she was overwhelming him, but when his eyes snapped back open they were filled with heat and hunger, and he licked his lips, grinning at her like the big bad wolf who would very much enjoy eating her up. He began to press reverent kisses into the soft skin of her inner thighs, the granite gray of his skin so different from her warm brown, but so *right*, working his way up to her sopping apex. He breathed deep of her scent, another shiver wracking his big body. Then, to her surprise, he leaned forward and licked at the wet fabric of her panties, the heat and pressure, even through the barrier, utter heaven.

Growling low in his chest, his hand came up and took hold of this last scrap of clothing on her body, his claws carefully slicing into the fabric and severing its connection to her body.

"*Yes*, Beast," she mewled, arching her back and squeezing her breasts; it was so hot, so indescribably naughty, and she thought she was close to coming just from seeing that.

Or at least, that was what she thought, until she caught sight of his face settled between her thighs, his arms sliding around her legs to hold them in place, the fingers of one hand carefully spreading her lips apart. He stared at her bared sex for a moment, a choked whine making its way past his slack lips, and then his eyes locked on hers, burning into her very soul.

His mouth descended, the difference in their sizes making it so that he was almost able to completely cover her with his mouth, and she was nervous, for a moment, that he'd be too enthusiastic, too rough, but she should have had more trust.

She'd read those Garnette Mason books he loved so much. He'd been getting passive instruction for years. He'd probably only asked her earlier because of his nerves. But those had fled from him entirely, and now he was a force to be reckoned with, playing her body like a master musician at his instrument.

No one had ever done this for her before, the selfish lovers of her past unwilling to bestow more than a quick lick, usually not even anywhere near her clit, but Beast was a whole new animal. He knew exactly where to go, knew exactly what he was going for, and he was watching her, listening to her, reading the subtle signs of her body to chase whatever gave the best reactions. His beautiful mouth sent bolts of pleasure through her that shattered the last scraps of her mind. He licked firm, slow circles around her swollen bud, moaning and taking deep breaths of her scent, his fingertips pressing hard into her skin, but there was too much pleasure for her to register his bruising grip as pain.

The noises flying from her throat were unrecognizable, barely human, but she couldn't stop them. The noises were the only thing keeping her tethered to this plane, the waves of ecstasy generated by his talented tongue flooding her, swamping her, driving her awareness further and further away. She was overwhelmed with the sensation, every muscle in her body tightening with sinful slowness, lifting her pleasure ever higher. She was writhing beneath him, trying to rock her hips into his face, desperate for more pressure, more friction, but Beast was in control, and she was helpless but to let him take it.

She was so close, held on the cusp and half-mad with her need, her hands fisted in his hair, her front half curled forward, desperate for more, when he did something that surprised her. He ceased his maddening circles, taking her throbbing clit into his mouth, and *sucked.*

She snapped with a scream, white-hot lightning bolting through her as she finally crested the wave of her orgasm, harder than she ever had before, stars and sparks lighting up the dark behind her eyelids. He was still lapping at her, capturing her slick and drinking it down like he was sampling the waters of the fountain of life itself. He moaned, fingers tightening on her hips again, tight enough that she felt the prickle of his claw tips, and then his spine snapped straight, his mouth leaving her pussy and his eyes squeezing shut with a groan. He shuddered once, twice, before sagging forward to kiss and nibble at her inner thighs.

"Vitrin's mercy, Claire," he breathed, rubbing his cheek against her tender flesh. "Thank you for that."

She couldn't help the laugh that brayed out of her. "*You're* thanking *me?*" she exclaimed, propping herself back up on her elbows. "Sir, you just sent me to the plane of the gods with that mouth of yours. *I* definitely need to be thanking *you.*"

The grin he gave her was sheepish but proud, and still so full of heat. "I'm glad you liked it," he said, blushing.

She hauled herself fully upright, resting her hands on his shoulders. "Oh, I did," she assured him, her muscles still shivering with the aftershocks. She felt so light, so boneless and liquid. She slid her hands up the thick column of his throat, curving around to the back of his neck and into the soft crimson waves of his hair. He sighed, closing his eyes, as she began to massage his scalp. "Would you like for me to take care of you, now?"

His flush deepened, his eyes snapping open. "Oh that uh…that won't be necessary," he muttered, avoiding her eyes.

Her brow furrowed. "I want to do it, that's why I'm offering. You don't have to be shy, sweetheart."

He pursed his lips. "No, I know. And thank you." He leaned forward and kissed her, the taste of herself on his lips making her clench again.

"Is everything okay?" she asked, nuzzling her nose against his when he pulled back. "I just didn't think it was possible for a person with a penis to turn down oral sex."

He swallowed, pressing his lips into a tight line and squeezing his eyes shut. He slumped forward into her breasts, forcing his face between them. "It's embarrassing," he mumbled, voice muffled by her flesh.

"What's embarrassing? Maybe I can help, somehow?" her brow furrowed, her hands coming up to cradle his head against her chest and comb through his hair again.

He pulled back, sighing deeply. "It's not necessary because…well…" he leaned back, gesturing towards his crotch.

Glancing down, her breath hitched, her eyes widening. There was a huge wet spot on the front of his trousers; he'd come in his pants, just from eating her out. She whistled low. "I guess you definitely enjoyed yourself, then," she murmured, leaning down and nibbling at his earlobe. "We'll have to try that next time," she promised huskily.

He shuddered against her. *Oh, this is going to be so much*

fun, she thought, fresh heat rolling through her.

CHAPTER TWENTY-SEVEN

The Past Will Not Be Buried

Beast wasn't sure if he'd ever get used to the fact that he could reach out and hold Claire, that he could pull her into a kiss, that he could test the heft of her soft flesh in his hands, and she would *welcome* it. He couldn't believe that she was as hungry for his touch as he was for hers.

He couldn't believe that he'd made her feel good. That he'd even impressed her a little. Sure, he'd embarrassed himself a bit afterwards, but even that couldn't sour the memory of feeling her come undone against his mouth, knowing it was all because of *him* that she felt that. He wanted to spend the rest of his life bringing her pleasure, making her wild for his touch only to sate her so well she was boneless and dreamy. He couldn't even imagine what it would be like to sink into her, to feel her clenching and squeezing all around him. Even just holding her, touching her idly in little ways, was proving potent and satisfying in a whole new way that defied all of his fantasies.

They were in the library reading after dinner. It was her turn to read, and she was lying on top of him, curled so perfectly into his chest that he'd lost track of the thread of the story almost immediately. He had pulled up a footstool and was lounging comfortably, with Claire nestled on her side facing towards him in his lap. She read carefully from the book, her expressive face telling the story as much as the words on the page. And while she was doing this he could wrap his arms around her, trail his fingers up and down her arm, along the column of her spine, over her flared hips, and she was completely fine with it—she even leaned into it, subtly asking for *more* with little wiggles and nudges whenever he flagged.

His heart had never felt so full.

"Soliei was trapped firmly in the mad king's curse, which Fausta was helpless to break," she read, her forehead scrunching with concern. "But Fausta remembered what the sage had told her: 'the power of your love is strong enough to weather any storm, to light up any night, so long as you claim it true'. And so she strode up to the mad king, though she trembled and Soliei begged her to stay away, to save herself. But brave, sweet Fausta found her courage and her voice, and claimed her mate as her own for all the realm to hear. Her act cleaved like a blade through the mad king's spell…"

All at once, he lost his patience for the pretense of story-reading. He pulled his arms tight around her, squeezing her against him, and she dropped the book onto his hip with an indignant squeak.

"You made me lose my place!"

He leaned down and nuzzled his face into the soft ropes of her braids. "I wasn't paying attention anyway."

"What?! But that was the performance of a lifetime! I was bringing their story to *life*. It was stunning."

He chuckled, kissing the top of her head. "You were. You're very good. You're just also very…distracting."

Her hand slid over his chest, her fingers digging slightly into his pectoral as she bit her lip. "You're pretty distracting, yourself."

He felt himself blushing. He didn't quite believe her when she said things like that, but he couldn't deny that it was good to hear them. He captured her chin and tilted her face up towards him for a kiss. Her lips met his softly, eagerly, her hand on his chest curling into a fist that tugged at his shirt, urging him closer, deeper. His hand slid down to her hip, then lower, to cup her ass and hoist her up higher on his chest. She let out an appreciative hum, nipping gently at his bottom lip in a way that made his cock jump in his pants.

She was so soft in his arms, so warm. Her tongue darted in past his lips, exploring his mouth in slow, sensual sweeps, the sweetness of her taste flooding him, making him drunk. He couldn't stop the groan that ripped from his throat as she invaded his senses, becoming the entire focus of his existence. If the entire rest of his life was kissing Claire, holding her tight, trading stories and jokes, then it would be a perfect life. Every ounce of pain and terror he'd endured was worth it, to make it here, to be with her. For the first time in two hundred years, he hoped he'd get out not just to end the madness, but so that he could live again. Or perhaps even for the first time.

You don't deserve to live, worm, Naja's chill fury hissed at the back of his mind. He tried to fight it, tried to keep his focus on Claire and her roses and vanilla scent, on the feel of her skin brushing against his, on the way she was leaning into him more firmly, her breasts pressed deliciously against his chest—

But it was a losing battle. He broke their kiss, his heart sinking in his cold chest as shadow creatures laughed and circled closer.

"Uh oh," she murmured, cupping his face and forcing him to meet her eyes. "I know that look. What's wrong, sweet man? Where did you go?"

He shook his head. Could he even explain it with the gag in place? And if he could, how could he watch the easy affection in her hazel eyes curdle when she found out the truth of him?

But he had promised her that he'd try. He'd promised to be better. And didn't that mean at least attempting to explain?

He sighed, pulling her hands from his face and tucking her tight against his chest. "I just keep thinking about how you don't know why I'm here. You don't know what I've done. And I worry that once you *do* find out that you'll realize how awful I am, and you'll—you'll leave me. And I couldn't even blame you for it."

She was quiet in his arms, thinking about what he'd said. "You can't tell me what it was because of the gag, yes?"

"Yes."

"Did someone get hurt?"

"Yes." So badly.

"Did you hurt them directly? Were you malicious or cruel?"

He considered that. "Not initially. I think I was a kind of cruel, though."

She pulled back to look him in the eye again. He wanted nothing more than to hide from the scrutiny in her gaze, but he didn't want to run anymore—not from her. "There was more than one moment when I could have acted," he said quietly, the words sticking in his throat. "And I never did, even though I knew I should have."

She searched his face. "And because of that someone got hurt? Did they die?"

He squeezed his eyes shut, unable to even test if he *could* answer.

At first, he'd accepted the story that Ingrid had taken her own life. But over the years, he'd come to doubt it. She had been earnest in seeking justice, determined to shine the light on the crimes of two very prominent families. Families with a lot to lose in a scandal and plenty of money to keep it from happening, resources Ingrid didn't have. But if he had joined her fight, if he'd lent her his voice, he would have also lent her the protection of his family name, their status. And he knew, in the twisted pit of his heart, that that would have saved her.

He could have done so many things to save her.

"Y-yes," he finally choked out, shame cloaked tight around him. He wanted to pull her in tighter against him, and he wanted to send her away from him. Protect her from his weakness and failure.

As if sensing his mood shift, she shifted closer against him, wrapping her arms around his neck. "Maybe once I find out what happened it'll be difficult for me to hear. Maybe I'll have to wrestle with the knowledge, and maybe it will even change how I feel. But I don't think it will. I think even if it's bad, the fact that you're so—so *tortured* about it counts for something. We don't necessarily enter into our relationship as our best selves, but there's nothing stopping us from trying to *be* better." Her light brown eyes bored into his, looking for something, something that he hoped she'd find.

She shook her head, her braids swaying around her head.

"Nope, you're a good person. Hate to break it to you, but you're an absolutely decent sort, Beast." Her hands slid down his shoulders to his chest and fisted in the front of his shirt once more. "Now come back here and kiss me."

And even if he was still uneasy, there was no way that he could deny her request.

CHAPTER TWENTY-EIGHT

Bath

"Will we be meeting back up in the library after dinner to continue our book?" Beast asked as he speared the last mouthful of duck on one of his claws. He hoped so—he liked the book of fae folklore they were taking turns reading to each other, but he was most excited for her to slide into his lap, her sweet scent wrapped all around him. Delightfully, it had become her preferred seat for their cozy evenings.

He could lose her at any moment, and while the thought ripped him apart it also made him determined to squeeze everything he could out of every moment he had with her. As much as she would give him, he'd take, and bless every god in every realm for that gift.

She bit her lip, giving him a look he couldn't quite read but that caused his pulse to start racing. "I was actually thinking of taking a bath," she said, her voice soft. After a moment of hesitation, she added, "Would you like to join me?"

He was stunned, unable even to breathe. Had he...had he heard her right? Surely not. But she was looking at him with shy expectation, and not a little bit of heat in her piercing hazel gaze. Pearly teeth worried at her plump lip again. He blinked, shaking his head as if to clear it. "I'm sorry, I think I misheard you. What did you ask?"

"I asked if you wanted to join me for a bath."

"Ah."

He sat staring at her with his brow furrowed.

And then he was up, his chair flung back and flipped over. He scooped her up, cradling her against his chest, her chair joining his on the floor.

She laughed, slapping at his shoulder lightly, before wrapping both arms around his neck. "Is that a yes?"

He grunted, his mind a wordless maelstrom. She laughed again, nuzzling into his chest. Her sweetness made him clench.

As he mounted the stairs he hiked her higher, re-balancing so that he wouldn't drop her, putting her face up to his neck. He was intent on keeping his balance and his hold on her, and didn't notice when her breath fanned against his cheek. But when her slippery little tongue traced the shell of his ear, flicking gently at the pointed tip, he certainly noticed that.

He choked, spine snapping straight, his already hard cock surging painfully in his trousers. She chuckled throatily, her teeth biting at his earlobe, only for her to pull it into her mouth and gently suck on it, erasing that small hurt.

He shuddered, his hold on her tightening as he fought to stay on his feet.

"Vitrin's mercy, woman. Do you want me to drop you?"

"Mmm. I couldn't help myself. You're just so…tasty," and to prove her point her mouth trailed teasing, licking little kisses against the side of his neck.

He groaned, shuddering again at the wild heat flaring

through his taut body. Truly, there was nothing more sweet or maddening than the slow tease of her mouth on his skin. He was so hard and aching for her that he felt slightly dizzy. He sucked in a shaking breath and put on a careful burst of speed, heading for his bedroom. He suspected her bathtub would be too small for the both of them, so they'd use his.

Underneath the wildfire of his lust, nerves prickled, washing the flames cold at the edges. He was a virgin in all ways except what she had introduced him to, and he knew he would be awkward and over-sensitive with her. She was so lovely, so sweet, so precious, and he wanted nothing more than to please her. He knew the mechanics of what he should do, thanks to the romance novels he loved so much, but the reality was sure to be different, and he didn't want to disappoint her.

She had lit up his whole life, brighter than any sun. She had awoken all the dead frozen things inside himself that he had thought Naja had strangled decades ago, giving him warmth and light and *hope*. The least he could do was bring her pleasure. He wanted her delirious, panting, boneless in his arms when they finally joined…but he didn't know if he'd be able to do it.

Maybe he was overthinking things, though. Maybe it was just going to be a bath. A sexy one, sure, given how hungry her mouth was on him, but that didn't mean *sex*. Maybe he was getting ahead of himself.

But he was still going to get to see her naked again. Completely, utterly naked, her rich brown skin bared and gleaming wet, her hazel eyes soft and hot—

No, he couldn't think like that, his control was reduced to one frayed thread as it was. He didn't need a repeat of last time, when he'd spent in his pants without her so much as touching him. He still flamed with the embarrassment of that one.

"I'll draw the bath," he said, his voice rasping and husky. He cleared his throat. "Do you want to get your soaps or anything from your room?"

She shook her head, her delicate fingers creeping up to the top button of her tunic.

He spun around, fumbling with the taps. He tried to surreptitiously press a hand to his aching length, willing it to calm down and not embarrass him, not now when he had the most stunning creature in all Cillure soft and eager and waiting to come to his arms.

He took a steadying breath, testing the water temperature and adjusting it to what he thought she'd like.

"How's this?" he asked as he turned to gesture she should feel the water.

But when he looked over his shoulder at her she was naked. *Naked.* And smiling at him, her eyes heavy-lidded and sultry. Her fine-boned hands trailed over her curves, squeezing at her supple flesh, making him ravenous for another taste of her sweetness. His knees grew weak, and he sank to the edge of the tub to avoid falling onto the floor.

Claire was a dichotomy of strength and softness, of firm muscle and curving plumpness. He wanted his mouth on every inch of her, felt his hands tingling with the desire to reach out and touch her. He was fascinated by the way her breasts shifted and jiggled as her arms raised, the deep dusk of her areolas pinning his gaze, as she pulled her braids into a bundle on the top of her head to keep them dry. The swell of her hips looked like it would fit perfectly in his palms, and the sight of the tight dark curls at the apex of her velvety thighs made his mouth dry…and then water with hunger. He hadn't been able to get the taste of her out of his mind in the days since he'd spread her out on the dining room table. Her flavor had been salty, sweet, musky, and delicate all at once, and nothing else had tasted as good since. He almost lost control at the memory of her gasping and crying out, trembling with the force of the pleasure he had given her. He squeezed his eyes shut and clenched his hands tight on his knees.

"Are you alright? Beast?" she asked, and he heard the pad of her bare feet on the tiles.

He grunted, unsure. *Was* he alright? Just the sight of her was proving to be his undoing.

A hand on his right knee pushed his legs wider apart, and he felt her step between them, her body so close to his. Her hands went to his shoulders, kneading and rubbing gently, soothingly.

"You okay, big guy?" she asked again.

He opened his eyes, meeting hers. "You're so beautiful," he rasped, keeping his hands on his knees, not trusting himself to touch her and keep his sanity.

"Is this too much?"

He shook his head. "I want to do this. Sweet Delenaa, do I want this. But we haven't even done anything and I already feel…so much. And I—I want to make it good for you. Whatever we're doing here, I want you to enjoy it. I *need* that."

Her face softened, but the smile she gave him was full of heat and mischief.

"What if I told you that seeing you lose control would give me pleasure? What if I said that if you're feeling…overfull, shall we say? That I'd love to be able to help you out with that."

He swallowed hard, his eyes locked on her face. He had no words. Surely she wasn't serious?

But her gentle hands were moving down his chest, his skin tingling with her touch, creeping to the buttons keeping his shirt closed. Slowly, she undid each button, tugging the hem out from his trousers to be able to get the last two. She smoothed her palms over his heaving chest, pushing the loose fabric back and off his shoulders.

"Gods, but you're beautiful," she breathed, freeing his arms from the tangle of his shirt fabric and leaning past him briefly to turn off the water, which he had forgotten utterly. Her breasts pressed against his chest, sliding over towards his arm as she pressed close, and the sound that came out of him was very nearly a whimper.

Straightening, she grabbed his clenched fists and put them at her waist. "You can touch me," she said, returning her own hands to their perusal of his chest and shoulders.

She lifted one of his limp, sweating hands and pressed it to the soft mound of one of her breasts. He sucked in a breath, his hand flexing carefully on her silky skin. She was soft everywhere, but the skin here was softer still, so delicate he feared he'd hurt her.

She arched into his touch, making a low sound of pleasure in her throat. "Use your mouth on my nipples," she breathed, and he was happy to oblige. He pressed soft kisses to the delicate flesh, tracing the shiny pale streaks of stretch marks on the underside with his tongue, then moving around in a wide spiral, gradually working his way to the pebbled peak of her nipple, already stiff from his attentions.

As his mouth wrapped around her firm nub of flesh, so soft yet hard at the same time, she moaned, her hands diving into his hair and gripping fistfuls of it. He teased at the firm tip with his tongue, swirling and flicking and making sure to imitate what his tongue was doing with his hand on the other breast. He sucked at her, experimenting, and as he did her hands tightened in his hair, her breath hissing through her lips.

He switched sides, looking up at her through his lashes, watching her face carefully for her reactions. Her eyelids fluttered, her lips pressed together as a delicious little whimper escaped her. He shuddered, the sound so lovely and erotic, and he decided there and then that his only goal in life was to wring more sounds like that out of her.

Deciding to be bold, he lowered his head to the valley between her breasts, where the scent of her skin got deliciously warm and intense, and ran his hands down her sides and around to cup the generous swell of her ass. Her eyes opened, her smile wicked and full of promise.

"That's more like it," she purred, lowering her face to his neck. "I love the way you touch me." She trailed hot kisses down the column of his throat, nipping and licking, teasing at his skin until he was panting, his hands flexing and clenching on her ass. "Why don't we get those pants off you and get in the water before it gets cold?" she asked with one last languid lick.

He stood shakily, his hands sweating and fumbling at the waist of his pants, desperate to do her bidding.

While he wrestled with his clothes she stepped gingerly into the large bath, groaning at the heat. She slipped beneath the water, sinking up to her collarbones. After an agonizing few moments, he finally managed to get his legs free and tossed his twisted-up trousers away, lowering his big body gracelessly into the water beside her. He tried to do it quickly, so she wouldn't see too much of his achingly erect cock, damp with precum already and bobbing obscenely with his steps. He was eager to touch her, but still so nervous about his own body. All of his insecurities were crashing around in his head, and he knew the only way he'd be able to stay in the moment was if he stayed focused on Claire.

As he settled on the bottom, his back against one side, she floated closer. The water only came up to mid-chest on him, their heights were so different, even sitting. He wrapped an arm around her shoulders, pulling her close and meeting her upturned face for a kiss. He lived for her kisses, for the perfect plushness of her lips against his, for the taste of her as their tongues slid against each other, probing and caressing and so, so slick. His free hand came up to knead her breast, rolling her nipple between his thumb and forefinger. She gasped against his mouth, arching closer to him, her skin pure slippery silk in the warmth of the bathwater.

One of her hands cupped the back of his neck, her fingertips digging into the base of his scalp, while her other hand began to drift low. Her fingers trailed over one of his pectorals, circling one of his nipples, sending a bolt through him that made him nip gently at her lip. And then she moved her hand lower, down his thick stomach with agonizing slowness, and when he realized what she was doing he pulled back, eyes wide.

"Is this okay?" she asked, her hand moving to his thigh.

"I...you want to do that?"

She nodded, smiling and kissing him again. "Oh yeah,"

she whispered, her fingers skating ever so lightly against his shaft.

Even that small touch was almost overwhelming, his entire body jerking and sending water sloshing over the side. His head fell back, eyes screwed shut, his breath ragged in his throat.

She leaned in to lick and kiss at his neck some more, her hand wrapping around him at the base of his cock and squeezing. "Easy, I've got you. You're doing so good," she murmured between kisses, and hearing her praise him like that did something to him, heightening his arousal and soothing his nerves all at once.

Her hand began to stroke him under the water, her other hand gently massaging his scalp, and he would not have been surprised to find his brain dripping out of his ears at that moment. He was already right at the edge, his whole groin aching in time with his pulse, and her hands—gods, her *hands*. He thought it would be something like when he touched himself, but it wasn't anything like that, it was an insult to her to have even considered it.

"What about the bathwater?" he growled, fighting to maintain his control.

"Who cares? We'll run more," she responded, her hand squeezing tighter as she stroked him from root to tip. "I want to see you come, Beast," she murmured, nipping at his earlobe again, "can you do that for me?" He was lost, he was falling, and when she rolled the pad of her thumb around the tip of him he came undone, his orgasm barreling through him and tearing the breath from his lungs. He'd never come so hard in his life—stars danced behind his eyes, his body rigid and arching off the bottom of the tub. He heard, dimly, from very far away, his own choking gasp. And he heard Claire—sweet, sinful, delicious Claire—whispering in his ear as she continued to work him, wringing him dry: "That's it baby, come for me. You're doing so good."

The sound he made was inhuman.

CHAPTER TWENTY-NINE
Deluge

Claire hadn't realized just how arousing it could be watching a partner come utterly undone in your hands. She was so turned on she thought that she might come alongside Beast, her sex clenching around nothing as she watched his mouth drop open, the cords on his neck going taut and his eyes squeezing shut in a look of such intense bliss she wasn't sure how it was possible she was the reason for it. She bit her lip, gasping and murmuring encouragement to him, squeezing her thighs together under the water and feeling just how slick she was getting, the wetness somehow so different from that of the water. She wasn't sure what had made her coo so many filthy praises at him, but it had satisfied something primal inside her, and it had seemed to get Beast even more worked up.

He insisted they drain the bath and refill it right away, and so they slipped out of the water, unable to keep their hands off each other while they waited.

This was the first time she was seeing him naked, and it was affecting her more strongly than she could have ever guessed. She had known he was big and muscular, but his clothes had obscured all of the finer details, and they were certainly *fine*. He wasn't lean, every muscle defined and on display like an athlete's would be—which made sense, given all his hobbies involved sitting around for long periods of time —but she found she loved that little bit of softness on him. It made her arousal spiral even higher, in fact, when she pressed herself into the front of him for a kiss and felt both solidness and softness molding to her. It allowed her fingers to sink deliciously into his flesh, let her grab handfuls of him that called for her mouth to follow where her digits led.

He sat heavily on the edge of the bath, his thigh muscles shivering faintly, and she felt a bright surge of satisfaction at how hard she'd made him come. She had been worried, for a brief moment, that she had actually managed to kill him, but he was all languid smiles and grabbing hands now.

She had been a bit concerned about just how proportionate his cock would be to the rest of him, and she was relieved to find that he wasn't obscenely well-endowed. It would be a tight fit, she thought, but she was confident she could take him. Her fingers had been able to just touch when she held him in her grasp, and his length might be enough to keep him from being able to get seated to the hilt before he encountered her cervix, but even then it might be able to work, with enough patience and care. She clenched in anticipation, and suddenly she was too hot, too tightly wound, and wasting more time in the bath sounded like torture.

"I changed my mind," she gasped in between feverish kisses, and to her dismay his hands immediately fell away from her.

"Not like that," she chided, grabbing his massive hands and placing them firmly back onto her breasts. "I meant about the bath." She leaned in and licked slowly up a tendon on the side of his neck, basking in the way he shivered against her, his hands tightening on her delicate flesh, kneading her breasts. Reaching his ear, she trailed her tongue along the outer shell and nipped at the sensitive point, making his cock twitch with the first signs of life against her pelvis. She grinned against his ear, moaning softly as his thumbs rolled over her nipples. "Come to bed with me, Beast," she whispered, nibbling on his ear again.

He pulled back, searching her face with eyes that were glazed and lidded. "You're sure?" he breathed, his eyes drinking in the sight of her from top to bottom, heating her skin further. She nodded, stepping back, pulling on his hands to bring him with her. He rose, following her easily, his already-hard cock jutting out, straining towards her. *Soon, my pet,* she promised it silently.

She led him out of the bathroom and into his bed by the hand, unable to stop herself from adding some extra sway to her hips as she walked. She wanted to drive him wild, make him lose his self-consciousness and nerves like he had at breakfast the other day. Already she was seeing his discomfort melting away, replaced with raw hunger...but he could stand to lose more.

Her hand was suddenly empty, and she half-turned to see why he had dropped it, but before she could complete the movement his arms were wrapping tight around her, one arm banded tight against her breasts, the other snaking across her belly to clasp her hip. She squealed as she was pressed back against his big barrel chest, her feet lifting off the floor.

"What are you *doing*?" she gasped as his mouth found her neck, nibbling and kissing at the sensitive skin and making her shiver.

"Too slow," he growled, the rumble of it seeping into her back and sending a bolt of need straight to her slick, swollen clit. In two more strides he had them at the bed, tossing her down onto the mattress, belly down, with a bounce that made her giggle.

Then she was being flipped onto her back, strong fingers taking firm hold of her thighs and spreading them wide. Cool air whispered over her hot, sopping sex, making her bite her lip.

"I have no words, Claire. To say you're beautiful just… isn't enough." he crawled onto the bed, settling on his knees between her spread thighs, making her gulp and arch towards him, her hips rocking in invitation. He pursed his lips, shuddering gently as a bead of precum dribbled down the swollen mauve head of his cock. He released her legs, grabbing her around her ribs instead and sliding her back into the mountain of pillows at the head of the bed. "Get comfortable, gorgeous," he ordered her huskily, Claire desperate to obey. *This* was what she wanted to see from him, what she wanted from him: his gaining confidence in himself and in her, taking equal part in the pleasure they were building together. She wanted him *present,* not trapped in his head.

"I've been thinking about eating this pussy nonstop since last time," he rumbled, sliding down onto his belly between her legs again, placing reverent kisses on her thighs, her hips, her mound. "I can't get the taste of you off my tongue. Nothing else tastes so good," he continued, nuzzling at her folds with his proud, jutting nose. She couldn't stop her hips from lifting up, trying to press up into his face, her nerves lit up blazing-bright and desperate for friction. She was burning up with desire, her body already slick with sweat as she panted and writhed on the bed, no room for anything in her mind except pure want.

"Then stop torturing me and eat it," she heard herself pant out, her hands coming up to massage her breasts, gently pinching and tugging on her nipples to punctuate her request.

He groaned, his mouth finally, blessedly, going to where she needed him, and the relief was so intense she nearly screamed. Her hips bucked and rocked against his mouth, though he was trying to keep her still with his thick, strong arms. But her need was so great, her body strung so tight, and she was already close, teetering on the edge of her orgasm. But she needed more, wanted him inside her too, filling the aching hollow at her core.

He shifted, one of his arms leaving her hip. He pulled his mouth away from her with a very wet sound, kissing her mound where her thatch of hair was thickest, making her whimper with how bereft she felt with it gone. "Don't stop, please don't stop. I'm so *close*," she begged, straining towards him.

"Don't worry, love, I'm going to take care of you." He placed a kiss right on her throbbing clit, making her gasp and sob at how terribly brief that contact had been. "But I wanted to ask..." his smoldering brown eyes caught hers as the hand that had left her hips slithered over her leg, leaving a trail of goosebumps in its wake, only to come up to stroke lazily through her sopping folds. "I wanted to try using my hands, too. Is that alright?"

She wanted to scream. Was that *alright*? "Be careful of your claws," she panted, her eyes locked on his face as his pink tongue darted out to circle her swollen bud with just the tip, just the barest tease.

He spread his fingers and wiggled them at her, and she noticed with a jolt that his claws were gone.

He'd cut off all his claws. Recently, because she could have sworn she saw them at breakfast that morning.

She moaned, throwing her head back. Why was that so *hot*? He'd prepared for this. Had realized those daggers didn't belong anywhere near her most sensitive parts, and had decided that that was just no good, and got rid of them. But only on one hand, she realized—she could see the glittering tips of his claws on the hand that was still wrapped around her thigh.

Sparks glittered along her spine as his mouth returned to her clit, his tongue working her firmly, precisely, giving her so much delicious pressure, and with his fingers sliding through her lips, gathering her slick, carefully circling her entrance, it was too much for her to hold in, and she did scream now.

A chuckle drifted up from between her legs and she pried her eyes open, looking down the length of her body at him again. "What?" She demanded as he let his index finger slip inside of her, making her gasp.

He released her clit with a pop, grinning up at her with those wicked teeth on full display. "There you go screaming again," he chuckled, and she couldn't help laughing along with him.

But then his finger pressed into a spot inside of her that she'd only ever read about, and all the laughter died in her throat. He pressed into it again, this time with a little more pressure, and she screamed again at the sensation. It was almost like she had to pee suddenly, but more tingling, more intense. "There it is," he purred, sliding his finger free of her sheath so he could add a second one. As he hit that wondrous spot again with his fingers he returned his mouth to her clit, suckling at it like she liked, and she was lost to madness. She squeezed her eyes shut against the explosive buildup of sensation and tension in her body, stars and sparks fizzing to life behind her eyelids.

The noises that were bursting from her throat didn't sound like her, but she was too far gone to care, her every nerve alight and straining towards the peak he was bringing her to. He sped up his fingers, and she shook her head. "No, slow. Slow and steady, like you had it," she panted, and he immediately obeyed, sending her rocketing towards her orgasm. It hit her so hard her vision went black at the edges and one of her ears started ringing.

She sank back into herself by degrees, her skin slicked with sweat and sticking her hair to her face, her neck. He was still between her legs, working her gently and bringing her down from those unthinkable heights...but also sparking fresh embers of desire in her.

With a rush of embarrassment she realized the bedding under her ass was *soaked*. Had she actually wet the bed?

"Why is it wet?" She asked in a panic, scooting back and pulling herself free of his hungry mouth.

"You gushed!" he crowed, grinning at her like he'd won some great prize.

"I—I wet the bed?" she asked in horror.

He shook his head, licking her wetness from his lips. "Don't think so. It uh...doesn't smell like that. Looked pretty clear."

"I didn't pee myself?" she asked breathlessly. She hadn't

known that she could do that—that she could...*gush*, as he'd said. It made her flush.

She clapped her hands over her mouth, shocked. She did remember reading something about that in one of the Garnette Mason books he'd lent her, but she thought that that was some sort of fantastical make-believe. "I didn't know I could do that," she confessed from behind her hands.

She still felt very loose and shivery with aftershocks. But when Beast rolled onto his side, his cock so swollen and flushed it looked painful, her hunger surged back to the forefront of her mind.

She wasn't done with him.

Not by a long shot.

CHAPTER THIRTY

Earth-Shattering

Beast was quite proud of himself and the spell he'd wrought upon Claire's body. She'd been surprised by some of the things he'd just wrung out of her, her body glistening with sweat and her own arousal, making her burnished skin positively glow in the low light. He couldn't stop the proud grin from plastering itself across his face. When her hazel eyes finally snapped into focus and locked with his, his smile froze in place and his breath stuck in his throat.

He gulped. The look in her eyes was *dangerous*.

She pounced before he could brace himself, landing on top of him and forcing him onto his back. Her mouth crashed into his, her kiss devoid of any soft edges and tenderness: it was all hunger and fire, making his cock weep with want for her. His hands had gone unsteady, gripping Her hips tight as they rolled and rocked, sliding her slick cunt along the tip of his cock.

He gasped into her mouth at the blast of sensation that impaled him at the feel of her on him, at the slippery heat of her, the pressure and friction she was gifting to him with her sensual movements. He groaned into her mouth, his fingers tightening into her soft skin.

She ripped her mouth away with a gasp, both of them panting and dazed. The grin she shot him was full of heat and promise. She kissed him again, then with one last rock of her hips began trailing more kisses down his body, lighting him up like a bonfire. When he realized what she was doing, where she was going, his heart stopped. He pulled a pillow over to prop his head on, because this…this he wanted to watch.

She settled between his thick thighs, her hands rubbing them slowly, combing through the fine down of his body hair. She bit her lip, staring down at his cock so intently it jumped, and she smiled again, looking up into his eyes.

"I'm going to have a lot of fun with this," she breathed, leaning down and slowly, so slowly, inching her parted lips towards the weeping head of his cock.

When her lips closed around him and he got his first taste of the hot wetness of her mouth, it took all of his self-control to stop himself from bucking his hips up into her mouth. He knew he was much larger than her, and that something like that, taking her by surprise, could so easily hurt her, and that was the last thing he wanted. His hands fisted the blankets, wrapping so tightly into the fine fabric that it tore, making her laugh throatily, and he *felt it*, felt her laughter like a sizzling hum against his member, and it took his breath away.

His world was rocked, shattered, vaporized in the wake of her tongue, her lips, her spit-slicked fingers. He could feel the pressure building already, his balls tight against his body as she kissed and nibbled and licked him like he was the finest meal she'd ever had.

He was making sounds, he realized: they didn't sound like him, and most of it was a kind of directionless pleading. He didn't know what he was pleading *for*, exactly, only that the waves of pleasure were sweeping his mind far out to sea.

Just when he was about to say something, his awareness coming in just close enough that he realized he should warn her about how close he was, she released him, sitting up and wiping the back of her hand across her shining mouth. He gulped down air, reaching for her, clutching at her, pulling her down for another kiss because he needed to ground himself somehow, and there was nothing quite as soothing as the smell of her. Roses and vanilla, his rock in the storm of his pleasure.

"Claire," he gasped, so awed by her, so in love with her, that it was an ache in his chest. He felt like he might cry, the feel of her skin on his, the weight of her body against his was so *right*, so *perfect*, more stunning than anything in this world had any right to be.

She pulled away gently, cupping his face in her hands, and he saw the impossible, saw the same love he felt reflected back at him, cracking him open, searing him alive, and he couldn't stop the tear that slipped out. She gave him a watery smile of her own, but while her eyes glazed no tears fell. "I know," she whispered. She kissed him again, lingeringly.

And then she slid down his body, her hands pressing into his pectorals as she lifted herself up, hovering in the air over his aching cock. She reached down, grabbing him firmly, and guided the head of him to her entrance. She pressed down, just the littlest bit, just enough that the head of him began to breach her, and they both seemed to hold their breath.

"You're okay with this?" she asked in a gasp, holding herself still. He nodded, his hands releasing the shredded wads of fabric from his late blanket, settling them onto her round hips. His thumbs traced the jut of her hip bones, then he thrust up into her, and he was well and truly lost.

If her mouth had been heaven, her cunt was above that, some forbidden realm that mortals were not meant to taste, and all he could do was cling to his composure and try to remember to breathe. She was so hot, and wet, and *tight*, and it was almost immediately too much.

She moaned, rocking her hips to take more of him, and he clutched at her hips, halting her movements, desperate for this not to be over yet. She stilled, her eyes sliding open to look at his face.

"You okay, big guy?" she asked, settling her hands on top of his at her hips.

"I...I think I need a minute."

She nodded, her brow lowering in concern. "Breathe," she urged gently, lifting herself off of his cock and sitting on one of his thighs. "My legs were going to give out if I just hovered like that," she explained, continuing to rub her hands on his body slowly, comfortingly.

"I'm sorry," he ground out, his voice dry and gravelly to his own ears.

"Don't be," she murmured, one of her hands leaving his skin and slipping towards the apex of her thighs. He swallowed as she dipped her fingers into her folds, moving in rapid circles that made her breath hitch. She moaned again, rocking her pelvis against his leg, soaking his skin with her arousal, and all he could do was stare at her, in awe. His hands began kneading at her legs, trailing up slowly to her waist, her breasts, having to curl up off the bed to reach her, but so caught up in the unearthly beauty of her chasing her pleasure that he didn't even notice the discomfort in his stomach.

"That's it, Claire," he breathed and she began to cry out, close to another orgasm already. "You're so beautiful, sweetheart. I want to see you come again."

Abruptly, her fingers stopped, sliding away from her pinkish-brown bud, and she climbed back onto his lap, slotting him back into her and sinking down with painful, delicious slowness that had them both moaning and panting.

"Gods, you feel so good," she gasped, her eyes squeezed shut as she braced herself on her hands against his chest. "I was worried you'd be too big but—" she gasped, her eyelids fluttering, "you're fucking *perfect*."

He had no words, but he agreed that what they were doing was perfection, was the most astounding thing that he had ever experienced, and despite the desperate way he was clawing for control, it was quickly overwhelming him.

She rocked into him, taking more of his cock into her sweet and sopping cunt with every rotation of her hips, until he was fully seated, their skin smacking together sinfully. His toes curled, his head falling back, as something that could only be described as a roar tore from his throat. His hands shot out to grab her hips, his only lifeline in the storm ravaging his insides, as each rock of her hips had him sliding closer and closer to his orgasm.

Her hand returned to her clit, making her scream as she rode him faster, harder, and he couldn't stop himself from thrusting up into her, meeting her pelvis with his own and squeezing still more friction in, more pleasure, until he was delirious. He could feel her tightening and fluttering around him, squeezing him with her inner walls, and it was torture, it was madness, it was salvation, and he was not going to be able to hold out anymore. But that goddess, that glorious creature bouncing and crying out above him, locked eyes with him and bit her lip.

"Come with me, baby," she gasped out, her voice little more than a whine at the end, and then it was like he was being gripped in a tight fist that was pulsing and shivering—her orgasm, he realized with a shock—and he could hold out no longer, his own orgasm boiling out of him, ripping through him like a bolt of lightning and flooding his body with pure ecstasy. She continued rocking on him, her movements erratic and slower, as he emptied into her.

For what might have been the first time in his life, he was calm and relaxed, utterly at peace. He had left his body behind, and at the same time he had never been more aware of it. Eventually he started to slide back into himself, every muscle feeling wrung out and tingling.

With a sigh, she collapsed forward onto his chest, causing his softening cock to slide out of her. She nuzzled into his chest, her hand stroking along his upper arm. He pulled her in tight, wanting there to be no part of his body that wasn't covered by her.

Neither of them spoke, instead gently panting and trading soft caresses. There wasn't anything *to* say, really; the tandem shuddering of their heartbeats, the warmth of her skin against his, the way their scents had mingled in the air, spoke of all of the love and passion that had just passed between them.

He tightened his hold on her, determined to never let her go. "I love you so much, Claire," he whispered into her sweaty hair, breathing her in.

Her arms tightened on him too, her face snuggling closer against his chest. "I love you too, sweet man. So, so much."

CHAPTER THIRTY-ONE

Adeela

As much as Claire wanted to spend the next three years in bed with Beast, learning his body and teaching him hers, there was quite a lot of work for her to do. The most terrible thing about this work, by far, was that it required she make another trip over to Edden. She needed to ensure that Kiernan was being handled properly and likely give a statement to the sheriff. Then she had to get the gears moving on the lengthy process of getting Consortium officials out to the manor to investigate the legitimacy of Beast's confinement. It wouldn't hurt to replenish some of her travel rations, either.

And beyond that, she thought it was time to break out the communicator. It was an expensive luxury, but one that had felt essential as she had been forced to reckon with her first prolonged absence from Adeela. She wanted—no, *needed*—to talk to her mother and get some clarity on her situation with Beast. Things were getting so serious with him, and even though it felt right in a way that nothing had before in her life, it also scared her, and there was no way to convey it all in a letter. Was this too much too fast? Should she be concerned about encountering barriers to their being together?

Was it too soon to be considering marriage?

She wasn't about to drag him to the altar right away, or even in the near future—but it had popped into her mind. She'd found herself thinking, with a warm kind of ache, of how happy she would be spending her whole life with him at her side, making her laugh, and think, and feel cherished. A lifetime of coaxing blushes and bravery from her gentle mountain of a man. And if she wasn't mad for thinking like that, then wouldn't it make sense for them to invest in their relationship accordingly now? Once he was free, things would look different if he was staying with her versus if he wasn't, after all. And she thought it might help him, to give him that kind of security.

But it was too scary for her to just talk about it with him, at least right now. She was worried that she was getting too invested too fast, and that once she'd aired all this out her feelings would shrivel and fall away somehow. That she'd break his heart beyond repair. So it was better to keep it locked up away from him for now, to save it until she was more sure of herself.

The day after their first time having sex was spent in bed. They only got up to use the bathroom and hastily scarf down enough food and water to keep them going between furious bouts of lovemaking. They would come together, sometimes slow and languorous and sweet, sometimes hard and fast and blisteringly hot, and then doze for a time, only to wake to one stroking, or licking, or sucking, and then they were in the thick of it all over again.

She had never orgasmed so often or so thoroughly in her life. She'd think that she was done, that there was no way he could wring another one from her tired, sweat-soaked body, only for him to get a very fervent and determined look on his face that would prove the harbinger of yet another delicious, shuddering peak. It was like it was a game to him, to outdo himself each time and make her come more times than he'd managed before.

There were worse problems for someone to have.

It was towards evening now. She was on her hands and knees, Beast pumping into her from behind, hitting that special spot inside her so perfectly with each thrust that she thought her limbs would actually collapse this time, her arms and legs already shuddering violently. The iron-hard grip of his hands on her hips was likely to bruise, and she didn't care in the slightest—it didn't hurt, it felt *right*, a delicious mark of their mutual possession.

"Spank me, Beast," she gasped out, surprising herself. But there was something about the way her flesh snapped when his hips met her body as he pumped into her that had her wanting *more*—more contact, more heat, more claiming.

He was so lost in her that he didn't even question it—he did as she asked, his hand with the short nails connecting with her ass cheek with a sharp sting of pleasure-pain that had her crying out, her orgasm building even quicker now.

"Yes, just like that," she groaned as he rubbed the sting out of her flesh. "Gods baby, you fuck me so good."

She felt him tremble behind her as he smacked her ass again, squeezing her before he soothed, and she knew he was as close as she was. She'd been delighted to discover earlier that he seemed to really enjoy it when she heaped praise on him, that he liked it when she directed him and took charge of things. And she was quite shocked to find that she enjoyed *being* in charge—she never would have thought of that for herself, but now that she was experiencing it, it was heady and fulfilling.

"You gonna make me come so hard, baby?" she panted, looking back at him over her shoulder. His eyes were closed, his jaw tense and brow furrowed in concentration, sending a hot thrill through her belly. "You better come with me, Beast."

His pace sped up, becoming more frantic, more uneven, and then he pressed deep into her and cried out, his hot length surging and pulsing inside her with his release, the sensation the last push she needed to tumble over the edge herself with a scream she muffled in the bedding. His hips twitched a few more times, his breathing ragged, and then he collapsed forward against her back. One of his arms banded around her middle, and then he guided both of them onto their sides, still buried inside her and twitching.

She patted his arm affectionately. "Good boy," she panted, grinning. "I knew you could do it."

He nuzzled his face into her damp, mussed hair and breathed deep, kissing her just behind her ear. "I live to serve," he rumbled, pressing kisses to her face and neck and holding her tight against him. She twisted her head back to capture his lips in a kiss. Neither of them was particularly fresh, but she found she didn't care, that even with morning breath his taste was everything, so sweet and *right*, and always somehow delicious.

They were quiet for a time, just holding each other, when she decided it was time to shatter their peace with her announcement.

"I hate to do this, sweet man," she began, spinning in his

arms to face him. "But I think I have to make another trip to Edden. Possibly tomorrow."

From the devastation on his face, it felt like she'd told him she was going to have to put him to death. "So soon?" he asked.

She nodded, pressing a kiss to the tip of his nose and adjusting so she could cradle him against her chest. She began finger-combing the snarls and knots out of his hair, her other hand stroking along his back. "I know, it's the absolute worst gods-damned timing. But the sooner I go in and get the process started on the investigation the sooner we can get you out of here. I really think they'll find that you're here illegally, and then the full strength of the Consortium will be behind us to break your enchantments. And then we can be together all the time. You can come with me wherever we need or want to go. You can make a life for yourself, do whatever you want. And I want that for you, love. Don't you?"

He was quiet for a moment, holding her tight. "I do," he finally agreed, burrowing his face closer to her chest, pressing light kisses to the tops of her breasts. "It's just so hard when you're gone. I feel…" He sighed, arms tightening. "I feel like I'm dying," he finished in a whisper.

She held him tighter, her heart breaking for her Beast. "Sweet man," she murmured into his hair, "I know it's got to be hard for you, and I'm sorry I have to do it. But I need you to hear this—are you listening?" He nodded. "I am always going to come back to you. *Always*. Do you hear me?"

"Yes." The word was muffled against her flesh.

"And just think: after this, the next time I leave the manor, you might be leaving with me. Isn't that exciting?"

He hummed, his face rubbing against her breasts in a way

that felt distinctly less sweet and more hungry. He shifted, rising up on an elbow and gently pressing her into the bed, nipping at her breasts, his shockingly pink tongue darting out to lave her nipple.

"If you're going to be leaving then I'll have to make sure you're clean," he murmured, licking her again, then beginning to slide down her body, leaving a tingling trail from his tongue and lips.

"You going to give me a tongue bath, is that the plan?"

His answer was giving her a long, languorous lick down the messy seam of her pussy, where their mingled releases were still damp.

All thoughts of leaving fled from her mind. She could think about her trip some other time, she reasoned.

Tearing herself away from Beast had been physically painful, the anguish on his haggard gray face making tears prickle at the back of Claire's eyes. But they both knew it needed to be done.

Between the milder weather and her added urgency, she made it to Edden in no time at all. She stopped by the jail to sign off on the arrest and give her statement. Kiernan was already on his way to Citrine, the officer told her, giving her a look like he wasn't happy about it. She vaguely recalled that Kiernan was the mayor's son, and no doubt there'd been a big fuss about it. But it was up to the judiciary office now. She left as soon as she could, though she was glad that it was done and no longer hanging over her head, and secured a room at the *Spur*, locking herself in to try and get ahold of Adeela.

She scooped the peat-smelling activator paste out of its jar and smeared it onto the mirrored face of the large pendant, using her fingertip to carefully scrape the runes listed in the instructions sheet into the thick, goopy layer. As soon as she finished the last rune they sank into the palm-sized mirror as if it were made of cheesecloth instead of glass, the silver bleeding out into the gray-brown color of the paste. Once the paste was completely absorbed, she lifted her arm so that the pendant was level with her face and waited. She had told Adeela to keep it close, that the pendant would shiver and change color when she was trying to reach her, but there was always the possibility that Adeela had misplaced it, or that she was busy, and that she would be waiting for hours or gods forbid *days* before Adeela found the pendant and answered her call. She hoped it wouldn't come to that, though. She was already antsy and unsettled from being away from Beast this long, and thought he must be feeling at least as bad. She was afraid of what that darkness of his would do to him if he was left alone for too long. She thought he was getting better, the longer they were together and working on it, but Claire was all he had, and that made the progress so painfully slow.

Her heart thumped wildly in her chest, her limbs loose and jittery with nerves as the minutes dragged on. She was beyond excited at the prospect of getting to see her dearest friend, her found mother, again after so many months away but she couldn't deny that her purpose for calling scared her enough that a small part of her hoped Adeela *wouldn't* pick up the pendant on her end. Though she trusted Adeela with anything, with *everything*, she'd never talked with her about things like what she was feeling for Beast, because she'd never been in love before. And admitting out loud to someone else, even if it was just Dee, felt…risky. Like by speaking it outside the safe closeness of the manor, she'd be able to call the wrath of the gods down upon them both.

Luckily it was only a matter of a few minutes before the glass cleared, her heart soaring in excitement at seeing the woman who had raised her and loved her as if Claire were her own daughter for the first time in months. Adeela would help —Adeela would know what she should do.

"Claire? Honey?"

Claire laughed, the image in the glass congealing into a closeup of Adeela's mouth and nostrils.

"I'm talking to the inside of your nose. Lift it up higher, Dee," she instructed, tears of relief threatening at the backs of her eyes. "Like you're looking in a regular mirror."

"How can you hear me if it's all the way up there?"

"It'll pick it up. That's how I'm holding it and you can hear me, right?"

The image shifted, Adeela's gently lined pale brown face coming into view. Her warm clove-colored eyes crinkled warmly as she beamed at Claire.

"Hi, baby," Adeela said softly, and now the tears were no longer threatening, they were gathering, and they were falling, as those two words sank into her heart and unlocked something she had been holding tight and tense for too long.

"Hey, mama," she murmured back, her voice wobbling. "How've you been, Dee?"

Adeela shook her head, her short salt-and-pepper curls bouncing gently against her temples. "Too busy for a retired woman. Catalina is engaged now, to that nice young man apprenticing at the bookshop, and helping her get ready has been a nightmare as much as it's been a blessing."

They chatted for a while, Adeela catching her up on the town gossip and assuring her that her sisters and father were doing well, and Claire outlining her progress on the quest since her last letter. She found herself second-guessing her decision to talk to Adeela about her situation with Beast. It was so much simpler now, keeping it all locked away. Even just telling Adeela would set things in motion, make the feelings more real, more heavy, and now that she was so close to speaking them aloud she wasn't sure anymore that that was what she wanted.

But of course Adeela knew something was bothering her, and when a natural silence fell she tucked in her chin and speared Claire with one of the intense, searching looks that had figured so prominently in her childhood. It was a look that she always dreaded, because she knew it meant something hidden was about to see the light of day and squirm with attention it didn't want. She braced herself, holding her breath.

"Now, as much as I love hearing from you and getting a chance to catch up, I know my Claire-bear and I know what that look is on your face right now: you got something you want to say. And it's not an easy thing, is it?"

She closed her eyes, drawing in a shuddering breath. "No, Dee. It's…I just feel like I can't get my head on straight."

Adeela nodded, her deep brown eyes locked on her face. Claire sighed, finding her own eyes drifting up to the ceiling of the tiny room she was renting.

"Well, you know that Beast person I was telling you about, how we get along really well and how he's been a really good friend while I've been here?"

Adeela nodded, and when she managed to look at the

older woman again she squirmed under the knowing in that shrewd gaze. Claire bit her lip, not sure how to phrase it now, all of her prepared speeches dissolving on her tongue.

"I love him, Dee" she whispered at last, her eyes squeezing shut, trying to contain fresh tears. "And we're…we're in a relationship now."

She heard Adeela click her tongue, and Claire's heart sank, thinking she was going to get a lashing, that judgment was coming down hard on her, even though Adeela had never been like that, had always accepted her and loved her as she was. But her own flesh and blood family rejected her, thought she was just too damn *much*, and a part of her was always bracing for when that same rejection was going to happen with Adeela.

"Sweet girl," Adeela said gently, and she opened her eyes, relief flooding her limbs and making them sag into the chair beneath her. "I take it you have some questions about these feelings then, since you're here talking to me about them rather than the man in question."

Claire nodded. "I guess I'm wondering if—if there's something wrong with me for falling for someone so fast. I've never felt like this before and it's…kind of scary. You know how I feel about marriage, right?"

Adeela nodded, smiling grimly. "Like it's a fate worse than death."

"Exactly!" Claire cried, flinging her free hand out. "But after just a few weeks with this man he's got me thinking about forever. That can't be right, can it?"

Adeela shrugged, smiling gently. "Sometimes that's just how it works. You meet someone and something in them calls out to you loud and clear and everything just…falls into place.

Other times, like with me and Harold, you gotta dig through things and figure it all out slowly.

"But for my two coppers, I think that if someone as smart and considerate as you has fallen for this man then he's got to be something special. Do you know how long I've been waiting for you to tell me you found someone who you've managed to forge a connection like that with? You're twenty-six, baby—I've been waiting a *while*. What does your heart say?"

She was quiet, considering. Her heart wasn't saying anything so much as it was *singing*, a bright and beautiful song that spoke of rightness, of destiny. But for once, she didn't know if she could trust it.

"My heart says yes. But it also says to be careful. I don't want to wind up like my parents, Dee."

Adeela nodded, her brown eyes soft and warm. "I get that. I don't think anyone would want to end up like that." She pursed her lips, considering. "Why can't you do both?"

"Do both of what?"

"Let yourself say yes but also be careful. Are they mutually exclusive?"

"Why does everything always have to be that much harder for me?" It was a question she hadn't even realized was hiding inside her, but as soon as it was out tears tracked wet trails down her warm brown cheeks, dripping onto her lap to stain the emerald linen of her trousers. She'd managed to fight through years of pain and abandonment, of insecurity and self-doubt, to get to a point where she was satisfied with the shape of her life—and she'd found a beautiful person to share it with, someone who lit her up and made her feel warm and safe. But now she had to fight *again*: she'd have to fight to get

Beast free, fight to make their relationship work, and might even have to fight for their ability to live their lives. She was sick of it.

Adeela clucked her tongue again, the pads of her fingers pressed, pale, into the glass, as if she would reach through it to wipe the tears from Claire's face. Yearning and a violent wave of homesickness swept through her. She swore she could feel the ghost of Adeela's touch tingling on her skin.

"Life has not been kind to you, baby—the gods know I wish I could change things and give you a kinder life. And I'm not going to sit here and try to sell you aerlanis-shit about how 'oh, everything happens for a reason' or 'the gods put mountains in your path so you can learn to climb them' because I don't think that's it. But I believe *Yun'Shaddeh falla ya*—the balance always guides us, and that when a thing is so wonderful and perfect that it can change your life, it makes itself hard to come by. And the kind of love that keeps you warm for a lifetime, the kind of love that—that me and Harold had...well, you have to fight for it, more often than not. You have to look for it, be open to it, choose it. And I can't tell you whether or not this is right, because I only know what you've told me, but I know you, and I know what a good person you are. And I know that every time you talk about that young man your face lights up like I've never seen it before. And I know you'll make the right choice. And I hope that it's the choice that makes you happy beyond your wildest dreams."

She was crying in earnest now, biting her lip to hold back the sob that threatened to choke her. Adeela always knew just what to say. She felt those tender words melting away the bitterness and frustration scratching at the inside of her chest.

She took a deep breath, letting it out slowly. She'd needed to vent, but she could feel her resolve re-firming itself. She was strong, and she could do this.

"I have to send out some letters to the Hall while I'm here in town, try and chase down a lead I have on getting Beast free, but if this works and he's free I think I'd like to bring him to Kesterin. To meet you and the girls. Would you…would you want to?" If he passed that test and won over Adeela and her daughters then Claire might have to propose to him then and there.

She had never been in love before, but she'd seen a lot of what people had to offer in her time, and there was no way she could deny that Beast was unique. There was something about him that filled in the cracks of her, that made *sense* being kept alongside her. She wasn't going to jump recklessly into a marriage—that just wasn't who Claire was as a person —but getting engaged felt…doable. Right. And she was no longer afraid of it.

Adeela beamed, bringing a hand to her chest. "Sweet girl, I would *love* to meet this man. Please bring him and come home soon. We all miss you something fierce."

"I miss you too, Dee." she said, unable to stop a matching smile from splitting her face. There was just something so *right* about the idea of all her favorite people gathered together and getting close. Now that she was letting herself think about it, Claire found that she could almost picture it: Adeela fussing over her massive gray gargoyle of a man, shoving food and small handmade things at him, literally burying him in her love while he blushed and tried not to let too much of his fluster show.

The picture in the communicator was starting to pale and

fade, and Claire knew that meant the call was about to be cut off, and she had no more paste. "Listen Dee, I think we're going to lose the connection soon so I'm going to have to go. Thanks for the talk. I love you, mama."

Adeela blew a kiss at the mirror and fluttered her knobby fingers in a wave. "Love you too, baby," she replied, her voice sounding fainter now. "Send me a letter when you can!" There might have been more, but the picture and sound stuttered and cut out, and then, much too soon, she was staring at her own face in the mirrored surface of her communicator pendant.

She sighed, heart clenching among her ribs. It hadn't been enough time, but things were progressing properly now, and if they continued going on like this then she'd be back in Adeela's cozy kitchen in no time. She hauled herself to her feet and stomped over to the desk.

She sat and penned a letter to Dretta first, explaining what she'd found and what she suspected. She made sure to be as detailed as possible despite the nervous energy creeping into her limbs, demanding she hurry up and finish her business and get back on the way to Beast. She missed him, and her talk with Adeela had only honed that into a razor-sharp edge.

At the very end, she made sure to outline the events with Kiernan. The Edden constabulary would have already reached out to confirm that she was licensed and able to make arrests, but the Guild would likely want an account of her side of things for its own records. And then, because it was the right thing to do, she let her mentor know that she'd entered a romantic relationship with the quest's subject. The Guild would have to look into it, but being up-front and honest would go far in keeping her out of trouble for following her heart.

She re-read the sheaf of papers several times, adding notes here and there and ensuring she hadn't left out anything important. If she'd been careful enough they'd send out an arbiter and a judge right away, but even if they opted to send out one of her fellow questers to get more intelligence from the manor itself instead it would at least be a step in the right direction. He would be that much closer to being free at last.

She sealed her letter and headed out to the post office. The belligerently apathetic clerk was back, and it took everything Claire had to avoid rolling her eyes. The clerk seemed equally as enthusiastic to see her, but in the end it was handled quickly. Claire decided she'd visit O'brenne for a bit and then check for a reply before turning in for the night.

O'brenne smiled when she walked in, startling her. Despite how O'brenne's lips stretched tight over her tusks the smile was warm and enthusiastic, and she was embarrassed to realize she had doubted that O'brenne even *could* smile up to that point.

"Was wondering if you'd be back soon," she greeted Claire in her gravelly voice. "You're something of a town hero, you know."

She blinked, shocked. "How's that?"

O'brenne grinned again, though there was a bit of a hard edge to it. "It was past time for someone to teach that prick Kiernan some manners. When he showed up bespelled and arrested and with piss soaked all through his trousers there were many women in this town who celebrated."

She grinned at that image, but her mood quickly sank. "He's done things like that before? To others?"

O'brenne's expression sobered as well. "Aye," she agreed,

her familiar frown settling back into place. "We've tried to do something about it, but he's the mayor's boy. Always managed to get out of it." O'brenne spat on the floor, crossing her arms over her chest. Her next words were surprisingly gentle. "You know how it is."

Claire swallowed, nodding. Yes, she certainly did know how it was. Countless vulnerable people knew all too well what that meant. "Not even the mayor can refute an arrest from a Guild member though," she said, pride sparking a fire in her belly. This was part of why she'd entered the Guild, why she was a quester: there was so much that wasn't right in the world, and not enough people who cared to fight to get it set right.

O'brenne nodded once, the movement sharp and curt. "Indeed." She uncrossed her arms and nodded her chin in Claire's direction. "If there's anything you need, you just come to me, alright?"

Claire smiled. "I'll do that. Thank you, O'brenne. I'm so glad I was able to help. If you ever have need of me again, I'll do whatever I can." She reached into the pouch on her pack that held her calling cards. She pulled one free and handed it over to O'brenne. "This will notify me if you need me. Just follow the instructions on the back."

After a moment of hesitation, the Orcish woman took the card and tucked it into her apron pocket. "My thanks," she murmured.

Claire clapped the quiet woman on the shoulder and flashed her another smile. It was time to check back in at the post office, she reckoned, so she took her leave and headed over.

The clerk actually did roll her eyes when she saw Claire

this time, but slipped into the back and grabbed her mail without a vocalized complaint. Still in a good mood from her talk with O'brenne, Claire smiled and handed a tip of four coppers to the annoyed clerk.

"Thanks for being such a good sport about all the mail," Claire teased, winking. Before the clerk could respond she'd spun on her heel and marched back out the doors. She tore open the wax-sealed letter as she walked.

She immediately recognized Dretta's haphazard scrawl. *Unsettling findings indeed, Odetima,* the letter read. *So sorry about your trouble with Kiernan Hastings. Hopefully you're doing well and don't have any more issues. Take care of yourself.* She smiled at Dretta's brisk concern. She got the impression that they had some trouble expressing themself, but they were a warm and caring person underneath all that. *I've requested Arbiter Vendelle and Judge Crawley be dispatched to the scene for further inquiry. I'd appreciate you and the subject sitting tight to await their arrival. Should be no more than three weeks. They'll also check into your relationship with the subject while they're there. It's protocol, of course. I don't think you'll have anything to worry about.*

She reached the doors of the inn just as she finished reading the letter. Her heart was soaring in her chest; with this all taken care of, she'd be able to return to the manor at first light. Back to her Beast.

She could hardly wait.

As excited as Claire had been to get back to Beast, she should have known something would muck up her plans.

She awoke to darkness and the cacophony of a brutal thunderstorm the next morning. From the way the inn shuddered and moaned from the fury of the wind and rain she knew that no amount of can-do attitude would get her to the manor that day. It sounded like one of those dangerous storms that swept through northern Cillure during this time of year, when the seasons changed. She flopped back onto her pillow and groaned, frustrated.

"Salerah's fires, you couldn't wait one more day?" she asked the storm, huffing. As if in reply, a violent crack of thunder shuddered through the morning air.

More often than not, storms like that would come in fast and leave just as quickly, but naturally this one lingered. For three days she was forced to huddle in her room at the *Spur,* her patience fraying until she was ready to charge out into the storm and risk the danger. So what if she got hit by lightning, or bludgeoned by hail, or caught pneumonia from the chill rain? She needed to *go.*

She tried to keep herself busy with work, organizing her notes and sending them on as reports for Dretta to pass along to the Consortium's agents, but even that ran dry. And then she was forced to seek out Teran and let him talk her ear off, just for something to do.

It wound up being surprisingly fun, chatting with the innkeep and listening to his stories, but her mounting tension prevented her from relaxing fully. As anxious as she was, with people all around her to distract her and soothe her, Beast would be going through much worse, and that was what really had her worried.

But just when she couldn't take it anymore, the storm finally broke, and Claire was able to set out at last.

CHAPTER THIRTY-TWO

Homecoming

Claire groaned in relief when the dull silver of the manor gates swam into view in the dusky twilight. Despite her aching feet and twinging back she jogged the rest of the way, the idea of finally seeing Beast again giving her a surge of much-needed adrenaline.

She huffed up to the slowly opening doors and threw them wide, wincing when the heavy wood slabs slammed into the wall.

She had expected him to meet her at the door like last time, but she saw and heard no sign of him, causing the manor's quiet to take on a sharp edge.

"Beast?" she called, dropping her pack on a side table. When only darkness and silence greeted her, unease began to prickle, ratcheting up her pulse. She began to call his name louder, more forcefully, her feet taking her to his study. Silence continued to press in on her, thick and heavy, and something tense inside her snapped, allowing blind panic to sink its teeth in.

When walking didn't eat up the distance fast enough, she broke into a quick jog, her unease thickening as the quiet continued to press in, heavy and unbroken.

"Beast!" she cried, her throat aching and dry, as the flung-open doors of the study revealed an empty room. Her heart sank.

Is something wrong? Is he hurt? she wondered. She kept running, checking the dining room, the kitchen, the library—all empty and cold.

Maybe he's in his room sleeping? She hoped desperately that he was upstairs, trying to keep her fear from freezing her up completely, because something was wrong, something wasn't right, she *knew* her Beast and there was no way he wouldn't have heard her by now and come to her unless something was wrong.

Air had begun to feel thin in her throat by the time she reached his bedroom, flinging open the door with enough violence that it bounced back towards her after it hit the wall, but that, too, was empty. Tears sprang to her eyes and she felt like she well and truly couldn't breathe anymore. She sank against the door frame, hugging herself and trying not to cry.

A gentle buzzing tickled her back and Claire gasped, spinning on her heel. She'd felt this strange sensation several times now, too many times for it to be nothing. She didn't know enough about magecraft to pin down what it could be, but she figured it was worth paying attention to. Especially because it almost felt like it was…tugging on her? Pulling her back down the hall, from where she'd come. She followed it, hope nearly choking her.

"Please, please, please," she prayed, realizing that the buzzing was leading her to her room, and that there seemed to be a little light flickering around the edges of the door. She surged forward, leaving the buzzing behind, and threw open the door.

All of the air in her lungs left with a great whoosh of relief —there he was, sprawled out on her bed, snoring softly, his face pressed into her pillow. As adrenaline ebbed away her legs went wobbly and weak, and she sank down next to him on the bed. He was deeper asleep than she'd ever seen him, his scent stronger than it usually was and with an unpleasant sourness lurking beneath. Maybe he *was* sick, after all.

She reached out and smoothed a thatch of his fiery hair away from his sweat-damp forehead.

"Beast," she called gently, brushing her knuckles across his cheek.

He snorted and twitched, moaning but not quite rousing.

She tried again, shaking his arm this time, and was rewarded with one extremely bloodshot eye cracking open.

"Beast?"

The eye squeezed closed, Beast groaning as if in pain and pressing his whole face into her pillow. He said something too muffled for her to catch.

"What's wrong? What happened, honey?"

His back stiffened. After a heartbeat he began to struggle to get his arms under himself, to push himself upright, but only managed to tangle himself up in the sheets and wind up on his back, panting from his efforts. He blinked up at her, squinting in the dim light of the single candle on the bedside, and she scooted closer to him, taking one of his hands.

"Claire?"

"Yes, I'm here. Are you okay?"

He stared up at her blearily, clearly struggling to pull her into focus, so she leaned down and kissed him gently. Her heart soared as her lips met his, no matter that he smelled sour and odd, because he was here, and he was fine, and she had so much to tell him.

He groaned, his free arm wrapping around her and pulling her to his chest. She went happily, heat pooling low in her stomach. She let him squeeze her tight for a moment before pulling away gently and sitting up.

"You're here," he rasped, closing his eyes and pressing one of his giant palms to his forehead and scrunching it as if it pained him.

"I am," she confirmed, concerned that he seemed so surprised. "Do you want to tell me why you're passed out in my bed?"

"No," he muttered, peeking at her from under his hand.

She snorted, swatting his arm.

"I wasn't *actually* asking, sir. What's going on?"

His bloodshot eyes slid to the side, avoiding her gaze. She poked at his ribs, earning her an indignant squawk. He rolled onto his side, preventing her from getting another shot in, wrapping his thick arms around his middle and glaring at her. If he hadn't been trying to suppress a smile he might have looked fearsome.

"Stop torturing me," he grumbled, watching her hands as they edged across the bedding towards him.

"Tell me what's the matter," she said primly, wiggling the fingers that had almost reached his bulk.

His lips pressed into a thin line as he glared at her again and scooted back from her. Claire slid closer, her fingers continuing their slow creep.

"Don't you dare," he snapped.

She grinned, inching closer. He tried to curl into a ball, his arms banded tight over his ribs, but she wasn't going for that anymore—she threw herself to the side and caught one of his feet, tickling at the sensitive skin in between his paw pads.

He jerked, howling from the shock. She squealed, holding on tight. "Tell me!" she shrieked, slotting his high ankle into the crook of her elbow and trapping it there. "Tell me what's wrong or by Salerah's wrath—"

"I thought you weren't going to come back," he choked out, breathless. "And the shadow monsters came for me. Now, unhand me!"

She froze, releasing him and twisting to look down into his face. He was still avoiding looking at her, keeping his hair flopped forward, and she realized his whole face was splotchy and puffy. And just peeking out of the neck of his shirt, now that it was rumpled and skewed, she saw an angry red wound, as if he'd scratched himself badly.

"W…what?" What was he talking about? "But…Beast, honey, there's no one here but you and me."

He shrugged, still folding in on himself. "I know. I'm… pretty sure they're not real. But I haven't been able to tell for sure."

Sweet Delenaa, was he…was he *seeing* things? Had he been hallucinating this whole time and she'd just never noticed? *How?*

"How long has this been happening?" she asked him, sitting on the edge of the bed and taking his hands. What in the seven hells was going on?

He sniffed, shrugging again. "Not sure. Awhile. Many years now."

She went cold, her stomach twisting. *Years?* "Oh gods," she breathed, throwing her arms around him and holding him tight. "Is it…are they still here?"

She felt him shake his head against her. "No. They go away when you're around. I think they don't like you."

"Good," she ground out. The terror she'd felt when she hadn't been able to find him was coming back, but now it was starker, harsher, because this was something she knew nothing about, something she was wildly unequipped to handle, something she couldn't fight, or outwit, or even magic away, even if she was gifted. "What happens," she asked him, trying to be gentle, "when the shadow monsters come?"

He pressed his lips together in a hard line. "They hunt me. Mock me. But they never manage to hurt me, so if they are real then I don't know what they're doing. But they're so loud, so persistent, and they drive me crazy. They scare me."

She held him close, her throat tight. "Of course, baby. It sounds awful. Is that why you came to my room? You were trying to get away from them?"

"Everywhere else was too open. And your pillows still smell like you, so it made them quieter."

"And now that I'm here, are they gone?"

"Yes."

She loosed a slow breath, her body still full of tension. She had to get him out of this cursed manor, and she had to get him out *now*.

She lay down next to him so that her front was pressed against his back, and wrapped her arms around him, pulling him close. Now that he was pressed against her, she could see that his hair was greasy and matted, his clothes smelling like they'd been worn too many days in a row. He'd had a very bad time while she was gone, and she couldn't help but feel a little guilty, even if she also knew she had no reason to.

"I'm sorry I wasn't back sooner," she murmured, her

heart breaking. "It was the rain. I couldn't walk through that storm."

"I know. It's alright, Claire—you needed to do it. You have to be able to get things done and—and do your job. I didn't tell you to make you worry. I just wanted you to know. I don't —I don't want you to have to baby me."

"Mmm," she hummed, kissing the side of his head. "But I bet you like it, don't you? You like when I take care of you," she said, her voice dropping and going husky. She couldn't stand to talk about this anymore right now, not when she was so tired and jittery with nerves—and what better way to distract than with a reminder of their favorite new activity?

His face flushed and he turned his face into the mattress. Yeah, he liked it. And Claire liked taking care of him. But what was she supposed to do to take care of *this*?

She'd known he was in rough shape mentally, and it hadn't really bothered her as long as he tried to work on it, but how did you work on this? How did you even begin to understand it? She mentally shook herself, trying to shove those thoughts away again.

She kissed his temple and smacked his round ass playfully, then released him and rolled off the side of the bed. "I'm going to go grab you water and some pepper tea. Otherwise, you'll probably spend tomorrow feeling like you've got a hangover. I love you but you look like you've had a long day."

He nodded, his red and swollen eyes watching her. He did his best to smile at her but it wound up looking more like a grimace.

She slipped out of the room and down to the kitchen, summoning a mug of the sharp and spicy tea and grabbing a glass from the cupboard as quickly as she could. She filled the glass with cold water and returned oh-so-carefully to her room.

He took the mug she offered and gulped it down obediently, sputtering when the first spicy mouthful licked at his throat. But he managed not to choke or make any more of a mess than that. He gulped down the water just as quickly, placing the glass and mug on the bedside table and wiping the back of his hand across his mouth.

"What now?" he asked.

She pinched her lip, thinking. She sensed he might need some more care, but she really was *so* damned tired, between the traveling and the panic. "Honestly? I'm so tired I can barely think straight." She sighed, unbuttoning her blouse and putting it in her hamper. "Unless you have any objections I think I'd like to just go to bed early."

She finished changing into a nightgown, pulling a scarf from her bag to tie around her hair. "Do you want to stay with me?" she asked as she deftly tied the knot on the top of her head.

He swallowed, smiling faintly. "I would. Sleep sounds… good. Should we move to my bed?"

She wrinkled her nose. "Your bed is too big. And you have *so many* pillows."

He laughed, his eyes glittering in the low light. "So you've said. What do you have against pillows, Odetima?"

She snorted. "I like pillows! But twelve is too damn many."

"It's *exactly* enough!" He got up and peeled the blankets back, untwisting them from the messy nest he'd made of them. "We could take the extra pillows off of my bed," he offered.

"That'll just make it feel even bigger! You could fit the entire town of Edden in that thing." She stooped to dig out her bottle of oil, rubbing it quickly into her skin. "I want to be able to find you to cuddle you."

"Alright then, how about this: we go to my bed, and move the pillows so that they form a ring around the outside of the bed, hemming us into a cozier space." He grinned at her. "That way I can still stretch out my legs. Your bed is too short, it hurts my knees."

She rolled her eyes. "Fine; we can't very well have your knees giving out on you, old man."

He finished making her bed and strode over to her, smacking his palm firmly against her backside. "Stop calling me old, it hurts my feelings."

"Stop saying things that make you sound ancient, then." She finished with her oil and yawned, her whole body shuddering with the force of it. "You know what? I no longer care where we sleep, I just want to lay down *somewhere*." She took his hands and threaded their fingers together. "I just want to settle down somewhere comfy with my big, sweet, strapping, completely elderly man."

They both burst out laughing, Beast playfully swatting at her again before leading them to his palatial bedroom.

As promised, he arranged all of his extra pillows around the outside edge of the mattress, using a sheet draped over the whole thing and tucked under the mattress edges to hold it all in place.

"There, that looks nice and cozy, doesn't it?" He rested his hands on his hips, examining his handiwork.

"Yes, it looks wonderful, sweet man. Bed? Now? Please?"

He nodded, and they both clambered into the middle of the pillow nest. She had to admit, it *was* pretty cozy and comfortable, and she settled in easily. Once she'd wriggled into the perfect position he surged and flopped over, his head landing on her shoulder and his arm and leg flopping on top of her body. She grinned, wrapping her own arms as well as she could around his broad shoulders and holding him close. She breathed deep, the smell of his hair filling her nose and wriggling deep into her chest, and something that she hadn't realized was still tense and frightened loosened there.

"So you're alright, then?" she murmured, needing to make sure. "No more shadow monsters?"

"Nope," he sighed. "Told you, y'scare 'em away…"

She had been so scared when she couldn't find him, and she couldn't lie to herself and say that the hallucinations didn't fill her with cold dread. But if she chased them away for him then she just had a really good reason to be clingy for the next while.

As tired as she was, her mad dash through the manor looking for Beast still haunted her. She couldn't shake the fear; it had been a deeper terror than she'd ever known before, something so horrible and primal that she'd forgotten to use caution in a potentially dangerous situation. What if someone else had slipped into the manor while she was gone, and had attacked Beast? They would have got her, too, with how she was stomping around. She had to be more careful, make sure she was thinking things through. She couldn't just go tearing off into potentially dangerous situations like she had during that golem attack with Jordan and Hereon. She had to keep her cool, no matter what she was feeling, because she was a professional, and on her own right now.

The shame and guilt for her lapse in judgment swirled and blended with her lingering fear and unease, making for a very tense and restless night.

CHAPTER THIRTY-THREE

Naja

It was hard to decide if the thick dryness of his mouth or the searing knife through his skull was the more unpleasant sensation Beast felt when he woke up the next morning. But he found he couldn't help but consider it a good morning anyway when he cracked a gritty eye open and realized the soft warmth his tender head was nestled into was Claire's chest—she really was back after all and it hadn't been another torturous dream. He breathed in, pulling the sweet scent of her in deep. The arm he had flung over her stomach tightened, and he thought that if she had any plans for her day she'd have to manage them with him wrapped around her and clinging like a barnacle.

The darkness had never before gripped him like it had this last week, when he began to believe that she was never coming back. He'd been hounded day and night by the shadow creatures, howls and snarls following him everywhere he went, glowing eyes and glittering tooth-filled maws snapping inches from his face. It didn't matter what he did, where he went—the creatures followed. He still felt cold, remembering it, even with the softness of her body pressed against his craggy face.

He didn't think he'd survive it, if he lost her.

Her breathing hitched, and after a moment she stretched under him, sighing and smacking her lips.

"Good morning, love," she murmured, a warm hand squeezing his shoulder.

He smiled. He didn't think he'd ever get used to her calling him that.

"How are you feeling?" she asked, yawning.

"Head's killing me," he moaned, shifting off of her to lay on his side next to her oh-so-carefully, so as not to send the knife deeper into his skull. "I'm sorry you had to see that," he added. "It was a tough week." He didn't think he'd be able to tell her that Naja had visited him again, taunting him and adding to how low he'd already been feeling with Claire gone, making the shadow creatures utterly relentless.

Most of the mage's visit had gone like it usually did, with her showing him an endless stream of memories showcasing all the things he had done wrong: his failures, his greatest shames, his foolishness. She'd spent an entire day on that this time. But just before she disappeared she'd decided to talk about Claire.

"I'm surprised that quester is still hanging around," Naja had drawled, sneering at him. "She must be especially stupid, to be willing to put up with you." He'd bristled at that, the urge to defend Claire riling him up instantly. He'd actually *growled*, making Naja blink at him in surprise. But the expression was gone quickly.

"She will get bored of you and your quest soon," she'd told him, a cold smile freezing on her face. "She will never want you."

Now that Claire was back, that moment struck him as odd; he'd long suspected that Naja had some means of monitoring him while she was gone, as she always knew when he was alone, and seemed informed of what he'd been up to at least in a general sense, so how did she not know that they'd come together? Claire had already proved multiple times that she wanted him, and had even told him she loved him. Had he been wrong about Naja being able to observe him? Or was it something else? Could it be Tully, shielding them from the mad fae mage somehow?

Good morning, love. More of the clouds in his mind broke apart as he thought of how she said such things easily, with no hesitation, her feelings written plain on her lovely face.

It felt selfish and greedy, but he couldn't help wondering how, exactly, she meant that she loved him. Did it mean that she fully, would-marry-him-and-build-a-life-with-him loved him? Beast didn't think he'd ever wanted something so badly in the entire bleak stretch of his existence, not even his freedom. The love of a woman like Claire *was* a kind of freedom. It had him thinking that if someone like her, so full of light and kindness, could love a monster like him, then maybe he wasn't so monstrous. Maybe Naja had been unfair all this time.

It meant that maybe he could be angry instead of lost in darkness.

"I didn't like seeing you like that," she admitted, her hazel eyes and warm brown skin gleaming in the golden morning light. "It scared me. Not being able to find you when I got home scared me, too."

He cupped the side of her face, swiping the pad of his thumb along her cheek. "I'm sorry."

She sighed, pressing her face into his hand and making his chest clench with feeling. "It's not going to be a regular thing is it? I might need to keep leaving to take care of my work so we can get you free, and I need to know you'll be alright."

"I know. And I want you to be able to come and go and take care of what you need to. It's just that…something…happened. I was—" but he choked, unable to say. He tugged on one of his horns, trying to think what he could say. "*She* visited," he said slowly.

Her eyes widened, her rich complexion going pale. "The mage was here? She visited you while I was gone?" He nodded, and she clucked her tongue with sympathy. "Well, no wonder you had such a bad time, then. I bet she just makes everything worse when she shows up." She scowled, then turned her head and pressed a kiss to his palm. "I'm sorry you had to face her alone. If I ever see her I might not be able to stop myself from trying to claw her eyes out, just to warn you." She pulled herself free with one last kiss. "I'm going to go freshen up. I'll see you in a little for breakfast?"

He winced, the pounding in his head making his stomach roil even though he'd barely eaten while she was gone. But even if he didn't eat much he still wanted to spend that time with her.

She smiled, a little crease between her eyebrows that showed she was still concerned about the fact that he'd been visited by Naja. Then she hopped off the bed and padded into the bathroom, the lazy swing of her hips stirring him despite how his head felt. He suspected he could be literally dead and she would still manage to rouse his corpse. She was *powerfully* beautiful.

By the time he made it downstairs, rumpled and wrung-out but clean, Claire had long since finished eating. She sat at the table, reading and sipping at a mug of tea.

He flung himself into his seat with a groan. "Pepper tea," he barked, pressing the heels of his hands into his eyes. He heard a soft *thunk* as the enchantment produced the mug on the table.

She clucked her tongue, and Beast heard the faint scrape of her chair pulling back from the table, which felt like it was scraping against the inside of his eyes at the same time. He hadn't had a drop of alcohol; it wasn't fair that he was feeling like this.

"My poor baby," she murmured, coming behind his chair and combing his still-damp hair back from his forehead and placing a soft kiss between his horns. He melted back against her, eyes closed, as her hands kneaded his shoulders and her vanilla and roses scent cocooned him.

He groaned low in his throat as the exquisite heat of her hands worked at muscles he hadn't even realized were tight and aching. "You spoil me," he declared, opening his eyes sleepily to study her face.

She smiled down at him, pearly teeth flashing. "I'm just addicted to touching you, it's not selfless in the slightest," she said, tilting his head back with a finger under his chin so she could steal a kiss.

When she straightened and resumed her ministrations, he felt a thick knot of emotion settle into his throat, making him swallow hard to try and dislodge it. "I love you, you know," he heard himself whisper, one of his hands coming up to snag one of hers. "I love you and I'll do anything for you. Anything."

She bit her full lower lip, pausing her rubbing, then

stepped around to the side of his chair and climbed into his lap. Her arms slipped around his neck, and then she was kissing him, her mouth hot and urgent on his. He groaned, pulling her tight against him and feeling like he could cry with the beauty of it, of this woman in his arms and the miracle of her wanting him as much as he wanted her.

She pulled away gently, grabbing his face and pulling him forward so his forehead rested on hers. "I love you too," she whispered, nuzzling her nose against his, and he thought he might actually cry now, it was too much, so much, and he never in a thousand years would have thought he'd ever hear someone say that to him. She was a wonder, his Claire, and he would endure the torture of his imprisonment again and again for just this one moment.

She cleared her throat and continued softly, "And I'd...I'd like to make it more permanent. Like maybe...maybe figuring out a way to get married. Someday. If you wanted something like that."

He kissed her again, a strangled noise ripping from his throat, still not quite letting himself believe the reality of this, that he was hers and she was his and that she was in his arms, soft and warm and willing. It had been relegated to a dream for so long.

"Do me a favor and hit me," he said, cupping a hand at the back of her head as he trailed kisses along her jaw.

"Mmm. Can I ask why?"

"Because this can't be real. There's no way."

Her head tilted to the side, baring her neck for him so he could continue teasing and nibbling at her, drinking in the delicious way her breaths grew panting and peppered with soft groans.

"I know you love being a masochist, darling, but this is very real," she murmured, her voice husky in his ear. Her hands dug into his half-dry hair, holding his hungry mouth to the sensitive skin of her throat. "You won me fair and square, sweet man—gods, that *mouth*—" Claire shivered against him, her hands tightening almost painfully against his scalp, sending heat spiraling through his stomach, "…so…so you better get used to this because I'm not letting you go. You're stuck with me…Now please stop teasing and answer me," she gasped as he gently scraped his sharp teeth against the cords of her neck, and he was so engrossed in wringing more of those delicious sounds out of her that it took a moment for her words to sink in.

"You are my everything Claire," he murmured, "you are the light of my life. Of course I want to marry you."

"Sweet man," she whispered, holding him close.

And the world fell away, focusing down to the sizzling heat of her kisses, of the soft strength of her body pressed tight against his.

But of course it couldn't last. Of course he wouldn't be allowed to keep something so perfect. He heard the unmistakable concussion, like thunder without the crash, that signaled to Beast that he and Claire were no longer alone.

In nearly two hundred years, Naja had never paid one of her visits when someone else had been at the manor. It was the only thing that was predictable about her arrival: if another soul was there with him, she kept away.

So it was the most natural thing for the furious mage to come now, when his wildest dreams were coming true. When he had a miracle in his arms that it would be so easy for Naja to twist into a nightmare.

He jerked upright, shooting to his feet with Claire cradled to his chest, adrenaline chasing away the last dregs of his headache. He set her gently on her feet, spinning her to face him and gripping her shoulders tightly.

"Claire, sweetheart, listen to me—I need you to run. You have to leave here, you have to *go*, please—"

"Beast, what's going on? You're scaring me—"

"You have to go *now*, you have to leave, please, baby it's not safe—"

"What *have* you done now, worm?" a voice like hot steel meeting cold water hissed from the direction of the open doors. While Claire stiffened and startled, Beast slumped, his head falling forward. This was it, then. His reckoning.

Naja had arrived. And she'd caught him with Claire. He drew a deep breath, straightening and pulling her behind him, trying to shield her from Naja's cold wrath. It wasn't likely that Naja would try to hurt Claire—her expansive cruelty seemed limited to just him—but no one had ever kissed him before. No one had ever loved him before. No one had ever *wanted* him enough to say forever before. And maybe that was enough to make her a target.

If Naja wanted her she'd have to tear through him first.

But Naja only shook her head and *tsked*, eyeing him with her cold ice-blue eyes. "I suppose I shouldn't be surprised that you'd eventually manage to defy me. With enough time even worms might grow a spine."

"What do you want, Naja? Why are you here?" he growled, Claire's hand on his back. To his relief, she seemed content to stay behind him and keep quiet. She could handle herself, of course, but if he could spare her from having to tangle with the mad fae mage, he would.

"I want to remind you of why you are here, Beast. Because you seem to have forgotten what you did, from your recent behavior.

"Tell me, girl: *do* you know what he did?" Naja called, head craning to see around Beast's bulk, "Do you know why I have locked this creature away in this manor?"

Claire stepped around to his side, grasping his trembling hand and squeezing it tight. "You know I don't, mage," she responded, her chin high and defiant. He loved this strong, brave woman. So, so much. "But I have to say, I have been curious. So why don't you come out with it?"

Naja's mouth curled into a barbed smile, fury and glee wrestling for control of her remote yet beautiful face. "As you wish," she purred.

Faster than he could move, the air thickened and pressed against him on all sides, squeezing him painfully. He kept a death grip on her hand, refusing to let them get separated, as the dining room grew shadowy and changed.

They were still in the dining room, but it was a version of the dining room he hadn't seen in nearly two hundred years: his family's crest and heirloom swords were on the wall, vases of his mother's favorite white roses sitting on little tables in the corners, and there were three young boys seated at the long table. It was a shock seeing Tollem and Deven again, of course, but the sharpest shock came from seeing himself, as a human, just sixteen and so, so desperate for his friends to like him. It broke his heart, seeing the longing in his own eyes as Tollem and Deven talked around him.

Perhaps the most obvious marker of this being a moment from a different time was the sound. Unlike now, voices murmured all around: there was the boys' conversation, but outside the dining room din from the kitchen trickled in, as did the quiet words and laughter of servants cleaning and the far-off whinnying of horses, the barking of his father's hounds. Here the world was *rich* with sound. For Beast, now so long used to silence, the layers of sound only made the vision unfolding around him more surreal, more *un*real, reminding him more than anything else that this wasn't really happening, that it was done and Claire and Naja were somewhere around him, likely witnessing this same scene.

He twisted, the air around him unsettlingly thick and cloying, as if he were moving through mud. His muscles screamed in protest, but he managed to turn, spotting Claire and Naja a few paces behind him, Naja's hand clutched tight around Claire's bicep. Claire met his eyes, clearly puzzled. He wanted to speak to her, to reassure her, explain to her, but the unnatural thickness of the air swallowed his words. He could only feel them as a vibration in his throat.

Eventually, he was forced to turn back around, the strain on his muscles maintaining that twist proving too much. His eyes settled on his younger self, on just how…frail, and *human* he had once looked. His hair was still the same, and while the face as a whole was unfamiliar some of the parts were still there, on his face now. He recognized his nose, the shape of his lips, the color of his eyes—though everything was shrunken and smoothed, and swathed in pale pink skin that looked more wrong than anything else. He'd completely forgotten he'd ever been so sickly pale.

"I've always thought Mirina had the best tits. What do you think, —?" the last bit was his name, he thought, but it had been badly garbled, indistinguishable.

His younger self blushed furiously. "I suppose they're

nice," he mumbled, pushing his food around his plate with his fork.

"Should have known you'd give a chicken shit answer. Do you even like girls, —?" Deven asked, Beast's name once again unintelligible. Deven broke a chunk off of a dinner roll and tossed it at young Beast so that it landed in his wild mop of red hair.

"'Course I like girls, Deven. I just...I dunno, it feels disrespectful to talk about people like that." His younger self combed his fingers through his hair, depositing the chunk of bread on the floor. He didn't seem to notice.

"Pussy," Deven scoffed, rolling his eyes. "She's never going to know. Unless you fucking *tattle*. You gonna go running to Mirina and tell her all about how we think her tits are great?"

Somehow young Beast managed to blush harder, his face an uncomfortable shade of scarlet not too different from his hair. "Of course not. I wouldn't betray you guys," he insisted, clutching his silverware hard enough his hands trembled.

"Of course you wouldn't," Tollem had interjected, smacking young Beast's arm. "We're just joking around."

Satisfied, the two other boys resumed their conversation, talking over young Beast once more. He watched his past self slowly shrink, his head sagging and thin limbs curling inward like a dying insect. For not the first time, he wondered how he could have ever thought those little assholes were his friends. Clearly, they had been using him for his father's influence. Clearly, they'd despised him. Clearly, there was nothing in that relationship for him. It would have been better to have been completely alone, he knew now. And not just because of what came next—but because living like this was awful, this was torture, and no one deserved it.

Suddenly, the doorbell rang out, announcing company. His past self froze, eyes darting to the nighttime darkness beyond the windows.

"Who's that? Your parents back already?" Deven asked.

Young Beast shook his head. "Shouldn't be. They're supposed to be gone another week, at least. And I don't think any visitors were expected…" he set his silverware down on the table and dropped his napkin next to his plate. He pushed back his chair from the table, but didn't yet rise. Even across the gulf of years, he could remember the sharp terror of this moment, of having to potentially act as the man of the house in his parents' absence and deal with a stranger. Not even Tully had been there, having gone along with his parents on their inspection of their latest purchase for their small fleet of merchant's vessels. Fear had been so cold and bitter on his tongue.

After a few minutes, a maid entered, bowing low to Beast and his friends.

"Pardon me sirs, but a visitor requires the young master in the foyer," she said.

His past self straightened, nodding once and meeting the maid at the door. As if tied to him by a tether, Beast slid forward as well, keeping a distance of perhaps six feet between himself and the vision of his past. He couldn't help but notice the slight trembling shaking his younger self's frame, and in that moment he couldn't decide if he hated this boy for his cowardice or if he pitied him for his fear and loneliness.

They reached the foyer, grander than Beast had seen it in so long, with the grand chandelier lit up and twinkling like a galaxy trapped among the eaves. Something else about the vision made the space look warmer, more alive and lived in, though he was unsure what that was.

The maid bowed again. "The lady Ingrid d'Naja-Baast, young master —."

Ingrid.

The woman he'd failed.

The woman he'd damned.

The woman he'd killed.

He'd forgotten just how small she was, and how soft. Where Claire was taut muscle gentled with curves, Ingrid was all softness, clearly a sheltered noble's daughter, too naive to be scared of what might happen if she tried to fling herself on the mercy of strangers. Her wide brown eyes watched his younger self approach her, a warm smile plastered on her pale pink face. Her clothes were simple but clearly of excellent make, and soiled from hard travel. Her brown hair was pulled back in a simple chignon, though several strands had escaped and hung haphazardly around her face, making her look even more doll-like.

"Good evening sir, my deepest apologies for intruding so late," Ingrid said in her low, gentle voice, so strongly reminiscent of a doe in that moment. "I've had an absolutely beastly evening and have gotten separated from my guards; might I impose on your hospitality for the evening? I can do some chores to earn my keep, or if you would accept my word I would be happy to pay you once I've joined back up with my party, who also have the trunk with all my possessions and money with them."

Ingrid's face was so full of hope, so open and ready to trust, that it almost brought him to his knees. He was a monster, a gods-cursed *monster* for letting it happen. He deserved this pain, deserved this agony, for what he'd done.

"N-no need miss. I'll have a room made up for you." His younger self nodded at the maid, who hurried away to get one of the guest rooms ready. "Are you hungry?" he asked shyly, combing his hair back from where it had flopped into his eyes. "We just sat down to dinner not long ago. Y-you can join us if you'd like."

Ingrid clapped her hands together and brought them to her chest. "I wouldn't want to impose!"

Young Beast blushed, waving his hand dismissively. "It's nothing, really. There's plenty. Come, the dining room is this way."

"If you're sure...I suppose I *am* rather hungry," Ingrid replied, smiling brightly at young Beast, making his face and neck a violent shade of red.

The two retreated to the dining room, Ingrid chatting quietly and young Beast silent and stiff.

"This is lady Ingrid d'Naja-Baast," young Beast announced as they swept back into the dining room. "My lady, these are my friends Deven Ridgewright and Tollem Sangrean."

"Please, just Ingrid is fine," she assured them, smiling and inclining her head in greeting.

"Hello, Ingrid," Deven said, the sharp edge in his voice unmistakable to Beast's adult ears. It was so obvious, the trajectory of things, now that he was paying attention.

Ingrid sat across from Tollem and Deven, on Beast's right at the head of the table, and folded her hands primly in her lap. A footman swooped over and arranged a place setting in front of her, filling her plate and goblet as soon as he'd finished the setting. Ingrid beamed and thanked him profusely, as if he had bestowed a great honor on her just by doing his job. He noticed that the footman seemed to carry himself straighter and step more lively after that.

Guilt burned cold in his gut.

"So Ingrid, where are you from?" Tollem asked as he speared a stalk of asparagus onto his fork.

"Oh, I'm from Citrine originally, but I'm returning home for the summer from the boarding school I attend in Kesterin."

"Is it an all-girls school?"

"Yes, it is. But very prestigious. Delenaa's Bounty Preparatory School; perhaps you've heard of it?"

"Ah yes, my older sister went there several years ago. It *is* an excellent school. Too bad about it being all girls though, eh? I'm sure you're more than ready for a strong male presence," Tollem said, his voice deadly soft.

Ingrid squirmed in her seat, her smile going stiff. "I suppose, though the girls there are lovely, I've made so many friends. Are you in school, perchance?" Beast didn't miss the desperate edge to her voice, as if she wanted nothing more than to steer the conversation elsewhere.

Tollem smiled, though it didn't quite reach his eyes. "Yes, I've got another year before I graduate, and then I'm set to take over my father's horse stables."

"Isn't that lovely," Ingrid said, nibbling on a heel of bread. "And you, Deven?"

"Do you have a boyfriend, Ingrid?"

"I—pardon?"

"Do you have a boyfriend?"

"I...I'm not sure I feel comfortable talking about

something that personal."

"Oh come on, Ingrid. We're all friends here. Tell her, —."

His younger self nodded, his eyes glued to his plate of food. Beast himself wanted to scream, to grab his past self by the shoulders and shake him until his bones rattled and he fucking *did* something. His hands twitched, but the thickness of the air kept him still and silent.

"You had so many chances, worm. So many moments in which you could have done the right thing and failed," Naja hissed from behind him. He could do nothing but squeeze his eyes shut.

When he opened his eyes again, he was in his bedroom, his younger self dressed for bed but reading a romance novel he'd slipped under his pillow by candlelight. He couldn't remember anymore what book it had been, but he supposed it didn't really matter.

A thud sounded outside the bedroom, from down the hall. Young Beast looked up, pale brow furrowing. He sat, tense, for several heartbeats. And then he heard it: more thumps, some rattling, and small stifled cries. It was a slight sound, barely there, but sharp and unmistakable. Young Beast's eyes widened, and the book fell from his slack fingers.

"Get up!" Beast tried to yell, his entire body straining forward, to try and reach his past self, to grab him and shove him bodily towards the door. "Get *up!*" he tried to yell, but no sound made it out. And he watched himself just sit there, frozen, as soft sobs started to shiver in the late-night air. He watched himself snap the book shut, snuff out the candle, and burrow into his blankets and cover his ears.

He wanted to throw up. He was so disgusted with himself, so horrified at what he'd done.

"Don't close your eyes now, worm. You owe it to Ingrid to face your failures. To witness the pain and suffering that *you* caused," Naja growled from behind him again, and he opened his eyes obediently. He hadn't even realized he'd closed them.

Then, breakfast with Tollem and Deven, both of them bright-eyed and flushed, Deven with scratches on his face that spanned from his ear to his nose across one cheek and Tollem with red and swollen knuckles. Nobody said anything about Ingrid.

Then—

Young Beast, alone in his room again, his thin chest heaving and his long fingers trembling around a letter he'd received in the morning post, written in an elegant female hand. A letter from Ingrid, informing him she was seeking justice, but that her testimony on its own wasn't gaining ground, that she needed him or someone in his house to come forward and lend weight to her story. She begged him, beseeched him, telling him she just *knew* he'd do the right thing and help her. She promised him she didn't blame him, that he hadn't known what was happening, but that surely he could help her, could at least speak to the character of Tollem and Deven…

His younger self crumpled the letter, his hands shaking and face pale. After a moment he'd strode to the crackling fireplace and tossed the balled-up letter in.

Then—

A cold and cloudy day, perfect for a funeral, but the body in this grave had been laid to rest weeks ago. Young Beast knelt in front of the polished granite stone, tears streaming down his twisted face. Sobs wracked his thin body, and in a low voice that was little more than a moan he apologized over and over:

"I'm sorry Ingrid, I'm so sorry, I'm *sorry*—"

Then.

His stomach sank, knowing what was next. They were back in his room, the late-night darkness thick. Some moon- and starlight-lit patches left silver pools on the floor, but his huddled form on the bed was swathed in shadow. The restless tossing and twisting happening in his sheets was the most visible thing in the room, but there, in the corner near his wardrobe—

"Your friends are already dead," a voice like hard-frozen ice hissed from that corner, and suddenly he was no longer an observer, he was sixteen again, huddled in that bed, stabbed through with cold panic and caught between nightmare and waking.

He bolted upright, heart hammering and his control over his bladder threatening to slip away. His wide eyes roved over the space of his bedroom, gone perversely unfamiliar, seeking who- or whatever had spoken...and hoping he would find nothing. *Just a dream. Please, let that have been just a dream.* His numb hands pulled his thick wool blanket up to his chin, as if he were six again instead of sixteen, when a blanket might actually keep the monsters away. But he knew now that the monsters weren't really like that, they didn't listen to anything but their own hunger. They took what they wanted with their greedy fingers and hungry mouths and laughed at all your tears.

"Wh-who's there?" he managed to ask in a hoarse whisper, his whole body shuddering and clammy and aching with the hope that it was all in his head.

A clutch of shadows peeled away from the corner and slid to the foot of his bed, coalescing into the figure of a woman. In the darkness of the room, it was difficult to make out much detail, but Beast imagined that in the light of day this woman would have looked like a painting of the goddess Delenaa—all soft creamy-pale skin, golden curls, and blood-red lips. But even in the dark the illusion of beauty was ruined by ice-chip eyes, by the wrath twisting that beautiful face as she sneered down at him. He flailed and kicked himself backwards, the back of his head slamming into the wooden headboard painfully.

"Do you not recognize me, boy?" the woman asked him, her voice like steel scraping along a whetstone.

He wanted to protest that he wasn't a boy, he was sixteen and a man grown and future lord of…this place—the name escaped him now, strangely. But his survival instincts told him to hold his tongue. Instead, he clutched the blanket tighter against himself despite being slick with sweat and shook his head.

The beautiful woman stepped closer, a deadly night cat cornering her prey. "And if I said I was Naja, high priestess of Vitrin, and mother to a beautiful girl named Ingrid? What then?"

His breath froze in his lungs, and now he did lose control of his bladder, the reek of urine mingling with the sour musk of his fear-sweat. He was filled so full of terror he couldn't even manage to feel shame about it; there was only room for blind panic. A low moan escaped his ice-cold lips as he recalled her first words: *your friends are already dead…*

Dead. Tollem and Deven—dead. He believed this woman, this Naja, knew that the angel of death before him had no reason to lie, not about this. He couldn't believe it, in the sense that they had always seemed so much larger than life to him, like a force rather than just two people much like himself, but he knew it was true: his only two friends were gone.

"Why are you here?" he asked in a shuddering whisper. But of course he knew, and he knew he deserved what was coming to him, but he was a spineless coward and the only thing he could think to do was to deny it, to try and save himself somehow, to escape this. "I n-never touched Ingrid, it was all them, they—"

"Shut your mouth, worm!" Naja roared, moving to the side of his bed with inhuman speed.

Where are the guards, where's Mother and Father, where's Tully? he thought, desperate, his ears straining for any sign that someone was coming to his rescue.

As if she could read his thoughts, Naja sneered and bent down to bring her face level with his. Her hand snapped out to grip his chin with fingers like cold iron. Tears fell from his wide eyes. "No one is coming for you, boy. No one will help you, just like no one came for my Ingrid. No one helped my baby, even though *you* could have, you pathetic coward."

His mouth worked, wanting to protest *No, I couldn't, I didn't know what they were going to do, please—* but no sound came.

Naja snarled, her expression in the dim light so ugly and full of malice that the last of her beauty slipped away, leaving only ghastly fury. "Not only did you fail her that night," she growled, fingers tightening so hard he whimpered, "but when she demanded justice and you had a chance to set things right and lend your voice to hers, you failed again. And now, because of you and those mongrels you called your friends, my sweet little girl is gone. She was light and joy and you snuffed that out because you were *afraid*."

He was sobbing in earnest now, thick ropes of snot oozing from his nose and making it hard for him to breathe, as he remembered, as shame sank its teeth in and ripped him apart. How when he'd heard that Ingrid had died, by her own hand according to the gossip mill, that he'd—gods, he'd been *relieved*, because now that was finally over, he didn't have to think about it or force himself to try and do the right thing anymore. The choice was finally taken from him, and bile was burning its way up his throat.

He lay on his side, sobbing, as Naja straightened and looked down on him coldly.

"Your friends I put down like the dogs they were," she spat, stepping back a few feet. "But I wasn't sure what to do with you.

"But I think I will teach you a lesson. You want to stay silent? Then I will give you your fill of it. Because of you, Ingrid will never know love or purpose, will never again feel joy or pleasure. Because of you she was shunned, treated with contempt by your friends' cronies, and called a liar, made so alone and beastly in her final days that not even *I* could save her." If he could have seen through his tears, he would have seen Naja's face slicked with tears of her own. He would have seen incalculable pain twisting her beautiful features like they were caught on the point of a knife. He would have seen the bleakness of her loss. But he couldn't see, and between one heartbeat and the next Naja's pain had given way to her fury once again.

"So here is your punishment, boy," she continued, her hands beginning to weave intricate patterns in the air between them. "You will be trapped, alone, in this house. Death will not find you, and though people may come and go none will stay, and none will love you. It will be difficult to earn love, after all, when you wear your true monstrous form," she sneered. "No one will remember you, no one will care for you, and no matter how much you may wish to speak of what has happened to you, you won't be able to."

Pounding began at his door, someone was wailing, shouting, rattling the doorknob and throwing their weight against the solid wood. But it was all so far away compared to Naja, to the spell she was weaving that Beast could feel tightening all around him like a snare. Pins and needles began to prickle over his skin, draining away his consciousness, pain flaring along every nerve to eclipse all else. His body felt like it was being stretched to breaking, muscles tearing, bones snapping, and he was screaming, screaming as something crashed, and there was more screaming that might have been his own or it might have been someone else far away and very close, the sound high and keening like a wyvern on the hunt, and then it was too much, and he was falling into the pain and the darkness.

CHAPTER THIRTY-FOUR

Confrontations

Claire was sick to her stomach at what she'd just seen. She couldn't believe that Beast—*her* Beast—had done something so pathetic and horrible. It was a stinging disappointment, to see him run and hide from stopping an innocent woman's worst nightmares from coming true. She was disappointed, and she was angry, and she couldn't believe that this was the same person who had stood by her against Kiernan.

The reason why Naja was showing this was obvious: she wanted Claire to hate Beast, to abandon him. It made her feel absolutely foul, but she forced herself to remember: the person she'd just seen had been only sixteen. When she was sixteen she'd done plenty of awful things, had had moments of cowardice and moments of bone-deep fear that froze her solid. Was this any different? And he had been paying for his crimes for nearly two hundred years. The real question now, she reasoned, might be whether or not he had changed. And if he had, whether it was for the better.

And the truth was that when Kiernan had attacked her, he'd shown no hesitation. He'd charged in and done what he'd failed to do for this other girl, Ingrid. He'd stood up. He'd helped. He hadn't been perfect, but he'd done well. He'd made sure she was safe, he'd demanded she be respected. He hadn't let Kiernan get away with inappropriate comments, with making her uncomfortable. And that said a lot.

He wasn't that sixteen-year-old boy anymore, and while it would likely take a while for her to shake those images, to be able to sit with this new knowledge, she was certain now that her feelings hadn't changed underneath all that.

There was something about Naja's monologue at young Beast's bedside that tickled at the back of her mind, something that had caught her attention that was slipping away now that she was looking for it. Hopefully, she'd find it again before it came up. She had the lingering impression that it had been important, whatever it was.

So that was it: she still loved Beast. She still wanted him, to take him from this horrible place and show him the world, to set him free, to help him fight back his darkness and keep him in the light.

Beast was *hers*.

And it was time that Naja know it.

"What do you think of your hideous lover now, girl?" that icy voice hissed from her side as the scene of Beast's transformation from boy to hulking creation played out before her.

"I think you need to let him go, mage."

Her body turned, Naja sliding into her line of sight, her beautiful face twisted with rage and the agony of grief. "Were you not paying attention? Shall I show you again?"

Claire tried to shake her head and found that she couldn't, she was locked in place, only her mouth and throat able to work under her own power. "No, I saw. Did you? That idiot was sixteen, Naja. A kid, and kids do stupid, selfish shit all the time. He deserved to be punished, not *tortured*. You are not a god, you cannot twist a person's fate like this. The law of this land is on my side. Release him to me."

Naja's face twisted further, becoming nightmarish, her blue eyes bulging and blazing from her face. "I will do no such thing, *child*. I do not wish to hurt an innocent, but if you continue to meddle—"

"Then kill me now, because I'm not going to yield. Release him to me. Give him up and mourn your daughter properly."

Claire knew it was the wrong thing to say as soon as it had slipped out of her. Naja hissed, color staining her pale cheeks. "How *dare* you speak to me of mourning? You pathetic wretch, I have mourned *endlessly* for almost two hundred years! That disgusting worm snuffed out the brightest light that has ever lit up my long life, and I will *never* forget it!" Her voice rose steadily, ending on a piercing shriek that made Claire flinch—at least, internally.

And then the world around her warped and melted once again. A small cottage lit from within by flickering candlelight bled into being before them. It was nestled snugly into a copse of pine trees, old and stretching high into the inky sky. She could feel the bite of Vitrin's breath prickling her skin, the wind cutting like ice through her thin linen summer clothes, making her shiver violently. Which made it all the more alarming when the keening wail of an infant pierced the looming night. She tried to look around, to find the source of that cry and protect the tiny life that had loosed it, but of course she was still frozen, and this was likely no more real than the visions of young Beast had been.

Faint footsteps hurried to the door from within, and then there was Naja, looking just as she did now, but softer, warmer, the edge of bitter ice missing from her blue eyes as she scanned the darkness.

"Hello? Who's there?" this Naja called, flicking her wrist and summoning a glowing orb. She raised her arm, searching in the dark, her other hand clutching the handle of a dagger. Past-Naja's eyes widened when her gaze landed on something just behind Claire. The world spun around her dizzyingly, making her stomach lurch, and then Naja was in front of her, crouching in front of a wriggling basket packed with blankets.

An impossibly tiny fist thrust from the pile of fabric, the fingers clawing towards Naja, the wailing growing louder and more frantic. Naja dropped the dagger and snuffed out the orb, snatching the baby from its basket and cradling it to her chest.

The baby's wailing eased into softer warbling cries interspersed with hiccups. Naja rocked the babe, spinning slowly and peering into the woods around them.

"Is anyone out there? Is this your child? Hello?" Nothing but silence greeted Naja's questions.

"It has been many years since a baby has been left in the care of a witch, little one," Naja murmured into the bundle in her arms. "And I have never cared for a baby before. But I promise you I will do my best. I promise I will love you and care for you and protect you, for you are mine now. A promise sworn thus is binding, dear child.

"Perhaps you were a curse to your parents, for them to leave you here in the woods, but to me you are a gift. A mark of Vitrin's mercy, who I have prayed to many years. If they come back for you they will not find you. Now let's get back inside, sweet little thing."

The scene dissolved again, and now another version of Naja stood tall and fuming, her smooth brow wrinkled with concern. Ingrid stood before her, her fists planted firmly on her wide hips, close to how old she'd looked in the other vision.

"I've been accepted already, Mother. You can't possibly mean to stop me from going to Kesterin. I *need* to go to Kesterin."

"You can study history here, with me. I'll get whatever books you need, make sure you have everything—"

Ingrid screamed quietly in frustration. "That's not the *point*. If all I ever do is read about the world I'll never really be a part of it. I need a chance to *live*. Please, Mother..."

"It's not safe out there, Ingrid. I hate to deny you anything, you know I do, but I've seen what this world can do to goodness, and it would destroy me if anything were to happen to you," Naja said, her voice soft and pleading. "Do you not love me? Do you not want to stay with me?" Naja asked in a whisper, as if she feared the answer would be "no".

Ingrid sighed, her hands dropping to her sides. She stepped close and clasped Naja's hands, squeezing them. "Of course, I love you, Mother. I just...I'm almost a woman grown. And I don't think I can keep growing if this is all I ever see. Please, I promise I'll be careful. I'll take whatever precautions you want me to. But I need to do this. Let me go."

Naja sighed, releasing a shudder as her eyes fluttered closed. Then she pulled her hands free to pull Ingrid into an embrace.

"Alright, my love. You can go to Kesterin."

Rain began to pour from a dull steel sky, drenching Claire

in icy cold. Before her the two women still embraced, but as the rain fell Ingrid's form began to crumble, the color leeching from her until Naja's arms were empty, a pile of ash and dirt lying at her feet. Naja knelt, sobs wracking her thin frame, as the pile smoothed and stretched into a long rectangle—a grave, too fresh for grass to have grown back over the spot. Naja rocked back and forth on her knees, her arms wrapped tight around herself, her sobs choking and rising into horrific screams that ripped apart Claire's heart.

Words began to take shape in between Naja's agonized cries. "They killed you," she was saying, over and over, "they killed you, they killed you, they killed you…" Claire wanted to leave this place, wanted to have never seen any of this, it was all too horrible, too nightmarish, but she was trapped, couldn't even manage to close her eyes now, Naja's pain and grief billowing all around her and through her like a polar wind.

"I couldn't keep my promise to her, in the end," the real Naja said from behind her, startling her. "I couldn't keep her safe. At first, I blamed myself. But then I found a half-finished letter among her things, begging your Beast for help, telling him he owed her that, at least, and I realized that it was no use blaming myself. Not when the real monsters were still out there, living and breathing without a hint of guilt for what they'd done."

Blackness sizzled up all around them, swallowing Claire whole. "I can't even begin to imagine what you've gone through, Naja," she choked out, "even with you showing me, I can't imagine. But you can't keep doing this." Claire wrestled with her surging emotions, trying desperately to remain calm. Keeping a level head now was essential for her and Beast's survival. She wasn't going to win this fight otherwise.

"You can't just lock people up like this. Not without a fair trial with at least two judiciary officials present. Which you know, clearly, because you've gone to such extreme lengths to hide everything about this situation." Claire sucked in a breath, trembling with rage as much as nerves. "If you were so certain that this was good and just and right then why didn't you ever petition for a hearing? Why not bring what had happened here in front of a court? Do you feel justice has been served in these two hundred years, Naja? Does it feel like what you've done here has been a return to *rorto*?"

As Naja seethed, too angry to respond, she remembered what had slipped away from her earlier. *None will love you*, Naja had said. But Claire loved him. She loved Beast enough to have proposed to him. But those words had clearly been a spell Naja had wrought, making it so no one should have been able to feel love towards Beast at all. It didn't make sense, it shouldn't be *possible*. Fae magic was supposed to be the closest thing mortals had to the powers of the divine: immutable, unbreakable, immortal. It was why scholars thought they were dying out: their existence on Cillure threw off the world's balance, and so the world was slowly getting rid of them. Claire wasn't gifted, there was no way she'd been able to dissolve or break through a spell like that.

Unless...

Unless Beast and Claire's relationship was made of the inconceivable. Unless they were bound by a magic that no fae spell could break or warp. Unless, against every single odd out there, they were enmeshed in the stuff of faelore.

Unless...they were *mates*. That ancient force that had tied together so many of the fae, so powerful and fundamental that not even fae magic could touch it.

But that was impossible, wasn't it? Claire was at best one-sixteenth fae on her mother's side. And Beast—wait, now that she was thinking about it he *had* mentioned some fae heritage as well. But there was no way that that had been enough to make a difference…was it?

It *did* explain some things, she had to admit. Why she wasn't tempted to be violent towards him like others had been. Why she'd fallen so hard and so fast for him. Why she'd never managed to fall in love before Beast. Why the idea of marriage felt right with him instead of terrible and horrifying.

Sweet Delenaa, that goddamn faelore they'd been reading to each other was going to come in handy after all. There was that one, Soliei and Fausta…*If he's my mate and I officially claim him, then that might break the curse. She'd be unable to keep him confined against a valid claiming without Consortium aid, and I've already figured out she's keeping him here illegally, so there's no way they'd help her.* This was madness…but it was also her best chance at freeing Beast without either one of them getting killed by the mage in front of her. At the same time, it felt too risky to try.

Naja snarled and swirled into being in front of Claire, her red lips stretched tight against her teeth, her sharp canines on full display. But she didn't say anything, and she didn't move. Claire plunged on.

"I'm a member of the Questing Guild, Naja. And I know as well as you do that this is completely illegal. And unlike Beast, when I go missing it *will* be noticed. Part of our induction is protection against spells like what you've done here. You can't erase me, you can't silence me. And you can't keep Beast here, either." She sucked in a deep breath, trying to swallow around the knot of fear in her throat.

"It's over, Naja. Let us go now and I'm willing to ask a judge for leniency given the nature of the crimes done to your daughter. But no matter what you choose now, it's over. Whether you keep fighting me or surrender…it's done."

Naja screamed again, the sound fury and grief honed into a blade. "*No!*"

Claire licked her lips, trying to think. What could possibly make Naja listen to reason? She had a sinking feeling Naja wasn't going to let them live, that she'd kill them rather than free them, and to hell with the fact that Naja would get the death penalty for killing a Guild member. Maybe there was no reasoning with her. Maybe Naja was too far gone, steeped in grief and rage for so long that all the sense and reason had been hollowed out of her.

Ah shit, I'm going to have to try claiming him. If it worked, Naja wouldn't be able to stop the curse from breaking—it should just happen, if the tale of Soliei and Fausta was to be believed. She had no idea if there was an official speech you had to recite to do it, or if she could just speak from the heart. Being fae folklore rather than a guidebook, the story hadn't been very clear—in fact, none of the texts she'd read had gone in-depth into the actual ceremony.

Shoulders square and chin held high, she looked down her nose at Naja and tried her best. "I, Claire Odetima, claim the beast of the manor as my love, my fiancé…my mate. You will not sever this sacred bond. He is free from your curse, Naja, and you will release him to me. His punishment is over. He is free," she finished uncertainly.

A gentle buzzing began tickling the nape of Claire's neck, shifting over to her shoulder. Her eyes flew open wide. It was the presence that had been lurking around the manor, helping Claire and Beast since she'd first gotten here.

Perhaps they meant to help now.

The buzzing left her skin, leaving her feeling cold, and she held her breath, waiting for something to happen.

She only had to wait a few seconds; Naja's body snapped taut, her eyes going glassy and distant, the tendons in her neck jumping against her skin. Whatever bonds had been holding Claire loosened, and she wrenched herself into motion, muscles screaming in protest. But as soon as she began moving on her own again the scene around them began to fade, began to warp and dissolve, the shadows thickening and swallowing the light, plunging everything into total darkness once more. But it was different this time, a darkness that felt like things rushing in, rather than falling away.

Sight and sound were nothing—all that was left of the world was the roiling black fire she'd been sunk into. Claire lost track of her body, unsure if her feet still hugged solid ground. She screamed and screamed, but without sound, without breath, her mind groping for a way out of the maelstrom, a way back to the manor and Beast.

With the loss of all sensation, she latched onto thoughts of him: she pictured the way he had smiled shyly at her when showing her his precious spinning wheel, his favorite books. She conjured the rumbling of his laughter, how it rolled out from deep in his chest. She focused on how the solid warmth of his flesh under her hand had felt, how his bulk fit so well against her side. She remembered the smell of him, warm and rich: clove and honey and autumn sun. She willed the dark fire all around her to cede to the rich loam of his eyes and how they had smoldered and sharpened when she admitted, at last, that she loved him.

Beast needed her. She had to fight this.

A sharp keening swelled around her, slicing through the tumbling oblivion. Claire's heart began thundering, her blood surging in her veins. This foul creature would not take him away from her. The shriek grew, thrumming all around her now, cutting through the morass of dark power still clinging like a shell. Claire sank into her own fury, whetting it, wrapping her trembling fingers around it, and thrusting it into the terrible husk around her, struggling back to where she came from. The skin of the nightmare realm began crinkling, peeling, until—

All at once it was gone: the howling, the black fire, the void of nothing that had become her flesh and bone. She was standing in the garden and Beast was there, collapsed on the ground, limbs akimbo and looking so, so still.

She surged forward, her heart stuttering in her chest. *No, not now. Not my Beast,* she thought in a panic, pumping her arms and legs with everything she had, urging herself faster, faster, *faster.*

She slid to a stop beside him and fell to her knees, reaching for his throat for a pulse. Dimly, she heard Naja behind her, repeating the same word over and over, the single syllable louder and more shrill each time: "No, no, no, no, *no!*"

It was faint, and far slower than she'd like, but she felt his pulse throbbing against her fingertips. Relief flashed through her, her eyes shutting briefly in silent thanks to the gods. She scrambled to crouch by his head, lifting into a squat while her hands sought to wedge themselves under his shoulders, struggling against his dead weight to lift him up enough to wind her arms under his; she'd never be able to carry him, but she might be able to at least drag him away so she could deal with Naja.

Naja shrieked, darting to Beast's still-frozen form, and Claire's heart shot into her throat—Naja was fast and so *furious*, and there was no way Claire would be able to make her stop this. If only she had been gifted, she could have made the arrest right now, without the paper charms, and finished this once and for all. The buzzing presence had given her time, had broken her free from Naja's memories, and she hadn't been able to do anything with that precious time. She had failed.

No.

No, it wasn't over yet. Claire wasn't gifted, but Naja wasn't trying to best her with magecraft. In her rage Naja had abandoned magic for a physical attack, and *that* she had some experience with. The fae were rumored to be stronger than humans, but as Caldus Love had said: most of the time, it wasn't about strength, it was how you used it.

Claire threw herself in front of Naja, tucking her tired body into a ball and rolling to a stop at Naja's feet. Unable to counter an obstacle so low or reverse her momentum Naja struck Claire's curved back, making Claire hiss in pain, before falling face-first into the dirt.

Claire surged to her feet, grabbing one of Naja's wrists and yanking that arm back and up, making Naja cry out—in fury or pain, she couldn't say. She straddled Naja's waist, using her body weight to pin her further as she tried to snatch up Naja's free hand. Realizing what Claire was up to, Naja's squirming intensified, reaching a crescendo that nearly bucked Claire off of her.

"*Naja*," she gritted out, pinning the wriggling mage under her. "He's mine. In all ways. You need to let this happen. Do you really think Ingrid would want this for you? For you to spend two hundred years torturing someone instead of living your life and finding happiness?" Claire huffed, feeling Naja's struggles weaken. "Ingrid seemed like a sweet person, full of love. How do you think she'd feel about what you've been doing with your life since she passed? Do you think she'd want that for you?" Despite everything, Claire was having a hard time staying mad at Naja. She was a parent mourning the abuse and untimely death of her child, and even if Claire didn't agree with her methods she couldn't honestly blame her. She couldn't say with certainty that she wouldn't try to do something similar, in her position.

"What was I supposed to do?" Naja rasped quietly from under her. "How do you just go back to your life when something like that happens?" Claire swallowed, her throat suddenly thick.

"I don't know, Naja. I-I'm sorry. I'm sorry for what happened to your daughter, and I'm sorry for the pain you've been in. And I understand why you did it. But that doesn't make it right. You can't just decide someone else's fate like that."

Naja snarled, struggling against Claire's grip, before going quiet and still all at once. Claire thumped into the ground, Naja's body suddenly gone, a sound like thunder without the boom echoing in her ears.

All she could do for a moment was blink, as if she could clear her vision enough to make Naja reappear somehow. But it really did seem like Naja was gone.

She crawled the remaining few feet to Beast, who was sitting up and looking around in a panic. Once his eyes landed on hers he pulled himself onto his side and dragged himself closer to her.

"Did she hurt you, Claire?" he asked, his voice hoarse.

She shook her head. "No. You?"

"A little. But it's no less than I deserve. For Ingrid. For everything, really."

It took a moment for them to grasp what he had just said, but they seemed to realize at the same moment. He'd said her name—he'd said *Ingrid's name.*

He looked at her, harsh gray features gone slack with shock. "Ingrid," he said again, looking around himself in a daze. She scooted closer, taking one of his big, clawed hands. "I'm here illegally," he said, testing it further, but it was gone: he was no longer gagged.

"Are you…are you *free*?" she whispered, as if by speaking too loudly she could undo whatever had been done.

"I don't know. I don't feel any different. A little unwell but otherwise the same as always." He squeezed his eyes shut, his free hand curling into a tight fist. "If I am free though, I don't deserve it. I deserve death, a life for a life, as the balance demands."

She squeezed the hand she was holding and reached out to take the other to stop him from hurting himself. "You've served your sentence and then some," she said gently, finding that she believed what she was saying. "We should try going now. I need my things, my arrest kit, my badge, so that if she *does* come back I can do something about it."

He looked over at her, his brow furrowed and his eyes

slightly unfocused. "You're going to arrest her?" he asked, voice slurring just a hair. Claire frowned, her grip on his hands tightening. Was he going clammy?

"Yes. She was holding you here illegally. Civil punishments are very highly regulated, you need to have a hearing and get approval from the Consortium to hand them out." It had been one of the thorniest units of her magical law class. "I still love you, you know," she blurted out, her cheeks heating. It seemed important that she say that, just then.

He looked scandalized. After several failed attempts at speech, he managed to croak out a very disbelieving "You *do*?"

"Oh yes," she agreed, tucking a loose curl behind his ear. "You're still stuck with me, I'm afraid."

"But I...you saw what I did. To Ingrid. How I...how I killed her."

She pursed her lips, keeping her grip on his hands as they sat there on the ground. "I did," she allowed, holding his gaze. "And I can't say that it hasn't changed anything, or that it doesn't matter, but I can say that I've seen enough of you to know that that's not who you are anymore. I knew when I fell for you that you'd done something bad—you were practically screaming about how guilty you were, even with the gag— but I think anyone could see that you've changed. That you're better than that now." She raised one of his hands to her lips and kissed his knuckles, holding his clammy gray skin to her cheek. "And I know we can work together to make what happened to Ingrid right. To get *real* justice for her, for everyone who has to go through what she did. I want to be the one to help you find peace, Beast. To help *Ingrid* find peace."

He sat staring at her, clearly stunned and at a loss. "You have to be joking," he rumbled at last, shaking his head. "There's no way."

"I've never been more serious. I just…keep falling deeper and deeper in love with you and I—" her voice failed her then, her throat locking up. Was it right to do this? Would she regret it in an hour, in the morning, in a week? She took a deep breath, letting it out in a sigh. "And I still want to marry you," she said, her voice pitched too high to her own ears. She'd shied away from it at the last minute, decided she'd hold onto the mates thing for now. She didn't want to overwhelm him, and if she was being honest with herself she didn't want him to feel like he had to wind up marrying her because of it. She wanted him to want that with her on its own merit. Call her old-fashioned.

She parted her lips to keep going, to explain that he didn't have to, of course, that it was his decision, that she'd respect his choice no matter what, but before she could get another word out, he surged forward and kissed her. Her hands drifted into his hair, tangling there, pulling herself closer and closer to the warm bulk of him. His large arms wrapped around her, pulling her to his chest, and they really were the perfect fit, like her body had been crafted to fit against his exactly. Everything else was so distant; all that she needed, all that she wanted, was his mouth on hers, his arms tight around her, his smell like a song thrumming through her blood.

He made a sound low in his throat, something that sounded partway between a growl and a moan, that set her blood on fire and knocked the air from her lungs. An answering sound rose in her. Need, hot and thick, began to heat her at her core, until she thought she would go mad with it. But she gathered her control, and broke away from the silken plush of his lips, meeting his eyes, so dazed, locked on her face.

And then he slumped, his eyes rolling back in his head, and it didn't matter how Claire shook him and shouted his name. The color in his gray skin started to bleed away from granite to pale dove, and panic like she had never known before seized her by the throat and squeezed.

Somehow, she knew: Beast was dying, and Claire couldn't save him.

CHAPTER THIRTY-FIVE

Tully

Claire had never felt so powerless in her life. She screamed again, a sound that came from someplace deep and cold and still within the earth, so primal it was wordless. *Please let him still be alive,* she begged the gods silently. *Please please pleasepleaseplease...*

The fear threatening to smother her eased off her throat as she realized that his chest still rose and fell. Weakly, shudderingly, but he was breathing and her shaking palm felt his heart beating sluggish pumps. She gasped in relief, her cold fingers tracing the lines of Beast's face, her lips moving in quiet, rasping pleas.

"I'm here, love," she whispered, kneeling close to his still, pale face, "I'm here, I'm here."

Her world had shrunk to the pained face of her Beast, to that desperate hope that this was not the end, not so soon, but a hand at her shoulder made her jump and whip around, her own hand reaching out, fingers clawed and wanting to draw blood. But her blow didn't connect, because of course it wouldn't, life didn't seem interested in fairness at the moment, in letting Claire take a heart for a heart, but it wasn't Naja standing behind her. Her wild rolling eyes landed on another woman, stout and handsome in a well-cut shirt and pants, salt-and-pepper hair pulled back in a neat bun.

"Easy, *maya groya*," the woman soothed, her weathered hands held up, palms open in supplication. She couldn't place her accent, thick and rolling but with an odd bounce between syllables. "I am a friend, I promise."

"Who are you?" Claire demanded, dragging herself closer to Beast, trying to use her body to block the stranger. "Where in the seven hells did you come from?"

"I am Tully," the woman crooned, keeping a cautious distance away. "I am a friend of Beast's, *seza groya*, for many years. I was his family's retainer mage, ever since he was a *menna boichik*. You must let me close now, I can help."

Claire didn't so much as shift her weight, every muscle locked tight and ready to pounce at the strange little woman's smallest twitch. It couldn't be Tully—Beast had said she was gone, and given that it had been two hundred years since he'd last seen her, she believed him. Claire's eyes darted around, looking for the trap she knew they'd never let her see so easily. "Who are you really?" she asked.

Tully shrugged, her hands still raised in a truce. "I have told you who I am, *maya groya*. Please, Claire, I beg you, I need to see to him. I cannot hold much longer and I need to set the break before the hold slips off."

None of that had made any sense to Claire, but she understood that the important bit was that this woman, possibly somehow Tully, was trying to help but needed to get closer. She searched Tully's face, her eyes straining and boring into the delicately-lined night-black eyes of the older woman.

She searched for the smallest hint of malice, determined to protect him at all costs, but all she saw was concern, and desperation, and panic.

After a long breathless moment, Claire's muscles relaxed, and though she kept herself facing Tully she moved to kneel by his head, letting her get close. "You make any moves I don't like and I'll kill you," she growled at the woman, her hands clenching into tight fists.

Tully loosed a breath, finally lowering her hands and coming to kneel at Beast's side. "Thank you," she said tightly, her hands already weaving and plucking at the air above his too-still form. Claire nodded, her eyes drawn to the spellwork that Tully had begun, her fingers fluttering and pinching as if she were combing through a woven fabric, loosening some knots and plucking up loose ends to unravel them elsewhere in the warp and weft. Tully began muttering, the words too breathy and strange for Claire to make out, but soon she could feel the air around her buzzing and warm, as if she was sitting inside an invisible beehive.

She gasped, her gaze snapping up to Tully's face. She knew that feeling. It had often teased at her senses, ebbing against her skin and tickling at the edges of her dreams—had it been this woman, Tully? It would certainly explain how she was still alive, if she'd been wrapped up with the manor's enchantments this whole time. And if she was free, then Beast must truly be free, too. He just had to survive whatever it was that was happening to him.

Tully continued her spell, her eyes closed now and her fingers a blur, sweat beginning to bead on her brow. Claire's eyes slid down to her mate's face, still so pale and still, but she noticed with profound relief that his chest was rising and falling more regularly, the movements stronger and fuller than they had been a moment before, and as she continued to watch his color returned, too. He looked so small and helpless on the ground, almost doll-like, and she couldn't stop an aching sob from climbing up her throat. *I will give anything, please. Please let him be okay.*

The fervor of Tully's movements began to ease, the frantic weaving and muttering slowing and smoothing, until she opened her eyes and sat back on her heels with a long sigh. She mopped her face with a shirtsleeve, then reached down to comb his wild red hair back from his face, every inch the mother tending a sick child.

"He will rest now," Tully declared, her voice softer but with an undercurrent of deep strength. "But he is safe."

Claire closed her eyes, sobs wracking her in earnest now. "Thank you," she choked out, reeling.

Tully gripped her shoulders, squeezing hard enough to hurt, and Claire was brought back into herself, tears flowing but no longer choking her. "You have been so brave, *seza groya*, and I know you have many questions. I promise I will answer them, but we must be strong now, yes?" Claire nodded, looking into the older woman's fierce black eyes and knowing, in that odd way that she seemed to simply *know*, that she was being told truths. "We have to move him, and we have to leave. Time is trying to rush back in and it will swallow this place up; it will not be safe soon. I am holding it but I cannot for very much longer. Do you understand?"

She didn't but she nodded anyway. "What do you need me to do?" That was the most important part, anyway.

Tully released her, pointing to the stables over her shoulder. "I need you to grab the cart from there, so we can move him from the grounds. If there is still time after, then we will need to go inside the manor and pack quickly, whatever necessities we can. Be swift, *Clarachik*."

Claire nodded again, sparing just a moment to lay a kiss on Beast's forehead before gathering herself and rising unsteadily to her feet. Her legs prickled and burned from sitting on the ground so long but she ignored it, running as fast as she could to the stable and throwing the doors wide.

Claire could see right away that something was wrong. The details of the space had gone askew, lines failing to stay straight, shadows slanting and sliding at odd angles. In the deep corners of her vision things had begun to sizzle and blur, and panic spiked through her chest and lent speed to her awakening limbs. She spotted the cart in question and hauled it towards the door, the rough wood chafing her palms. Blessedly, the wheels turned smoothly, easily, and in a moment she was out of the stables and hurrying across the grass to where Tully still crouched over Beast.

She set the cart down and squatted by his head. "I'll grab him under the arms, you get his feet," she suggested, suspecting that Tully would be worn from her magecraft. She let more prayers fly that her wrung-out body would find the strength to hoist his massive form up and over into the cart with just Tully's help. Weren't people always telling stories about fantastic feats of strength made possible by desperation and panic? Maybe they'd prove true.

Tully nodded, getting into position. The older woman still carried herself well, her movements clean and straight, but shadows bruised her under eyes. On Claire's count, they lifted, her legs and back burning with the strain of lifting Beast's limp bulk. But by some miracle they got him settled into the cart.

Panting and sweating, Tully took up the posts of the cart and waved Claire towards the manor. "If you mean to grab supplies from the house now is the time. The spell is breaking and I think you only have a few more minutes. Fifteen, maybe. I will take him beyond the gate, *Clarachik*. I think I am too tired for more running."

Claire nodded, uneasy at the idea of taking her eyes off him for so long, but even her ungifted senses could tell that something was going quickly, horribly wrong with this place. She turned on her heel and ran as fast as her wrung-out legs could carry her into the manor.

Once again she was struck by how tilted and off-center the familiar bounds of the space had gone. It felt like she had been spinning around in circles for too long, the world gone dizzy and slippery all around her. When she put her feet down, trying to eat up the distance to her room, her foot no longer connected with solid wood, and several times she stumbled or slipped.

At last, she found her room. She slid to a halt and threw the door open, lurching inside and heading straight for her wardrobe. Luckily, she hadn't fully unpacked from her last trip to Edden, taking out her clothes and toiletries but leaving all of her road gear neatly tucked away. She spun around the room, which spun dizzyingly with her, grabbing everything she could, then tied her pack shut and threw it on.

The manor had begun to groan and shudder, metal and stone deep inside the structure squealing in protest. Her breath came in pants now, her heart hammering away inside her chest like it wanted to crack through her ribs and escape. She gulped air, swallowing past the burning in her throat, then dashed out of her room and down the bucking length of the hall, turning left at the juncture and making for Beast's bedroom. There, she repeated the process, ripping the sheets from his bed and tossing armfuls of his clothes in the center. She tried to select the hardiest pieces, but as she heard the sharp crack of stone breaking panic flooded her senses and she began flinging whatever she could into the bundle. The manor shuddered violently all around her, and she screamed, flinching from the horrible groaning, then tied up the bundle and flung it over her shoulder, praying her trembling legs would be able to carry her to safety.

The manor bucked and rolled and began to sag, and she pushed even harder, her lungs burning and her blood roaring in her veins as the wood and plaster all around her began to crack and slough away. She sailed down the grand staircase, her feet barely touching the risers. The marble floor of the foyer slid like ice beneath her feet and she almost fell, tipping dangerously far backward, but she managed to keep her feet and strained for that last stretch between her and open ground. As she crossed the threshold she heard a great tinkling crash, and a quick look over her shoulder showed the enormous chandelier crumpled in a heap where she had been seconds before. She whipped her head back around, sunlight and a curiously strong wind striking her face as she crossed the threshold onto the lawn.

She groaned in her head, her breath too spent to do it aloud, as she realized that the manor wasn't the only thing crumbling: huge jagged rends in the grass were splitting wide like hungry mouths, threatening to catch her feet and swallow her up. She searched ahead and saw with relief that Tully was waiting outside the silver gates with Beast in the cart, waving frantically at her to hurry, hurry. She didn't let her stride break, her bundles heavy and bouncing on her back, as she dodged and leaped the cracks in the ground. She came heart-stoppingly close to the edge of one, noting that it looked like there was no bottom to it, and a surge of panic so sharp it made her dizzy knifed through her stomach.

They were so close now, Beast still and unconscious and Tully hopping and waving and shrieking, more and more of the ground crumbling away around her. As she got within the last few feet she wrung the last bit of strength from her legs and leaped, landing hard on her stomach near Tully's feet, her meager breath knocked from her lungs.

Stomach aching from the impact, she lay still on the trembling ground, sucking up air with limited success, for several heartbeats. Gradually she was able to fill her lungs, the black spots on the edge of her vision fading, and she shucked off her pack, pushing it and the sheet-wrapped bundle of Beast's things off to the side. She flopped onto her back, moaning a little at the sharp protests of her muscles, and closed her eyes against the bright sunlight beaming onto her sweaty face.

"What...in the ever-loving shit...just happened?" Claire panted, rolling her head to the side to take in Tully, wilted to the ground herself, sitting propped up against the cart.

Tully sighed, leaning her head back and closing her eyes. "Time," she responded breathlessly. "A lot of time, all at once. I think it was one last trap that *mala crujzta* set for us. It almost took him, our Beast, but we are too clever for her, *maya groya*."

The two women lay on the ground, limp and spent and trying their best to gather their wits about them. Claire had begun to drift gently into sleep when Tully cleared her throat and began to speak.

"Our Beast will sleep still for some time, maybe a day or two, and while he does this we will need to make our way to town. Does Edden still stand?"

Claire rolled over and half-crawled over to Tully, joining her propped up against the side of the cart. "It does," she responded, groaning as pulled herself up. Tully's warm rough hand clasped hers, squeezing.

"You did so good, *seza groya*," Tully rasped, her eyes closed. "Better than I think I would have done in your position. You have saved my son, and I am forever in your debt for that. I can never thank you enough." Tully's eyes cracked open, studying Claire's face.

"So you really are his mother?" She swallowed, trying to moisten her throat. "He mentioned you a bit."

Tully shrugged. "Yes, and no. I did not give birth to him, but from when he was just a little boy I took care of him, raised him, and in that way he is mine."

Claire nodded, smiling weakly. "You were there this whole time, weren't you?"

Tully nodded. "Yes, but also no, as is always the way with the sticky things in life. I was not allowed to be there, to intervene, but I found a way to be near. In another layer of the world, one that touches but is not here, where I could watch and send small magics to help. Where I could wait for my *boichik* to be free."

"I felt you," Claire whispered, her throat still burning from her mad dash through the crumpling manor. "I didn't know what it was but I felt you."

"You are very sensitive, I think," Tully replied, searching

her face in earnest. "I don't feel much magic in you but there is some, maybe only enough to be able to feel little whispers and hints. You see people clearly, more clearly than an ungifted person should. And I think this drop of a gift also lets you feel some of the magics of others."

Claire snorted. "Handy. There's some fae way back in my ancestry, you think that's where it comes from?"

Tully shrugged. "Very possible. The gift is strange and wily. Beast also has some of this same ancestry, and I think with so much time steeped in the magics of others, it has given him some giftedness."

Claire's brows rose. "That shouldn't be how that works," she scoffed, but turned to Tully with a smile. "Lucky him. It explains some things he's said to me, if he's been secretly gifted."

"Oh yes, it would be very secret. Even to him. I watched *maya boichik*, and I do not think he even really saw what he was doing."

The two women remained seated on the ground, catching their breath for several minutes, while Claire tried not to look too closely at the massive pit on the other side of the silver gates that had once been the manor.

"Since you're a mage, do you think you could explain to me how that worked? Are me and Beast…are we really… *mates*? It seems so unlikely."

Tully nodded, beaming at her. "It is no more unlikely than one woman enchanting a man and an entire manor home to be frozen in time as punishment for a crime against her daughter. It is no more unlikely than this same *stroga nazsam* managing to find a way to alter the boards at the Questing Guild, making it so that her tracks are almost completely covered. If you want, perhaps think of it more like soulmates. This is a human concept, yes?"

Claire nodded. It was less weird to her than thinking her one-sixteenth fae blood had been enough to forge the mythical mate bond, at least. "So all the weird stuff with the boards and other questers…Naja somehow did that?"

Tully nodded again, rolling her eyes. "Yes, though by all accounts she should not have been able to. The Consortium infused those boards with powerful magecraft." She sighed. "She could not stop the surge of magic registering on the boards, but she was able to alter the information on it to obscure what she was doing. She made it unappealing and easily forgettable so that few would even look at it. And for those that *did* look, she had her nasty fear enchantment to make sure no one was successful."

Claire cocked an eyebrow. "Fear enchantment?"

Tully nodded, her face contorting with pain. "On Beast. To make everyone who looked upon him go mad with fear. Everyone who came here before you either ran from him or tried to kill him. If—" she swallowed, tears making her eyes go glassy. "If not for the enchantment keeping him alive, he would have died dozens of times over."

Feeling like she might be sick, Claire pressed a shaking hand to her mouth. Tully pursed her lips and grabbed Claire's other hand, squeezing firmly. "Well, at least it explains why everyone was so violent towards him," Claire said faintly. She squeezed Tully's calloused hand and then let go.

Muscles that had begun to stiffen at rest seared back into life as Claire hauled herself to her feet, leaning heavily on the rough wood of the old cart. As her eyes settled on Beast's slack face, the panic threatening to claw its way out of her stilled and settled. She raised her trembling hand up to cup his long face, now fully back to its usual pewter gray color. He looked serene and relaxed, his breaths deep and even. He was fine, he wasn't dying. Claire sighed, shaking her head to try and clear it of how he'd looked splayed out on the ground, pale and fading fast. She leaned down to kiss his forehead lightly, hoping that he, at least, was having a good rest.

As her lips brushed his warm skin his eyelids twitched and fluttered, then cracked open and locked dazedly on Claire's face. She beamed at him, relief so profound it made her dizzy cutting through the confusion and fear darkening her thoughts.

"Sweet man," she breathed, taking one of his hands and squeezing it gently. "Welcome back."

"You're here," he murmured, his gaze going a bit unfocused.

"Of course," she assured him, "and Tully's here too. She saved us."

His face crumpled, his eyes drifting wider as he looked around. "*Madjem?*" he asked.

Claire heard a sob from down by her hip and felt Tully hauling herself upright beside her, panting faintly with the effort. But the older woman was clearly cut from steel rather than cloth, and managed to stand, swaying slightly and tears glittering in her eyes. Tully clapped her hands to her face, covering her mouth and nose as sobs began to work their way out from between her tightly pursed lips.

"*Maya boichik,*" she rasped, and then she bent down and wrapped her arms around Beast as best she could, his arms coming up as well to wrap around her shuddering shoulders, and she took a step back to give them more space, emotion welling up in her throat and causing tears to prick at her eyes. They held each other like that for a long minute, murmuring things that Claire couldn't hear. But they did part, Tully planting a huge kiss on his damp cheek, and with red glistening eyes Tully announced she would give them a moment while she set up a little camp.

Claire returned to Beast's side, and while his eyes shone bright and clear she could see that exhaustion was pulling at him again, trying to drag him back down into sleep. "You're safe now, love," she said quietly, picking at bits of grass and dirt that had embedded themselves in his clothes. "And you're free of the curse. Naja let me have you."

He smiled up at her, his eyes drooping. "Good. I can't wait to be your kept man."

She laughed, squeezing his hand again. "You should sleep," she said, leaning down to kiss him gently. She was afraid of hurting him, of losing him, that she would do the exact wrong thing and he would burst like the rind of a bubble and effervesce into nothing. But his lips felt as solid and warm as they ever did, and she breathed his smell of spice and amber deep into her lungs.

"Love you," he whispered as his eyes slid shut and his breathing began to deepen.

"And I love you," she whispered back, brushing her knuckles along the sharp ridge of his cheekbone. "Sleep well, sweet man."

CHAPTER THIRTY-SIX

Sam

In the end, all three of them had needed quite a lot of rest. Claire had offered to take a watch and given Tully her bedroll. The two women had wedged some clothing under Beast's head and tried to make him a little more comfortable in the cart.

Mother and son sleeping, Claire set to work sorting through what she'd grabbed in her mad dash through the manor. In her pack, she had most of her clothes, and all of her traveling gear, including her little cooking pot. She was useless at hunting, but maybe Beast or Tully could manage to catch something. If not then she could forage and make a vegetable stew. She couldn't name any of the pretty flowers that had decorated the manor grounds but she'd done fairly well in her survival classes and was confident she wouldn't poison them all. She had her travel kit of toiletries in there, but didn't think she'd grabbed anything for Beast, and certainly not for Tully. *Well, I guess we'll all get smelly, or have to share.* Sharing with Beast wasn't completely horrid, considering how intimate they were, but she'd only just met Tully.

She also had her half-knitted scarf stashed at the very bottom of her pack as well as the two skeins of yarn he'd gifted her, but her heart sank as she realized that all of Beast's spinning was gone now, lost in the sinkhole. He'd probably manage to take it in stride, especially because now he was free, but it hurt anyway. And when she realized her spindle was gone, too, she couldn't help the disappointed groan that slipped out. "Dee's never going to believe me now," she grumbled.

Her arrest kit, diviner, and baton were still strapped to the front of her pack, thank the gods, as was her badge, and she found her dagger wadded up with a pair of pants, so all told she was reasonably prepared to be able to make it to Edden. She studied the sun in the sky, then her sleeping companions. They'd be camping tonight for sure, but if they rested well they might be able to make it in tomorrow.

With a heavy sigh, she tackled the chaotic tangle of things she'd grabbed for Beast next. At the very least she could fold things neatly and keep her hands busy without having to get up anytime soon, which sounded absolutely perfect. She wanted to keep busy, her residual nerves resisting idleness, but she was *very* tired and aching for her turn at some sleep. She un-knotted the sheet she'd thrown everything in and started sorting things into piles. It was mostly clothes, but given the size of him he'd likely have trouble finding clothes that could be made to fit him until they got back to Kesterin, so this was good.

Back to Kesterin. Beast was free, and he was coming with her back to Kesterin. He'd meet her family, see the places she'd grown up. A huge smile unfurled across her face. Adeela was going to love him, her bashful giant. Adeela loved nothing more than mothering and Beast was the sort that attracted mothers like flies to honey.

But then she remembered that she didn't have a home waiting for her back in Kesterin. Her father didn't want her, and as much as she loved Adeela it wasn't right to expect her to house so many people. The Guild would at least provide shelter for Beast and Tully, and then Claire might be able to find a cheap room while she did some more quests to save up for a place of her own.

The idea wasn't as terrible as it had been when she'd first considered it at the beginning of this quest. So much had changed for her. She wasn't alone anymore, for one—even if Beast was just as clueless as her about how to make it in the world he was someone to help her, someone to figure it out *with*, and that made it a lot less scary. And that was another thing—she'd done a lot of scary things since setting out on the road to Edden, and compared to the soul-deep fear of thinking her mate was going to die right in front of her, having to figure out how to make enough money to keep a roof over her head was nothing.

She paused in her folding, looking over at him asleep in the cart. It had been very hard, seeing what he'd done. It was definitely something she'd have to sit with, that she'd have to figure out where it fit, exactly, in how she thought of him. But she'd been correct when she'd told him that it wouldn't change how she felt about him. She knew he'd never let that happen now, that he'd do what was right even if it scared him. She still loved him, still found herself wanting to build a life with him. Butterflies rioted in her stomach at the thought. Ordinarily, she'd never rush into something like that, but with Beast it felt inevitable, it felt natural, even before she'd realized the true nature of their connection. *Mates. What were the odds of* that *one?* She thought with a dry huff of laughter.

They probably wouldn't get married right away. No doubt there'd be miles of paperwork in their future: there'd be some for wrapping up the quest, some for getting Beast and Tully citizenship, and who knew how much would come from sorting out how they'd live their lives now that they were free to live them for the first time in two hundred years. There'd be time for her and Beast to keep getting to know each other, to feel out what it would be like to live together in the real world, to work as a single unit. Beast had mentioned that he'd like to be a healer, and Claire honestly thought he'd make a good one. He'd certainly done well at nursing her through her food poisoning, and he was very warm and calm when he wanted to be, and not at all squeamish. That would mean getting him enrolled at a questing preparatory school, and she thought it would be just grand for him to go to her alma mater. In fact, she'd pay good silver to see how Caldus Love would react to a seven-foot tall gray-skinned giant strolling into his practice arena.

She finished the last of the folding, pleased to see she'd grabbed the three Garnette Mason books Beast had had stashed in his room. That would be some comfort to him, even if other things might have been more useful. She'd also grabbed his hairbrush, to her surprise, and a packed kit that wound up being for shaving and nail trimming.

Everything at the makeshift camp sorted, Claire groaned and staggered to her feet. She'd be stiff and sore tomorrow for certain, but for now she was alright once she got moving. She decided to try foraging on the edges of the clearing they'd settled in, or at least try and gather some firewood. She didn't think it would be too risky to start a fire, all the way out here and so far from the beaten paths popular with bandits and thieves. And it would keep night cats away once the sun went down.

Luckily, it hadn't rained recently, and the season was beginning to turn, so there was plenty of dry firewood and dry grass and leaves for timber. She was less lucky when it came to food though. She found some wild onions and chestnuts, but no berries she recognized as safe, no mushrooms, no streams for water. Likely she'd have to go deeper into the woods for all that, but it was getting late, the afternoon tipping into evening and darkness, and she was completely drained. It would be best to stay close to her companions for now. She returned to the center of camp and built up a small fire.

Once the flames had gotten big enough to crackle, Tully stirred and sat up, wiping her hand over her face.

"Good morning, *Clarachik*. How have things been? Quiet, I hope," Tully yawned, stretching her arms up.

"Good morning. Though I hate to tell you it's actually more like late afternoon." She smiled at the older woman, suddenly shy. For all intents and purposes, Tully was going to be her mother-in-law, and that thought suddenly made her much more intimidating.

Tully waved away her correction. "Time has not meant anything to me for many years. All I know is I wake up from big sleep, then it is morning. *Kasza pruje*," she said, clapping her hands together as if that was that.

Claire smiled, deciding she liked Tully, even if Tully didn't wind up liking her. "I tried scrounging up some food while you were sleeping but didn't have much luck in the immediate area," she offered, getting Tully up to speed. "I could try looking deeper in the woods now that you're up, but I didn't want to leave you two defenseless." She hugged her knees to her chest, not looking forward to having to trudge through the darkening forest—but as a quester, it was her job to take care of the victims of violence and disaster.

Tully yawned again, shaking her head. "No need, *seza groya*. You have done so much, you should rest now. I can handle the food." Tully hauled herself to her feet with several audible cracks and snaps, making Claire wince in sympathy. "I will let you take back your bed, *Clarachik*, and get your own rest. I will take watch and get food while you sleep."

"Are you sure? I don't want to leave you without any defenses. I can stay up a bit longer, help with dinner."

Tully put her fists on her wide hips, glaring down at Claire. "You are *not* fine to stay up longer, young lady. I can see your exhaustion plain on your lovely face." Tully's look softened into a smile. She waved Claire over. "Come, rest. You will need your strength in the coming days. Getting my son to Edden will not be easy."

Claire got up from her seat next to the fire, brow furrowing with concern. "Why's that? Is he still ill?"

Tully shrugged, looking over at Beast in his cart. "He may be, after the shock to his body when the enchantment snapped. But I think the harder thing will be getting him ready to be in a place with many people again. Nothing will be like he remembers, and I am sure you have noticed *maya boichik* is very delicate, very nervous. He will need our support."

As tired as Claire was, she couldn't resist walking over to the cart and looking down at his sleeping face. "My poor sweet man," she cooed, combing her fingers through his hair and brushing her fingertips over one of his cheeks. "You're right, it's going to be very difficult for him." She looked over her shoulder at Tully, who was picking through Beast's clothes. She pulled out one of the rattier shirts in the pile and began ripping it apart. "Will it be difficult for you, too?"

Tully shrugged, setting a strip of fabric aside. "It will be… an adjustment, I think. But I am not afraid of stepping back into life. This one, though…I think he will need to be eased into things. I am glad he has you, to lead him and comfort him in ways I cannot."

Claire blushed. She realized that there was a very good chance that Tully had witnessed just how well Claire could "comfort" him, her face flaring so hot she worried she might faint for a moment. "I'm—" She cleared her throat. "I'm glad you approve of me," she admitted quietly, turning back to the bedroll so that she could set it up directly beside Beast in his cart.

"How could I not? I want only the best for my boy, especially after all he has suffered. And I do not just say this because of being mates. It is because I have seen you with him, have known for many weeks now that you are so good for him. No parent would be disappointed to have you in their family."

Well damn, if that didn't have Claire choking right up. She blinked away tears, swallowing several times to dislodge the knot in her throat enough for her to speak. "Thank you," she croaked. "My father would probably disagree with you, but I appreciate it. I love Beast with all my heart. I will protect him, I promise you."

Tully nodded, smiling. "Of course. I trust you in this. And

your father is a great fool, I am sure you already know. I will be your father now, have no worries *Clarachik*."

Claire laughed as she settled onto her bedroll. "Well, thank you, Tully. For…for everything. I couldn't have done it without you."

"Pah," Tully said as she began braiding the strips of fabric she'd torn. "You were already on your way to it. That *stroga nazsam* tried her best to defy you, but you had a plan. And it worked! So sleep now, Claire. I will take care of dinner. Rest."

She didn't have to get told twice. She curled up on her side, her travel cloak pulled over her like a blanket, and closed her eyes.

When Claire woke it was to the sound of night insects chirping and the warbling of a strange bird.

Wait. No, that was singing. She rolled over and saw Tully cooking over the fire, whatever it was smelling utterly delicious. Claire sat up, stretching and looking over at Beast, who was still out cold. She hauled herself to her feet, leaning over to kiss his brow and brush her fingers along his jaw.

"Good morning, *Clarachik*," Tully trilled, shooting her a smile. This time Claire didn't correct her. It *was* pretty funny, and she liked it.

"Good morning, Tully. That smells amazing. What did you manage to find?"

"I managed to get nice fat rabbit with a snare, and some maska root in a patch not too far from here. So we shall feast on stew!"

Claire was impressed. "That's amazing!"

Tully grinned, stirring the stew. "It was good to brush the dust off. I have not had to hunt since I was a *groyachik*, a little girl. It is good to know I did not lose my skills."

"I was hopeless at all things hunting in my survivalist class," Claire admitted, sitting down on a rock near Tully. "My strengths have always leaned more towards foraging, if anything." The two women sat in silence for a time, Claire shaking off the last delicate cobwebs of sleep. "If you don't mind my asking, what did you do before you got trapped at the manor, Tully?"

Tully sighed, sitting back on her heels. "*Tch*, it seems silly now. I was royal high mage for some years—no, don't look so impressed, it was not such a good thing. I was like a nanny, cleaning up messes for the royal family of Viskege. So after I had served my minimum I left, came to Citrine. My plan was to join the Consortium's officers, do some real good in the world. But then I met Beast's parents, who had an interesting job offer for me, to be their retainer mage. And I saw *maya boichik* hiding as best he could in a corner, far too quiet for a little thing, and I had to accept. When you feel the threads of fate tugging you must follow, yes?" Tully took a branch and poked at the fire, rearranging a log so that it would burn more evenly.

Claire was dumbstruck. She had been a *royal high mage*? And she'd wound up *here*, trapped by an enchantment?

"Naja must be really powerful if she was able to keep you trapped here for so long."

Tully snorted. "She is tricky, and brutal, but no match for me. I could have freed myself any time. But *maya boichik*…it was too dangerous to try and pull him from her web. There were so many thorns, so many traps built in. It was safer to wait, to make him comfortable as I could, and hope someone could free him safely. I did not want to free him only to lose him, you see?" Tully looked over at Beast's sleeping form with a soul-deep heaviness. "It is my greatest failing in life, that I could not free him. That I could not help him more." Tears glazed her dark eyes, and Claire reached out to take her hand, squeezing gently.

"You did everything you could," she said softly. "You're the reason he didn't go completely mad. I couldn't figure out how he could have kept his wits about him for so long, but if you were there that whole time, and he knew it, then that's it: he wasn't alone. He had his mama there, and that counts for a lot."

Tully's lower lip trembled, but she managed to firm it up into a smile. "Thank you, *seza groya*. You are a treasure, truly."

Claire was blushing now, unsure how to take a compliment like that. After a lifetime of lacking, she still had a hard time accepting kind words and soft feelings from others. But it felt good. And considering Tully was going to be family eventually, it was still more amazing to know she was already loved and accepted.

Once the stew was done, Claire and Tully helped themselves to heaping bowls of the thick, rich food. Claire burned her tongue in her eagerness, having to eat with her fingers because her spoon had gone missing. "It's so good," Claire moaned, licking her fingers. "Do you think we should try and wake him to get him to eat and drink?"

Tully cocked her head, thinking. "I do not think he will wake, but it would be good for him to get some nourishment." She stood up and walked over to the cart, rolling up her sleeves. She held her hands out over his chest, her fingers plucking and smoothing at the air, her hands occasionally twisting into shapes Claire swore she almost recognized.

He groaned softly, his hands and feet twitching. Claire stood and jogged over to the other side of the cart with her bowl. Slowly, his eyes fluttered and cracked open.

"Well, how do you like that," Tully murmured. *"Maya boichik*, we wish you to eat and drink. Can you do this?"

He groaned again, his eyes falling shut. "Alright," he sighed, though he made no move to sit up. Claire smirked, handing Tully her bowl.

"Come on, big guy," she said, wedging her arm under his shoulders and hauling him upright.

His eyes slid open part way, but it seemed like a mighty effort for him to keep them open.

"Better feed him quick, Tully," Claire grunted as she got a firmer grip on his upper body to keep him upright. She kissed his temple just below his horn, whispering in his ear: "If you're a good boy and eat and drink something I'll suck your cock once we're alone."

That perked him up: his eyes opened fully and he whipped his head around to look at her, narrowly missing her face with that horn of his, face flushed deeply. *"Claire,"* he said, sounding scandalized, but looking excited.

She laughed, pecking another kiss to his face and squeezing his shoulders. "Eat," she commanded, and he obediently took the bowl from Tully and ate. He took several long swallows of water from the skin, then belched lightly and slumped. "You did great, sweet man," Claire told him quietly as she helped him back down. "I'll work on that reward as soon as I can."

He smiled, asleep almost as soon as his head touched the wadded clothes that were serving as his pillow. Claire admired how relaxed and peaceful he looked, her fingers combing through his hair, her heart aching with love.

"He'll be like this for days, you said?" she asked, turning back to Tully.

The older woman nodded. "At the worst. He may be up and about tomorrow. But two hundred years…this is a lot of time to recover from."

Claire sighed, rolling her neck. "Then we'd best get our sleep tonight, since we'll have to drag him in the cart." She brushed her fingers over his cheek, then forced herself to step away from his sleeping form to help Tully get the camp ready for the night. "I can take first watch."

But Tully waved her hand dismissively. "You rest. I am too awake still. I have much to prepare for the journey, besides."

"You're sure?" Claire couldn't help the rush of relief. With food in her belly she was back to being utterly exhausted and ready to drop.

Tully nodded enthusiastically. "Of course. Sleep, *seza groya*." A coy look stole over her gently lined face, making her dark eyes glitter with mischief. "You will want to be well-rested for when it is time to give Beast his reward, yes?"

Claire's face flamed hot. "You uh…you heard that, huh?"

Tully laughed, the sound full of joy and delight. "It's alright. Believe it or not, I was once young and in love. Just do not make me see it, please."

Claire squealed, burying her face in her hands. This was *not* how she wanted to spend her first day with her eventual mother-in-law. "Right, I'm going to bed. Please forget you heard that. Or at the very least do *not* let that man know you heard. He might literally die of embarrassment."

Tully laughed even louder, saying something in her native tongue, then closed her mouth and twisted her finger in front of her closed lips like she was locking a door.

Face still flaming hot, Claire lay back down and tried not to let herself get worked up thinking about the things she'd be doing to Beast when they finally got some time to themselves.

The last thing she needed was to get aroused around Tully, too.

It wound up being another full day before Beast woke up on his own. Claire and Tully were taking turns lugging the cart, the other person shouldering the heavy pack. They marched through the forest for as long as they could that day, but the cart kept getting caught on roots, on rocks, on uneven patches of ground, sinking into muddy patches, and slipping on leaves. It was making traveling miserable and slow, and they agreed early on that as soon as he could walk they were abandoning the damned thing.

It was perhaps two hours into their slog on the second day when Claire, who was having her turn with the cart, heard a gasp behind her and felt the cart rocking. She stumbled to a stop and called out for Tully, who'd scouted ahead a little ways, clearing what she could to make the cart's path smoother.

"I think he's awake, Tully!"

Claire heard a squawk, then the sound of foliage being trampled. She set the front of the cart down and turned to

Beast, who was sitting up and scrubbing at his face with his hands. He noticed her and held his arms open to her, and she climbed into the cart without hesitation and threw herself at him.

"You're finally awake!"

"How long was I sleeping?"

"A little over two days."

He made a little strangled sound in her ear. "Sweet Delenaa, that long?" He pulled away from her slightly, looking around them. "Where are we?"

"A few miles outside of Edden. If you can walk now we'll make it there by sundown, I should think." Tully had finally made it back to them, but Claire couldn't stop herself from pressing a lingering kiss to his soft lips. His arms tightened around her, holding her close and making her melt.

"How are you feeling, *maya boichik*?" Tully asked from the side of the cart.

He broke their kiss, blushing again and pursing his lips. "Stiff. Hungry. Thirsty. What happened, Tully?" Claire squeezed his hand, then hopped off the cart.

"Ack, it is a long tale to tell, sweet boy, and me and your lovely Claire are tired from dragging this *crujzta* cart all over this forest. We will tell you all once we are at the inn with good food in front of us. Trust me."

"Of course," he said. He slowly clambered upright, taking a moment to make sure he had his balance before sliding out of the cart. Once he was out he twisted and stretched, every joint cracking loudly as he did.

"Vitrin's mercy, are you alright?" she exclaimed.

"Yes, I think so. Nothing hurts too terribly." He continued stretching for a bit, then took the water and jerky Claire held out to him. Once he'd eaten they continued on their way, making much better time now that the cart was left behind.

He kept close to Claire's side as they walked, his hand clasping hers tight.

"You really don't hate me, knowing what I've done?" he asked quietly, his voice sounding so tight and scared.

She squeezed his hand tighter. "Nope! I told you I'd still love you after, and here we are with me still loving you."

He managed a small smile. "You just love being right, don't you?"

She laughed, nudging him playfully. "It's the best." She sobered, leveling a hard stare at him. "You're not getting any pigheaded ideas about leaving me, are you? Because you think I deserve better but just don't see it?"

He shook his head. "No, I think I learned my lesson there." He had the decency to look embarrassed. "But I do still think it. What I did it's…unforgivable."

"I won't lie to you; it was hard to see. But I think unforgivable is too harsh, even for you." She squeezed his hand again, leaning into him as they walked. "You're not that person anymore. And that counts for a lot, in my book. I've known too many people who wind up the same awful person their whole lives—or who get *worse* over time. And now you're free. You can keep growing, keep working on yourself and doing better. You can give back to the world and try and make your little corner of it better."

"I'm free," he breathed, his brown eyes going liquid. "I can't believe it, after two hundred years—" He paused in his steps, surprised joy on his face. "I forgot the gag was gone! I can talk about Naja and Ingrid and everything again!" His brow furrowed. "I…I can't remember my real name though.

Or my parents'."

"Give it time, dear," Tully called back from ahead of them. "You are recovering from a near-death experience."

His brows drew together. "I almost died?"

Claire tugged on his hand, urging him forward. "Later, dearest. We need to get to Edden by dark, first."

"It would be nice if you both stopped saying things that upend my life, then," he grumbled. Claire and Tully laughed brightly, and after a moment a smile quirked up his slate lips. They continued on, quietly deciding to save the heavier conversation for later, when they could focus on it.

It was perhaps an hour later when Beast's spine suddenly snapped straight, eyes going wide. Claire drew up, alarmed. But fear turned to confusion as he began to laugh—great, deep-seated belly laughter that had him doubled up and gasping.

"What in the name of the gods has gotten into you?" she asked, bemused.

It took a moment for him to get it out, to get air enough *to* get it out: "I've remembered my name, Claire."

Confusion settled deeper, drawing her brows down low over her eyes.

"My name," he gasped, still giggling, "was Blare. Blare Malterran III."

Her eyebrows shot clear up to her hairline, eyes going wide. "*No.*"

He'd begun laughing again, nodding, and this time Claire joined him, doubling over and shrieking. Ahead of them, Tully drew up and spun on her heel, looking at them like they'd grown extra heads. "What is so funny, you two?"

He repeated the news, but Tully only nodded and smiled.

"Yes! Yes, I remember this: Blare Malterran, *maya boichik*. It was a good family name, I recall. I don't understand what is so funny."

Claire managed to straighten, wiping tears from her eyes and gasping. "Tully—Tully our names are Blare," she pointed to Beast, "and Claire," she pointed at herself, then began laughing all over again as she choked out: "we rhyme!"

Tully shrugged and shook her head at them. "This explains nothing to me. Except why you like each other so much: you are strange in the same way. Maybe a little crazy in the same way, as well."

As Beast and Claire regained their composure and resumed following Tully through the woods towards Edden Claire looped her arm through his and pulled close against his side.

"Thank goodness I was going to change my name anyway," he said, his other hand coming up to rest on top of hers.

"You were?"

"Gods, yes. That's not who I am anymore, like you said. He died a long time ago, and I'd like to leave him that way."

"Do you have any ideas about what you *would* like to be called, then?"

"No. I was thinking I'd probably take your family's name, once we're officially married. If you're alright with that, of course."

Claire snorted, squeezing his arm, "Of course. My father will be ecstatic. He is obsessed with his lineage, even if Odetima was actually my mother's name, since he insisted on the fae affiliation. But what about your first name?"

He lifted a shoulder in a gesture that was almost a shrug.

"I thought perhaps my mother would want to try her hand at naming me."

Ahead of them Tully stopped, whirling around and covering her mouth with her rough hands. Emotion surged in Claire's chest, threatening to choke her. "What do you think, Tully?" he asked softly. Tears gathered in Tully's dark eyes, her fingers on her lips beginning to tremble. In a few quick strides, she had stepped up to him and thrown her arms around his neck. They embraced tightly, Tully rocking side to side, before pulling back to look at his face. She kissed each of his cheeks, sniffling.

"It would be an honor, my boy." Tully swiped at her nose with a knuckle, blinking away tears and beaming at Beast. "I think you are a Sam," she said immediately, squeezing his arms once before letting go and continuing along the path. "I have already thought on this these long years. Tully is always prepared, yes? Or perhaps a Jorichko, if you do not like Sam."

"I like Sam, it suits you," Claire barged in, unable to wrap her head around how she'd be able to keep from mangling Jorichko...or how she'd manage crying it out during their intimate moments. She slung her arm across Beast's—no, *Sam's*—back as they followed Tully. He settled his arm around her shoulders.

"Sam Odetima. I like it, it has a good ring to it."

A shy smile tugged at Sam's lips. "So do I."

The plan had been to wait until they were alone and more settled to tell Sam about what she'd learned about their relationship, but the longer she sat on the information the more it felt like a betrayal, like she was hiding it or lying to him by not telling him right away. Claire squared her shoulders and looked up at his rough-hewn face.

"Listen, I have something I think I need to tell you. About why I was able to break Naja's curse," she began, nerves making her stomach flutter and swoop.

"Oh? What is it? Is it bad?"

"Not at all. *I* think it's fantastic, and I'm fairly confident you'll feel the same. But it is…odd. And unexpected. At least, I wasn't expecting it."

Sam arched a heavy brow, turning his head to look at her while they walked. "Well, you seem awfully nervous about it, whatever it is."

"I'm not *nervous*—oh by the grace of the gods, fine: we're mates, Sam. Fated fae mates. I don't know how, but the reason Naja let you go is because I spoke my claim on you and forced her."

Managing to keep his feet, Sam nonetheless looked like he'd tip over on the next breeze. "Alright," he breathed, dazed. "You were right. It's good but I don't understand it. Neither of us is fae. Right?"

"I have a theory!" Tully called over her shoulder, slowing down to draw closer to them. "Would you like to hear?" she asked coyly.

Sam huffed. "Of course we do, *madjem*. Please, enlighten us."

Beaming over her shoulder, Tully began outlining her thoughts. "I have already told Claire this, but it is worth saying again. I think it is because you both have some fae heritage. Not much, just a drop, and normally this would not be enough for a bond to be possible. But you, *maya boichik*, have been steeped in heavy magic for two centuries, longer than I have ever heard of anyone being kept in an enchantment as layered and complex at that *mala crujzta's* curse. And I think it has changed you, and given you some things you did not have before. You are no longer ungifted, as another example."

Claire's brow furrowed. It was all so gods-damned convenient, but she couldn't deny it was the first thing about what had happened that made any kind of sense. "And that was enough to waken a bond in me, too? To allow me to make a valid claim?"

Tully shrugged. "Perhaps. But you have a great sensitivity to you, more than someone who is ungifted should have. So I think maybe there has been something in your life that awakened a kind of gift in you, that connected you more to your fae heritage than nature made you."

No such moments stuck out in Claire's memory, but she supposed it was possible. She turned to look up at Sam, starting at the intense look on his face. "What is it?" she asked him, squeezing his hand.

"If we're mates then I guess that explains why you would fall for someone like me. You couldn't help it. It was your body forcing it." Sam looked almost…sad about that.

"Stop it right now with that," Claire scolded, swatting at his arm. "You've been locked up for a while, but medical artificiery has come a long way and I hate to break it to you, but no matter what love is just 'your body forcing it.' All of our emotions are just different things firing off in our bodies. And I don't think that makes it any less beautiful or wonderful," she finished tartly.

"What things?"

"I'm not sure about the finer points but it's a whole bunch of different chemicals zinging around in your brain and setting off chain reactions. It's fascinating but beyond me.

Maybe if you wind up going into healing you'll find out."

Sam nodded thoughtfully. "I suppose, if I'm honest with myself, knowing that my feelings for you are because of the mate bond does nothing to change them. If anything, it might make them deeper. More…firmly rooted."

Grinning, Claire tugged on his arm. "Because it means we're stuck with each other. You can't separate mates, which means you legally cannot abandon me out of a misplaced sense of duty. And we might as well get married, since it'll help you get your citizenship, I'd think."

Sam blushed, smiling sheepishly. "Gods, you make me sound like such a-a *buffoon*."

"Well you're *my* buffoon and I love you. And you're mine forever, so yay for us."

Abruptly, Claire was yanked off her feet and swept up in a bridal carry. She flung her arms tight around Sam's neck, squealing in delight and surprise. He spun them in a circle, laughing, and Claire joined him, going breathless and giddy. The kiss he planted on her when they stopped was searing, knee-melting, and she was quite glad she didn't have to trust her own legs to hold her up.

Tully coughed uncomfortably from ahead of them, and Sam broke their kiss and started walking again. Claire bucked and wriggled in his arms. "Aren't you going to put me down?"

"No. I don't want to."

She combed her fingers through his hair like she knew he liked, making sure to dig the pads of her fingers into his scalp a little. "You're already carrying the pack; let me walk, love."

But he just shook his head. "If I want to carry my *mate*," he blushed, grinning wide and looking starry-eyed, "then I will."

Claire clicked her tongue, her own smile blooming on her face. Ooh but she *liked* hearing him call her that. "So bossy," she murmured, deciding after yesterday's hard traveling that maybe it would be nice to be carried for a bit.

CHAPTER THIRTY-SEVEN
The Real World

When their little party finally, blessedly, made it to Edden, the sun had begun setting, and people were settling into their homes for the evening. Claire led her two exhausted companions through town to the *Dragon's Spur*, praying Teran would have at least one room for them.

It was good that there weren't many people around, because what few people *were* around drew up and looked at Sam with naked fear. Tired beyond social niceties, Claire glared at every one, making sure she held tight to Sam's hand to show they were together and hopefully discourage violence.

It seemed to work, as they made it to the inn unmolested, though Sam was clearly deeply discomfited by the stares and whispers. Claire squeezed his hand. "I've got you, sweet man," she assured him, glaring at yet another person who'd stopped to gawk and point. "I won't let them hurt you."

Tully went over to his other side and took his arm in hers, saying something low and comforting to him in her native language. Claire entered the inn, seeking out Teran in the cozy and rather full common room. Spotting him at the back by the bar, she waved and headed over.

"Miss Claire!" he exclaimed, wiping down the bar counter with an old rag. "How wonderful to be seeing you again so soon! Will you be needing a room then?"

"Yes, please, Teran. If you have it, I'll need two, actually. I have two companions with me, waiting outside."

"I have two, though one's a little on the small side. That alright?"

"Yes, that'll be lovely."

"Do y'mind my asking who these guests might be? I thought you were out in the forest tinkering with the manor quest."

Ever the gossip hound, this one. "I've actually solved the quest. My companions are the denizens of the manor. It collapsed when the enchantment broke, so they're homeless and coming back with me to Kesterin." Teran had stopped in his mopping, his eyes wide and mouth slightly agape. Claire leaned in closer and lowered her voice. "One of my companions is the beast of the manor. His name's Sam. I need you and your other patrons to remain calm when he walks in. He's a person just like any other, and he's very gentle. He won't hurt anyone, so no one needs to panic and get violent."

Teran nodded, glancing over his shoulder at the kitchen. "There's a back way you could use, through the kitchen. Some of these fellas are fair deep into their cups and I'd hate for you or your friend to come to harm. I'll just let Sil know."

Claire was shocked to see the innkeep so somber, but she nodded her thanks and waited while he went into the back to talk to his husband. A moment later he returned, several clean mugs in his grasp, then nodded his chin at the front door. "Sil's going to meet you at the front door, Miss Claire. He'll get you all settled in." He leaned in and grinned, the brightness Claire was used to seeing lighting his blue eyes. "Sil's shy but he's mighty excited to get to meet an honest-to-gods quester and an enchanted person. Don't mind him if he stares a bit." Claire laughed despite her fatigue and foul mood.

"I'll keep that in mind. You have my thanks, Teran." She pulled her coin purse from her belt and slid a pair of silvers across the bar to him. But Teran refused to take it.

"Pleasure's all mine," he insisted, pushing the coins back to her. "The look on Sil's face when I told 'im was plenty of payment."

Claire tried to insist on paying, but Teran was stubborn, shooing her out and into the night to meet back up with her party.

Out in the deepening night, Claire squinted, looking for Tully and Sam. She spotted them huddled against the side of the inn, away from the prying eyes of foot traffic. Claire waved them over just as Sil rounded the opposite corner. Seeing them, he halted in his tracks, eyes going wide as a beaming smile spread across his face. He clapped his hands to his chest and bowed at Claire and her companions.

"Hello, and welcome to the *Dragon's Spur*," he said softly, a flush creeping up his neck. Sil was about Claire's height and rail-thin, with golden skin and a thatch of dark curly hair. His face was broad and warm, his mustache quivering with excitement. "If you'll follow me…" He led them back around the way he'd come, wiping his palms on his soiled apron.

Claire took Sam's hand again, beyond excited to be able to take her mountain of a pack off her back and get some rest. She'd promised Sam some things on the walk into town, but she didn't think he'd object to getting some food and rest first.

Sil led them through the warm, fragrant kitchen and up a back stairwell that allowed them to bypass the common room, then showed them to their rooms. Claire was delighted to see that they were across the hall from each other, rather than next to each other. She wouldn't have to worry quite so much about Tully overhearing the things her and Sam would get up to in their room.

Sil left them with their keys, promising he'd bring up some food and drink in just a moment, and then they were left alone to get settled. Tully took the small single room without being asked, which Claire could have kissed her for doing, and her and Sam let themselves into the other. It was still a small room, but with a double bed and a *bit* more floor space.

"Oh, it's perfect, Sam," Claire said, unbuckling herself from her heavy pack and letting it clatter to the floor. She eased her boots and cloak off next, stretching her tight, aching muscles. Sam set his bundle with his things next to her pack and sat heavily on the edge of the bed, looking as tired as Claire felt. She stepped between his legs, cupping his face in her hands and kissing him tenderly. "We did it, you're free. Can you believe it?"

Sam smiled up at her with a flash of sharp teeth. "No, it still doesn't feel real. Or it does, and it feels…big. Scary."

She bit her lip, watching him carefully. "Are you…are you seeing the shadow creatures, baby?"

He blinked, looking around. A smile stretched across his face with sweet slowness. "No, not a hint. Nothing since I woke up." His brow furrowed. "You think Naja was behind that, too?"

"I wouldn't put it past her. But that's good, isn't it? If it's gone now?"

He nodded, smiling and tilting his face up for another kiss. "You're right. It'll be nice, not having to worry about that on top of everything else."

Claire kissed him softly. "Yeah, your life's really gone sideways, love. But I hope you know you've got me, and Tully. And once Adeela meets you she'll probably adopt you, too." She pulled back a little, sliding her hands to his broad shoulders. "Have you thought any more about what you want to do with your life now that it's yours again?"

Sam shook his head, his arms coming up to wrap around her waist and pull her in closer. "Not really. It's still too new, I think."

"Sure. We'll tackle it when you're ready." Sam pulled her down into another kiss, this one lingering and full of heat, his lips firm against hers and his tongue sweeping slowly into her mouth. Heat swept through Claire, desire arching through her and making her clench. Perhaps she was not too tired after all...

A sharp knock at the door shocked them apart. Claire chuckled. "That'll be dinner," she said, pulling out of Sam's strong arms. "We'll have to continue that later," she shot at him, wiggling her eyebrows. Sam's smile was bright, full of so much love and softness.

As they settled in to eat, Claire was struck by an intense wave of feeling. This was the start of their lives together. They'd rest here for a day or two, Claire would send an update to Dretta and Adeela, and then they'd make their way to Kesterin. She'd introduce Sam to her family and friends, get him set up as a citizen, help him get his feet under himself. They'd get married, maybe travel. It was a thought that was so beautiful, so powerful, that it took her breath away. She looked at the man seated beside her on the bed eating thick slices of a roast with a singular focus, spatters of grease on his shirt, and she smiled. In many ways, this quest had been exactly what she needed.

She'd proved that there was a place in the world for a quester who approached things with kindness and gentleness. She'd shown herself that she was strong and capable. She'd proved her father and sisters wrong for doubting her. And Sam had shown her that she was worthy of love. Further, that she was worthy of love on *her* terms, that she deserved to get what she needed from her partner, and that the right partner would be thrilled to give it to her.

There was a chance, Claire had to admit, that Sam had saved her as much as she'd saved him. And it was going to be a beautiful life they'd build together.

CHAPTER THIRTY-EIGHT

Epilogue

Raspian and Valis had settled around their campfire, cleaning and mending their gear, when steps crunched on the gravel just outside the ring of firelight—the very reason Raspian had chosen this location for their camp. Beside him Valis's grip tightened on the dagger she was sharpening, and Raspian reached out to peel a handful of flickering flame away from their fire, molding it with careful strokes of his fingers into a blade of his own. They sat in ready silence, straining to hear more. An animal, perhaps?

But then a voice called, smoky and female.

"Hullo! We're from the Questing Guild and mean you no harm; may we approach your fire?"

We? Then there was more than the one woman who'd spoken. Raspian's eyes slid over to Valis. Her lovely face was tense, dark eyes flicking over to his only briefly, her mouth pressed into a hard line. She nodded though, and he returned his gaze to where the voice had come from.

"Very well," Raspian called, rising smoothly to his feet, his flame dagger still ready in his grip. "We are also from the Guild," he added.

"I know, we spotted your badges on your packs" the voice responded, crunching footsteps closing in. *Ah. So that is why they felt safe to approach.*

Raspian could hear another set of steps now crunching through the gravel, but it seemed to be just the two. If they proved hostile then Raspian and Valis would be evenly matched, at least. Well–Raspian stole a look at Valis, standing tall and tense at his side, two daggers held ready in her palms–perhaps not *truly* even. His sweet Valis was more than a match for most people. He bit back a smile despite the tension, forcing himself to focus on the strangers blooming from out of the darkness.

The first to come into view was a dark-skinned woman, perhaps only a couple of inches shorter than Raspian, her hands held up with her palms out. The newcomer's arms were well-shaped with muscle, and she moved with the casual grace of someone used to combat. But of course, Valis was much stronger, her arms almost as thick around as Raspian's slim thigh, he couldn't help comparing with pride. He saw a glint of silver on one of the newcomer's pack straps, and recognized it a moment later as a Guild badge. *Good. Less likely they are lying, then.* The woman wore some light leather armor and had a short sword and a dagger sheathed at her hips.

Just behind her was an extremely tall man walking with a strange gait that Raspian realized, with a start, was because he walked on large paws with high ankles, like a dog's. His skin was even darker than hers, and looked like it might have been steel gray in the flickering firelight. His hair was such a shocking shade of crimson that it had to be a trick of the light, too. His features were all a little too big for his face, but his eyes were soft and kind, for all their wariness. Short horns swept back from his temples, the shape graceful and dignified. Raspian thought that they were both bold to approach them like this, in the dark, even being Guild members and with half their party being a terrifying monster.

As a show of good faith, Raspian released his flame dagger back into the campfire and gestured for their guests to join him and Valis by the fire pit. Valis put one of her daggers away and resumed her seat, keeping the other out to finish sharpening it.

"My name is Claire," the woman said, unstrapping her pack and slinging it to the ground. "And this is my husband, Sam. He's a healer, if you have any need for it."

"Good to meet you," Sam mumbled, removing his own pack and settling into the ground beside his wife.

After a moment Raspian gasped, suddenly recognizing them. "You are the Odetimas!" He exclaimed, a grin spreading across his face. He barked a laugh, elbowing Valis. "The Beauty and the Beast!"

Claire rolled her eyes but chuckled, while Sam ducked his head and combed his long fingers through his shaggy red hair. "Gods, that nickname. It's so...*silly*," he bemoaned.

Valis offered a small smile, the whetstone dragging along the steel of her blade with a rasp. "It's so catchy though," she murmured, her voice so soft and raspy it made Raspian flush with heat. Truly, he would go mad if he could not manage to woo her into his bed soon.

"And you cannot deny that what you did was impressive: solving the longest-lived quest in Guild history, besting a fae mage, rescuing a damsel in distress..." Raspian added.

Sam cleared his throat, grinning at Raspian sheepishly. "I

wasn't much of a damsel," he protested.

Raspian laughed and reached past Claire to pat Sam's arm, the heavy black marks of his many tattoos dancing in the flickering firelight. "Not you, my friend," he assured Sam, "I am referring to the illustrious Tuluuchimeg Borosovski, trapped alongside you, yes?"

Even in the dark Raspian could see that this made Sam blush furiously, and his gut sank as he realized his teasing may have shamed the strange-looking man. He took in a breath to apologize, but Claire took her husband's hand and squeezed it. "You were more of a damsel than you realize, love," she cut in, smiling up at Sam wolfishly. It seemed impossible, but poor Sam blushed even harder, but he looked pleased all the same.

The heat in their eyes as they looked at each other, as they touched each other casually, made Raspian ache with longing. He dreamed of sharing moments like these with Valis. She was so maddeningly perfect, yet remote, and he couldn't seem to find a way to draw her in.

Claire and Sam shared their rations with their hosts, allowing them to cobble together a decent meal. They shared gossip as they all ate, and the couple revealed that they were also traveling to the Sabarathian Guildhall to answer the summons. They all speculated about what had made the Consortium so nervous as to call such a large Guild meeting. They all agreed it was likely that tensions between Ba'Thell and Sabarath had something to do with it.

Raspian was tempted to be ashamed of his Ba'Thell heritage in moments like these, to try and hide it from these newcomers and the woman who made him ache with longing, but it proved only a passing fancy. It was not his fault that the power games of others brought the threat of war to Cillure for the first time in over two centuries. It was not his fault that the earth he was born upon sat within one imaginary boundary and not another. He did his part to keep the peace—he was a proud member of the Guild, after all, and his research in runic artificiure would change lives. He had nothing to be ashamed of.

Eventually, the night grew long, and he and Valis offered to take the first watch. Claire thanked them profusely, her jaw cracking with the force of her yawn, and the Odetimas lay out their bedrolls close together by the fire. Claire tied a silk scarf around her wild nest of dark curls, and they settled in together under their blankets, Claire's head resting on Sam's shoulder, her hand on his chest.

It was almost time for him and Valis to rouse the couple to take their own shift sleeping when Raspian's attention was drawn to their sleeping forms. Sam was twitching in his sleep, moaning and whimpering. Just as Raspian was about to get to his feet to investigate and make sure Sam was well, Claire woke beside him. She shifted in their bedrolls so that she could wrap her arms around his shoulders and tuck his head in against her chest. Her hands moved over his shoulders and upper back, her chin resting on the top of his head as she made soothing sounds. Raspian could see him shiver in the dim light, and he burrowed in closer against her, holding her tight. "I'm here, I've got you," she murmured several times, her own eyes still closed. "It's just a dream, sweet man."

Raspian's heart clenched in his chest. This is what he wanted in life, what these two infamous strangers had: easy closeness, shameless affection, giving his whole self to another person. He wanted the feel of their hands around him, lifting him when he fell. He was a romantic man.

He watched them for a moment more, then averted his gaze, feeling as if he was intruding and rude. His eyes landed on Valis, drinking in how soft her face looked in the heavy shadows cast by the flames. The stubborn lock of hair that resisted all of her combing was flopped onto her forehead, and his fingers twitched as he suppressed the urge to brush it back for her.

Valis caught him watching her, and he grinned widely at her, even as his ears heated. She snorted, but he didn't miss the twitch of her lips, or the way she peeked at him from the corner of her eye. And when he shifted subtly closer to her, his heart soared when she let him claim that space.

Perhaps his feelings were not so one-sided. Perhaps seeing such a happy couple had filled Valis' quick, clever mind with thoughts of romance as much as it has filled Raspian's. He grinned again, hopeful.

Author's Note

It really does take a village to raise a child and this baby is no different. I could not have made this book what it is without the invaluable insight, support, and advice from my beta readers, my sensitivity reader, and my fellow monster romance indie authors. So from the bottom of my heart, thank you (in no particular order): Desi'ree, Norris, Mattie, Crystal, Amanda, Michelle, Jenn, Lark, Catrina, Frost, Katie, and Wulf. If I missed anyone I'm sorry for my neurospicy swiss cheese brain that forgets literally everything!

If you especially liked the first seven chapters, you have my partner to thank for that—so please mention it in the reviews so I can stop hearing him joke about how people are going to think those chapters sound like the ramblings of a mad man. I might be biased, but I think he did a great job helping me with the pacing and worldbuilding there, and figuring out how to ease people into this story that's been rattling around in my skull for two decades.

That's right: it took me more than 20 years to write this book.

Well, not 20 years *straight*. That's kind of wild, even for me.

No, it was about 20 years ago that I first read *Beauty* by Robin McKinley and said to myself, "holy shitballs—I've got to write my own version!" and started writing fics in my fancy B&N notebook. But I'm going to count it, because it took writing the wrong story dozens of times to get to the right one. Of course I'd been exposed to other versions of the fairytale before I found McKinley's, but I give this particular novel credit for being the impetus because it wasn't until I read McKinley's book that I saw the potential to craft my *own* version of my favorite fairytale, one that didn't stick to the Disney narrative and found itself in some wild yet beautiful places as a result. It's not an adult romance, but it is still one of my favorite books of all time.

I started writing *this* version while I was still working at a factory full time, about three years ago. Because of the nature of my job, and other demands on my time, it took ages and ages to make progress. I don't work there anymore, for which I am eternally grateful, so writing's going a lot faster these days. As of writing this, I have a second novel written (an alien romance I'm calling *All or Nothing)* and at least four others planned, two of them sequels to ALITD. The second book might be more of a novella, following my dear sweet babies Sam and Claire around as they acclimate to their new lives. The third book is where we watch sassy, debonair Raspian try to convince gentle giant Valis to give him a chance while the world plunges into chaos. Raspian and Valis are both characters that have been kicking around for more than a decade, and I think I finally found their story. As a fun fact for the one of you who's reading this and cares, the fantastical land of Cillure was created at the same time and Ras and Valis. OoOoOoOoOoOoh!

Speaking of young me, like many monster lovers (hey, y'all ;)), sexy animated monster men were my gateway drug, and Beast from Disney's *Beauty and the Beast* really rocked little me's world. I remember being disappointed that he changed into a human man at the end—barf, ammirite? So boring! And now here I am, letting my freak flag fly with a fully-beast Beast who stays hulking and delicious. Mmmmm. I also threw a little (okay, more like a lot) of both Goliath and Demona from Disney's *Gargoyles* into Beast's design. Hands up if that movie/show (YES there's a movie, it's pretty great) was a little bit of a bi-awakening for you too ;)

But while young me was obsessed with fantasy lands I could escape to, adult me is more interested in making monsters who fuuuuuck and showing all the beautiful flavors of humanity. Representation is important to me, and something I'm always challenging myself to do more of. Whenever I create a character I ask myself: does this character need to be white? Cis? Straight? Neurotypical? Slim? Conforming to the gender binary? And if the answer is no (which, spoiler, it generally is) then I ask myself how I might diverge from that "standard". I myself am white, but none of those other things, and my spouse is a person of color, so I see all the time how impactful and important representation is.

If you don't like reading books that feature representation (which I truly don't get, but you do you), then you don't have to pick them up—there's plenty of media out there you can still consume. But I'm going to do my best to represent diverse viewpoints, and if ever I fall flat or put my foot in my mouth, *please bring it to my attention.* I am eternally grateful for the many people who have called out the problematic thoughts and behaviors I've had over the years. Their courage and love in doing so has truly been invaluable to me and made me a better person.

I would love to hear from my readers, so feel free to reach out to me on social media! I'm on Instagram and TikTok as @mirandasapphirewrites or via email at mirandasapphirewrites@gmail.com . Hopefully by the time this publishes I'll have my website sorted out and a newsletter you can subscribe to to help stay in touch and on top of updates and exclusive content (come oooon Future Me, you can do it!). That'll be at: MirandaSapphireWrites.com .

—Miranda Sapphire (December 2022)

PS: Extra internet points for anyone who figures out what real-life author Garnette Mason is a (probably clumsy) homage to! B)

PPS: Someone on Goodreads (who I cannot for the life of me find —UGH!) correctly guessed: Garnette Mason is Ruby Dixon, AKA my intro to monsterfucking and total fave.

Viske (Tully's Language) Glossary and Pronunciation Guide

Tully's native language is Viske (VISS-kuh), a language spoken in the kingdom of Viskege (viss-KAY-guh).

- Madjem (MAH-gem): a form of "mother" which is approximately as familiar as "mom" but less familiar than "mommy"
- Maya boichik (MY-uh BOY-chick): my (baby/young/ little) boy
- Stroga nazsam (STROH-gah NAH-zsa*m): dark expletive, approximately "horrible witch"
- Seza groya (SEH-za GROY-uh): sweet/darling girl
- Stroga facha (STROH-gah FAH-cha): another expletive, approximately "horrible woman"
- Mala crujzta (MAH-lah CROOJ-tah): (Tully has a pottymouth, it's another expletive) approximately "bitch"
- Kasza pruje (KAH-zsa PRUE-yay): idiom approximating "and that's that"

*"zsa" is pronounced like in the name Zsa Zsa Gabor

Lore Notes and Pronunciation Guide

Lore Notes and Pronunciation Guide
*Feel free to pronounce this stuff however you want — this is
just how I pronounce things, but the fun of language is getting
to play with it! And this is doubly so for fantasy languages!*

The Cillurean Religion (the Old Gods)

The core of the old religion (that most of Cillure observes)
centers on Yun'Shaddeh, the great scale, keeper of the
balance. All things in the world exist in balance with all other
things, and when there is inequality they will always attempt
rorto: a return to this sacred balance. Entropy and chaos exist
with this balance; they are not its antagonist.

The Deities:
- Delenaa (del-LAY-nah)(Feminine): Lady of the dawn,
  goddess of light, spring, beginnings, births.
- Frichta (FRICK-tah)(Neutral Gender): Liege of the
  dusk, ruler of night, endings, journeys, and autumn.
- Salerah (sahl-AIR-uh)(Neutral Gender): Keeper of the
  sun, bringer of summer. Deity of fire, harvest,

purification.

- Vitrin (VITT-rin)(Masculine): Keeper of the moon, bringer of winter. God of snow and ice, of dreams and death.

In recent years, a monotheistic religion has begun taking hold in some parts of Cillure. This religion is much stricter in its beliefs and means of worship, and has led quickly to abuse and corruption. Its emphasis on the power of men and the importance of legacy is widely-regarded as its greatest misstep.

Nouns (people, places, and things)
Claire (KLAIR)
Beast (BEEST)
Tully (TUHL-lee) / Tuluuchimeg Borosovski (tuh-LOO-chih-meg bor-oh-SOHV-skee)
Adeela (uh-DEE-la)
Dretta (DREH-tuh)
Teran (TARE-uhn)
Sil (SILL) / Silvio (SILL-vee-oh)
O'brenne (oh-BREN)
Kirnan (KEER-nuhn)
Draseus (DRAZZ-ee-us)
Vanessa (vuh-NESS-uh)
Danielle (dan-ee-EL)
Jordan (JORR-duhn)
Hereon (HEER-ee-on)
Naja (NAH-zsa)
Ingrid (INN-grid)
Caldus Love (CAHL-duss LUHV)

Fausta (FAUW-stuh)
Soliei (SOL-ee-ay)

Cillure (sill-OOR)
   Kesterin (KESS-ter-in)
   Citrine (SIT-reen)
   Edden (EHD-en)
   Sabarath (SABB-uh-reth)
   Ba'Thell (bah-THELL)

aerlanis (air-LAHN-iss)

Time and the Cillurean Calendar

Every time there is a cataclysmic event they reset the year count and name the following era "After X" where X is the event. So the events of ALITD are happening in the year 230 AW: After the War. This was a long and bloody multi-nation war that had ravaged the Cillurean continent, similar to WWI/WWII. Beast was locked up in 30 AW. The previous era was AFL: After Flood, and before that AFA: After Famine. AFL lasted 392 years, and AFA 137.

Beyond that, the Cillurean calendar has eight months instead of twelve, two per season, and the names of the months are related to the patron deity of each season: spring is Delenaa, summer Salerah, autumn Frichta, and winter Vitrin.

The beginning of the year is at the beginning of spring.

The first month of a god's season starts with the same letter as their name, and the second ends with their suffix, mirroring the path of their reign through that season. In order, the months are: Dima, Salenaa, Setar, Calenah, Fiel, Gishta, Vost,

Hectrin.

Each month is twenty-eight days, or the duration of one full lunar cycle.